In a South Seas Paradise,
They Were About to Plunge
into an Inferno of Fire and Fear....

Admiral Peter MacKenzie—The submarine commander has repeatedly proven his honor, resourcefulness, and courage under fire. Now, at the helm of a fifty-year-old sub, he confronts the most destructive weapon in the world. Before the battle is done, he will be forced to make a choice no man should face.

Justine MacKenzie—A Senior Covert Operations Director for the CIA, the Admiral's wife is a woman trained and prepared to kill in the line of duty. Taken hostage by terrorists, she must balance her sacred oath with a sacred trust: the life of her unborn child.

Praise for Bart Davis,
the Master of International
Submarine Suspense Fiction

ATLANTIC RUN

"More twists and plots and intriguing characters than any three adventure tales . . . tough to tear your eyes from."

—Clive Cussler

Akiro—Curator of the Atomic Bomb Museum in Hiroshima, he saw the devastation wrought upon his poeple. Now, disgusted as his nation forgets its tragic past and marches toward a nuclear future, he prepares a dramatic demonstration: a distant fire in the sky. . . .

Shuto—Even more than his father Akiro, Shuto knows firsthand the horrifying effects of the Hiroshima blast. He wants only revenge upon the nation responsible for his suffering—the United States.

DESTROY THE KENTUCKY

"A winner in which people, not gadgetry, are paramount and adventure is delivered at a satisfying clip."
—*Publishers Weekly*

"Bart Davis has a unique way of looking into the heart of naval officers. His depictions of the price of command and the pain and triumph of leading men in combat are superb. His narration of the events leading up to the riveting climax is wonderful. A terrific sea story which kept me going long after my bedtime."
—Gerry Carroll,
author of *North SAR* and *Ghostrider One*

Viktor Lysenko—A nuclear physicist whose star rose under his former Soviet masters, a man of strange and violent desires, he's now willing to sell his skills to the highest bidder—and he has promised the terrorists a weapon unimaginably more destructive than any ever seen before.

Dr. Philip Keller—One of the hostages taken by the terrorists, he is a physician with a remarkable gift—for saving his own skin. Schooled in the art of treachery, betrayal, and deceit, he may well prove a greater threat than Shuto himself.

RAISE THE RED DAWN

"A rip-roaring yarn beneath the polar ice pack."
—Charles D. Taylor,
author of *Boomer* and *Deep Sting*

"Suspense as chilling as the Arctic seas."
—Ed Ruggero,
author of *38 North Yankee*

Books by Bart Davis

Atlantic Run
A Conspiracy of Eagles
Destroy the Kentucky
Full Fathom Five
Raise the Red Dawn
Voyage of the Storm

Published by POCKET BOOKS

BART DAVIS

VOYAGE OF THE STORM

POCKET BOOKS

New York   London   Toronto   Sydney   Tokyo   Singapore

This book is a work of fiction. Names, characters, places and incidents are products of the author's imagination or are used fictitiously. Any resemblance to actual events or locales or persons, living or dead, is entirely coincidental.

An *Original* Publication of POCKET BOOKS

POCKET BOOKS, a division of Simon & Schuster Inc.
1230 Avenue of the Americas, New York, NY 10020

Copyright © 1995 by Bart Davis

ISBN: 0-671-76905-7

First Pocket Books printing December 1995

10 9 8 7 6 5 4 3 2 1

POCKET and colophon are registered trademarks of Simon & Schuster Inc.

Printed in the U.S.A.

For Sharon, Jordan, and Ally,
the best part of my life;

and in memory of Gerry Carroll,
a friend gone too soon.

Author's Note

His Majesty's Submarine *Storm* was built in the shipyards at Cammell Laird's in 1942, at the height of the war. Her captain, Commander E. P. Young, wrote in his classic work *Undersea Patrol* (McGraw-Hill, 1952) that he first saw her "in the dusty water, riding high because she was still very light, unmistakably a submarine from the shape of her long, rounded pressure hull and the tapering bulge of her ballast tanks, but still, it seemed a long way from completion." By the end of her wartime commission, the *Storm* had traveled seventy-one thousand miles, and spent over fourteen hundred hours underwater, the equivalent of sixty days and nights. Her combat accomplishments are a matter of proud record.

Unfortunately, old boats, unlike old soldiers, do not just fade away. In October 1947 the *Storm* was approved for disposal. For a time she was used in underwater explosion tests. On September 15, 1949, *Storm* was handed over to Shipbuilders W H Arnott Young and Company, and scrapped.

It was with great respect that I resurrected the *Storm* and placed her where she could suit the demands of my story. I am well aware that the *Storm* was quite well known during the war, and can only hope that those who remember her, including those who served on her, will be pleased that her namesake could rise to be valiant once again, and end with a more poetic fate, albeit fictional, than the scrapyards at Troon. Commodore Rowe is a fictional character and bears no resemblance to the remarkable Commander Young, and the exploits and history of my boat are a compilation of many of the exploits of the boats of that time. Exercising an author's right, even geography was bent to my story's needs.

I want to thank Mr. George Murphy, who told me the story of salvaging the U.S.S. *Threadfin,* over lunch at the AUTEC officers' club on Andros Island, and later provided me with details of that mission. *A World War Two Submarine,* by Richard Humble and Mark Bergin, let me peer inside the hull of a British S class boat. Commander P. R. Compton-Hall, RN (ret.), of the Royal Navy Submarine Museum in Portsmouth, England, was generous with his time, knowledge, and cautions. Dr. George Billy, Chief Librarian at the United States Merchant Marine Academy, has always been extremely helpful with my research. Finally, Commander Young's book should again be mentioned as an invaluable source, and a great read.

My sincere thanks to:

Paul McCarthy, my editor at Pocket Books, for always giving the best guidance. The growth of the MacKenzie novels owes most to him.

Robert Gottlieb, a visionary, right more often than any person I've ever known.

Chiquita McCarthy, so much a part of our union, for holding my hand that day.

Rear Admiral Weldon Koenig (ret.), who inspired me.

My wife, Sharon; after twenty years, she is still everything to me.

And Jord and Ally, the kids without whose help I could have completed this novel in half the time.

Contents

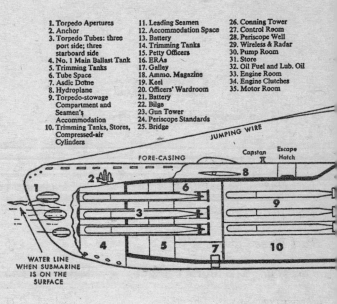

1. Torpedo Apertures
2. Anchor
3. Torpedo Tubes: three port side; three starboard side
4. No. 1 Main Ballast Tank
5. Trimming Tanks
6. Tube Space
7. Asdic Dome
8. Hydroplane
9. Torpedo-stowage Compartment and Seamen's Accommodation
10. Trimming Tanks, Stores, Compressed-air Cylinders
11. Leading Seamen
12. Accommodation Space
13. Battery
14. Trimming Tanks
15. Petty Officers
16. ERAs
17. Galley
18. Ammo. Magazine
19. Keel
20. Officers' Wardroom
21. Battery
22. Bilge
23. Gun Tower
24. Periscope Standards
25. Bridge
26. Conning Tower
27. Control Room
28. Periscope Well
29. Wireless & Radar
30. Pump Room
31. Store
32. Oil Fuel and Lub. Oil
33. Engine Room
34. Engine Clutches
35. Motor Room

Diagram of

HM SUBMARINE "STORM"

The heavy lines represent the pressure hull. Everything outside this (except the torpedo tubes) is open to the sea and floods up when the submarine dives.

The double vertical lines between compartments indicate watertight bulkheads, built to withstand the same pressure as the pressure hull.

In this diagram the for'ard periscope is shown raised, with the after one lowered into its well.

The jumping wire is designed to enable the submarine to ride under antisubmarine nets and other submerged obstructions. When both periscopes and the radar aerial are lowered, nothing projects above this wire.

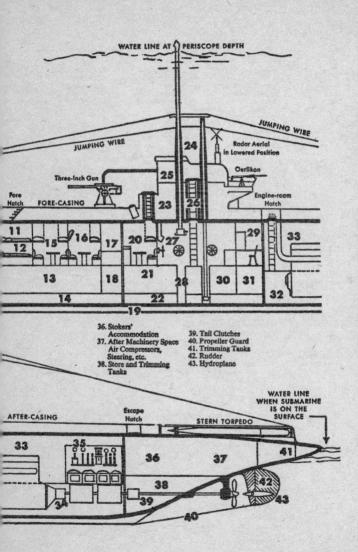

WATER LINE AT PERISCOPE DEPTH

JUMPING WIRE

JUMPING WIRE

24

Radar Aerial
in Lowered Position

Oerlikon

25

Three-Inch Gun

Engine-room
Hatch

Fore
Hatch

FORE-CASING

23

26

11

12

15

16

17

20

27

29

33

13

18

21

28

30

31

32

14

22

19

36. Stokers'
    Accommodation
37. After Machinery Space
    Air Compressors,
    Steering, etc.
38. Store and Trimming
    Tanks

39. Tail Clutches
40. Propeller Guard
41. Trimming Tanks
42. Rudder
43. Hydroplane

AFTER-CASING

Escape
Hatch

STERN TORPEDO

WATER LINE
WHEN SUBMARINE
IS ON THE
SURFACE

33

35

36

37

41

38

42

34

39

43

40

PART ONE

The Lamplighter

1

Hiroshima

HIS ART WAS THE ART OF SEEING. WITHOUT CAMOUFLAGE.
Extraneous elements removed. A grain of sand suggested the universe. The center held everything. All
else was illusion.

Akiro placed a single sprig from the *katsura* tree
outside into a black bowl on the lacquered wooden
table before him. Autumn was still several weeks
away, so the leaves contained only a slight hint of the
lush purple they would turn. His ancient eyes studied
the sprig till he was lost in it.

The sun's last rays settled like rice flour on the vast
open structure of the Atomic Bomb Museum across
the courtyard. Akiro was the museum's curator and
this was his house, just a short walk from the Museum
down the Path of White Stones. The sea smell was
strong. The ocean was only a few hundred yards away.
Gulls soaring above the cliffs cried occasionally. Soon
Shuto, his son, would bring the Russian sea captain.

Like the *katsura* branch, the Russian had many secrets to reveal.

Akiro traced the sprig to its end. It made him contemplate his own death. It was nearer than sooner, his doctors had told him, averting their eyes out of respect for his age and rank. It wasn't the first time Akiro had faced death. As a young pilot he had been ordered to be *Kamikaze*. Only the atomic blasts at Hiroshima and Nagasaki that had resulted in Japan's surrender had spared him. The blasts brought him Shuto, too, but that was later. *Kamikaze;* the god-wind. Insanity. Nothing godlike about it. Just the criminal ambitions of men.

And now they were back.

He meditated to regain composure. The tide. The setting sun. The *katsura* leaves rustling in the breeze. Freshly raked grains of sand cooling in the gathering darkness.

"I am the Lamplighter," he said softly.

Akiro was surprised he had spoken the thought out loud. He ran a long finger down his cheek and stroked his wispy beard. Age had taken his physical strength, but he knew what had to be done. That was his Art; seeing. Falsehoods stripped away. Conflict reduced to a single course of action.

Maki, his old servant, brought the tea as she did every afternoon at this hour. She had performed the ceremony daily for more than forty years. She knelt beside the table, pausing for a moment to inspect his placement of the branch in the black bowl, the only decoration in the room. Her mouth softened and she began the tea ceremony without wrinkling her nose in disfavor. Good, he thought. Lately she was getting easier to please. The two of us. Old dogs coming to an end.

He sought the curve again. A tiny sprout made him feel something. He realized he was only afraid of dying if he didn't finish what he had come to think of as the culmination of his life's work. After the war he had dedicated his life to building the museum so that no one would ever forget, and he had seen it grow in national importance till every Japanese schoolchild and millions of their silent and grief-stricken parents made the stomach-churning trip down its corridors. It was Akiro's reminder that the Japanese, of all people, must make certain such things never happened again. But showing them the past hadn't been enough. He saw that now. He had to show them the future.

"Akiro-san?" Maki's ears were cocked.

"I hear, Maki. Bring them to me."

Maki left with a rustle of her kimono. Moments later he heard her returning, along with the Russian captain's heavy tread. As always with Shuto, he heard nothing at all till his son was almost next to him. Even that was a courtesy to the elder. Had the reedlike Shuto wished, his arrival would have been as silent as the space between heartbeats.

"Akiro-san," said Maki, bowing. "Captain Kasimov."

"Konichiwa, Captain-san."

The blunt-faced captain wore a uniform jacket over a gray turtleneck sweater. Akiro motioned him to sit at the low table, but Kasimov pushed his officer's cap back and stood his ground as if balancing against a swaying deck.

"Old man, I've got what you asked for. You have the money?"

Akiro nodded politely. "Would you care for some tea?"

"I don't suppose you've got any vodka?" asked Kasimov.

Shuto coughed. Kasimov heard the warning in it and stopped. His black boots squeaked on the polished floor.

Akiro was pleased. A stupid man wouldn't know Shuto for what he was. Pencil-thin, age indeterminate, eyes averted so that their intense amber color—like a tiger's—remained hidden, baggy shirt and trousers. It all bespoke one who was unimportant. Kasimov was smarter than he let on, Akiro thought, which, of course, was why he had been able to secure the information.

The Russian handed Akiro a packet of papers. "These are the sailing orders for the *Marshal Korlov*. She left three weeks ago, escorted by the *Akatsuki Maru*. Everything's there. Her route through the South Pacific. Crew list. Satellite relay system. Cargo manifest. They've been haggling over politics for months and couldn't agree on much. Security's a joke as far as I can see. You can check it."

"That won't be necessary." Akiro touched a piece of inlay on the side of the table. A cleverly fitted door opened, revealing a briefcase filled with gold bars. "An intelligent man knows the wisdom of honor."

For a moment Kasimov's coarseness faded. Akiro motioned for Shuto to carry the case, and made a sign. *He goes free.*

Kasimov mumbled his thanks and followed Shuto out of the room. Akiro placed the packet in the drawer. Only one thing remained before he could set things in motion. He called Maki to bring his traveling clothes and went back to studying the *katsura* branch. It was slightly askew.

Akiro spent time pondering that.

Kasimov and Shuto stopped at the stairway at the edge of the cliffs. The Russian's small motorcraft bobbed in the surf below.

"Pleasure doing business with—" Kasimov began.

Shuto flowed like water and struck Kasimov in the solar plexus with stiffened fingers, paralyzing his breathing center. Kasimov fell to the ground and pain filled his eyes. What had gone wrong?

"Akiro gave his word," he managed to gasp.

"And he kept it," said Shuto, speaking for the first time. "My father is an idealist, with strong principles."

"Then . . . ?"

Shuto shrugged. "I have different burdens."

Too late, Kasimov saw his mistake. Shuto wasn't the loyal servant of his father as he had been led to believe. Kasimov also realized that Akiro didn't know it.

Shuto's fist shot out and Kasimov went slack. Shuto took the gold, then searched the Russian for anything else of interest before shoving the body off the cliff.

In Akiro's dream: *His intended bride tried to tell him a joke, but she was laughing too hard to tell the end. He laughed with her. It was a fine summer day. He and some of his fellow pilots had gotten leave from their squadron. The mood of desperation in Tokyo in the summer of 1945 was abated for a while by their good spirits. They borrowed a car and sped to the lush picnic gardens in the hills outside Hiroshima.*

Then Akiro saw the Light . . .

The wheels hitting the runway woke Akiro with a start. He had slept the entire flight to Tokyo. As soon as they stopped, Shuto went outside, seeing to things. Their limousine turned out to be a Mercedes, evoking a partnership that never failed to alarm Akiro. Shuto drove, equally as lithe in traffic. Ido Miagi, the man they were going to meet, would be late, but not overly so, a compromise between the demands of his position as the leader of his political party, and the respect that Akiro was due.

Mind-sets. Akiro saw everything through his experience on one single life-changing day. Hiroshima was a lens welded into place which could never be removed. Traffic, for him, became a sea of tightly packed, melted coffins. The crowds were plains of ash. In downtown Tokyo, the government buildings' vast columns only reminded him of how easily atomic winds toppled the mightiest works.

He grimaced when they passed the Yasukuni shrine near the Imperial Palace. Few things aroused Akiro's hatred like the old Shinto institution, once the center of the government-sanctioned cult of militarists who had spawned the Second World War. The grand notion of sacrificing oneself for the Emperor had been born here, the lie of nobility in death. There was still a military museum on the grounds with flags and letters painted in blood, and displays venerating the suicide units. For years, no one in office dared visit it for fear of resurrecting the antiwar sentiment that ran so deep in the nation. Now politicians stood before it posing proudly for pictures, glorifying the past. Akiro turned away in disgust.

His meeting with Miagi could not be at his office. They drove instead to a small teahouse where privacy was insured by long family tradition. It was dark and quiet. Akiro shed his shoes and was taken into a room that held only a table surrounded by cushions.

A screen slid open and Miagi walked in. He wore a dark business suit. He bowed and extended his hand. Akiro took it gravely. Miagi slid to the cushions across from Akiro. It was a fluid movement, interesting because Miagi was a big man.

"They've gotten their way," Miagi said without preamble.

"How big is the order?"

"By the end, one hundred tons of plutonium. Weapons grade."

"*Aie,*" Akiro swore. "They can never use that much."

"For the reactor, anyway," Miagi agreed. "You were right, I see that now. I would not have believed it possible."

"Anything is possible, human stupidity being what it is."

"History must not be allowed to repeat itself. Are you ready?" Miagi asked.

Akiro put the two objects he had brought from Hiroshima on the table. An old hand-drawn map of Japan and the southern islands, and a lamp. Both were works of art, vividly colored. Akiro put a match to the wick. The flickering light made the mountains, lakes, cities, and towns all seem as if they were in flames.

"You see?" he asked.

Miagi passed him a small leather notebook. Akiro felt Shuto stir, somewhere out of sight. Had Miagi intended harm, his hand would never have reached Akiro.

"You will find all the account numbers in here.

Forgive me, Akiro-san, do you understand wire transfers and the like?"

"Shuto handles all that."

"A last matter. I am Zen enough to approve your plan in spirit." Miagi sighed. "But practical, too. Do you know you can never come back? They will hunt you. Are you prepared to sacrifice yourself?"

Akiro thought of his grim-faced doctors. "It is not so great a price to pay for the enlightenment of a nation."

Miagi smiled. "A good phrase. You should have been a politician. That is what I will call it. Afterwards. Good-bye, my friend."

"Arigato, Miagi-san."

Akiro doused the light and rolled the map into its case. Shuto stepped out of the shadows and thumbed through the notebook.

"A lot of money here," he said.

"Disburse it as necessary."

Shuto pocketed the book. "I'll tell the driver where to take you. It's better for me to go alone where I have to."

"When will I see you again?"

"On the ship."

They bowed formally. Akiro was reminded of the woman who birthed the boy, of her painful life and death, and of the marks Shuto bore because of it. Shuto was already gone by the time he walked out the front door into the sunlight outside. Even among the vast crowds, Akiro felt isolated.

He was remembering the Light, and everything that came after.

2

S.S. Tuscany

"MY DEAR, ARE YOU ALL RIGHT?"

Justine MacKenzie looked into the pair of concerned elderly English faces standing over her deck chair on the French passenger yacht *Tuscany*, cruising the South Pacific Ocean. She wasn't all right. She felt light-headed and weak.

"Please, could you call the ship's doctor?" she asked.

"Yes, of course. I'm Lady Emily Rowe. This is my husband, Lord Alex Rowe. Everyone calls him the Commodore."

"I'm sorry to trouble you," Justine said.

Lady Emily's smile shined through the lines and wrinkles of her seventy years. She took off her high-collared black-and-white-checked cloth coat and laid it over Justine.

"It's no trouble at all, my dear. Alex?"

The gaunt, silver-haired Commodore had a military man's inherent distrust of illness, but Justine looked truly unwell. He straightened his tweed jacket and tugged at his mustache.

"Hmpf. No, of course not, Em. Pleased to do it."

Rain clouds had moved in, bringing a brisk wind. Lady Emily wore loose cotton pants and a white cable-knit sweater. She and Justine were the only passengers left outside. A steward asked if he could be of help. Lady Emily sniffed primly. When did an English royal ever need help?

"You're very kind," Justine said weakly.

"Nonsense, my dear. And call me Lady Em, everyone does. What's your name?"

"Justine MacKenzie."

"Do you know what's troubling you?"

"I'm pregnant."

Lady Emily looked surprised. "But, my dear, you have the figure of a gymnast." Truly, Justine was striking even in a simple skirt and blouse. Her body was lean and strong. Her jet black hair, pulled back as tight as piano wire, showed off her dark Latin eyes, straight nose, and full red mouth. *Aristocratic* was the word to describe her.

Justine managed a smile. "I'm only ten weeks. Not really showing yet. There are complications."

Lady Emily patted her staunchly. "We women know about *that*. I had a friend. Healthy as a horse. Her happiest day was when she delivered. Put an end to the misery."

"How long did she throw up every other minute?" Justine asked.

"Not long. I believe it was replaced by the shakes."

Further discussion was cut off by the Commodore returning with the ship's doctor and nurse. Dr. Keller had watery brown eyes and a face that was more pretty than handsome. Parisian, he had a touch of that city's arrogance. His English was flawless.

Lady Em wagged a finger. "Take good care of her, Phillip."

Dr. Keller winked at Justine. "Nurse Carter and I know Mrs. MacKenzie."

Keller's brunette nurse, an American named Carolyn Carter, was a handsome woman in her late thirties, with knowing gray eyes and a buxom figure that strained the seams of her white uniform. She wrapped a blood pressure cuff around Justine's arm and took her pressure with a reassuring smile.

"One-twenty over seventy, Doctor."

Lady Emily hovered nearby. She knew Alex was thinking that she'd picked up another hurt soul to fill her inner void. But he would indulge her, strong for them both, loving her dearly beneath his public gruffness, easing her pain even after all these years. Not for the first time, she wished she could do the same for him.

Dr. Keller opened his bag and prepared a syringe. "As I explained earlier, Justine, your gestational diabetes is getting worse. This insulin will help. Eat a good hot meal and get some bed rest." Keller handed the spent syringe to Nurse Carter and pulled his cap over his wavy, brown hair. "I'll see you at dinner."

"Thank you, Doctor."

"Not at all."

Nurse Carter stayed after Keller left. "How are you feeling now?"

"Like I didn't need this on top of everything else," Justine said bitterly.

Carolyn put an arm around her shoulders. "Pregnancy's a little scary at first, but you'll get through it. Your body's storing sugar for the baby. The problem is it's just storing a bit too much. You have to be careful, the weakness can sneak up on you. Listen, I have two at home. Want to talk a little?"

Nurse Carter looked like she'd seen a lot of life, Justine thought. But her earthiness was charming.

"Perhaps it would help," she said.

"Good. I'll meet you back here at three."

"Okay." It was Justine's turn to smile. "And thanks."

Lady Emily said thoughtfully, "Does anyone know if that charming Dr. Keller is married?"

There was no mistaking Carolyn Carter's interest in the matter. "He's not," she said. "But I'm working on it."

Lady Emily positively beamed. "Perhaps I can help."

"Emily, you promised," said the Commodore sternly. "No more matchmaking."

Lady Em winked at Carolyn Carter. "Of course, dear."

The Commodore gave an exasperated sigh. "It's blowing up a bit. Let's go into the lounge."

Lady Em and the Commodore helped Justine inside. The yacht's lounge had ample room to relax and read. There were three dozen Japanese men on board, some kind of museum travel group taught by an old curator named Akiro. There was also a Norwegian couple in their forties, Drs. Ivor and Carla Bernhardsen; traveling with Italian colleagues, Drs. Tony and Bette—pronounced "Bet"—Rietti. They were all geologists, going to Japan for a scientific expedition. Last, there were the Rowes. Till today, Justine had kept to herself. No one on the ship knew she was a Senior Covert Operations Director for the

Central Intelligence Agency, a specialist in armed and unarmed combat. Pregnancy had taken her off the active list. In fact, a whole new life had seemed possible, until that cold Bethesda morning . . .

She pushed it out of her mind. She was going to Tokyo to meet her husband, Admiral Peter MacKenzie. It had fallen to Mac's newly formed section under the Joint Chiefs, and her shop at CIA, to plan a shipment of Russian plutonium to Japan. It was a dangerous cargo, a tempting target for terrorists. In the end, Mac, the ranking officer, decided to go on the freighter himself.

"Can I help you to your cabin, my dear?" asked Lady Emily. "You should rest."

Alex made a distinct *harrumpf.* "Emily, *you* are here to rest."

"I don't want to be a bother," said Justine. "I'm sure this will pass. Do you have children yourself?"

Sadness clouded Lady Em's eyes. "We had a boy. Gerald. He became a missionary in South America. Contracted a disease there. He never recovered."

"I'm sorry."

"He was dedicated," she said proudly, "Like his father. The Commodore was a war hero, you know."

"Mrs. MacKenzie isn't interested in all that, Emily," said the Commodore. "Your husband's in Tokyo on business?" he asked Justine.

"Special assignment with the navy."

The Commodore brightened perceptibly. "A navy man? Why didn't you say so? I commanded submarines in the Big War. Why, we sailed these very waters. What's his name?"

"Peter MacKenzie."

"He wouldn't be Rear Admiral MacKenzie, would he?"

Justine's own pride showed. "That's Mac."

Her stock rose markedly. "Dash it all, I've met the man. Fine CO. He sank that stolen minisub, the *Kentucky,* if I remember correctly. How good to have you among us."

Lady Emily looked amused. To the Commodore, a naval heritage was better than a listing in *Scott's Peerage.*

"Do you play cribbage, Mrs. MacKenzie?"

"No, not really."

"Game of kings," said the Commodore happily. "Game of kings. Admiral MacKenzie. Quite good. Sit *down,* young woman."

3

South Pacific Ocean

THE HUNDRED-THOUSAND-TON RUSSIAN ORE-BULK-
OIL Ship 101, *Marshal Korlov,* shouldered aside
another wave, shuddered mightily, and plunged on
through the South Pacific Ocean. On the bridge,
Captain Nikolai Vladimirovich Raskin lowered his
binoculars and clapped his old friend Admiral Peter
MacKenzie soundly on the back.

"A fine life, eh, Peter?"

"Sunburn, storms, and seasickness," MacKenzie
said idly. "I wish I had my old submarine back."

Raskin knew something was wrong with his friend.
For three weeks he had been trying to get him to open
up, without success. Raskin expanded his considerable chest.

"Stop brooding. Fresh air. Open sea. We never got
those on our submarines."

MacKenzie shielded his eyes. "Where's the
Akatsuki Maru?"

"She'll be steering wide in these seas."

"Okay. I see her."

"I'm sick of staring at the ocean," said Raskin. "Let's go to my cabin and drink some of the best pepper vodka on earth."

"Not on duty," MacKenzie reprimanded mildly.

"A man reaches the upper ranks, he forgets what it was like on the bottom," Raskin muttered.

"You're a Captain First Rank in the Russian navy," he said. "That's hardly the bottom, Nikolai."

Raskin winked. "But not an exalted Admiral like yourself, responsible to three governments. A man to respect." His pompous tone made MacKenzie laugh.

In a way, MacKenzie *was* surprised he had been selected for this post. But his friend Admiral Ben Garver, Chief of Naval Operations, had fought for him with the Joint Chiefs. MacKenzie remembered the pride in Garver's voice when Garver told him.

Mac, you're going to run a new agency that monitors those infernal brush fires springing up around the globe, and puts out the ones that threaten to grow into infernos.

For six months he'd been trained in intelligence work, including time spent with the Navy SEALs working on combat skills. MacKenzie had never felt more mentally capable and physically able. Yet at this critical moment his heart was so full of worry, it took all his strength just to keep going.

"Peter, a drink will loosen you up. Get you talking. Remember?"

Raskin had been the captain of the Soviet submarine *Riga,* serving as MacKenzie's executive officer on the mission to destroy the *Kentucky.* He also helped MacKenzie survive a personal tragedy that almost destroyed him. Raskin's cure was a steady supply of vodka and a marvelous grasp of feelings.

MacKenzie remembered the night it all came tumbling out, in a dingy seamen's bar on the docks of Odessa.

"Nikolai," he had said, "when we're born, God places us on the starting line and we trot off innocently and begin our lives. What we don't know is that thirty seconds later He puts a slavering, horrid monster on that same starting line and points to us and says, Get him!"

"For the first time you feel despair," Raskin had said.

"Yes."

"And you think you are less of a man for it."

"Yes."

"Then you are a fool, and because of it I will drink to you," Raskin had said, raising his glass. "Peter, we Russians drink because we have *always* known there are grinning monsters behind us. That is the truth of the Russian soul. But we have also learned, any day it does not come for you is a good day. So drink, and if God loves you even more than His own son, he may never catch up. Drink, Peter, because one day is all you get, and today we did not die."

So long ago, MacKenzie thought. When Raskin's name appeared on the list of captains the Russians submitted for the *Korlov*, he requested him at once.

First Officer Chenko looked up from his chart table. "Sir, three minutes to check in."

"Very well," Raskin acknowledged. "Get the codebooks."

Chenko removed two thick loose-leaf binders from the safe. He handed one to Raskin and the other to MacKenzie. They placed them on an NSA security console installed back in Russia, and found the correct codes for this transmission. They removed the keys for the console's two locked keyboards from around their necks.

"Unlock," said MacKenzie.

They inserted their keys to free the boards, activating the attached monitors.

"Codes on line," said Chenko.

"Acknowledged. Transmit."

Heavily armed fighter jets stood ready to scramble instantly from air bases and carriers stationed along their route should the correct codes not be received by the National Security Agency's orbiting satellites every hour, on the hour, every day she sailed.

"Codes acknowledged," MacKenzie said. "End transmission."

They withdrew their keys, the codebooks went back into the safe, and the console shut down for another fifty-nine minutes.

Raskin picked up a clipboard. "Chenko, we'll make the inspection now."

"Yes, sir."

Down on the deck, MacKenzie felt the sea more keenly. The waves broke into white foam as far as the eye could see, a million crests marching along. He tugged his cap over his black hair. Age and responsibility had matured him, there was more silver in his hair, but his gray eyes were still sharp and bright, and the rugged planes of his face and body lean and strong, a blend of Scottish and midwestern ancestry.

MacKenzie strapped on a service Beretta. Raskin was trying unsuccessfully to buckle his.

"Obviously food shortages haven't reached your part of the service, Nikolai."

"Moderation is for those of meager spirit," observed Raskin.

"'Cupolas in Russia are gilded with pure gold,'"

quoted MacKenzie. "And so's your stomach, old friend."

"You're quoting the poet Vysotsky!" exclaimed Raskin happily. "You remember him."

"You'd think I'd forget my savior?"

"*I* was your savior. He was merely a voice." Raskin clapped one of his great arms around his friend. "Peter, I've seen for weeks you are saddened by something. Let me help. Did you learn nothing in Russia?"

"Maybe you're right, Nikolai."

"It's private in our bubble."

"Okay."

In the *Korlov*'s cavernous main hold, Russian engineers had constructed a special containment area for the plutonium. A glass bubble covered a hundred stainless steel cylinders set into a turntable-type retriever machine with a pneumatic arm that could move them one by one to a transfer belt. Their polished surfaces glistened softly in bright blue racks. Red and green coils of wire on the pneumatic arm looked like blood vessels. Yellow and black radiation warnings were posted everywhere.

"Sergeant Porter." MacKenzie saluted one of the American Marines on board, who returned it crisply.

"Afternoon, Admiral. Captain Raskin."

"Nice way to see the sights, eh?"

Porter looked around. "Admiral, a swimming pool's just about too much water for me. I'm fine down here."

"Not worried being so close to the hot stuff?"

Porter displayed his usual equanimity. "You going in again, sir?"

"Yes."

Porter smiled. "Then I'm not worried."

21

Mac and Raskin put on radiation suits. The Geiger counter showed only normal background radiation. Raskin secured the outer door and they went through the inner lock.

"I haven't told you everything," MacKenzie began, once inside. "They have these tests to tell you about the baby. One of them measures something called alpha-fetoprotein in the spinal fluid. They find a little, it's okay. The central nervous system is developing normally. Too much means the spine isn't closing. What's supposed to be inside the baby, is outside." MacKenzie's voice almost broke. "You get a number. One to ten. One, okay. Ten, well, it's pretty horrible. The brain might not be developing at all."

"What was your number?"

"Six. Inconclusive. Trouble is, by the time you know for sure, it's past when you can do anything about it."

Raskin shook his head sadly. "How is Justine?"

"She's depressed, Nikolai. Confused. Honestly, I can't say she's the same woman anymore."

"Time, Peter. Perhaps, in time . . ."

"Sure. I know. We figured a long cruise might help. That's why she's on the *Tuscany*."

"And you?"

"Nothing stays the same, Nikolai. I learned that."

Everything had been looking up. New job. Secure marriage. First child. A bright future. Then it all came crashing down. He'd wondered more than once if his personal problems had kept him from concentrating fully on his task. Had he spent too much time with Justine and not enough on his job?

They finished checking all the seals and recording the radiation readings around the cylinders and the oxygen tanks. Care here was essential. Plutonium was one of the most toxic substances on earth. A speck could cause cancer.

"Nikolai, talking about problems. Will you let me return the favor?"

Raskin looked at him curiously. "How did you know?"

"It was in your dossier. First your wife dies of cancer, then a month later your parents are killed in a car crash. I'm truly sorry. Can I help?"

"The time for help is over, Peter, I failed Irina. My wife died because the country is poor, and medicine is scarce. In the end my rank meant nothing. I live with guilt every day. I tell you, when my parents died, it felt like . . . punishment."

"That's crazy."

"Peter, I am sixty-two. They knew my pleasure to work with you again. This voyage is to honor me. But the *Korlov* is my last command. I am being retired."

That, MacKenzie hadn't known. "What will you do?"

"I don't know. I have no wife, no parents, no children. Normally Irina and I would have retired to a good life. A pension. A small cottage. But she is dead, and those promises cannot be kept. The economy is bankrupt. You can't even get a decent apartment. There are no jobs. What kind of future is that?"

"Come to Washington."

Raskin smiled sadly. "I don't want to leave Russia, Peter. I wouldn't be a good American. With the exception of yourself, you are too meager a people for me."

"When this trip is over, we'll make plans. There are options . . ."

"Now that you are such a big shot, eh?"

"I was thinking street sweeper."

"In Russia that's a good job."

It was almost time for the next transmission. They sealed up the containment area and climbed back to the main deck. MacKenzie's shoulders were bowed under the weight of his conflicts. He felt very much afraid and alone.

4

Tuscany

JUSTINE HAD SPENT THE AFTERNOON PLAYING CRIBBAGE
with Lady Emily and the Commodore, then met
Carolyn in the lounge. Afterwards, as she lay in her
stateroom, her mind just churned endlessly, so she
went out to walk the polished decks, avoiding other
passengers. By nightfall, a thick fog bank had rolled
in, suiting her isolation.

Her life had stopped that morning in the doctor's
office in Bethesda Naval Hospital. The pictures of
infants born with open spines were so terrifying, she'd
rushed to the bathroom and thrown up. Later, despite
Mac's hand in hers, the coldness had crept in. She
could be nourishing a monster inside her. The fog
swirled before her like dreams. No balls to throw. No
dances to teach. No school plays to attend. Nothing
but protracted misery, and death at an early age.

She tried to remember there was a chance the child
was normal. Could she take the chance? Maternal

feelings welled up. Could she kill her child on a possibility? Mac told her to have faith. She'd sneered at that and pushed him away. It wasn't in *his* belly. *His* blood wasn't feeding what might be in those terrible pictures.

The ocean raced past, an endless series of pools and eddies leading her nowhere. The sole pleasant time in her day had been spent with Carolyn Carter.

"I'll tell you," Carolyn had said, her white uniform filled to the point of bursting, munching a celery stalk from a second Bloody Mary, I'm-off-duty-thank-you-kindly. "The first year of motherhood is like being a POW. Sleep deprivation and torture."

"Should I file that under things they don't tell you?"

"Believe it, dearie. And more. Men wrote the book, and what do they know about anything? You're walking around fat and ugly, and they're saying it's beautiful. Sure, for them it's beautiful. *They're* not pregnant."

It was the first time Justine had laughed in days. It felt good.

"You gotta laugh, hon," Carolyn said. "World's too tough to take otherwise. Besides, at least you're meeting someone in Tokyo. I'll just sit here and put in calls to my mother back in San Diego."

"Divorced?"

Carolyn lit a cigarette. "Widowed. One of those stupid things you hear about and never figure will happen to you. He was playing ball with his friends like he did every Sunday. He had a heart attack running for second base. We had an okay marriage. Just not a lot of insurance. I went a little crazy for a while, but the kids needed taking care of, and food had to be put on the table. So I dried the tears and went back to work."

"How'd you get here?"

"I got tired of being pawed by hospital docs used to pretty young nurses rolling over easy on the chance they'll get married. If you haven't noticed, I'm not exactly underdeveloped. The guys in the bars and clubs? Gimme a break. Out here it's quiet. People are nice. And Phillip, well . . ."

"You like him, don't you?"

"It's scary how much. He snaps those cute fingers and I jump."

"Don't underrate yourself."

"Sweetie, I'm too old not to know how old I am. But thanks." Carolyn drained the last of her drink. "We'll talk more later, okay?"

"I'd like that," Justine had said.

Stewards were already serving in the dining room. The Japanese sat at two long tables, the curator, Akiro, at the head of one, with a vacant place to his right. The handsome blond, blue-eyed Bernhardsens and dark, professorish Riettis were dining together. Justine caught part of their animated discussion as she passed by.

"We can't get the pictures with the robot, Tony. I tell you the angle's too steep," Ivor Bernhardsen said.

"What if it blows while we're inside?" Rietti responded. "You remember Peru. Or don't you care?"

"You know damn well I do."

"You're not being fair, Tony," said Carla. "Bette?"

Bette took her husband's hand. "Whatever Tony thinks best."

"If you both feel that way, why did you come?" Bernhardsen demanded.

"To keep you from killing yourself," said Rietti. "You've lost your mind."

Bernhardsen's chiseled face was filled with anger. "At least I haven't lost my nerve."

Justine missed Tony Rietti's reply when Lady Emily called out, "My dear, join us, won't you? Alex and I have a place all ready for you."

They were at the captain's table with Dr. Keller and Carolyn Carter. Justine couldn't avoid them without being rude.

"Thank you. I do have an appetite."

She turned to lay her jacket across a chair and found herself face-to-face with one of the Japanese men. For a second, instincts trained by years of combat sounded an alarm. There was something in the man's manner, an aura she had learned to watch for, one she knew well. It was a familiarity with the ways of death. Even in baggy clothing, he moved with the fluid containment of a trained *Karateka,* a combat master. His eyes were the color of fire. Her mind registered that she was facing one of her own breed. Then someone called, "Shuto!" and he was gone, and her own troubles returned to dull the brief contact.

"Mrs. MacKenzie, Captain Moré." Alex Rowe presented her to the portly, bearded master of the ship.

"Madame MacKenzie, we have seen too little of you. You walk the decks like a ghost."

"I'm here to rest, Captain."

"I hope you are enjoying the voyage."

"It's been very pleasant."

Moré speared a shrimp. "We have had to rely on the Commodore for news about you."

"My husband and I are vacationing in Tokyo."

Carolyn's thick hair fell to her shoulders. She wore

a dark skirt and sleeveless blouse. Stockings and heels showed off her fine legs. "Vacationing from what?" she asked. "I forgot to ask what you do."

"I produce educational media."

"Oh, that's nice."

It had taken Justine years to find something she was never asked to explain, absolutely no one had any questions about, and about which there was nothing further to say.

Moré poured more wine. "As a military man, of course, I appreciate your Admiral's exploits. I imagine he'll rise to great prominence, like Commodore Rowe."

"You embarrass me, Captain," said the Commodore.

"Don't be so modest, Alex," said Lady Rowe. To the rest she said, "He was awarded the Victoria Cross for sinking five enemy ships in one night before his sub was hit. He barely survived. He was stranded on some deserted island or other. Sophie something."

"Sōfu gan, dear. But I'd prefer to be known for my European Community service. The war was over a long time ago."

Justine lifted her wine and looked questioningly at Dr. Keller. He mouthed the words *just one*. She sipped it gratefully.

"Admiral MacKenzie wouldn't be on the *Marshal Korlov*, would he?" Moré had a twinkle in his eye. "We're going to pass very close to her tonight."

"I can't say."

"Madame, everybody sailing these seas knows the *Korlov* is passing through, and exactly what she's carrying. All those countries telling her to stay out of their waters, eh?"

For a moment she thought about threatening to

report the Gaelic braggart to his superiors as soon as they docked, but she let it go, and changed the subject.

"Phillip, did you always want to be a doctor?"

"Always. I used to go on rounds with my uncle. He forever seemed to have a letter from a grateful patient to show me. It affected me deeply."

"And going to sea?"

"I'm from an old French Jewish family. A branch of the Rothschilds. Social responsibility was drummed into me from the start. I suppose I rebelled after all that school and training. Perhaps it was irresponsible to go to sea, but I wanted to see more of the world."

"You have a kindred soul in Nurse Carter," said Lady Emily.

Phillip patted Carolyn's hand. "We share more than the desire to travel. Carolyn is a wonderful partner."

Carolyn blushed. "Why, thank you, Phillip."

Judging from Keller's reaction, Justine thought, Carolyn might have more of a chance than she thought. Justine didn't know why she didn't warm to Keller. Maybe she was just too damn picky. If he made Carolyn happy, she had no reason to question it.

"Steak for you tonight, Justine," Keller said. "You need the protein."

"I had my heart set on the duck with black cherries."

"Too much sugar. Even the wine is pushing it. High-protein diet. Meat, chicken, fish. Or the weakness comes back."

"The baby's in charge now, my dear," said Lady Emily. "You might as well accept it."

"When are you due?" asked Captain Moré.

Maybe never. "Late spring."

Carolyn picked up her glass and the others followed. "Here's to the old saying that babies bring luck."

Later on, Justine was reminded of the toast. And just how wrong people can be.

Justine went to sleep right after dinner, only to be awakened by waves of nausea in the middle of the night. It was all she could do to make it into the head and throw up. It was getting worse. She could barely keep any food down.

She pressed a cold towel to her face.

"You look horrible," she said to her reflection.

What time was it? Three in the morning. Damn. She'd never get back to sleep. The stateroom felt like a cage. She wished Mac were here. Moré had said they'd pass near the *Korlov* tonight. Maybe she could see its lights. Anything to feel closer to Mac. And the air would do her good.

She slipped on jeans and a gray sweatshirt, sneakers, ankle-warmer socks, and tied her hair back. Her jeans still closed without strangling her. She pulled on a jacket and hit the door handle, but it was locked. At first she thought it might be jammed, but it was locked from the outside. And the phone on her night table was dead. She looked at the wall compass. They were heading west instead of north. Alarms began to go off in her head.

For a full five minutes she sat on the bed, deep in thought, so motionless she looked frozen. Contingencies. Equations of possibility. One thought kept emerging and could not be ignored.

We're passing close to the Korlov.

Was the *Tuscany* being used for a raid? If it was, who was behind it and how were they staging it? What did her play have to be to put herself in the best position if it couldn't be stopped? Her advantage lay in knowing the *Korlov*'s security arrangements. She had an idea. She'd have to improvise as time went on, but under the circumstances it was the best she could do.

She used the screwdriver in her Swiss Army knife to remove the door plate and disengage the locking mechanism. She took two pieces of ID from her wallet and tossed the rest out the porthole. She threw out all her expensive dresses and suits, keeping only the simplest skirt and blouse and a pair of tan shoes. Those she cut the labels out of, and stuffed them into a big leather handbag.

She dumped most of her makeup and scrubbed her face clean. She threw her Dior underthings out the porthole and changed into the inexpensive packaged brand she used when she worked out. Jewelry went next, without remorse. She put her jeans, sneakers, and sweatshirt back on. She was all business, moving quickly, propelled by years of experience.

How easily I change, she thought. How much I hate it.

Weapons next. She had no gun, but she wasn't unarmed. The handle of her suitcase came away when she unscrewed the clasps, leaving a weapon from her childhood, a narrow four-inch oak rod with rounded ends called a *pesas* because it was shaped like a tiny dumbbell. Specially built for her, it fit neatly into her fist, as deadly as a gun or a knife if you knew how to use it. She knotted her hair and used the *pesas* to secure it. It looked like a simple hair accessory.

She couldn't afford to think about the baby now, not and do what was necessary. She had to find the rage inside, the primeval thing that let her kill if she had to. *Are you listening in there? Do you know what Mama's planning?* Someday she would tell her baby how she led the Angel's Chorus when she was a child herself. Their screams scared the hated National Guard into running so the guerrillas could kill them. Then later, she was in charge of a rebel group, an accomplished killer. And as a woman, Doña Justiñana, the leader who broke her brother out of jail in Managua itself and escaped with half the army chasing her. That was when she'd met Captain Peter MacKenzie and her life changed. She would tell her child all of it.

If she's born.

She steeled herself. None of them might make it if what she feared was happening. *Be safe, little one. Mama has things to do.* She cut up her suitcase and fed it out the porthole. She made the bed, cleaned the bathroom, and repaired the lock. When she was done, no trace remained of anyone ever occupying the cabin.

A different woman opened the door and slipped into the corridor. Plain. Of simple carriage. A Latino working girl with nothing but a handbag. She tried other cabin doors, just to be sure. They were all locked.

She made her way aft to the staff quarters.

5

Tuscany

AKIRO ENTERED THE *TUSCANY*'S BRIDGE. SHUTO HAD taken control of the ship.

"Opposition?" he asked his son.

"Eliminated."

"Do we have sufficient hostages?"

"Italian, French, Norwegian, American, and Russian. The whole UN would have to mount a rescue mission if it comes to that. But it won't."

"It is still prudent to have them."

"They take up space and occupy my men."

"They won't, on the island."

"I still disagree."

"Considering that," said Akiro, "you acted with admirable restraint."

"That's an interesting perspective, Father. At least twenty are dead. Some of ours, too."

"But not my special ones, eh?" Akiro patted Hiroki's and Ito's black-clad backs as they worked at their stations. Hiroki had come to him two years after

Shuto. He was six foot three with muscles a power lifter would envy. Ito, working communications, was the opposite, small and lithe. Akiro had rescued them both, when the Museum was built. They and Shuto were like brothers, inseparable since childhood, all sharing the same secret.

"How do you see in this fog, Hiroki?" asked Akiro.

"Instruments, Akiro-san."

"We're drifting toward the *Korlov*," Ito explained. "The *Akatsuki Maru* is trying to raise us on radio, warning us off."

"What will we do?" asked Akiro.

"Continue to drift," Shuto said. "Every few minutes we broadcast a weak SOS, then go dead. Soon they'll come to check."

Akiro was the leader, but Shuto was his general. Hiroki was Shuto's second-in-command. Ito was third, the communications expert. Mori was the fourth child. Akiro always thought of him as Shuto's stolid sergeant. He was out securing the passengers. The rest of the men had been "adopted" by Akiro as children, over the years. Now grown, they were loyal to him, all joined by what they were.

"Look towards the bow, Father. See how we spent Miagi's money."

The men were opening crates from the storage hold marked Museum Expedition. Shuto's men moved with confidence born of meticulous training. Some inflated rubber boats. Others attached silenced motors or assembled weapons. They all wore black T-shirts, black boots and pants. Each carried an automatic rifle and a combat knife, and wore night-vision goggles.

"The course is locked in, Shuto," Hiroki advised. "I should be in the boat."

"Go. I'll be there in a minute."

Hiroki went to the main deck and ordered the boats into the water. He got into the first with five men. They checked their weapons. The ocean was calm, the fog remained thick. Perfect conditions. He picked up his walkie-talkie and signaled they were ready to go.

Justine watched the terrorists from the shadows under the bridge stairs. They were well trained. The engine room crew was already under their control. Captain Moré and his officers had been disposed of quickly and efficiently, all but Dr. Keller. Evidently the doctor had value, which sparked her second idea. The rubber boats confirmed her worst fear. They were going after the *Korlov*. It was too late to stop them. She couldn't take all the terrorists alone.

She drew farther back into the shadows. A guard was coming, carrying a big ring of keys. Probably the one who locked them all in. She was in high gear now. The idea was evolving. She swung around the railing and drove both feet into the guard's chest. He slammed into the bulkhead and went down without seeing who hit him. She used the *pesas* deftly, avoiding the killing blow. He'd be unconscious for at least an hour. She pulled him into the corridor and used his keys to unlock the infirmary door.

"Dr. Keller?"

He was cowering by the instrument cabinet. She shoved the guard into a closet.

"Justine, how did you get here? Those men killed Captain Moré and the others. They locked me in."

"I know. I saw."

"Someone called Shuto told me to get the medical supplies ready. What do they want?"

"They're using the *Tuscany* to hijack a military ship. They'll want you to treat their wounded."

"What are we going to do?"

"No time to talk. You'll have to trust me."

He was still shaking. "What can *you* do?"

She ducked the question. "Just stay here. Don't do anything brave. I'll be back."

Carolyn was asleep when Justine slipped in. She put her hand over Carolyn's mouth and shook her.

"Shh. Be quiet. It's me."

Carolyn came awake fast, eyes wide. "What are you doing here?"

"Listen. I don't produce educational media. I'm with the Central Intelligence Agency. Covert operations. Look at my ID. You understand what I'm saying?"

"I read the papers. A spy. Is this for real?"

"We're in danger. What Moré said about my husband's ship is true. The Japanese passengers are terrorists and they've taken over the *Tuscany*. They're going after it. I need your help. Get dressed."

Carolyn swung her feet onto the floor. "I'm going to call the captain."

"He's dead," Justine said bluntly. "So are the officers."

"What about Phillip? Oh God, not him."

"No. I just saw him."

Carolyn shook her head. "This can't be happening."

"It happens all the time. You want proof?"

"What could you say that would convince me?"

"Not say. I had to go through a tango to get to you."

"Tango?"

"*T*, tango, terrorist." Justine led Carolyn to a closet in the corridor.

Carolyn stared at the dead man. His clothing and weapons certainly weren't tourist issue. "Look at the size of him. His neck's broken. How could you?"

"It's what I do. Now, decide. We have to hurry."

Carolyn was fighting for balance. "This morning we were two regular people. I don't know you now. Leave me out of it."

"It's too late for that. You want to see your kids again?"

"You've got a baby inside. What do you think?"

Justine ignored the stab of pain. "Then I'm your only chance. Decide."

Events sometimes propelled you despite what you wanted, Carolyn thought. She certainly knew about that.

"What do you want me to do?"

"Stop talking and get dressed. Pack as much as you can in a suitcase. Makeup, toothbrush. The whole works. I've got to get rid of the body."

"Pack? Why?"

"You're getting married."

The fog was all around them in the water. Shuto rode in the second boat. In five minutes the *Korlov* was due to transmit to its satellite watchdogs. He signaled Hiroki to proceed. Loyal Hiroki. Always there for him. Hiroki gunned his muted engine. Fifty feet away, his boat was lost to sight.

Shuto looked back to the bridge. Akiro's arms were folded; he was composed even at the height of things. A thought intruded into Shuto's mind before he could shield it. He was worried Akiro might catch it. There had been times as a child when he would have sworn the old man could read his thoughts.

More than you know has been unleashed this night, Akiro-san.

Shuto unlimbered the missile launcher. Beside him, Ito was watching his instruments. If Hiroki was one part of him, Ito was the other. The little one understood so much.

"Have they sent the signal?"

"Transmitting now," Ito said. "*Akatsuki Maru* approaching."

"They won't come any closer. Let's go," Shuto said.

The small boat sped over the waves. There wasn't a radar in the world that would spot its low profile on the surface. Shuto activated the shoulder-fired missile launcher. The warhead was armor-piercing.

"One mile," Ito said.

Shuto peered into the fog. Lights showed. He could see the outline of her stack. The bridge.

Ito pressed his headphone tightly to his ear. "Hiroki reports he is on the *Korlov*."

The *Akatsuki Maru* began to turn. The captain wasn't going to take his ship any further. He'd wait for the fog to lift and call in the jets to see if the SOS was for real. The missile's sighting mechanism amplified starlight. Shuto had a good image. There was a sudden color shift. The crosshairs merged.

"Target ranged and acquired," Shuto said.

The needles on Ito's gauges jumped. "They've sent the signal."

Shuto pressed the trigger and the missile flew off his shoulder on a trail of fire. The bridge of the *Akatsuki Maru* exploded. His second shot pierced the engine room. A more violent explosion followed. Deck fires flickered in the fog. The ship began to break up. It sank quickly. Silence rolled back over the ocean.

"What about survivors?" asked Ito. He could see them. They all could.

Shuto said, "There are none. Head for the *Korlov.*"

6

Korlov

MacKenzie plunged down the bridge stairs and ran for cover. Gunfire was hot in the air and he had nothing but his walkie-talkie. The Japanese had burst in with a hail of automatic weapons fire, cutting down two of Raskin's officers as they tried to transmit an SOS. Only Raskin's quick reaction with his pistol killing one terrorist had allowed them to escape.

"Nikolai?" he whispered into the walkie-talkie.

"Main hold," came the curt reply.

MacKenzie heard cutting and drilling. The terrorists were working inside the bridge. Guards had been posted outside. He went forward and found Raskin in the shadows under the big loading crane.

"You all right, Nikolai?"

"Barely."

"We're in trouble. These guys know exactly what they're doing. They're working on the security console."

Raskin fingered the chain around his neck. "Even with the codebooks, they need our keys to unlock it. What should we do?"

"Find Porter and his men. Try to retake the bridge and call for help."

"What about the *Akatsuki Maru*?"

"Just hope it sent an SOS," MacKenzie said soberly.

Down in the main hold there were more casualties. MacKenzie looked thoughtfully at the containment area. It was time to make his new training pay off.

"Nikolai, take the transmitter out of your walkie-talkie and open the airlock."

Raskin brightened. "A plan?"

"More like an act of desperation. You'll probably hate it."

"Why?"

MacKenzie told him.

"You're right. Airlock open."

MacKenzie removed the cover from his own walkie-talkie and discarded the speaker.

"Empty the powder from some of your cartridges into your handkerchief."

Raskin did as he was instructed.

"Now put the handkerchief against the speaker wires and tape the receive button down. That's it. Secure it to one of the oxygen tanks by the valve. All right, close it up."

"It's inventive, in a macabre sort of way," Raskin admitted.

MacKenzie hid the transmitter section of his walkie-talkie in his shoe and discarded the rest.

"How do we get to the Marines' quarters?"

Raskin opened a hatch into a foul-smelling walkway between the hull and the hold wall. "We'll use this service corridor. They'll have the decks secured by now."

Footing was slippery, the deck wet and moldy. After a few minutes Raskin said, "We should be right below the Marines' deck now."

The hatch opened into a deserted corridor. They made their way quietly up the decks.

"Guard," Raskin whispered, drawing his gun.

MacKenzie stopped him. "Too much noise."

Raskin thought for a moment. "Follow me."

Twenty seconds later, MacKenzie walked into the corridor and threw his hands up.

"I surrender. Don't shoot!"

The guard relaxed, and Raskin hit him from behind with a stream of high-pressure water from the fire hose. He sprawled into MacKenzie's arms and Mac hit him the way the SEALs had taught him. Raskin dragged the unconscious guard inside.

Sergeant Porter sprang up. "Am I glad to see you, sir. I didn't know if anyone was left alive."

"Report," said MacKenzie.

"They just burst into the containment area, five of them. Took us totally by surprise. Kelly and Rawlins bought it right away. It was over in five seconds. I never got my gun out. If I had to say, sir, they were ready to kill me, but only if they had to. I guess they didn't." He exposed his neck. An ugly red welt was visible.

MacKenzie nodded. Professionals. A group of international hostages would be a valuable bargaining chip in a volatile situation.

"You did what you could, Sergeant."

"I'm just sorry I didn't get any of the bastards."

MacKenzie gave Porter the terrorist's rifle and night-vision goggles.

"Could you hit the guards outside the bridge from the main hold?"

"Yes, sir. I'm qualified long range."

"Captain Raskin and I will try and make it to the security console. Nikolai?"

Raskin checked the corridor. "All clear."

"Let's go."

Raskin led them to a ventilation tunnel with metal rungs set into the walls. Porter climbed first, then Raskin and MacKenzie.

Security for this voyage had taken a backseat to expediency from the beginning, MacKenzie thought miserably. Now the problems had come home to roost. Japan had pushed hard to get the plutonium to keep its multibillion-dollar breeder reactor project going, Russia grabbed it for the hard currency, and the United States went along to speed the destruction of former Soviet ICBMs. Yet no government took full responsibility for the dangerous cargo.

Eighteen minutes to the next signal. The jets would come if it wasn't sent. He'd already considered tossing his key over the side. The fog was the unforeseen element. They were already miles off course. The jets might never find them. He had to take the bridge, whatever the cost, and transmit their position.

"Five minutes, Sergeant."

Porter adjusted the night-vision goggles. "Yes, sir."

The deck was deserted but for rolling shadows. Overhead, cargo lines creaked in the sea breeze. They could have been on the moon, it was so isolated. MacKenzie and Raskin made it to the bridge and waited. Porter was very good. There were two shots, and the guards pitched over. MacKenzie went up the stairs and kicked the door open. Raskin bowled into the lone terrorist at the controls. The man went down easily. Too easily.

"Peter?" Raskin held up a black shirt and pants stuffed with rags.

"The guards, too," MacKenzie said. "And the security unit's gone. It's a trap."

A voice behind them said, "I am Shuto. My brother Ito assures me he can activate the unit without your keys, but I'd rather not put him to the test. Give me the keys. Your part in this is over."

MacKenzie reacted just as Justine had taught him. Don't think, do. He raised the .45 and pulled the trigger, but Shuto was no longer there. The shot shattered the bridge window, showering them with glass. Amidst that shower Shuto moved like quicksilver, suddenly alongside them, his hands and feet flashing. The gun dropped from MacKenzie's hand as he fell. Raskin grunted in pain.

MacKenzie lay on the deck, helpless. Shuto hovered over him. Death was written on his face. MacKenzie's senses narrowed to pinpoint focus as the Japanese lifted his hand to deliver the final blow. But as Shuto's amber eyes bored into his, something completely unexpected happened. A connection coursed between them like some kind of electrical circuit closing. Suddenly MacKenzie was trapped in a universe of agony inside those burning orbs. Wonder overcame Shuto. MacKenzie was equally shocked.

One shared thought: *We are the same.*

A wordless question: *How can this be?*

Unanswerable, it changed death to life.

MacKenzie felt the key torn from his neck, then a brief stab of pain, then nothing.

7

Tuscany

JUSTINE PUSHED CAROLYN INSIDE THE INFIRMARY. THE loss of Captain Moré and his officers had hit the nurse hard. She had to get over it if she was to bear what was coming.

"How could they kill those men?" she asked Justine.

"They were excess baggage."

"So they just killed them?" Carolyn was horrified. "Is it what you would do?"

"Depending on the circumstances. Yes."

"I don't like you as much," Carolyn said.

"Sometimes I don't like myself much either. Come out, Phillip."

Keller hugged Carolyn. "Thank heavens you're all right."

Justine pulled off her sweatshirt and bra.

"Justine, I'm as liberated as the next woman, but—"

"What are you doing?" Keller demanded.

Justine faced him, naked. "I'm sorry, Phillip. When you wake up, try and remember I had no choice."

She drove the terrorist's knife into Keller's side. Blood spurted onto her skin.

Keller cried out in agony, clutched himself, and sank to the deck.

"No!" cried Carolyn, grabbing her.

Justine pushed her aside roughly. "Stop it! I didn't kill him. Look for yourself." There was a lot of blood and pain, but Keller wouldn't die. That wasn't her plan.

"Why did you do it?"

"I had to. Help me get him in bed."

"I don't know who's worse, you or them," Carolyn said bitterly. She began to dress Phillip's wound.

"I'll do that," Justine said. "Get me a nurse's uniform."

"Why?"

"Do it!"

Justine washed herself off, then took the basin and spilled the bloody contents on the still unconscious terrorist.

"Listen to me, Carolyn. The officers were killed, the crew is expendable, the passengers will be prisoners. But they have to give a doctor a degree of freedom to do his work, and if the doctor is disabled, his nurse gets it. All this, for that. You understand?"

Carolyn glared at her. "Here."

"Thank you."

The white uniform Carolyn filled to the point of bursting was short on Justine, and loose in the bust, but wearable. She put the rest of her things in Carolyn's room, *her* room now, and put Carolyn's bag in Keller's adjoining quarters.

"Unpack. Make it look like you live here. From now

on, you're Mrs. Keller. Understand? And I'm the nurse, Justine Segurra."

"You can't treat patients," Carolyn scoffed.

"You'd be surprised what I know about wounds."

The door rattled. Justine pressed the knife into Carolyn's hand.

"Here they come. Get ready to act up a storm. Defend your husband."

Akiro entered, followed by Shuto. Carolyn did her job.

"Stay away, you murderers." She brandished the bloody knife. It wasn't such a stretch. Her concern for Phillip was genuine.

Shuto stepped forward and did something too quick to follow. The knife dropped into his hand. Justine blinked. *Fast* wasn't the word to describe him. There was a plane of movement beyond mere physicality that the true Masters spoke of. The knowing-before. Not quite prescience, but so close it was spooky. In that moment, she realized Shuto was better than she was. It made her afraid.

"Don't hurt him," Carolyn pleaded.

"What happened here?" Akiro demanded.

Justine shielded Keller. It was a delicate moment. Thank God she had been a virtual hermit all voyage.

"Dr. Keller jumped your man out there and ended up with a knife in him. We just got him stabilized. Please, he was just doing what he thought he should to protect his wife and me."

Shuto spoke in Japanese and the guard was brought in, looking groggy. He responded sluggishly.

"Mori says he has no memory of this."

"Okay," said Justine. *"I knifed him."*

Akiro snorted. "This is foolish, Shuto. No one has any blood on them but Mori. He reacted as trained."

"Maybe." Shuto turned his gaze on Justine. She willed every muscle to relax. He would sense the slightest aggression. She reached inside to her baby. *What are you?* she wondered. Infant or monster? Sadness welled up inside her. Fear, too. The warrior saw it, and relaxed.

"We need you," Akiro said. "There are wounded. My men will bring your supplies."

"Mrs. Keller is a doctor's wife," said Justine. "She can help me."

"I won't leave my husband."

Carolyn was warming to her role.

Shuto turned to Mori. "Bring him."

They went out on deck. The *Tuscany* was moored next to the *Korlov*. Shuto's men were transferring the security console onto the *Tuscany*'s bridge. Akiro was clever. The *Tuscany* would continue to sail the *Korlov*'s prescribed route, sending the correct signal every hour, no one the wiser. Justine was desperately worried about Mac. Oh, please be alive, she prayed.

The terrorists herded the passengers onto the *Korlov* with the few clothes they could carry. Awakened in the middle of the night, they were groggy and scared. Fog dimmed the ship's lights. The air was cold. Commodore and Lady Emily stood together, shivering in their nightclothes. The Bernhardsens and Riettis huddled against the chill.

"Please," Justine said. "Let me get them blankets."

Shuto nodded. It took but a moment to get them from the *Tuscany*'s deck chairs. She draped one around Lady Emily's shoulders, whispering in her ear.

Lady Emily nodded, surprise and understanding showing in her wise, gray eyes.

"Of course, my dear. I will. And thank you for thinking of us."

49

8

Korlov

MACKENZIE WATCHED THE *TUSCANY* SET SAIL WITH GRIM
foreboding. The security console would draw the
satellites away. They were alone now.

The passengers stood together, a multinational col-
lection of hostages. MacKenzie, Raskin, and Porter
exchanged names and countries with Alex and Emily
Rowe from England, Ivor and Carla Bernhardsen
from Norway, Tony and Bette Rietti from Italy.
MacKenzie almost died when he saw Justine wasn't
among them, then his heart abruptly jump-started
when she came on board wearing a nurse's uniform.
She was carrying a medical bag, and with another
woman was tending to a medical officer on a stretcher.
What was she up to?

"Admiral MacKenzie?"

"Yes."

"I like the way you look at her," Lady Emily
whispered, eyes shining. "We're not to give her away.

She said to tell you she's fine, and to remember Segurra. What does that mean?"

It means she's gone back to what she was, MacKenzie thought. He couldn't contact her, or indicate he knew her in any way.

"It's her maiden name," he explained. "Tell anyone else who knew her to call her that."

"She never spoke to anyone else, not who's still alive," Lady Emily said quietly. "Only Alex and me and Carolyn."

"Is that Carolyn with her?"

Lady Emily nodded. *"She* was the nurse. Now she looks like a passenger."

"Who's the wounded man?"

"Phillip Keller, our ship's doctor. I don't know how he got hurt."

MacKenzie's admiration for his wife grew. She'd made herself as plain as possible—no makeup, hair in a bun—and taken the nurse's identity. What must it be doing to her, called to action with a child inside her? This close, not being able to touch her was almost a physical pain.

Voices were raised. Across the deck, Akiro and Shuto were arguing. The passengers watched them anxiously.

"I wonder what that's about," said MacKenzie.

"Ivor and I speak some Japanese," offered Carla Bernhardsen. "The younger one says they don't need this many hostages."

"That's Shuto." MacKenzie's last contact with the terrorist was still very much on his mind.

Commodore Rowe turned to MacKenzie. "I'm sorry to meet you again under these circumstances, Admiral. We served together in Holy Loch. Commodore Alex Rowe."

"I remember you, Commodore. This is Captain Nikolai Raskin of the Russian navy."

"Difficult times, eh, Captain?" said the Commodore.

"*Da.* So it seems," Raskin agreed.

"We can't just stand here," argued Bernhardsen.

"We can until those guns go away," Raskin advised him.

"I'm not waiting to be shot." Bernhardsen made straight for Shuto. "See here, you!"

Carla went after him. "Ivor!"

The terrorists clubbed him to the deck.

"Help him," Carla cried.

Shuto and Akiro were watching. Shuto's expression seemed to say, See? More trouble than they're worth. He lifted his hand in an unmistakable gesture. Weapons rose.

Bette Rietti cried out, "No!"

Lady Emily began to pray.

MacKenzie pulled the transmitter from his boot.

"Shuto, I'll sink this boat at the first shot. Believe me. I'm not bluffing."

Akiro said calmly, "How?"

MacKenzie stepped away from the hostages. "Send a man to the containment area to check the oxygen cylinders. Don't try to defuse the mechanism or it will go off."

Ito detached himself from the others and went into the hold.

"Dr. Bernhardsen needs treatment," said Justine.

For an instant she held MacKenzie's eyes. Tensions were rising. Something had to give soon. She moved closer to him in anticipation of a fight. Her hand dipped into the medical bag and came out with a scalpel.

Ito came back. "There is a bomb."

Shuto nodded. He wouldn't underestimate the Admiral again. The man continued to disturb him. What exactly had happened on the bridge?

"Tell me what you want," Shuto said.

"A lifeboat. Food and water. A compass." MacKenzie couldn't actually use any of those things, but they were expected. He had to stay with the ship and the plutonium.

Shuto shook his head. "We went to considerable lengths to insure our security. And I don't believe in standoffs."

"Shoot, I push the button. There's enough pure oxygen in that room by now for a fireball they'll see in Tokyo."

"An interesting thought," said Akiro. "Admiral, if I can convince you that we have an entirely different purpose than you imagine, would you put the detonator down?"

MacKenzie wished he could look at Justine. What would she tell him?

"What is your name?" Akiro asked.

"Rear Admiral Peter MacKenzie, United States Navy."

"I am Akiro, Admiral-san. Curator of Japan's Atomic Bomb Museum."

It was an odd moment, killers and victims held apart by one frail old man.

"I give you my word, Shuto will not harm you. I just want to tell you a story."

The fog enclosed them, a room in the mist. MacKenzie cradled the transmitter.

"I'm listening."

"My story begins in the hills of Hiroshima," said Akiro. "I was with my fiancée and friends. It was the summer of 1945, a very time long ago to most of you."

"My wife and I remember it quite well, sir," said Commodore Rowe. "It was our war, too."

Akiro bowed his head. "Forgive me for not recognizing our shared years, venerable one. My friends and I were pilots. We were on leave, celebrating in a kind of desperate way because our unit had been selected to be *Kamikaze.* To die for the Emperor. I did not want to die. I hated the war. I'd watched my countrymen turn the code of the warrior into the code of the barbarian. I was sickened by the unthinking slaughter. Nanking. Battan. The death camps. What we did as a nation should have condemned us forever in the world's eyes, but we found our absolution that day. An inferno hotter even than our guilt burned away our crimes. The ultimate punishment. Nuclear destruction.

"We had all heard tales of the monster weapon the U.S. was building, but we thought it was a tale to frighten us. To make us better *Kamikaze.* It was no tale. The first thing I saw was the Light. My fiancée was blinded when it struck her eyes. My comrades died within days, suffering horribly. I was lucky. My fiancée fell against me and we tumbled down a hill. It saved our lives. When the wind passed, I climbed back to the top to see the city. I'm an old man now, yet I can still see the mushroom cloud rising above it as clearly as I see you here now.

"People wandered blindly, their clothes burned off what was left of their skin. Cars were filled with corpses. Buildings were swept into oblivion. I helped where I could. The children bore the worst of it. Homeless. Parentless. When there was no meat, they ate . . . what they could. So many died. Tens of thousands. An entire city was thrown back to prehistoric times by ten minutes of the full fury of Man. I watched it all, and if that wasn't enough, again at Nagasaki.

"When we'd cleaned up the city as best we could, and the military that had led us into such disaster was gone, a group of us vowed that such things must never happen again. We built the Museum for everyone to remember. So they would never permit such stupidity again. The world saw the pictures because *we* collected them. Heard the stories because *we* published them. We never wanted them to forget. I am the last curator. All the rest are dead."

MacKenzie was unsettled. This was no terrorist as he had fought them before. But if Akiro was so opposed to nuclear destruction, why did he want the plutonium?

It was almost as if Akiro read MacKenzie's mind. "My countrymen *forgot,* Admiral. They forgot! All journeys begin with a single step. We protested that step, but the government said we will buy just a little of this plutonium to make the reactor run. So we relented. Then someone wondered, What if we should run out? All our TVs and games and computers would stop. So we'd better stockpile. And yet another voice spoke up and said slyly, Let us remember that China has nuclear weapons, and North Korea. With the U.S. pulling back, we cannot stand naked anymore. Why not take just a little of this enormous pile of poison we are bringing to our shores and set it aside for weapons of our own? You see, Admiral? It goes on and on. One step leads to another until the Light returns to the sky. No one can tell me it is impossible. No one can tell any of us. Shuto, show him."

"Akiro-san, I beg you. Let me do this my way."

"Do as I say. I cannot countenance unnecessary death."

Shuto removed his tunic. There was a collective gasp. He was a mutant. Scales covered him almost to his waist. The skin on his back and shoulders was hard and scaly as turtle shell, all the way from his spine to his breastbone. Underneath his arms were webs. Shuto was as ashamed of his difference as he had always been, but he refused to show it. His eyes sought MacKenzie's, expecting the disgust so many others had felt. He waited for the cruelty that had been shown him again and again, till all his emotions had fused into just one: the desire for revenge. But MacKenzie could only think of what the baby inside Justine might be, and so he felt pity for Shuto, despite the killing. How terrible it must have been for him as a child. He began to understand the rage he saw behind those amber eyes.

Shuto's face shone with surprise. Nothing else would have made him look away, but this did.

Akiro was not finished. "Hiroki," he commanded.

The big Japanese removed his shirt. On his chest, the stump of an extra limb, surgically removed.

"Ito."

Ito put down his radio and lifted his hair from the bare skin where his right ear should have been. One by one the Japanese revealed themselves. All had some form of genetic mutation.

"Generation to generation. We still suffer," Akiro intoned. "The girl who was blinded that day became my wife, Shuto's mother. She suffered for many years. It was a miracle she could conceive at all. The strain was too great. She lived only a few years more. Shuto was born the way you see. In Japan we do not love what is different. The doctors wanted to kill him. The boys at school tormented him. Several older ones caught him and tried to slice his webs with broken glass. He would have bled to death if not for his skin. I sent him to a monastery for his own survival. He learned the martial arts there."

"Why did you take my ship?" MacKenzie demanded.

"To dissuade my countrymen, by reminding them of Hiroshima."

"Remind them how?"

"I will use the plutonium to set off a nuclear explosion. They will see it in the sky. A lamp to light the new way. A beacon. Fear will make them wise. Sadly, it is the only thing that ever does. At the height of the ensuing panic, the opposition party will call for a vote of no confidence. They will be swept into office and end this madness."

"The damage will be catastrophic."

"It will be too far away to cause any," Akiro said.

"You don't need the entire shipment for one bomb," said Raskin.

"We'll scuttle the rest. I am assured that the containment vessels will hold."

"It's piracy," said Commodore Rowe. "You can't let him get away with it, Admiral."

"Just a moment," said Tony Rietti. "I must confess I have some sympathy for Akiro's ideas."

"A terrorist is a terrorist," said Lady Emily flatly.

"But he has principles," said Bette Rietti. "You can see that."

"I see Ivor's head almost caved in," said Carla Bernhardsen angrily.

Justine spoke up. "Admiral, whatever you do, do it fast. Unless we're all going up in a fireball, if you get my meaning."

"We should vote," said Ivor Bernhardsen.

MacKenzie vetoed that. "This is a military ship. I'm in command."

"What will you do, Admiral-san?" asked Akiro.

"Captain Raskin and I will stay as hostages. Let the rest go."

"Sadly, I cannot," said Akiro.

"Then if we must stay, I want a guarantee of everyone's safety. No one is to be hurt."

"If they do not rebel. Agreed."

"The plan you just outlined is the truth?"

"I give you my word," Akiro said.

MacKenzie needed time more than anything right now. Bette was right. In his own way, the curator was principled. He handed him the detonator.

Akiro refused it. "Give it to Shuto; I might do us damage."

"Unlikely," said MacKenzie.

"I don't understand, Admiral-san."

Shuto examined the detonator. His face reddened. "This cannot work, Akiro-san."

"The bomb's a fake, too," MacKenzie said. "I dumped the powder."

Commodore Rowe chuckled. "By Jove, well done, Admiral."

The Bernhardsens showed MacKenzie new respect. He'd just bluffed a boatload of armed terrorists.

"Fascinating," said Tony Rietti.

MacKenzie knew he hadn't won yet. Shuto might well ignore Akiro. Raskin shifted his weight. Justine was ready with the scalpel. Only naive civilians thought this game had rules. It could go either way.

Akiro said quietly, "I gave my word."

Power flowed between the two. He stood his ground.

Shuto's violent energy ceased. He bowed. "As you wish, Father."

9

Korlov

THE *KORLOV* SAILED INTO A VOID. HIROKI KEPT THE SHIP
in fog banks, and used thermal currents to mask their
engine noise as well as any submariner. The heat was
oppressive, the air damp and close. The humidity was
above ninety around the clock. In the cottony silence,
it felt like they had dropped off the edge of the earth.

Rumor had it they were going to an island to
conceal the ship while the nuclear device was fash-
ioned. The men were to be kept there, the women on
board. They were already separated. The men spent
the first night locked in the hold, cramped and un-
comfortable. The heat sapped their strength and
frayed tempers. MacKenzie spent the time planning.
Nobody thought of everything. There were weak-
nesses he could exploit, especially if he could talk to
Justine. But the only time the men got out was for an
exercise period under the watchful eyes of armed
guards. The women spent their day working kitchen
and laundry duty and were bunked at night in the

Marines' old cabin. The Japanese seemed to appreciate Justine's tending to them. It pained him to see her. He alone could not approach his wife.

The following morning they were taken out to exercise.

"Move around," MacKenzie said quietly. He organized them for this first step in fighting back. He wasn't going to be put on the island with nothing if he could help it.

"I want that buoy over there in the hold. Mr. Rietti, jog a bit. Get their attention."

"Gratefully, after the air down there," said the dark-eyed Italian. In T-shirt, jeans, and sneakers, he looked more like a college student than a professor.

Akiro and Shuto led the rest of the Japanese in *akido* exercises. Akiro wore a white *gi*, Shuto a black one. Both had black belts. Akiro was quite limber, but Shuto moved with sublime grace and power. Men came up against him during the *Kumité,* fighting, and he felled them like a scythe.

MacKenzie did a few push-ups. Sergeant Porter was doing them Marine style, one-handed. MacKenzie consoled himself Porter was a lot younger. When he guards yelled at Rietti to get back to the others, Mac used the diversion to knock the white buoy over to Raskin. Raskin kicked it soccer style to Bernhardsen, who spun it into the hold.

Raskin sidled over. "Got this." He had a file concealed in his fist.

"Admiral?" The Commodore briefly showed them the top of a flashlight.

"Good work," said MacKenzie.

On the first day of their captivity, that much was accomplished.

"We make great pack rats," Bernhardsen said

scornfully. He was a strikingly handsome man with straight blond hair, and steely blue eyes. "I thought you were a man of action, Admiral."

"Where appropriate, Dr. Bernhardsen," MacKenzie told the Norwegian. "And when."

Rietti smirked. "You got your head bashed in, Ivor. We need better planning."

"Brave as usual, Tony."

"They've got our wives. Or don't you give a damn?"

Bernhardsen wiped the sweat off his face. His slacks and shirt were damp and baggy, his Gucci loafers useless.

"This isn't Peru, Tony. You'd better remember that."

"That's enough," MacKenzie said sharply. "This is my ship. You're under my command. I don't know what's bugging you, but this is a dangerous situation and you're not helping. So file it. You understand me?"

"Here, here, Admiral," agreed the Commodore.

"You're right, of course. Sorry," said Rietti.

Bernhardsen walked away muttering.

"Peter, he isn't our only problem." Raskin pointed.

There were angry voices on deck, over by the *akido* class. Porter and the guard named Mori faced each other aggressively. Violence was in the air.

"Sergeant!"

Porter spun around. "Sir?"

"Apologize and walk away."

"But, sir, he took my last cigarettes, and the lighter that belonged to Corporal Kelly."

"Hard to get smokes out here, Sergeant. It's time to quit."

Porter looked threateningly at Mori. "He might be the bastard who killed Kelly."

"Belay that."

"But—"

"It's the wrong time, son." MacKenzie said it mildly, but Porter heard the steel underneath.

Porter lowered his eyes. "Sorry, sir. Must be the heat."

MacKenzie tried to say something, but he fell to his knees and clutched his stomach.

"Nikolai . . . !"

"Peter, what is it?"

MacKenzie's skin was sickly yellow and his face was covered with perspiration. Raskin called to the guards, "We have a sick man here. He needs help."

Shuto himself came and felt MacKenzie's pulse. It was fast and thready.

"Take him to the infirmary."

Justine had managed to get through the first few tests of her nursing ability by relying on her own combat experience and some help from Carolyn. Phillip was awake and resting, but still groggy from the painkillers. Being the medical authority on ship was working as she'd hoped. She had freedom of movement and had used it to build an intelligence network by taking the women into her confidence. They were anxious to help. Lady Emily said it reminded her of London during the war when everyone pitched in. Carla Bernhardsen spoke some Japanese. She listened to the guards as she served meals and collected laundry. Lady Em was able to learn things from Akiro himself, who respected her age and experience. The war, it seemed, had been the defining moment for both. From her reports, Justine was slowly building psych profiles of Akiro, Shuto, Hiroki, and Ito. Bette's keen analytical mind kept track of the

Japanese's movements, and such physical plans for building the bomb as she could scrape together.

For Justine, the hardest part was passing Mac and having to treat him like a stranger. She didn't know how much time they'd have when he came. She just knew he would, sooner or later.

She tried not to show anything but a nurse's concern when Shuto brought him in. He looked terrible. For a moment she worried he was truly ill.

"The Admiral is sick," said Shuto.

"Put him in bed."

She avoided Raskin's eyes and slid a thermometer into Mac's mouth.

"What happened?"

"He passed out on deck," Raskin said.

"His temperature's almost a hundred and two." Shuto checked it to be sure.

"This man isn't going anywhere," she said.

"Do you know what's wrong with him?"

"Not without an examination."

"Do your best," Shuto said.

It struck her as an odd thing to say. Why would Shuto care about Mac?"

"Go now, please. Both of you." She waited until Shuto and Raskin left. "Mac?"

His eyes popped open and he managed a weak smile. "Hi, honey."

She fell into his arms. They held each other for as long as they dared.

"I can't stand this," she said. "I've lost me *and* you at the same time."

He stroked her hair. "It's all I can do not to run to you when I see you."

"Mac, how are we going to get through this?"

"We'll have to be creative. Like your becoming a nurse. What's your status?"

"I can get around the ship. They trust me." She told him about her women's network.

"Excellent."

"You, too. That was a neat bluff with the bomb. They taught you quite a lot in your fancy spy school."

"I saw you pick up the scalpel. Who would you have gone after first?"

"Shuto."

"Would you have won?"

"No," she said honestly. "I don't think so."

It was the first time MacKenzie had ever heard her say that. Was it true, or was this what the baby had done to her?

She wiped his face with a cool cloth. "What did you do to yourself?" she asked.

"Drank gunpowder dissolved in water. The stuff I didn't put in my bomb. An old sailor's trick to get on sick list. Nikolai is the only one who knows. It looks worse than it is. Tell me what you've learned."

"Akiro bought himself a Russian nuclear expert named Viktor Lysenko. He's coming to build the bomb."

"When will it be ready?" he asked.

"Ten days from today."

"Where will they detonate it?"

"I don't know yet," she said. "The island we're going to is called Sōfu gan. Akiro's supposed to be able to hide the *Korlov* there. Carla got it from the Japanese. We'll arrive tomorrow. Lysenko the day after."

"We have to fight a delaying action. Sooner or later someone will catch on to the *Tuscany*. I have some ideas," he said.

They might not have a chance to talk again. A long list of possibilities had to be planned for. They went over procedures until they were satisfied.

"Mac, one more thing. I can't be sure, but I get a feeling something else is going on here. It's just bits and pieces the women pick up, but Carla thought she heard Hiroki say something like 'a larger lamp than Akiro intended.'"

"What does that mean?"

"I don't know. She wasn't even sure she heard it right. Her Japanese isn't perfect. Then Ito used the phrase 'a bigger payback.' Again, if she got it right."

"Shuto could be planning something on his own," MacKenzie mused.

"He wouldn't be the first son to go his own way. By the way, he looked genuinely worried when he brought you in. Like on deck the other day. What's between you two?"

"I can't explain it." He told her about the episode on the bridge, and again during Akiro's speech. "It probably saved my life."

"Some kind of ESP? Don't laugh," she said. "I'm serious."

"So am I," he said. "It's more an emotional connection, an understanding. And eerie enough at that."

"He'll be back any second," she said. "Roll up your sleeve. I'm going to give you a vitamin shot."

"If Akiro sets off his bomb, it will send a signal to every fanatic on the globe to try it. No matter what we think of him or his motives, we have to stop him."

"I agree, of course," she said. "But then?"

He knew she wasn't talking about the terrorists.

"Just, every time we almost called it quits, every time either of us got hurt or broken up inside, we found our way back by believing in each other." He held her. "This is no different. The baby's part of us."

She said desperately, "I want to kill it, do you know that? I used to lie in bed on the *Tuscany* thinking of ways I could get hurt so I'd miscarry. Then it wouldn't be my responsibility. That's what this child means to me. Praying for an accident."

"You're frightened."

Tears ran down her cheeks. "I want to die."

"You have to be strong."

"I don't know how to anymore."

There was so much he wanted to say, but Shuto chose that moment to come back. Justine turned to prepare her instruments.

"What's wrong with him?"

"An intestinal infection. I gave him a shot."

Shuto checked the mark. "When will he be fit?"

"Quickly, if there aren't any complications."

"Good. Leave us now."

"I'll stay with my patient, thank you."

Shuto slapped her. "Do as you're told."

MacKenzie wanted to tear Shuto apart, but his greater fear was that Justine would react violently and blow her cover. Her face reddened. She didn't move. Shuto went to hit her again.

MacKenzie caught his arm. "Don't."

It was suddenly very close in the small room. Shuto could break his grip with ease. Justine tensed. She wouldn't let Shuto hurt him without a fight. He had to prevent that.

Shuto looked at MacKenzie's hand curiously. "I could kill you with a single blow."

"I know."

"Is it the woman?"

MacKenzie kept his face closed. "No."

67

"Then why do you risk getting in my way again?"

In that instant MacKenzie knew that their battle against Shuto had to be psychological. Physically, he was indomitable. But perhaps he could find a chink in his emotional armor and pry it open. He let his mind free, hoping to plug into whatever connected them. Suddenly it was there again. Blazing energy from Shuto. Anger. Shock. And the smallest beginning of fear.

"Her pain won't pay them back, Shuto."

"How do you know me?" he gasped.

"I don't know you," MacKenzie said honestly. "I *feel* you."

"Then you should know the pain of thousands wouldn't pay back all the people who hurt me." Shuto's hatred was almost a physical thing. "What Akiro told you on deck was the smallest part of it. Beneath our civil masks, we Japanese are a cruel people. I found that out early. I had to burrow in a garbage dump on the way home from school to avoid the gangs chasing me every day. When they caught me, they stripped me to look at me. And hurt me. The girls . . . they watched. Sometimes they did things, too.

"Every day I came home stinking from garbage. I had to clean myself outside of the house even in winter, and change my clothes so my mother wouldn't see what they'd done to me, and it add to her pain. She never got up from bed again after her illness. When she died it was a release." He looked stricken. *"Aiee!* Why am I telling you this?"

"Because it helps," MacKenzie said. "I learned that." It was almost impossible not to look at Justine.

"I'm sorry," Justine said. There was no subterfuge in it, but it was a mistake.

Shuto's temper flared. "Be sorry for yourself, Nurse. If not for Akiro, I would have killed you. You mean nothing to me." He made to hit her again.

Justine clutched her belly reflexively.

Shuto stopped in midstrike and looked at her curiously. "A woman normally protects her face. I've seen your reaction before, when the doctors told Japanese mothers that their children were to be born without arms, or legs. When the baby was threatened. You're pregnant, aren't you?"

"Yes," Justine whispered.

"The father?"

"Back in the States."

Shuto touched her almost innocently. "Your first?"

"Yes."

He was so gentle. It was difficult to reconcile with the man who had killed so many. In the quiet, MacKenzie understood what joined them for the first time. The baby. Shuto's pain, his own, and now Justine's. It all had the same root. The connection was beyond anything he'd ever experienced. He understood things solid and real. Earth, ocean, the deck of a ship under his feet. But Shuto's monastery had given him a vastly different spirituality, Mac realized. His control, his uncanny ability to anticipate, his strength, even his fighting prowess, stemmed from it. And somehow it joined a midwestern farm boy, a Nicaraguan rebel child, and a Japanese mutant-warrior. Was Shuto a portent? Was the baby doomed to live its life in pain, too? Or did it mean something entirely different? Hope and despair warred in all of them.

"We three," Shuto said, feeling it. "Knowing without knowledge. I can't claim to understand it."

"Is there nothing I can say to stop you?" MacKenzie asked him.

Shuto helped MacKenzie to his feet. "Nothing. But listen to me, Admiral. For whatever reason this strange thing between the three of us exists, I make you this promise. If you do nothing to get in my way, I will let you and the others live. It is the best I can do."

"It's not the best," Justine insisted.

"There is more at work here than you understand. We must make a country remember."

"There are better ways."

Shuto sighed wearily. "I've never seen one. Now go, Admiral. Hiroki is waiting to take you back."

"All right."

Justine handed him a pair of pills. "Admiral, these will help you sleep."

MacKenzie looked at the pills twice, to be sure. "I hope they're not necessary, Nurse."

She said nothing.

They separated, strangers again, unable to risk a final look for what it might betray.

10

Korlov

THE MEN PRESSED MacKENZIE WITH QUESTIONS WHEN HE came out on deck. He still felt dazed from the encounter with Shuto and Justine.

"Did you see our wives?" Bernhardsen asked.

"The women are doing fine."

"Lady Emily, too?" asked the Commodore.

"An inspiration to the others."

"What are Akiro's plans?" Raskin asked.

"A Russian scientist named Viktor Lysenko is coming to build the bomb. It will take ten days."

"Lysenko." Raskin frowned. "I know him. Everyone in military circles does. An arms designer who flaunts conventions. Especially sexual ones. Some say he's a genius, others say he's mad as Rasputin. Certainly he's capable of building such a device."

A genius arms maker to build a simple bomb? It suggested Justine might be right, there was more to this than Akiro had let on. Was it more than he himself knew?

"You better speak to Sergeant Porter," Raskin said. "He tried to take on the Japanese single-handed while you were gone."

"Again?"

"I think he feels he should have gone down in a blaze of glory with his comrades. And he may yet. Look."

Porter was putting on an impressive display of one-handed pull-ups on a crossbar. His stomach muscles rippled and his body glistened with sweat. Every pull-up strained his entire body, but he made it through twenty. It was a show of great strength. The Japanese came to watch. There was even applause when he finished.

"That'll show them, eh, Admiral?" Porter crowed, dropping down to the deck.

"At ease, Marine. I thought I made myself clear. I don't want to provoke a situation."

Raskin said softly, "Too late."

One of the Japanese elbowed Mori and said something in a provocative tone that Bernhardsen translated as roughly "Bet *you* couldn't do that." Mori snorted and stood his rifle against the railing.

"You, me," he said in English, slapping Porter on the back.

"A contest, is it?" said the Marine, grinning.

"No, Sergeant," said MacKenzie, but the guards pushed Porter back to the bar.

"Don't worry, Admiral, he can't do ten." Porter held up his fingers.

"Ju?" said the Japanese disdainfully. He shoved Porter out of the way.

The Marine lifted a fist. Rifles rose.

"Sergeant!"

Porter bristled. "Admiral, I don't see why—"

"You aren't required to. It's an order."

"Yes, sir. Sorry, sir."

The Japanese bowed and pointed to himself. "Mori."

The Marine nodded. "Porter."

Mori grabbed the bar with both hands and did a few quick pull-ups, two-handed. Then he dropped one hand to his side and pulled himself up.

"Ichi," said the other guards.

"Ni."

Mori did another three in quick succession, his arm pumping like a piston.

"San. Shi. Go."

"The first five are easy," said Porter contemptuously.

Mori kicked Porter in the chest. It brought cheers from the guards and spurred Mori to greater effort. Porter was hot. Mori did another pull-up. It cost him, but he had their honor to uphold. They shouted at him to go on. He managed three more.

"Rok. Shishi. Hashi."

The rest of the guards came over. It was a hot, boring day and this was the first excitement since taking the ship. For a moment MacKenzie thought Porter might actually have provided a diversion sufficient to take them, but he hadn't. They were still covered from three different angles. They'd be cut down before they got halfway to the bridge. And Shuto could be anywhere.

"Ku . . . !" the Japanese cried, nine.

Mori was in agony. The veins in his neck looked about to burst. He gritted his teeth. The guards' attention was on him. He strained valiantly, but try as he might, he couldn't pull himself up one last time. He dropped from the bar as if the muscles in his arm had ripped.

MacKenzie didn't see Porter's grandstand play coming till it was too late. It was badly timed and conceived. He grabbed Mori's rifle and shot one of the guards.

"Admiral," he shouted. "We can take the bridge."

MacKenzie reacted the only way he could. He yelled, "Down!" pulling the frail Commodore to the deck and covering him with his own body. Gunfire poured down from the bridge. Porter leaped on the hatch and returned fire.

Shuto dropped from the crane. Porter never saw him coming. His strike hurled the rifle from the Marine's hands and sent him to his knees. He hauled Porter back to his feet and hit him again with the edge of his hand. Porter swayed weakly. Two guards were dead. MacKenzie and his men were flat on the deck. Shuto caught MacKenzie's eye. An example was to be made. MacKenzie raged at watching the brave sergeant suffer at his hands. Greater goals, he reminded himself, but his fists were clenched so tightly, they hurt.

"That's your man out there, Admiral," said Bernhardsen accusingly.

"Don't you think he knows that?" Raskin said. "He's saving your life, man."

"Sergeant Porter disobeyed orders, Admiral," said the Commodore. "I, for one, do understand."

"The hell with orders. Do something," demanded Rietti. "Shuto's killing him."

MacKenzie said, "Everybody stay where you are."

Every one of Shuto's blows was calculated to hurt, but not so much that Porter blacked out. The lesson was meant for all of them, guards and prisoners alike. This was what would happen if anyone slipped again. Blood poured from Porter's mouth. MacKenzie couldn't guess how he was still standing. For a moment he thought Shuto might let Porter live. He was totally unprepared for what happened next.

Shuto clasped Porter's head between his hands. His amber eyes grew hazy, almost liquid. Breathing deeply, his elbows at chest level, he pressed Porter's head. His muscles knotted. Porter cried out. The pressure must have been excruciating. The Marine tried to rally. He drove an uppercut into Shuto's stomach, but Shuto was protected there by his scales. He never even flinched. Bernhardsen yelled support across the deck, but he might just as well have been yelling at the sea. Porter hit Shuto another staggering blow to the midsection, but it didn't stop the pressure on his head. The blow would have broken the ribs or ruptured the abdomen of a lesser man. Porter hit him till his hands bled. Shuto just took it. The merciless punishment continued.

Porter tried to pry Shuto's hands apart. The muscles on Shuto's arms just bulged as if by some ancient means he drew the other man's strength out of him. The bones in Porter's jaw gave way with a sudden crack they could hear all the way across the deck. Blood strangled his cry. Shuto's eyes blazed. If muscles had a voice, his would have been screaming. There was a final sickening sound as Shuto's palms crushed Porter's skull. Gray ocher spurted onto the deck. Shuto dropped the dead Marine and his gaze swept over the others with a message: Remember this.

MacKenzie vowed he would. He'd remember Porter and the other Marines, Raskin's officers, and the crews of the *Tuscany* and the *Akatsuki Maru.* No matter what bond he and Shuto shared, no matter how deep his wounds, he'd remember this cold-blooded murder. It was the difference between them. Vital and important.

There was silence on deck but for the sounds of the ocean.

MacKenzie said, "I'll bury my man."

"As you wish."

They wrapped Porter in a tarp. It was too much for Rietti. He ran to the gunwale and threw up.

"Lift him," MacKenzie said. The one called Mori came over to help. MacKenzie saw his regret. Their simple contest should not have ended in death. MacKenzie wanted to tell him there weren't any simple contests anymore. Not here, not anywhere.

The Japanese and the hostages bore silent witness as MacKenzie spoke.

"Dear Lord, we commend this man's soul to Your mercy. He died in the service of his country, fighting for the right to be free. He was a brave warrior.

"The disciple Peter said that God shows no partiality. He said the prophets bear witness that everyone who believes in Him receives forgiveness. I know our friend and companion will receive His blessing. We will miss him. Let Sergeant Alexander Raymond Porter find his final peace in the ocean depths. Amen."

They slid the tarp into the sea.

PART TWO

The Island

11

Korlov

FROM THE DECK OF THE *KORLOV* THE NEXT DAY, MAC-
Kenzie and the men got their first look at their future
home, the island of Sōfu gan. The fog was thick
enough to cut off the sun, and the ocean lapped at a
scraggly beach bordered by tall palms. The *Korlov* was
anchored just beyond a line of rocky breakers a mile
from the beach. The heat and humidity were blister-
ing. Inland, the active volcano Niigata Yakeyama
broke through the rain forest tree canopy, towering
over the island. Smoke trailed from its summit. The
last mining operation here had been hastily ended by
its eruption only a few years before.

MacKenzie rubbed his sprouting growth of beard.
"Akiro's nobody's fool. The fog eliminates aerial
observation. Even the heat-tracking satellites can't
see with the volcano masking us."

"Look at that riptide," Bernhardsen said. "We
won't be able to get off the island."

"What causes a fog like this?" Raskin asked.

"The cold Oyashio Current and the warm Japan Current meet here," said the Commodore, staring at the island. Returning to Sōfu gan had hit him hard. "The fog rarely dissipates. Akiro's been bloody clever."

"What is it like there?" Raskin asked.

"The humidity is bloody unbearable. But that isn't the worst of it. Flies, snakes, wild boar, and a hundred-degree heat all day and night."

MacKenzie put a hand on the Commodore's shoulder. "We'll be all right."

"It's just life's twists and turns, I daresay. After all these years, I'm having trouble adjusting. It was ages ago."

"Why were you here the first time?" asked Rietti.

"I was the commanding officer of Her Majesty's Submarine *Storm* back in 1943. She was a fine ship, I tell you. I saw her built myself in the shipyards at Cammell Laird's. Two Admiralty-pattern eight-cylinder Brotherhood diesels. Metro-Vickers motors. Even had radar and some air conditioning, can you imagine? She was an improved S-type sub with bigger tanks for long-range cruising in these waters." Pride swelled his voice. "We were on night patrol when we spotted a Japanese convoy. I'll never forget it. We had to get in close. Under a mile was the best range for the Mark Eight torpedoes. We sank five enemy ships before they hit us. I sent an SOS and managed to limp in here. The *Storm* sank on the other side of the island. We held on for weeks till we were rescued. Out of a crew of forty-five, I lost ten men in battle and as many on the island."

"It's an odd name, Sōfu gan," said Bernhardsen. "What does it mean?"

"Lot's Wife," said the Commodore. "The Jesuits

were the only ones thought this unholy place deserved a name."

"Lot's wife was turned into a column of salt for looking at the destruction of Sodom and Gomorrah after God warned her not to," MacKenzie said. "Fits well with what Akiro has in mind."

"The volcano's a monster, eh, Tony?" Even in their predicament, there was excitement in Ivor Bernhardsen's voice.

"Niigata Yakeyama's last eruption was in 'eighty-six," his partner responded. "It was recorded all over the world."

"I'd sure like to get inside," said Bernhardsen.

"Why on earth?" asked the Commodore, appalled.

"It's what we do," Rietti explained. "We're volcanologists. Ivor and I have been taking measurements before and after eruptions to try and predict when volcanoes are going to erupt. Sometimes we take measurements inside."

"At least some of us do," said Bernhardsen caustically.

There it was again, MacKenzie thought, tension between them. They might be partners, but it was a strained relationship.

Rietti ignored Bernhardsen. "You see, Commodore, we still can't predict when volcanoes are going to erupt. Too many people every year get caught napping. We call it the Pompeii Effect. You'd know how dangerous volcanoes can be if you lived in Tokyo or Manila."

"But actually going inside one that's erupting?"

"Partway," Bernhardsen said, adding, "It depends on how much your partner is willing to risk."

Rietti ignored him, but they could see the cut bothered him.

"Robots do more of it," he explained. "Far more prudent."

Bernhardsen snorted derisively. "Prudence doesn't win awards."

"I never thought science was about awards." Rietti finally blew like one of his volcanoes. "Neither did you once."

"One of us better, if we ever expect grants again."

The argument was ended when Mori and several guards rounded them up to carry crates up from the hold. MacKenzie, Raskin, and the Commodore worked together. They lost sight of Rietti and Bernhardsen, and didn't see them again until they were returned to the hold, listless and exhausted. They waited for their dinner, each man picking a spot and resting quietly, trying to endure the heat.

"Admiral?"

MacKenzie was resting against a crate. His damp shirt refused to dry. He stripped it off.

"Yes, Dr. Bernhardsen?"

"Yesterday. What I said about helping Sergeant Porter. I'm sorry. I know you were protecting the rest of us."

MacKenzie nodded. "Something else?"

"You and Captain Raskin are trying to figure out a way to stop them. I want you to know, well, you can count on me. That's all."

"Thank you."

"Captain Raskin wants to see you."

Raskin had been working since the guards locked them back in. MacKenzie went over.

"Peter, we have quite a haul."

"Let me see."

Raskin unrolled a blanket. A few tools, nails pried

out of packing cases, a pocketknife, wire, screws, plugs, even batteries."

"I pinched the screwdriver when they took you to the infirmary," said the Commodore proudly.

"The knife was in the hold," said Rietti. "It must have belonged to one of the Marines."

"You make good thieves," MacKenzie said.

Raskin loaded everything into a canvas sack pinched while they were working, and tied it to the buoy.

"All you have to do is get it into the channel, Peter. It should make the beach."

"A neat trick with that riptide pulling at you," said Bernhardsen.

"I'll go as soon as it's dark," said MacKenzie.

The guard came for their dinner trays a little after eight. He made a bed check, then settled outside.

Raskin said, "Let's go."

MacKenzie wasn't looking forward to this, but it had to be done. He slipped a line over his shoulder.

Bernhardsen showed him a seam on the hull. "The fingers, Admiral. They're what you grab with. Friction will do most of it. Stay pressed against the wall."

Five feet below the ceiling was a ventilating shaft Raskin said went clear to the top deck. It looked damn far.

"I'm ready, Nikolai."

Raskin stood against the wall like he was being frisked. MacKenzie swung Rietti up onto Raskin's shoulders. Bernhardsen climbed over Raskin and Rietti, the third in the tower. The ventilating shaft was still ten feet over his head.

"Go, Admiral," said Bernhardsen.

"Without a net," MacKenzie muttered darkly.

He put his feet on Raskin's back and pulled himself onto Raskin's shoulders, then climbed till Ivor Bernhardsen grabbed his hand and helped him up.

"Try for the shaft," he said.

"Do be careful," called the Commodore.

MacKenzie belayed the end of his rope around a pipe. He wouldn't hit the ground now if he fell, he'd just be cut in two. He found a seam overhead. His fingers felt as if they were breaking till he found purchase for his feet. He was perilously close to falling.

"Footing six inches to the right of your right foot, Admiral," said Bernhardsen.

MacKenzie pushed with his legs and slid up the wall. The ventilating shaft was just beyond his reach.

"There's a pipe about a foot higher. Can you reach it?" said Bernhardsen.

MacKenzie was weakening. He'd fall if he didn't get inside the shaft soon.

"Three inches more . . . two . . . That's it, your hand is almost over the lip now."

"I can feel it."

"There's a handhold inside," Raskin shouted.

MacKenzie wrapped his hand around the steel rung and pulled himself up. He chest-landed with a walrus belly flop and wriggled in. Squirming around, he fed his rope out. Raskin and Rietti attached the buoy and he hauled it up. He crawled into the shaft till it angled upward, pushing the buoy ahead of him. There was a ladder. He draped the buoy over his shoulders. He was sweating profusely by the time he reached the top.

He risked a peek out. They were anchored without

running lights. Two hours till the next bed check. He had to get moving. He stripped and tied his clothing to the rungs. He dropped to the deck clad only in his briefs. The darkness worked for him. He made it to the bow and slipped over the side, working his way down the anchor line to the water. It was cold and choppy. Precious little moonlight filtered through the fog. Waves broke noisily on the rocks in the distance.

The trick was to get the buoy into the channel without being pulled into the riptide. He wrapped his arms around it and kicked out. A strange pale phosphorescence on the rocks helped guide him. His skin soon matched the water temperature. The splash of the waves lulled him. His mind wandered.

He thought about taking Justine off the ship and making for the island. They'd be better off than with the others. But even as he framed the thought, he knew he couldn't. The keynote of his life was responsibility. That's what commanding a sub had meant. Now his responsibilities were larger. If Akiro succeeded, it would mean a wholesale race for every terrorist to make his point with a nuclear weapon. Some group's point might be made by setting it off in Washington or Los Angeles. A ton of construction dynamite had shut down the World Trade Center in New York, killing and wounding scores. A four-thousand-pound bomb of fertilizer and fuel oil had destroyed the federal building in Oklahoma City, the worst terrorist attack in U.S. history. What would a nuclear bomb do?

Akiro had to fail. He had ten days to stop him.

The current yanked him out of his reverie. He was close to the channel, but he was cold and tired. The sea was rough, with clashing tides. The ship seemed a far way off. The sound of the waves on the rocks was louder. He had to get into the channel to release the buoy, or it would be lost in the ocean. Worse, it might catch on one of the rocks and Shuto would see it.

He was jerked around by a vicious current. He lost the buoy trying to break free. The tide swept it past the channel into the open sea. He felt a bleak sense of failure. He was tiring fast. But he had to get back. If they found him gone, he was certain Shuto would execute everyone. He struck out with all his might towards the ship. He had to get out of the riptide. The undertow dragged him down. He fought back to the surface. A wave slammed into him and he swallowed seawater and vomited. It weakened him further.

The opposite of responsibility is release. For a moment he felt the sweetness of letting go, of quitting. Never mind Justine or the *Korlov*. The world would survive without him. Rest. Sink. Forget. But there was a child who needed to be born, and its survival was a reason to live. Dark rocks flashed by as the waves slammed him under. He struggled in the underwater silence. He couldn't orient himself in the darkness. His lungs threatened to burst, but the current thrust him back to the surface. He fought back. He gulped in air. The breakers receded. He swam into calm water.

He was almost totally depleted. Only twenty minutes left till the guard changed. His arms trembled when he grasped the anchor line and pulled himself up. He made it to the gunwale and hung there shivering with cold. His legs were fast losing feeling, but he couldn't afford to trail water across the deck. He heard someone coming. It was Ito, the communications man, with Shuto.

Most of their conversation was in Japanese, but

there were a few scientific terms in English. He heard *Magnus Field,* and he recognized the word *tsunami.* He didn't understand anything else. He needed to get warm, to sleep. He was shivering uncontrollably. They went below and he made it back to the ventilation shaft. It was too cramped to dress, so he just shoved his clothing down the shaft. The men were waiting for him. He saw their relief when he stuck his head out, especially Raskin's. He knotted the line the way Rietti had showed him and slid to the deck.

"Move it, man," said Bernhardsen. "They'll be here any minute."

MacKenzie almost fell, he was so tired. Raskin helped him dress. "It went all right?"

"The current almost sent me into the rocks. I lost the buoy."

The Commodore handed him a blanket. "Dry yourself."

"The riptide's too strong," MacKenzie said bitterly.

"Rather good show to try, though, Admiral," said the Commodore.

Bernhardsen yanked the line. It pulled the knot free and both lines came down from the shaft. He shoved them under a tarp. They extinguished the lights. The sounds of the hatch opening sent them to their pallets. The guard checked, saw the right number of sleeping bodies, and left again.

MacKenzie lay in the darkness. There was nothing else he could do. They'd have to face the island without the tools they had painstakingly gathered. They'd be alone tomorrow, with only ten days to prevent the first nuclear blast set off in anger since World War II.

He'd made a real mess of things. Having Justine on the *Tuscany* had thrown her into the fight of her life, at her weakest time. He'd let his own ship fall into terrorists' hands. He'd even lost the buoy in the riptide. The baby was a constant torment. Was there anything he couldn't screw up?

Ten days.

MacKenzie felt close to breaking. They had trained him to fight the enemies outside. How much harder it was to fight the internal ones.

Ten days.

He slept the way he felt, troubled and exhausted.

When the rest were asleep, he rose carefully and went to where he'd hidden the tool he stole. He might have a special need for it, one he alone knew. The wicked four-inch needle on the awl was so thin, it was almost invisible with the bulb-shaped wooden handle concealed in his hand. Funny how things worked. Fate took a sudden turn and you had to face your greatest fear.

And your greatest guilt, he reminded himself.

The awl broke into two pieces when he worked on it awhile. He slipped the needle into his shoe, and put the handle in his pocket.

Ten days more he had to survive. Ten days.

It was comforting to know he could deal with the future now. He could wait, he knew. He had waited before. He recited his old bedtime poem to calm himself, the way he had always done.

> "The time has come, the Walrus said,
> to talk of many things:
> of shoes—and ships—and sealing wax—
> of cabbages—and kings—

And why the sea is boiling hot—
And whether pigs have wings."

He might not know about pigs, but he knew why the sea boiled. He thought about that for a long time, till sleep came.

12

Sōfu gan

SHUTO AND HIS MEN BROUGHT MACKENZIE AND THE
others to the island in a lifeboat. It was an unceremo-
nious landing. They were herded through the surf at
gunpoint and their provisions were dumped on the
sand. Shuto left without a word. The island was as hot
as a blast furnace even on the beach. Niigata Yakeyama's all-too-frequent rumblings shook the ground.
Despite Rietti's and Bernhardsen's assurances that
it was normal for a volcano of this type, it was frightening.

It was impossible to wear clothes. MacKenzie and
the others stripped down to their shorts and pulled
the crates under the trees.

"We need an inventory. Nikolai."

"I wonder if putting the captain in charge of the
food isn't a little like giving a tippler the key to the
liquor store," asked the Commodore wryly.

"More like giving a sommelier the key to the wine
cellar," retorted Raskin.

Bernhardsen looked over their stores. "Shuto was hardly generous. Food, a saw, some bottles of water."

"At least he let us bring our minis," said Rietti.

Bernhardsen was unimpressed. "A lot of good computers do us here with no electricity to recharge."

MacKenzie thought "mini" was somewhat underdescriptive for the scientists' portable computers. They were the size of small suitcases, containing a printer and battery.

"Always the bright side with you," Rietti shot back.

The tension was increasing between them. MacKenzie cut it off.

"We're alive. Under the circumstances, that's a lot."

Shuto could have killed them, he thought. The man remained an enigma. One image: touching Justine's belly gently. The next: crushing Porter's head between his hands.

"Shuto had *some* feeling for us," said Raskin. "There's toilet tissue and cloth and mosquito repellent."

"Water won't be a problem," said the Commodore. "There are plenty of springs. And we should cut our pants into shorts. Wearing much of anything is asking for a bad rash in this humidity."

"If only he'd included some vodka," Raskin said wistfully.

MacKenzie shielded his eyes. A mile of ocean and deadly riptide separated them from the *Korlov*. He looked around. Green jungle, white sand, gray water, fog-bound sky. The colors of his new country. He wished for a breeze, but the broad, leafy vegetation didn't stir. They were covered with sweat after the slightest activity. Birds screamed. Insects buzzed incessantly.

"Commodore, see if you can find some vines for lashing. And those sarongs sound like a good idea."

"Right, Admiral. You've got to treat this island with deadly respect."

They used four sturdy palms as corner posts for a shelter. Rietti and Bernhardsen sawed saplings for roof joists. Raskin cut palm fronds to cover them. The Commodore found vines and they were carted back. The island extracted a price for every effort. The bugs were so voracious, they had to run into the ocean every few minutes to stop being eaten, despite the repellent. The heat demanded frequent rest stops and left them enervated and listless. But it was good to work. It made them feel more masters of their fate. They dug a fire pit and a latrine and looked over the camp with satisfaction.

"How about this, Admiral?" Rietti held up a sign he had printed out on his computer: Hotel Sophie. There was a murmur of agreement.

"Hotel Sophie, it is," MacKenzie agreed. "Anybody wanting maid service is going to be disappointed, though."

They waded into the surf. The Commodore sank gratefully into the water. MacKenzie wondered how long a man of his age could stand these primitive conditions. He wondered how long any of them could.

"Nikolai, make sure that the Commodore gets whatever food he needs," he said to his friend privately.

"I will, Peter."

"Are you okay?"

Raskin shrugged. "Some days are bleaker than others. I make myself fight, but a big part of me keeps asking why I bother."

"Because you're not a quitter."

"A man has to have a purpose. If I leave here, I return to nothing."

"That's an assumption," MacKenzie said flatly.

"No, my pension won't be—"

"I meant that you'll leave here."

It caught Raskin by surprise. A grin split his big, bearded face. "So drink, because today we did not die?"

"Exactly."

Some of his spirit returned. "You teach me my own lesson."

"What are friends for? How many hours of daylight left, you figure?" MacKenzie asked.

"At this latitude, seven or eight."

"Want to take a stroll?"

Raskin shuddered. "Take our volcanologists. For some absurd reason, they seem to like physical exercise. The Commodore and I will protect the Hotel."

"We'll be glad to go, Admiral," said Rietti.

"Maybe we can get a look at the volcano," Bernhardsen said hopefully.

MacKenzie flattened an area in the sand. "Commodore, do you remember enough to draw us a map?"

"I do."

"Admiral, we can do this a little more high-tech," Rietti said. "Ivor?"

"Use yours. Mine is acting up."

"Should I take a look?"

"No."

"Whatever you say. Commodore, draw right on the screen. We'll print it afterwards."

"The island is roughly triangular," the Commodore said. "The beach we're on is here at the base in the south. The volcano is in the center. There's a lava field around it, very active, very hot, then more jungle.

There's an abandoned mining camp beyond the volcanic region."

"Is that where the *Storm* went down?" asked Mac-Kenzie.

"Yes. We landed here in a terrible squall. The winds gusted to fifty knots. It was hellish on the surface."

"I can imagine," said Raskin. "I commanded submarines, too. In fact, that is where I met Peter." They were lying on the beach. The late afternoon sun turned the fog golden. Raskin was a born storyteller. It was a pleasant diversion.

"Peter was in command of my boat, the *Riga*. During a combat trial, a Soviet Admiral tried to ram us. Peter ran straight at him. At the last minute the Admiral turned, but rammed us in the sail. We had some flooding and mast damage, but the worst was that it took out the hydraulics. We ended up in a jam dive."

"What's that?" asked Bernhardsen.

"The planes get stuck in a down angle and you can't surface the ship," MacKenzie explained.

"I thought we weren't going to make it," Raskin continued. "We went below crush depth. We had to pump the planes up manually. We came very close to dying, but Peter got us through. I expect he will do so again."

"Thank you, Nikolai."

"We're all in it together," Rietti said. "An odd lot, eh?"

"I daresay," agreed the Commodore.

"What do you think, Admiral?" said Bernhardsen. "Do we have any chance of rescuing our wives and stopping Shuto?"

"We have one advantage. My wife would call it having an agent in place." He explained who Justine really was. "The women are her network. That's why we know about Akiro's plans."

"I never imagined," said Rietti. "The beautiful dark-haired woman who never spoke to anyone. She must be very clever."

"I saw she was a truly formidable person, even in her condition," huffed the Commodore.

MacKenzie wished he hadn't mentioned the pregnancy. It threatened his equilibrium.

"Nikolai, there won't be enough light to make it back tonight. Expect us around noon tomorrow. Break out food and mosquito repellent."

"Three orders, coming up."

He followed Raskin over to the crate. "Are you going to be okay without me?"

"Better to leave me where I will do no harm."

"I don't want to hear that, Nikolai. We're in deep trouble. You gotta stay with it."

"I'm trying, Peter."

"Sing me a song," MacKenzie said suddenly.

"What?"

"You heard me. Sing me a song. That's an order."

Raskin muttered a few notes halfheartedly. "This is stupid."

"Sing!"

MacKenzie began to clap. Raskin sang louder. MacKenzie pulled him into a stumbling dance. Raskin's hoarse, rumbling voice grew stronger, like a storm building. Soon they were both stomping in the sand, clapping together. MacKenzie didn't speak Russian, but he joined in the repeated verse anyway, and Raskin laughed at him. MacKenzie made Raskin dance until he was panting for breath. He made him sing louder. They romped around the beach like drunken bears until Raskin finally collapsed in the sand, bellowing with pleasure. Laughter bubbled up between his gasps for breath.

MacKenzie weaved over his friend, panting. "The monster won't get you today, Nikolai. I promise."

Raskin embraced him. "You're good medicine."

"Two fools."

Back at the Hotel, the Commodore shrugged and said something about the modern military. Rietti and Bernhardsen didn't know what to say.

13

Sōfu gan

MACKENZIE HAD SPENT MOST OF HIS LIFE AT SEA AND WAS grateful for it walking across the island. The insects were ravenous. The very air was oppressive. He didn't love snakes at the best of times, and finding them hanging from branches and slithering out from under logs was every bit as frightening as the sight of larger animals.

"The Commodore's wild boars," supplied Rietti. His dark hair was wet with perspiration. "Very dangerous. They'll attack anything."

"Ever been in a rain forest, Admiral?" asked Bernhardsen.

"Never. I was raised on a farm in the Midwest. I've been at sea since college."

"We've been in quite a few," said Rietti. "Most of the world's active volcanoes are in remote areas. There's actually a well-defined volcanic zone called the Ring of Fire that runs down the west coast of the Americas from Alaska to Chile, and down the east coast of Asia from Siberia to New Zealand. We're in the zone now."

Talking helped take MacKenzie's mind off his discomfort. "What causes the zone?"

"Instability at the boundaries of the plates under the Pacific Ocean and the surrounding continents," Bernhardsen said, adding, "North Americans don't think much about it, but there have been over seventy thousand deaths from volcanoes worldwide in this century alone. That's more than your Vietnam war. There are over eight hundred and fifty active volcanoes in the world."

"I hadn't realized."

"Like Tony said, you would if you lived near one."

MacKenzie turned to Rietti. "What part of Italy are you from, Tony?"

"Florence. The city of artists and lovers."

"And pigeons."

Rietti laughed. "You've been there."

"Once. Justine and I loved it. Wonderful food, kind people. We strolled around at night eating gelati, and sat in cafés drinking wine and watching people. I didn't see any volcanoes."

"It was Pompeii," Rietti explained. "I went there with my family as a child. It intrigued me. I read all I could. The fascination lasted a lifetime."

"Where did you all meet?"

"Bette and I came to Tokyo to do research. Ivor and Carla were teaching there."

"That's the reason we speak a little Japanese," Bernhardsen informed him.

"We became friends, and later, partners," Rietti said.

And now seemingly enemies, MacKenzie thought. He wondered what had caused it.

"If we ever get off this island, Admiral, you and your wife will come to Florence, and Bette and I will show you the city as we natives know."

"I'll hold you to that. How about you, Ivor?"

"I was born in Oslo."

"I loved the sculpture park there," MacKenzie said. "With all those beautiful blond children playing in the fountains."

Bernhardsen smiled in remembrance.

"You know it well, Admiral. I broke my leg when I was thirteen trying the ski jump."

"That big monster ramp?"

"I thought I could stop. I went right over the edge. My father was furious."

The slide had been built for the Olympics. "No wonder you don't balk at going into volcanoes."

"You always took too much risk, even then," said Rietti.

"And you used to appreciate it," Bernhardsen shot back.

MacKenzie didn't need to break them up this time. It was too hot to argue. Both men lapsed into silence.

The volcano towered over them, dominating the island, reminding them that what it had created, it could destroy. A shock was waiting for him at the volcano's base. They broke through to an area that was devoid of everything except rounded layers of black rock. Not a single stick of vegetation rose from the rock, but small fires erupted like geysers.

Rietti said, "The magma vaporizes everything. When it cools it leaves these syrupy-looking layers of rock. If you've never seen a lava field before, it makes quite an impression."

MacKenzie had never witnessed such total destruction. Not a single blade of grass was left. The boundary between the lava field and the rain forest looked like it had been cut with a knife. The lava covered everything, a solid shroud of rock. Above them, the summit was lost in the mist.

"It's frightening," MacKenzie said.

"A volcanic eruption shows up on every seismograph in the world," said Rietti. His boots crunched on the rock. "Everyone comes flocking to see it, within hours sometimes, to get the best measurements."

"Stay behind us," warned Bernhardsen. "The crust is thin where the magma's close to the surface. And it's going to be *hot.*"

Bernhardsen used a long staff to test the ground. Scorching heat rose off the lava. It felt like they'd walked into a barbecue pit. Smoke drifted out of small vents. Columns of fire shot out of nowhere, dying just as quickly. Sulfurous smells clogged Mac's nose and lungs. He thought hell must be like this, doomed souls dancing on burning rocks, forever in pain. The volcano looked down with complete indifference.

It happened suddenly. Bernhardsen's staff broke through the rock and the black crust fell away. Underneath was a pit of bubbling magma fed by an underground volcanic pipe. Bernhardsen lost his balance and fell.

"Tony . . . !"

Bernhardsen hung over the fiery cauldron. Rietti reacted quicker than MacKenzie expected, throwing himself forward and managing to grab his partner. His stick fell in and ignited like a match.

"Help me," yelled Rietti, "or he'll burn!"

The soles of Bernhardsen's shoes were gluey from the heat when they pulled him out. His feet must have been on fire. Mac poured water on them. It spattered onto the rocks and hissed into steam.

"Okay," Bernhardsen panted. "Go. Now."

They crossed the rest of the field. MacKenzie was silent. The volcano's lesson had not been lost on him. There was a majesty about destruction of this magnitude that dwarfed the affairs of men. When the rain forest closed in again, he was almost glad to see it.

They reached the mining camp just before nightfall, a ghost town outlined by gray moonlight and mist. There had been life here once, but time and the volcano had plowed it under. Doors and windows had blown away. Most of the structures were covered with lava, like pudding. The buildings left standing hung at disturbing angles. All that was left was an office, a bunkhouse, some storage sheds, and a shop. The road leading out to the cliffs and down to the sea was cracked and broken. Rusted railroad tracks ran alongside it from the mine to the pier.

"Spread out and see what you can find," MacKenzie instructed them.

The volcano was blowing red sparks off its summit as Mac went into the machine shop. Ash coated everything. Vegetation had crawled through holes in the walls. There were pools of rot and rust. But lathes, presses, grinding machines, and compressors still stood in neat rows, all covered by protective tarps. They'd help reopen the mine, he thought dryly, but he was hard-pressed to see any other use for them. He was wondering what to do next when Bernhardsen and Rietti came in with the results of their foraging.

"We found these in the storage sheds," said Bernhardsen, showing him four rusty machetes. "There are explosives, too. Look."

MacKenzie put up a cautionary hand. "Treat it carefully. That's CVX plastique. A small block could blow up this building. It's stable enough long term. Just keep it away from fire."

"There's a ton of canned food," said Rietti. "Lanterns, blankets."

MacKenzie examined the machetes. "None of this stuff is easy to come by in this part of the world. Why leave it all behind?"

"You betray an American's ignorance of volcanoes. Would you care about a few company tools, or anything else for that matter, if Niigata Yakeyama was erupting?" asked Rietti.

"Not at all," MacKenzie agreed. "Ivor, rig some lanterns and get a space prepared in the bunkhouse."

"What are you going to do?" Bernhardsen asked testily.

"To see if for once in my life something is going to be easy."

"What's that?"

"Maybe in their rush to get off this place, someone left a radio."

There were ash-covered desks, file cabinets, and tattered Japanese calendars in the main office, but no radio. Mac brushed off a chair to sit and take stock. Rietti accepted his command, but Bernhardsen was still chafing. They weren't his biggest problem, though. Time was. He had enough tools to build a housing development, but that still left the *Korlov* untouchable, a mile offshore on the other side of the island. No matter how secure they could make themselves, he could never for a moment forget he had to stop Akiro. One day was almost gone. Nine left.

Light was emanating from the bunkhouse when he walked over. Rietti had found fuel for the lanterns. There were other nice surprises. Bernhardsen might not like taking orders, but he had cleaned a wooden table and chairs, and found enough blankets to set up three bunks comfortably.

"All this and dinner, too?" MacKenzie said appreciatively.

Bernhardsen divided a tin of stew onto three tin plates. "I wonder what our wives are doing."

"Justine won't let anything happen to them."

"I wish I shared your optimism," said Bernhardsen.

Rietti took a plate. "If there's a downside, Admiral, Ivor will find it."

"What gives with you guys?" MacKenzie was reaching the end of his patience. "You don't stop."

"Forget it," said Bernhardsen.

"It's useless," Rietti agreed.

"Then put it away for the duration."

Bernhardsen turned on him. "I'm not in your navy, Admiral. I'm not even an American. What gives you the right to order me around?"

Something in MacKenzie changed. People who had seen it before likened it to a storm gathering. Suddenly there was an intensity about him, an energy. His intense dark eyes were no longer calm, but turbulent. He emanated an indefinable force. MacKenzie made no explanation of his "right," as Bernhardsen put it, although it began as soon as Bernhardsen came aboard the *Korlov,* nor did he list his skills. He didn't need to give an answer when there was no question.

"I'm in command. Everyone on the ship and this island is my responsibility. You included."

Bernhardsen looked like he was going to protest, but the determination on MacKenzie's face stopped him. Instead, he said acidly, "Give all the orders you like. They won't change a thing. I'm going for a walk outside, *if* you don't mind."

MacKenzie didn't try to stop him. Let him cool off.

"I'm sorry, Admiral. Ivor's mad at me, and he's just taking it out on you. We've been at each other's throats for months."

"Why?"

"It's hard to explain."

"Try me."

Rietti set his plate down. "It started in Peru, but it goes back farther than that. We've been partners for more than fifteen years. Since our Tokyo days. We were well respected. Full professors. The grants came in regularly. We weren't rich, but we did well. Useful. Important. Not a bad life."

"Quite a good one. What happened?"

"We got older. It changed things. Made us different. We always used to complement one another. No matter what risks Ivor took, I'd always have us backed up. If we got into trouble, we always made it out. But it got so he wasn't just aggressive, he was reckless. He wanted the big find. Our names in the textbooks. He went to more dangerous lengths. Deeper into craters, exposing us to inordinate risk. All I could think about was not coming home to Bette. I guess I felt my mortality. I started to pull back."

The light from the lanterns flickered on Rietti's face. "We were in Peru testing our theory that the magnetic field around a volcano changes when it's ready to erupt. Carla and Bette were back at the base with the computers and communications gear. Ivor and I were up at the rim. We had four doctoral candidates from USC with us, two men and two women, all young and eager. They looked up to us"—he half smiled—"the old pros."

"Things were happening fast. All the signs said it was going to blow, but we had to get monitors inside the crater. I said abort, Ivor said go. He said we'd all taken risks before in the name of science. If we proved the theory, it would be a milestone. The students agreed. I still felt it was too risky to go in. I wanted to do it by robot. Ivor blew his top. It would take too long, he said. I wouldn't budge. He was furious.

"The robot planted the first and second monitor, but the angle got too steep and it failed on the third. Ivor told everyone it was my fault for sending it; now we had to go in anyway. It was too close to erupting and I said so. There'd be other volcanoes. Ivor overruled me. He called me all kinds of names, and threatened to fire the others on the spot. He said I was a coward." Rietti looked ashamed. "I couldn't stand it. I relented. We went in to plant the last monitor by hand.

"Magma was close to the crown. You could feel the heat through your boots. The underground pipes that bring the magma up were near bursting. It was hell inside the crater, but we got to the robot. Ivor thought we could salvage it and told the others to make repairs while he and I went across the ridge to plant the last monitor."

Rietti's eyes grew haunted. "We should have just gotten the hell out. While we were across the crater, a pipe blew and took out the other side of the ridge. The students were incinerated." Rietti covered his face. "Ivor and I barely made it out. He was badly burned.

He blamed me for everything, said it was my cowardice that made him wait to go in. I blamed his ambition. I don't know who's right anymore."

"Who was in charge?"

Rietti shrugged. "Ivor sort of naturally made those kinds of decisions. But those four students died, damn it. He was wrong. He should have listened to me."

"Listen, Tony," MacKenzie said gently. "I know what you're going through. People died, people who were your responsibility. And you're right. The commander has to judge risk, and balance possible loss of life against the value of the mission. But things get blurred out there. Maybe this, maybe that. If it rained, if it snowed. You aren't a coward, and he may not be a monster."

"He was wrong, damn it."

"Was there a hearing of some kind?"

Rietti nodded. "At the university. They said what you said. No blame was fixed, nothing criminal, but we ended up on a kind of professional probation. Foundations refused to give us grants. Ivor got private funding from somewhere for this expedition. It's supposed to get us going again."

"But it isn't the same."

"It's over for me," Rietti said sincerely. "Bette and I came because of how it would have looked if we didn't. But I won't go back into a volcano. Ever. I keep seeing them falling into the magma. I keep thinking what it would be like to be one of them." He shook his head. "That fear never goes away. It's ruined other men in our field. Ivor is kidding himself that I can ever go in again."

"You reacted well enough today. You saved his life."

"It's different up there," was all Rietti would say, and he said it in such a way that MacKenzie knew the matter was closed.

It was late and MacKenzie was tired, but he couldn't sleep. He kept thinking about Rietti's story. If the eruption had come ten minutes later, Bernhardsen was a hero. Ten minutes earlier, Rietti was a sage. It was impossible for him to know who had been right, but one thing was clear. The healthy mix of agression and caution that had made them a great team was clearly gone, undermined by one's ambition and the other's fear.

MacKenzie walked out to the cliffs. Bernhardsen and Rietti weren't the only ones time had changed. Everyone got older and wanted more, needed more, and it was easy to lose faith when the old priorities failed to sustain. Was it better back then? Will it ever be better? Tough questions, Mac thought, stuck on this island with Justine pregnant and in danger, with a mission to accomplish and nothing to accomplish it with. He was about to turn back to the barracks when a wildly excited Bernhardsen ran up to him, panting.

"Admiral, you've got to see this. I can't believe it!"

"What is it?"

"Just come on, man."

MacKenzie ran with him out to the edge of the cliff. It was low tide. The smell of ocean was strong. Enough light filtered through the fog to see. A string of sandbars lay exposed a few hundred yards out, like whales basking in the wan moonlight. But one of the whales . . .

"Is that what I think it is?" Bernhardsen said wonderingly. "Or is it a ghost?"

Seaweed hung from her wires and masts. Her gray

and black hull was encrusted with barnacles. But MacKenzie could still read the designation **P. 233** painted on her sail in faded man-high letters. She was pocked and pitted, listing awkwardly on the sandy spit, yet the once graceful silhouette was unmistakable. They stood transfixed as the rising tide crept over the hull till only the periscope standards remained, ancient fingers reaching for a lifeline. Then they, too, were gone.

"It's a ghost for sure," said MacKenzie, equally awed. He had no way to explain it. Long after the ocean covered it again, the image stayed in his mind.

After fifty years, His Majesty's Submarine *Storm* had surfaced once more.

14

Korlov

JUSTINE CALLED IT THE LADIES TABLE.

Lady Em and Carla Rietti cooked for the Japanese in the galley. Bette Bernhardsen and Carolyn served them. Justine had to help the women clean up before they could all sit down and eat. They kept conversation to a minimum when the guards were around, and the women weren't seen as a threat, just the way Justine wanted it. Alone, together, they talked.

"It's lonely with the men gone," Bette said.

"I watched them go today." Lady Em looked troubled. "I hope they'll be all right. That island is an awful place."

"Mac will take care of them," Justine said reassuringly. "Tell me what you heard today."

"Akiro instructed me to expect six more people to feed," Lady Emily said.

"Did he say when?" Justine asked.

"I think it'll be tomorrow," Carolyn interjected.

"I'm supposed to clean out the cabins and put fresh bedding in them."

"Ito was working on the crane today," Carla said. "There was talk about their having to use it to bring crates over from another ship."

"So six people are coming tomorrow by ship. Probably Lysenko and his bomb team. With their gear. You ladies are doing fine." Justine beamed. "A regular intelligence network."

"I thought spies were supposed to look like Mata Hari," Carla complained jokingly. "What I wouldn't give for a change of clothes and some makeup."

The others laughed. They all looked worn and haggard. They hadn't taken any cosmetics from the *Tuscany,* and they were permitted few showers. A ponytail tied with a rag sufficed for hairstyling. They wore a minimum of clothing to deal with the heat and humidity. Carla had on denim shorts and a halter top, both stained with food. Bette wore a cotton T-shirt and a sarong she had made from a linen tablecloth. Carolyn had cut down her jumpsuit and ended up showing enough skin to turn the guards' heads when she passed. Lady Em had sliced her skirt into a fringe for comfort, and tied the ends of her cotton blouse above her stomach. Justine's uniform was sweaty and bloodstained.

"What are we going to do, Justine?" asked Lady Em.

"Buy time. Slow them down. Every hour helps Mac."

"It must be nice to feel that way about your husband," said Carolyn wistfully. "My Johnny was a love, but I couldn't count on him to take out the garbage."

"The Commodore always made me feel so safe,"

Lady Em said. "I'll never forget our first encounter. He was just out of the hospital, and the War Office decorated him for his actions on his sub. All the newspapers played it up, you know. It was wartime and we needed the lift. He was a guest at all the finest homes." She sighed. "It was such a sad and lovely time."

"Go on, Lady Em," prompted Bette.

"We can talk inside the galley, ladies," said Justine. "Carla, I'll need your help."

"Right."

"And, Carolyn, don't empty that ashtray."

Carolyn looked surprised, but complied. "Whatever you say, girl."

They cleared the dishes into the stainless steel galley. Justine showed Carolyn how to rub an empty can along the knife-sharpening blocks to make a fine powder, while at the big sink Bette washed and Carla dried. Lady Emily kept watch, continuing her narrative as steam filled the room.

"My father was a newspaper publisher, and there was a dance at Lord Claridge's house," said Lady Emily, her voice warm with the memory. "My mother had been hurt in the bombings, so he took me. We were very sheltered in my day, not like you girls. I was twenty-two and it was practically my first formal occasion. It was wonderful. I danced with my father. He looked so proud. I turned down all the other lads who asked me."

"Finer powder," Justine directed Carolyn.

"It'll break my nails, but okay."

"My father's friend, Admiral Binns, introduced Alex and me, actually." Lady Em suddenly interrupted herself. "Guards."

She grabbed a towel. Justine scooped up the powder. By the time the guard looked in, all he saw was five women busily washing dishes.

"Hai," he said, and disappeared.

They went back to work. "More, Lady Em," Carla urged. "It takes my mind off things."

"Well, dear, Admiral Binns said there was a man who had been watching me all night, and he wanted to meet me. He told me all about Alex, what he had done. How could I refuse a war hero?

"We danced every dance. Later, there was an air raid and I was separated from my father. Alex took me to the shelter and held me till it passed. I was afraid, but it was so romantic. I felt no harm could come to me in Alex's arms. He brought me home and asked my father if he could call round the next night. We were inseparable after that. I was so afraid he would go to sea again and be hurt or killed. But his time on the island had taken too much out of him. He was made to stay ashore, and we got married."

"What a lovely story," said Justine.

"A lot different than mine," Carla said, toweling a big steel pot. "I met Ivor at Oslo University. He was a geology professor. Very popular. And handsome. All the girls wanted to take his class. I was a grad student. Bright, innocent, and sexy as hell even though you might not know it to look at me now, birds are going to nest in my hair. Ivor and I took to each other like magnets. All passion and not a care in the world. Next thing we knew, I was pregnant. I finished my degree while I was weaning my first son, and I've been hopping to volcanoes all over the world with Ivor and Bette and Tony ever since." Carla's blue eyes twinkled. "By the way, if you must know, the passion part's better than ever."

The others laughed. "Bette, you can't be the only

one not to tell how you met your husband," said Justine. "He seems like such a nice man."

Bette pushed her dark hair off her forehead. She had a sweet smile, like Tony's, and the same gentleness of spirit.

"I was already in the field when I met Tony," Bette said. "I went to a conference in Rome. He was there, but we didn't know each other. One day a group of us went walking near the ruins by the Colosseum. It was glorious. Things were so ancient and beautiful. I suppose it was why I was so surprised by the dog. Some horrible boy must have done it, hung him in a doorway. There were flies all around. Everyone turned away except Tony. He cut it down with a little penknife and dug a shallow grave. Someone asked him why he bothered. I'll never forget what he said. It was: We can't permit cruelty to stand. That's all. I think I knew then that anyone who felt that way about the death of a poor animal would never hurt me. I helped him wash up, and later we had dinner. We went on from there."

In its way, Justine decided, it was the nicest story of all.

She pushed the aluminum powder into a small plastic bag and knotted it. "I'm going now. The rest of you go to bed."

"Be careful, my dear," said Lady Emily.

Justine knew she meant the baby. She remembered telling Mac how she prayed for an accident. It would be so easy . . .

"I'll watch it," she heard herself say.

Justine went to check on Phillip Keller. He was recovering, and very bitter.

"You could have killed me!"

"Phillip, if I wanted to kill you, you'd be dead now. Be quiet and listen." She explained who she was.

"CIA?" he gasped. "It's incredible."

"I'm sorry I had to do it, but I was improvising. Can I count on you?"

Keller was still visibly upset. "What can you do alone?"

Justine thought of Carla and Carolyn, Bette and Lady Em. And Mac and the men on the island.

"I'm not alone."

"You're risking the baby," he warned.

"I know that," she said coldly.

"Yes, I'm sorry. Of course you do."

"I need you now. Can you make it up for some exercise?" she asked.

"I'll throw up."

She rolled up her sleeves. "Then let's get it over with, because you're going anyway."

It was pitch-dark outside. The moon was blocked by thick fog, and the ship's lights were extinguished. A guard helped her get Keller's wheelchair out on deck. The air seemed to do him some good. Color returned to his face, and he actually talked about walking on his own. Mori looked at them curiously. She inscribed circles with a finger. A few times around. He nodded. After the first circuit she pushed Keller behind one of the lifeboats.

"Wait here and don't make a sound," she instructed. "If I'm not back in ten minutes, we've got problems."

She stripped off her nurse's uniform. Underneath she was wearing a black bodysuit, compliments of Carolyn. Her hair was tied in a bun, secured by the *pesas*. She had planned this during the afternoon when they were out on deck. It wasn't going to be easy to get to the crane the way she'd chosen, but going across the deck was too exposed. She stretched her muscles. Up the radio mast to the rigging, over the rigging to the crane arm, down the crane arm to the motor housing. Back the same way. Not so tough in daylight. In darkness she'd have to be damn careful.

She climbed the bridge stairs, surefooted and quiet. There was a guard on duty. He could see the base of the radio tower from his position, preventing her from just climbing the access ladder. He tapped his foot and hummed. She wondered why till she saw the snaky black wires running to his ears. Of course, a Walkman. Music to while away the boring hours.

She used the rail under the catwalk to get past him and onto the superstructure. There she used the ladder to the bridge roof, the top of the ship. She moved gingerly. The terrorists had gone in this way, and the hatch covers were splintered and jimmied.

The radio tower was in front of her, between the bridge island and the crane. Guy wires secured it to the deck. There was a network of hooks and pulleys and wires and lines. She remembered going to the circus once and looking into the rigging. It looked like that.

Three steps and a jump. The night air flowed over her. She caught the beam and the tower swayed dangerously, but righted and stood firm. She climbed higher. The crane was a three-story box that moved on tracks set into the deck. A big diesel motor was on top next to the control cabin and the crane arm. It was about twenty feet away. One of the guy wires from the radio tower led past it. It was solid half-inch cable. Her weight wouldn't be a problem.

She pulled the *pesas* from her hair and lubricated it

with butter from the galley. She settled the wire in a groove she'd notched with a kitchen knife. It was quiet. The guard on the bridge below was still listening to his music. The guard on the foredeck was talking to his mate. Nothing else stirred.

She launched herself into space. The *pesas* slid along the wire with oiled ease, soundless save for a slight *thrum*. The crane sped towards her. She had to time it right, only seconds to pick her landing point. If she slid past, she'd end up on deck in front of some surprised guards with some fancy explaining to do. She saw an open area by the control room at almost the same instant that her mind/body directed her to jump. But at the last second she remembered to protect her middle and it threw off her timing. She hit the open spot, but far too hard. Her ankle twisted painfully.

She lay on the metal floor in the darkness. No alarm was raised. She took a oily cloth hanging over a valve, tore it into strips, and bound her ankle tightly. She could put her weight on it, but just barely. One thing was certain. She wasn't going back the way she came.

She hobbled over to the motor. Russian ships weren't know for their spotless maintenance, especially merchant vessels. There was a thick coating of grease and oil on the engine, a nice mess to ignite. She packed the powdered aluminum into the electrical contacts, and covered them with grease. The rest went into other hot spots.

Now how do I get out of here? she wondered. Only a few minutes remained. There were still guards on the foredeck and bridge. Shuto could be anywhere. She couldn't just saunter down off the crane with a smile. She needed a diversion of some kind, but how could she arrange one from here?

There was a platform ten feet above the deck. She waited till the guards were occupied, then slid down the crane ladder the way sailors did on ships, using only the railings. The platform gave her a good view, but time was up. In fact, one guard looked at his watch and peered into the darkness, waiting for her and Keller. The *pesas* was in her hand. If need be, she was going to have to take both guards. But how would the missing men be explained? She tested her ankle. It might not hold in a fight. She looked up to the crane. It was too late to remove evidence of her sabotage.

She watched helplessly as the guard moved off to find her and Keller. There was no way off the crane that she could see.

Below her, the guard stopped, nodded to himself, and went back to talking to his companion. Justine was completely surprised. Right on time, Keller in his wheelchair, pushed by his nurse in her unmistakable white uniform, was making another casual circuit of the deck. They came to a rest not five feet from her.

"Justine?" Carolyn whispered. "Are you up there?"

"Over your head. No, don't look."

"You were late. Phillip said—"

"Shh," Justine said softly. "Tell me later." She whispered instructions and dropped something at Carolyn's feet. "Start a fire, and plant these nearby."

"Okay."

Justine sighed with relief. Maybe she was going to get out of this after all. As she watched, Carolyn put a match to one of the big crates on the stern and wheeled Keller away. It caught almost immediately. Within minutes, the Japanese were racing to put it out. Shuto arrived. It didn't take him long to find the cigarette butts Justine had taken from the mess and given Carolyn to plant. Shuto waved one in front of one guard's face, yelling angrily.

Justine slid off the crane and slipped back inside.

"Carolyn, I could kiss you," Justine said, as she hurriedly changed. "How did you know?"

"I went to check on Phillip. A guard told me you were up on deck," Carolyn explained. "Phillip saw me. Nearly gave me a heart attack popping out. He was worried you were so late. When I saw the uniform, and it was so dark . . . Did I do right?"

"Better than that, lady. You did great."

"How's the ankle?"

"Hurts."

"Lie down," Carolyn instructed. She put an ice pack on it and gave her some anti-inflammatory tablets.

"How's Phillip?"

"The exertion drained him. He's not a strong man to begin with, and infection could set in."

"I'm sorry I had to do it."

"We all have to do what we can. But, Justine, Phillip's paid his dues."

"A lot have paid higher."

"You know how I feel about him," Carolyn said with a trace of anger. "I don't want you to hurt him again. Do you understand?"

Justine admired the strength of Carolyn's devotion, even if it was misplaced in Phillip Keller. She had real feelings for him. It made no sense to tell her Justine would sacrifice Keller or anyone else, for that matter, willingly, if necessary, to stop Akiro. What the hell did Carolyn think she'd been doing on that crane?

"I won't hurt him, Carolyn. I promise."

"Elevate that ankle," said Carolyn, mollified. "the

sprain's not bad. It'll feel better by morning. I'll be with Phillip."

"He's a lucky man."

"Maybe he's starting to know it," she said hopefully. "Get some rest."

"Okay. And thanks."

Keller lay inside, feigning sleep. He'd heard it all. His guts hurt where the knife had penetrated and he felt hot. He wasn't healing properly. As a doctor, he had been taught to value human life above everything. He did. His own.

The facilities on the freighter were appalling. He needed a good hospital. In a pinch he could give up Justine to Shuto, in trade for his life. But that was tricky. Terrorists weren't noted for paying debts. And Justine was evidently quite well trained and resourceful. She might just be able to stop Shuto. Finally, there was always the chance they might be rescued by a search party of some sort. He decided his best play was to lie low, and see how things went.

"How are you feeling, Phillip?"

"Better, now that you're here, Carolyn."

"Ready for your shot?"

"You take good care of me."

He saw her grateful smile. He could read the signs. She was devoted to him. Obviously in love. She wasn't the first. He had almost married his nurse in Paris. He didn't like to think about her, about what he had done, but she had left him no choice.

"I've grown very fond of you, Carolyn," he said. It made her glow.

She turned down the cabin lights and sat by him, holding his hand.

"Rest, Phillip. You've got to recover your strength."

"Justine is gone?"

"Yes."

"That woman frightens me. She's very dangerous."

"We're in a difficult situation, Phillip. She's trying to protect us."

"Us, or her?" He touched the knife wound. Justine had scared him deeply. He destroyed things that scared him. His mother had taught him that. Hadn't they protected his father that way?

"I won't let her hurt you again," Carolyn said protectively.

She leaned closer. Her breasts pressed against him. He said, "I feel better when you're here."

"Then I won't leave."

"I'm cold, Carolyn."

There was a rustle of clothing in the darkness. He felt the covers lift, then the comforting plumpness of her naked breasts against him. Moist heat rose from her.

"I'll warm you," she said.

15

Tuscany

EVERY HOUR ON THE HOUR, CAPTAIN KOBIASHI SENT THE
signal to the orbiting satellites. As instructed, he kept
out of the shipping lanes, lessening the chance of
accidental contact. The course changes weren't
enough to cause alarm, just the kinds of corrections a
prudent captain might make to pursue better weather.
Actually, Kobiashi was doing the opposite. He sailed
into every rain squall and fog bank on the route to
Japan, and stayed in them as long as possible for
concealment.

"Could be fog due north, Captain," said his navigator, Noburu. "Water temperature's right."

"Lay in a course. What's on the screen?"

"Overflight at thirty thousand feet," said Sasaki,
the radar operator. "Probably a passenger jet heading
for Tokyo."

"Can you verify that?"

"Not without an AWAC. The amplification we did
was good. But not *that* good."

121

Kobiashi nodded. All the training he had received, just to do this one thing, captain this ship. Others in his naval class went on to command coast guard ships and merchant vessels. And he had, too, for a time. But Akiro had sent him to school for one purpose, and Kobiashi had always known his debt to the old man would have to be paid.

They were still nine days out of Japan, but the *Tuscany* would never make port. Near Tokyo, another ship would remove him and his crew and they'd scuttle her. The *Korlov* would appear to have vanished without a trace. It would be days before anyone linked the Russian freighter to an overdue French passenger yacht.

"Fog bank, Captain." Kobiashi heard the pride in his navigator's voice. Noburu liked to be right.

Outside the bridge window a fluffy gray blanket was rolling in, separating sky and sea. To Kobiashi, sailing inside the fog felt like being hidden in the cotton batting his family had used to wrap the musical instruments his father made. The memory caused a stab of pain and an involuntary closing of his once-webbed fingers, surgically altered. No music for him as a child. Only the dark rooms of the factory basement until Akiro and Shuto found him.

"Captain?" Sasaki sounded concerned.

"Yes?"

"Either that jet is breaking up, or we've got trouble."

Kobiashi looked over his shoulder. There were three contacts on the radar screen where one had been. Three jets, flying close enough together to fool the radar. One was coming down. Maybe the pilot had instructions, maybe it was just a friendly look-see.

Either way, Kobiashi had to avoid it. He looked back outside. The air was getting hazier. It was a race now.

"Twenty thousand feet," Sasaki called out.

At that distance they were invisible.

"Ten thousand."

The fog was thicker now, but not thick enough. And if they hit an open pocket . . .

"Make smoke," Kobiashi directed the engine room. It came in seconds, thick and black. The smell penetrated the bridge.

"Five thousand, four, three . . . He's starting his approach."

"Noburu?"

"Suggest right ten degrees rudder, Captain."

Kobiashi gave the command. The light changed almost at once as the fog thickened to the point of opaqueness. He threw open the door and peered upwards.

"Three hundred feet and overhead . . . now!" Sasaki called out.

Kobiashi heard the jet and felt the turbulence in the water its passage caused. But he couldn't see it.

That meant they couldn't see him.

"He's rejoining the others," Sasaki reported.

"How thick is the fog bank?"

Noburu said, "Twenty miles, maybe more."

By the time they got out, the jets would be in Japan.

"Maintain present course," ordered Kobiashi.

16

Korlov

MORNING BROUGHT PEARLY LIGHT FROM THE FOG-filtered sun, and Viktor Lysenko's luxurious yacht, *Odessa*.

"Beautiful," said Akiro. He and Shuto watched its approach from the main deck. "He must be very rich."

"At two million dollars a week, he damn well ought to be. A good part of Ido Miagi's money will go to him."

"Ido can afford it."

Shuto said, "I'm told Lysenko loves that yacht. He spends most of his time on it. The crewmen are well-paid mercenaries who protect him."

"Will that be a problem?"

"Shouldn't be."

The *Odessa* swept in alongside the *Korlov*. Shuto's men placed the crosswalk.

"By the way," Shuto said. "I am also told he is a

pervert. Sleeps with his staff. Men and women. Arrogant. A bully. Quite possibly insane."

Akiro considered that. "Will *he* be a problem?"

Shuto gave one of his rare smiles. "Shouldn't be."

Lysenko came out on *Odessa*'s deck. He was short-bodied, Napoleonic in his carriage. Lysenko was legendary among physicists for his violent temper, sexual excesses, and unmatched brilliance. A day-dreamer and a social outcast like so many prodigies, at twelve he solved one of the Rothenberg equations and set the world of physics on its ear. Overnight, the tiny boy with the unruly shock of black hair and the eyes of a grown man was propelled into national prominence.

"Begin the transfer as soon as possible," Shuto told Hiroki.

"Hai."

Lysenko's shock of dark hair was gray now, his eyes older, but he moved with the energy of a nuclear pile, never at rest. His assistants, two men and two women, stood behind him at a respectful distance.

Hiroki crossed to the yacht, bowing politely.

"May I offer you assistance, Dr. Lysenko?"

Lysenko grabbed Hiroki's shirt as if it were a strap in a bus, and strode across.

"Why aren't you ready for my arrival?" he demanded without greeting or introduction.

Shuto bowed, ignoring the disrespect. "My father is honored to meet you."

"Tell the old man whatever. Are you ready to start? I've come a long way and my time is valuable."

"You do us honor to have such great expectations," said Akiro humbly. "We are prepared to unload your yacht."

"Fine. Let's get on with it."

The Soviet machine loved Lysenko. He was proof it produced geniuses. At fifteen, Lysenko had been given almost unlimited research funds, and lived a life of luxury. By seventeen, he fulfilled his promise by producing dazzlingly elegant atomic weapons. But at eighteen, he savagely beat and raped a woman who refused to sleep with him. When he was twenty, a car cut him off and he ran it off the road, killing the family inside. No one could say for sure how much human misery Lysenko was responsible for over the years, but he had never served a single day in jail or, to anyone's knowledge, voiced a single regret.

Shuto signaled Ito in the crane control room. The diesel roared into life and the crane moved on tracks to line up with *Odessa*'s foredeck, which opened like the cargo bay on the space shuttle. Ito used the crane arm and lowered cargo nets into the hold. Lysenko's men secured their crates and the first load swung over to *Korlov*'s deck. It was a good start. Akiro said so.

"My crew knows better than to fail me," Lysenko responded.

"They are completely loyal?" asked Shuto.

"They do what I say." It was a fact. Like numbers.

"A tribute to your brilliance," said Akiro.

"More to each man knowing working for me allows him to sit on the *Odessa* earning a small fortune every contract, instead of fighting some stinking jungle war."

"Self-interest rules everything, then?" Akiro inquired, interested.

"I've studied the universe my whole life. It's the only truth I've ever found," Lysenko said flatly.

Another shipment cleared *Odessa*'s hold and swung out over the water. It gave no prelude to disaster. The

]powdered aluminum on the electrical contacts finally heated to its ignition point. A flash fire set the oil sludge on the engine burning, which melted the fuel line. Diesel fuel poured out and ignited. Ito had no time to get out of the cabin. He was engulfed by fire. They could hear his screams.

Shuto shouted, "Ito!" and tried to climb to him, but the heat was too intense. The fuel tank exploded and tore the superstructure apart. The crane cable unwound like a dead snake. Cargo fell into the sea. Shuto pushed his father and Lysenko to safety and tried once more to get to Ito. When he was halfway up the ladder, a hot metal bar fell against him. His shirt caught on fire. Shuto ripped it off, hanging on in midair, ignoring agonizing pain. The entire crane was on fire. He had no choice but to drop off. He prowled the deck like a stalking cat. His grief and fury were terrible to see.

Hiroki's men got the fire under control. The damage was extensive. The crane was useless. A portion of Lysenko's cargo was lost. And Ito was dead.

Lysenko said, "I'm not responsible if the project can't be completed on time."

Akiro spoke in Japanese. Shuto began issuing orders. His men streamed over to the *Odessa*. Hiroki was the first. His muscles bulged as he lifted a crate and carried it to the gunwale. Two of his men took it and passed it to another two, bucket brigade style. They passed crate after crate. It was backbreaking work in this heat. Shuto came to the gunwale. The crane was still burning overhead. Ito's pyre. The men doubled their efforts. Lysenko's mercenaries were a hard lot, but they watched in admiration as the cargo in *Odessa*'s hold was brought to the *Korlov*.

Justine arrived amidst the smoke and fire and ran over to Shuto.

"I heard the alarm. I brought my things."

"Treat the men," he said.

"What happened?"

"The crane caught fire. Ito is dead."

"I'm sorry," she said, thinking: I caused it. She could feel his grief. She wondered if he could feel her guilt.

"He was a brother to me," Shuto said simply.

A charred smell filled the air. Hot, dirty water rolled over the deck. Justine saw they had lost cargo. Ito was dead. She'd succeeded, but her duplicity and violation of trust were terrible things. They weighed heavily. It was important to remember what these men were trying to do.

"Send the burned ones to me, Shuto."

"All right." He was lost within himself.

Lysenko looked at her covetously. The carnage hadn't affected him. A steak might have been burned.

"Who are you?"

"Justine Segurra. Ship's nurse."

He kissed her hand. His lips felt positively reptilian. "Shuto picks his people well, I'll give him that."

"Are you hurt, Dr. Lysenko?"

"No. Why aren't you Japanese?"

"I was on the *Tuscany*. I'm a prisoner."

"Charming," said Lysenko. "I'll ask him to make you my prisoner, too."

She wished she didn't feel too crummy to hit him.

"Would you like to see my yacht?" he asked.

Justine was interested. Yachts had radios. An hour after she was on the *Odessa*, Lysenko would be dead, and a call for help made.

"I can arrange it," he said.

Before she could answer, he put his hand on her breast. It was a rude, insensitive gesture. He would have plucked a grape the same way. Justine left his hand there, and studied the little man who barely came up to her chin as she would an insect. A piece was missing. Something essential to the feeling part. He had no boundaries, freely violating even the most basic rules of human interaction. He did what he did because he could, the moral equivalent of a German shepherd.

Lysenko was stung by her contempt. He looked about to slap her, but at that moment Akiro and Shuto joined them.

Shuto said, "Is there anything else on the yacht you require?"

"No."

"You're certain?"

"Everything is in those crates. Or was. Prefabricated back at my warehouse. I won't know what we lost till I take inventory. Just send a man for my private papers. In my stateroom. A black case."

Shuto called to Hiroki. Shortly Lysenko's briefcase was on the *Korlov*.

"That is all?" asked Shuto. "You're certain?"

"You are insufferable. Yes. Yes!"

"Then go to your cabin."

Lysenko's lips curled disdainfully. "I don't take orders from you. And don't wave guns at me. My men are armed. Also, I agreed to stay on the ship while the work was progressing, but I didn't expect such a garbage scow. I'll remain on my yacht."

Shuto walked away.

"Please reconsider," asked Akiro.

"No. And I want this woman brought to—"

A sudden explosion rocked the deck and everyone

on it. Smoke poured over the side where the yacht had been moored.

"What in Lenin's name . . . ?" Lysenko began.

"The matter of your men and where you are staying is settled," Shuto said, removing the shoulder harness. He hated to use the last of his missiles, but a lesson was definitely in order.

The *Odessa* was burning violently. Lysenko watched in horror as Shuto's men pushed it away from the *Korlov*. It sank without survivors.

"My yacht! There were thirty men on board," he gasped.

Shuto ignored him. "One more thing. Don't put your hands on this woman again. She's part of my crew."

"You can't build the bomb without me," Lysenko said defiantly. "What if I refuse to work?"

Shuto turned to Hiroki. "Drown him."

Lysenko was many things, but slow wasn't among them. A man who would kill thirty to make his point couldn't be bluffed or threatened.

"Of course, I *wouldn't* refuse, having a contract and all," he said quickly.

"As you wish. Hiroki, take the doctor to his cabin."

Hiroki led him away.

Justine thought it was too bad about the loss of *Odessa*'s radio, but she had to admit that Shuto's style was growing on her.

Justine finished bandaging the last Japanese. He thanked her several times. Heal them by day, kill them by night, she thought. The irony weighed heavily on her. She was in no shape to live this kind of lie. Pregnancy and the diabetes drained her strength. She couldn't keep food down, but she had to eat to avoid the weakness. The heat sapped her resolve. She felt worse every day. How long could she last?

"One moment, Justine, please."

Shuto was the last on deck. His *gi* top was draped over his bare shoulders. She stopped packing her things.

"Are you hurt?"

"Ito was my best friend. A brother."

"I'm sorry. I meant physically."

Wordlessly he removed the tunic.

She winced.

He expected it. "Ugly?"

"Only the burn," she said. His scales were blackened and charred. "Move your hands. Let me see."

He pulled away. "It hurts."

"Baby," she scolded. "Stand still."

She cleaned his scales with peroxide and applied ice to the worst of it. He watched as she worked. "You're very gentle. And you don't mind touching me. Why aren't you disgusted?"

"I have a theory about people."

"Yes?"

"We come in all shapes and colors. Evidently"— she rapped a knuckle against him; it made a sound like tapping a turtle shell—"we come in a variety of textures, too."

"No prejudices?"

She shrugged. "I try and make myself an alien."

"Explain, please."

"Is an alien with three mouths and eight legs and two purple antennas different than one with three mouths and eight legs and *one* purple antenna? Would one of those aliens feel anything about human skin being pink or tan? Of all things," she said disgustedly.

Shuto said something in Latin.

"Now you explain," she said.

"It translates roughly as 'Nothing human is alien to me.'"

"Or . . ." Justine smiled and tapped his chest again. "This is bullshit."

It was Shuto's turn to smile. "Even more succinct."

"That's me."

"I have a question," he said, after a while.

"All right."

"Why did you let him touch you?"

She knew what he meant. "Why does it matter?"

"It . . . angered me."

"I don't belong to you. I'm a prisoner, remember?"

"Events occur on the surface of the sea and they occur underneath. Others occur deeper still. Separate events in the same sea. Are they related or not?"

"I'm not Zen enough to answer that, Shuto. Keep it simple."

"The heart does not always recognize politics."

She was caught off guard, flustered. "You don't think . . . I mean, I never . . ."

"You've done nothing. Honor is intact. There are reasons I can ask freely. Believe me, I mean you no harm."

He was like a little boy reaching out in grief and confusion, hurt by Ito's death. She tried to explain.

"Lysenko's a pig. He's been slapped before. It wouldn't have mattered."

"So?"

"Scorn made him small. I knew he'd hate that."

"What if I were to do it?"

"Touch me? You wouldn't."

"Why not?"

"You'd see my pity, and that, *you* would hate."

Shuto lowered his eyes. "You know so much. How?"

Justine said it the way she thought Carolyn would. "I've been around."

He shook his head. "It's more than that. I want to tell you something. The reason I can speak this way." He looked out to sea as if he had a special understanding of its emptiness. "I never have . . ."

Justine spared him saying it. "Because of this?" She touched his chest.

"Another result of my birth."

Justine found herself again torn by this gifted, lonely man. How he had suffered. She understood what that did to you. For a long time it had sent her inward, till she met Mac. The difference was, Shuto was no innocent child caught up in a war. He'd killed Sergeant Porter with his bare hands, and destroyed the men on the *Akatsuki Maru*, the *Odessa*, and the *Tuscany* without remorse. He was the enemy. She had to remember that. If he found out she'd sabotaged his operation and killed two of his men so far, one his best friend, he would kill her. If events permitted, if she had the chance, she'd have to kill him. Unless she could dissuade him.

"Don't do it, Shuto," she pleaded. "It can't bring any good."

"Akiro wants his enlightenment."

"What do you want?"

"I used to ask myself that constantly," he mused. "When I found the answer, it became the most important thing in my life. The only thing. Justine, do you know what I did when I came back from the monastery Akiro sent me to?"

"Collected stamps?"

His eyes blazed. "Don't mock me. I waited for those boys who tormented me, by the very garbage pile I once had to hide in. When they came I broke their arms and legs and stuffed garbage into their mouths till they stopped breathing."

Justine was suddenly frightened. "That isn't enlightenment."

"It's never been about that for me. The Admiral, you, and I. We're alike. I've meditated on it. We want the same thing."

"What?"

"More than enlightenment. Justice." He savored the word.

"Revenge isn't justice."

"The hell it isn't!" In that instant she feared he would kill her with a single blow from those terrible hands. His fire threatened to engulf her. There were any number of strikes she could have tried, he was vulnerable for a split second, but she was too weak, and his anguish burned her senses. She turned away from the heat.

"The secret is balance," he said. "Before anything else, I learned that. Don't worry about Lysenko. He won't bother you again. Thank you for treating my men."

Justine looked at the crane, still burning with an oily smoke.

"I do what I can," she said.

17

Sōfu gan

LOW TIDE WAS COMING AGAIN. MACKENZIE, BERNHARDsen, and Rietti had worked all night scavenging parts from the mining camp to fix the power winch in the boathouse. It had rained twice, making the work more difficult. The humidity made food left out spoil while you watched. Simple cuts festered into infections in hours.

MacKenzie finished splicing cable. "What will the Commodore say when he sees the *Storm* again?"

"It can be painful to recall a lost youth," said Rietti.

"Can't be more painful than being here," said Bernhardsen, swatting a fat mosquito.

"I wonder what kind of shape she's in." Mac was dead set on going out to the sub. Rietti had supported the idea. Bernhardsen wasn't as easy to convince.

"After fifty years, what kind of shape *could* she be in?" he protested. "She's a fish tank."

"Not necessarily. Depending on how she went

down and what the damage is, she might be salvageable."

"You're both crazy," Bernhardsen said flatly, but he lent a hand. MacKenzie was beginning to understand him. Bitch and moan, and in the end join in.

They got the motor running. Rietti hefted the metal hook on the end of the winch cable.

"I've done some deep-sea fishing, but this is one for the books, eh, Admiral?"

"Lose that formality, Tony. Friends call me Mac."

"Why does Captain Raskin call you Peter?"

"His accent. I couldn't stand being called Muck. Ivor?"

"Mac it is."

It was an eerie feeling waiting for the sub. They all had doubts. Maybe it had been just a ghostly apparition or a fantasy of tired minds. Yet once more when the water receded, the *Storm* came into view.

"Remarkable," Rietti said, seeing it for the first time.

"After all these years," MacKenzie said. "How is it possible?"

Bernhardsen supplied part of the explanation. "Feel how warm the water is? The whole slope's riddled with volcanic pipes. Heat makes for big tidal movements. It might have shifted a dozen times over the years, maybe even moved up from the bottom before, only nobody was around to see it."

"In the Caribbean," Rietti added, "storms bring up ships overnight."

MacKenzie stripped down to his shorts. They packed tools, strong line, and a miner's generator-light into a waterproof bag and secured it around his waist.

"Don't get caught out there when the tide comes

in," warned Bernhardsen. "If you can't get in right away, swim back and try again later."

"Good luck, Admiral," said Rietti.

Like most submariners, Mac found submarines themselves fascinating, and he had more than a passing acquaintance with the ancestors of modern navy boats. The *Storm* was just over two hundred feet, and displaced only eight hundred tons, far smaller than his last command, the Los Angeles–class fast-attack sub U.S.S. *Jacksonville,* which was 365 feet long and displaced seven thousand tons. *Storm*'s twin propellers were powered by diesel engines or electric motors. She had six bow torpedo tubes. Commodore Rowe said she carried 48 men. *Jacksonville* carried 135.

What was it like to command her? MacKenzie wondered as he swam for the *Storm.* Air-gulping diesel engines forced these old subs to spend much of their time on the surface, including during an attack. Her top surface speed was about fifteen knots. Modern subs could do more than twice that on the surface, and were even faster underwater, where the *Storm* was slowest.

The *Storm* was resting on a sandbar. Blowholes for her saddle-type ballast tanks ran all the way down her gray length. Why had she come back? MacKenzie wondered. For what purpose? She was built in an era of dogfights and convoys, of wolf packs and battleships. But make no mistake. She was the most efficient warship of her day. Submarines had made up only 2 percent of the Allied naval strength in the Pacific, but they sank 240 warships and over 90 percent of Japan's merchant shipping fleet.

Mac hauled himself up on deck. The hull was slippery with sea slime, crusted with barnacles and sharp coral growth. The deck listed almost fifteen degrees. Footing was precarious. He used the handrail for balance. The "jumping wire" still ran overhead, a cable strung the length of the boat that enabled it to slip under antisubmarine wire.

He ran a hand over the pitted surface of the three-inch gun in front of the sail. An experienced crew could get its first shot off within forty-five seconds of surfacing. They left the breech open so water could drain more quickly when they surfaced. Behind the sail was a 20-mm Oerlikon cannon mounted on a railed platform. It was easy to imagine the *Storm* racing along a horizon glowing with the fires of burning enemy ships, gunners slamming shells into their guns and firing even as water drained out the barrels.

A deep scar ran along the port side of the sail, from the bridge back to the shattered radio antenna, called the W/T mast, for wireless transmitter. It was the shot that put the *Storm* out of action, he assumed, and it had probably come close to flooding her till they secured the valves. There were auxilary controls in the bridge. Periscope standards towered overhead. The upper sail hatch was directly below his feet, with drainage holes all around. Below the hatch was the conning tower, then the lower sail hatch leading into the control room. The hatches seemed secure, giving him hope.

MacKenzie had an inner conviction that he'd been given one chance, and if he didn't take it, he would lose her. The capricious sea might take the *Storm* for good. But it was risky. The tide was creeping back up the hull. If she flooded, he might sink her for good. He made a decision. Clearing the hatch of debris with his tools, he hit the locking levers a few times to loosen them, then used the pry bar. They gave an inch or so. A few more minutes of concentrated effort and the locks released. It was a solemn feeling. No one had entered here for over a half century.

Back on the pier, Bernhardsen and Rietti were signaling him to come back. The sea was rising fast. He decided to play his hunch that the *Storm* was still watertight, that her hand-milled stainless steel valves would still hold after all these years, and that she had enough compressed air in her tanks to blow the ballast and hold her above water. Old and encrusted, she might be, but she was a fighting ship of the line. He needed the *Storm* too badly to let her go now.

Stale dead air from the days of Roosevelt and Churchill poured out when he cracked the hatch. He climbed down the brass rungs set into the conning tower. The lower hatch was his last obstacle. The walls were dry, a good sign. He opened the lower hatch and let fresh air flow in, impatient to go, anxious about what he might find. The ship was rocking. The tide was rising fast. He had only minutes to find the emergency switch and blow the main tanks. If he couldn't raise her immediately, he'd have to scramble to seal the hatches and pray they held for another tidal cycle. He doubted they would.

The darkness in the control room was broken by the first shaft of light in over fifty years. He got the miner's generator-lamp from the waterproof plastic bag and cranked it into life. The control room was agonizingly small. Steel and brass levers and controls were arrayed in a complicated display. Glass gauges. Riveted seams. A host of things unfamiliar. Modern conns were cramped, but compared to this, they were spacious. "Life under the kitchen sink" was how one submariner had put it. There were two brass periscopes and a single sonar station, asdic, the British called it, with a set of bulky earphones and a sweep-hand tracking screen. No computers or fire control stations, no global positioning systems or electronic tracking and communications devices. Orders to and from the bridge were passed by voice pipe.

He had no time for further exploration. The air was stale and he staved off a wave of dizziness. The rocking was more pronounced, the first trickle of water coming down the hatch. He shone the light around the conn, looking for the emergency blow ballast levers. His knowledge of the S class wasn't detailed enough to know its controls.

A gap-toothed skeleton almost made him drop his light. It was a ghastly sight. The seaman was still wearing the heavy white roll-neck sweater of the British submarine service, parchmentized to his mummified body as if it had been découpaged. The tally on his once white cap read, H.M. Submarines. His feet were encased in black boots with white socks rolled over the top. His hollow eyes were unseeing, yet his bony hand still groped for the levers labeled Ballast Control. Fifty years after dying at his station, he was showing the way. MacKenzie pulled the levers. Seawater was pouring through the hatch now. In seconds he would know if time had accomplished what the *Storm*'s enemies could not, scuttling her for good. The sub might be his grave if he couldn't raise it. He yanked the auxiliary tank lever, hoping to jar the valves open. All at once the *Storm* began to tremble. Compressed air blasted through long-unused tubes. The hull rumbled and groaned as seawater trapped fifty years before was forced out of ballast tanks, and the immutable laws of physics decreed that the *Storm* rise because she was once again lighter than the water she displaced. Seawater stopped streaming through the conning tower hatch. She showed her sail proudly and held steady on the surface.

MacKenzie touched her ancient controls reverently. It might be impossible to make her motive again. There was a staggering amount of work to do even before the ship was secured at the pier, but they'd made a start. But he imagined the throb of her diesels, and men racing to their stations when Commodore Rowe gave the command to "start the attack." The past seemed to reach out for him. He listened closely. What did the *Storm* want to tell him? Why had she come back? He hoped someday he would know what power raised the *Storm* at the very moment he so desperately needed her, and the part he was to play in her final destiny.

He saluted the dead seaman, and covered him with a blanket, before returning to the bridge.

18

H.M.S. Storm

OUT IN THE FRESH AIR, MACKENZIE FILLED HIS LUNGS and gave a victory yell. Bernhardsen and Rietti waved excitedly from the pier. Lines were coiled and ready.

MacKenzie had been given some unique commands during his career, including a deep submergence rescue vehicle and a Russian nuclear sub. Now it was a World War II relic, old and rusted, shaky at best, future uncertain. But he knew he would always treasure these first moments alone on her bridge, and the sense of empowerment they gave him. His first great love, commanding a warship, was something he had thought lost to him forever. The *Storm* had given him another chance.

The *Korlov* was formerly unreachable. Now he had a weapon and a plan to try for it. Distances were deceiving, though. In his day he had hunted the rogue sub *Kirov* to its death in the Caribbean; dueled a Soviet *Akula*-class submarine under the North Pole; and pursued the minisub *Kentucky* across half the world to destroy it. Here, all he had to do was navigate the *Storm* around a tiny island and sink a bulky freighter less than a mile out to sea, but he had no doubt that the last voyage of the *Storm* was going to be the most difficult one of all.

Below the sail was a watertight compartment for a folding boat. With typical British efficiency the oars were still stored there and fit neatly into the oarlocks. He secured a line to the bow capstan and slid the boat over the side. They were fortunate the current was heading in. The sub had already moved a hundred yards towards the beach. Rietti started up the motor of the power winch. Bernhardsen was swimming hard for the *Storm*. MacKenzie was glad to see them working together. Perhaps the team could be salvaged after all, like the *Storm* herself. Right or wrong, Bernhardsen didn't shirk hard work. Swimming with the winch's big hook and cable wasn't easy. He was nearly exhausted when MacKenzie finally got to him. He pushed the hook over the side and pulled himself in.

"Heavy?" asked MacKenzie innocently.

"It must be the way you navy types dispose of people."

"Only civilians."

They rowed to the *Storm* and MacKenzie fixed the hook to the capstan. Bernhardsen signaled Rietti in the boathouse and soon the winch cable tightened, drawing the *Storm* to land. It was a great moment.

"We thought you were going down with the ship," Bernhardsen admitted. "We could barely see it."

"It was close. And by the way. Not 'ship.' Boat. And not 'it,' her. She has feelings."

"Superstitions, from you?"

"Traditions."

Bernhardsen scanned her length. "She's been through the war, eh?"

"Ivor, I don't suppose you were ever depth-charged."

"Hardly."

"I was once. It was only an attack simulation, but I have never, ever, been so frightened in my life. I couldn't think straight. I was sure I was going to die. Fifty years ago, the crew of this boat went through the kind of night most people can't imagine. They had to get in close and trade shells while being hunted by destroyers. They fired their torpedoes on the surface through burning oil. Underwater, 'on watch' as it was called, the air was stale and the boredom unrelieved for days on end. No videotapes, no radio or television, no messages from home. The pressure was often unbearable. Believe me, they were a rare breed."

"And the Commodore was one of them?"

"A great one."

The winch drew them to the pier at about half a knot. Rietti had the lines ready. There was enough clearance to bring the sub in.

"Secure the bowline," MacKenzie ordered. "Watch yourself. We're going to hit hard without engines to slow us."

"Okay. And, Mac?"

"Yes?"

"Tony told me what you said about Peru. I don't think it will change anything, but I appreciate it."

"I hope it helps."

"Tony thinks it was about money, or fame. Maybe that was part of it. I'm older. There are things I want. But it wasn't all," he insisted. "We always took risks. Every time we went into one of those monsters, we knew we might not come out. But knowledge is hard-won. Doctors are exposed to disease. Astronauts sometimes die. You want safety, be an accountant. If a different pipe had blown, Tony and I would have been killed instead of them." He ran a hand over his blond beard. "I hurt for those students. Tony just won't see it. And I won't accept we're finished. I put this expedition together to prove it. And I will," he added, "if we ever get out of here."

"We will."

Bernhardsen shook his head. "That's not what I mean. The funds have a time limit. If we aren't in Tokyo in two weeks, we lose the money."

"Does Tony know that?"

"Sure. But the way he feels, he'd be just as happy to miss it."

"I think you two should talk."

"I said too many things that hurt him when it happened. He's stopped listening to me. Maybe rightfully so. You see, I still think he was wrong."

MacKenzie watched the pier draw closer.

"Ivor, I used to think there were answers to things like this. Navy regs. The military code. Parents and teachers. I've learned the hard way there aren't any answers."

"So what's left?"

"The attempt," MacKenzie said firmly. "One of the few things left to believe in. The try. For reasons that appear good at the time, even knowing that they may be wrong later. Knowing also that motives are often too complex to figure, and that bad men sometimes prosper, all of that. The attempt, bolstered by a rational belief that you are trying to do good, is one of the few moral choices left."

Bernhardsen whistled. "You're quite a philosopher."

MacKenzie gestured to their ancient warship and gave a self-mocking laugh. "Look around, Ivor. I'm a fool. And a coward. And a hero, like you and Tony and the rest. Now, get ready. We're going to hit."

The *Storm* rammed the pier with enough momentum to splinter timbers and shake barnacles off the hull, but the pilings held and the boat came to rest. He imagined he heard her sigh as she settled against the pier. She'd made port at last. Rietti tossed lines to Bernhardsen. Mac watched them work. Both brilliant, yet so different. One forged ahead, the other planned escape routes. The tension between them was palpable, the tragic events still very near. It was impossible to tell if they could ever be a team again.

He put Bernhardsen and Rietti's problems aside and finished securing the *Storm*. She was a sight to rouse the blood. The Storm was no longer a young boat, and the sunlight revealed her every flaw, but she had dignity, and the strong lines of a well-bred craft. She had a heart, too; MacKenzie could feel it.

Was it strong enough for one last voyage?

19

Korlov

JUSTINE HUNG HER RAIN SLICKER IN THE INFIRMARY shower and wrapped a towel around her damp hair. A nasty squall had moved in on their second day at Sōfu gan, whipping rain across the ship like buckshot. She'd just come back from bringing salt pills to the Russians, who were feeling the effects of the heat and humidity along with everyone else. Lysenko was programming their computers, forging ahead. It reminded her they had only eight days left.

She opened the adjoining door to Keller's room.

"Carolyn?"

"Just a minute."

Justine heard them dressing. Carolyn's new relationship with Keller was changing things, as if a choosing of sides was taking place. Her attitude towards Justine was increasingly antagonistic. Carolyn shut the door behind her, patting her hair back into place.

"I was feeding Phillip. What is it?"

147

"I need help. Bette and Carla are serving dinner. Lady Emily is with Akiro. That leaves you, *if* you can tear yourself away from the suffering Dr. Keller." She regretted her sarcasm as soon as she said it.

"That's not fair. Phillip still isn't well. It's not right to leave him."

Justine made a sour face. "He's been lying around for days."

"Phillip's not strong. And he's not a killer like you."

"Isn't that a little harsh?"

"I don't know. Is it?" Carolyn didn't meet her eyes. "All I know is that Philip and I intend to get through this alive."

"Phillip and you. How tidy."

"It's not like that. The stress of the situation just brought out feelings that were already there."

"What's gotten into you?" Justine asked angrily. "I thought you had a head on your shoulders. He's faking it and you're making excuses."

"I'm not. He'll be up and around when he's ready. That's all."

There was no use carrying it further. Carolyn's loyalty was to Keller.

"What do you want?" Carolyn asked.

"These nightly chats Shuto and Lysenko are having in the bridge," Justine said. "I plan to sit in on one."

"How?"

"You did pretty well the other night. Willing to try it again?"

"All right," Carolyn said grudgingly.

"Get Phillip ready."

The rain soaked Justine's black leotard. Carolyn was out on deck pushing the wheelchair. Keller was so bundled up, it was impossible to see any part of him. The sight of the nurse walking him around again provoked little attention.

The squall was Justine's ally. Her ankle hadn't fully recovered, but the guards were all inside, enabling her to climb to the bridge roof using the ladder. She moved carefully past the hatch covers and ventilators. The rain cut down on the time a nurse would logically keep her patient out, and on the time she could allow herself up here. She pulled Keller's stethoscope out of her leotard, and lowered it into one of the ventilation tubes.

". . . how we control the wave," a voice was saying. Lysenko's, she thought.

There was a garbled response, and then the single word ". . . problem." Shuto's voice.

She shifted her position.

". . . the brilliance of it," Lysenko was saying. "No explosion on earth has ever had the power. It will go down in history. Isn't that what you want?"

"Explain it to me again."

Lysenko tried to keep the exasperation out of his voice.

"The device Akiro hired me to construct, the kind the Americans dropped on Hiroshima and Nagasaki, is quite simple. We compact radioactive plutonium sufficiently so neutrons are emitted at an ever-increasing rate. Each atom captures a neutron, becomes unstable, and splits, yielding two smaller atoms, more neutrons, and a quantity of energy. All that energy released in a tiny span of time is called an explosion."

Lysenko's voice became more animated. "But the world's gone further. The energy you get if you fission atoms is negligible compared to the energy you get if you fuse atoms together. We take two enriched hydrogen atoms with two protons each, and fuse them together to make one atom with three protons. Ah, but where is the extra proton, you ask? It has become energy. That is the power of the sun itself. But you need the heat of an atomic bomb to trigger it."

"What's our problem then?"

"The enriched hydrogen was what your crane dropped. I can make a fission bomb using the plutonium, but it won't be enough to explode the Field. Without the Field, no wave. Just the pretty light your father wanted."

"Can it be done anywhere else?"

"There is only one Magnus Field. Hundreds of undersea volcanoes in a small area. Some are over seven thousand feet tall. I've seen the charts. When they erupt together"—there was the sound of lips smacking together deliciously—"the pressure front will create a tidal wave over five hundred miles long and three hundred feet high, with a velocity of over two hundred miles an hour. The Hawaiian islands will be inundated. Seventy hours later, it will hit California. That's what you hired me for, and I can deliver it. More than enough payment for old sins, eh? Don't get me wrong. I like the poetry of it myself. But I've got to have more enriched hydrogen."

"How long?" Shuto demanded.

"Two days. Maybe three. I wanted you to understand."

Justine was staggered. Shuto and Lysenko had just coldly outlined a plan that could kill millions. Akiro's desire to teach his countrymen had opened the door to Shuto's far deadlier revenge on the authors of his deformity.

"One other thing," said Lysenko. "Your father is

still giving me orders. Tell him he isn't in charge anymore. How you do it is your problem. But do it soon. My business is with you alone."

Justine lost Shuto's reply in a peal of thunder. The sky seemed to split open. The rain knocked her towards the edge of the roof and she had to grab a hatch cover to keep from going over.

"What was that . . . ?" she heard Shuto say through the stethoscope.

Damn his senses. He'd be up in seconds. There was only one chance to avoid detection, and after hearing their plan, she had to take it. She shoved the stethoscope down her leotard and went to the edge of the roof. The rain hit her like fists. She extended her arms, curled her toes, and launched herself out into space.

Nothing fancy. No points for form out here. It was at least six feet to clear the edge of the ship. Fifteen more to the water. She flung herself as far forward as she could and prayed it was enough. She cleared the gunwale by a scant six inches, but she flipped into the dark sea on her back. The shock knocked the air out of her lungs. Consciousness faded. She sank, unable to get her body to function. Part of her welcomed it. You can only fight so long before death stops being an enemy and becomes a partner. Her senses seemed to retreat. It had finally happened. This time, her spirit said, let it be over.

She might have, except for the child. Whether or not the baby actually spoke to her, or it was just her maternal instinct emerging in a moment of crisis, she would never know. But it gave her the strength to get back to the surface and gulp air into her aching lungs.

The sea fizzled all around her from the raindrops. The worst was past. The wind slowed, calming the water. She swam to the anchor chain and pulled herself up just as her husband had done days before, but she didn't know that. Nor did she know that he had been saved by a similar voice reminding him of the people who needed him. All she knew was that she had been renewed by the life within her. That small miracle sobered her, even as it awed her. She crawled onto the deck. Carolyn was coming past the lifeboats to get out of the rain.

"Here," Justine whispered.

Carolyn pushed the wheelchair over. "What happened?"

She wanted to say, *I felt life.*

"They heard me. I had to go over the side and swim back."

Carolyn threw the towels that made up Keller's form over the side and wrapped the blankets around Justine.

"Get me back. Quickly."

Justine wished she could lie down and sleep for about twelve hours. A wave of weakness passed over her. She remembered Keller's admonition. She hadn't eaten in hours.

Her job wasn't over yet, though. She had to talk to Mac.

Shuto came by the infirmary as Justine anticipated, checking on everyone. Phillip was sleeping soundly, cool and damp from a washcloth. Justine had just emerged from the shower to hide her wet hair. She was trying to examine her shoulder in the mirror when Carolyn walked in.

"What happened?"

"I hit it when I dove off the bridge."

There was an darkening bruise. "Hurt?"

"I've had worse."

"What's your range of motion?"

Justine raised her arm over her head and winced.

Carolyn got some pills. "These Tylenols are okay."

"Thanks, Doc."

"I'll send you a bill."

Carolyn was in a quandary. She liked Justine, and she felt Justine liked her. But Phillip warned her that was just a cover, natural to a woman like her. They couldn't trust anything she did. Carolyn had to admit there was evidence to support that, but wasn't Justine trying to protect them? The image of her crawling out of the sea in pain was hard to reconcile with the self-centered woman Phillip described.

"Why do you do it?" she asked suddenly. "All the heroics. Phillip says you're just protecting yourself, but you aren't, are you?"

"What do you think?"

"I think if you were really selfish, you'd get off this ship. They'd never find you on the island."

"But I don't."

"I can't figure that."

"It's hard to explain," Justine said. "I guess I've been at war since I was a child."

"Is that where you learned to fight?"

"I'm from an old Nicaraguan family. When Somoza came to power we joined the revolution. I was trained with the other children. I was just better at it than most. Ow!"

"Stay still. You tore some skin. Your father let you fight?"

"He encouraged me, and my brothers. He was a concert pianist. So was I, for a time. I distracted the border guards with my playing so that he and my brothers could kill them."

"For God's sake, why?"

"To bring weapons and ammunition over the border. If it means anything," Justine went on, "I didn't want to fight anymore. Not after I got pregnant. But this happened."

Carolyn made a frustrated sound. "For two cents I swear I'd let Akiro have his explosion. At least it'd wake people up."

"I wish it were only that." She told Carolyn about the conversation between Lysenko and Shuto.

Carolyn's eyes widened with fear. "My kids are in San Diego. Did I just say . . . ?"

"See? Nobody's safe. People on planes. Secretaries in a skyscraper. Babies in a Federal Building. All innocent. All targets. There are more killers every day. We try and stop them."

"The good guys against the bad."

"You'll never hear me actually say that."

"But you think it," Carolyn said. "Someone's got to be responsible; that's it, isn't it?"

Justine nodded. "Yes. That's it."

"Phillip says—"

"Carolyn, don't let Phillip do your thinking for you."

Justine shouldn't have said it. Phillip was a sacred cow. Carolyn got defensive. "You don't listen to your husband?"

"It's not that."

"Every woman on this ship is married except me. I just want what all of you have. What I *had*. There's nothing wrong with Phillip. He's a fine doctor, a good man."

"I'm sorry I said it, okay?"

"And he's not wrong. You're hitting your head against a brick wall."

Justine shrugged. "Sometimes the wall falls down."

"Answer me honestly. Can you really stop Shuto?"

"I don't know." Justine suddenly felt woozy. The weakness was coming back.

Carolyn saw it. "All right. Forget it. C'mon, you've got to eat."

Carolyn helped Justine to the galley and left. The distance between Carolyn and the other women was growing. Bette and Carla made Justine some food. Lady Em served it with royal manners. Justine had developed a real liking for them. In their stained, makeshift clothing and stringy hair, all three looked like prisoners of war, but they "carried on," as Lady Em put it, despite the heat and their worries about the men. Each had real character, was quick on the uptake, and tough.

"Shoot," Justine said.

"They're building the bomb on that platform on deck. It's supposed to float," Carla reported. "The *Korlov* will take it to the explosion point and detonate it by radio."

"But they need something or other that ended up in the ocean the other day," Bette said. "It's holding them up."

"Enriched hydrogen." She told them about the Magnus Field. "We bought time with the crane accident, but not much."

Carla was shocked. "The Field is on the edge of the Pacific plate. An explosion could push the whole region into instability."

"It's that serious?"

Bette confirmed it. "Volcanic activity on the ocean

floor doesn't usually reach the atmosphere. That many eruptions at once could create enough heat to change climate on a global scale. We can't let him do it."

"And we won't," Justine said firmly. "Not this team. Did you find a flashlight?"

"Swiped it during dinner," said Carla. "Binoculars, too. The red cellophane came from the fruit wrapping in the refrigerator."

"Perfect. Give me some time to compose. I'm a little out of practice with Morse."

She read her message a few times and made changes. Finally she was satisfied.

"Lady Em, get the lights. Carla, keep watch outside. Bette, start cooking something for show."

Lady Em doused the lights and Justine opened the porthole. The island was a dark patch sitting on a dark sea. The squall had passed and Mac had started a fire on the beach. She was grateful for the intelligence training he had been given before this mission. It had made planning communications a lot simpler in the infirmary that day. She wrapped the red cellophane over the hood of the flashlight to eliminate glare, and pointed it at the fire, her target. Morse code was never her specialty, but urgency lent her ability. She sent twice, at ten o'clock, and again five minutes later.

Her sending wasn't risky, but a blinking light on the island was too easily seen by anyone on the ship. She wasn't sure what he would do. It depended on conditions on the island. The flickering firelight partially illuminated the palm trees and nearby boulders. She checked her watch. Her time to receive. Where was his signal? She swept the beach. Darkness at one end, fire at the center, then darkness again. She couldn't spot Mac. She swept again. The fire. Palm trees. Boulders. Wait a minute. The light flickering on the boulders was too regular. Mac was shining his light on the rocks to send the code. To all but the most discerning eye, it blended in with the firelight.

She read his signal and could hardly believe it. The *Storm* raised after all these years, and he believed they could make her seaworthy. He acknowledged the delay she had caused, and told her he needed more time.

She acknowledged reception and closed the porthole, then wiped the tears from her eyes so the others didn't see.

I love you both, he sent. *Don't.*

She understood.

"We love you, too," she said softly.

Phillip was awake reading when Carolyn got back.

"Where have you been?" he asked petulantly, snapping the book shut.

"Justine needed my help. Oh, Phillip, it's horrible what Shuto plans to do."

She told him everything. He made her go over it again to make sure she hadn't left anything out. After she finished, he seemed satisfied.

"It's a terrible thing they're planning," he said. "But from what you've told me, this ship will be safe."

"I suppose so. But . . ."

"But nothing, my dear. I'm just thinking about the future. *Our* future. And protecting your children. Don't you like that?"

"You know I do, Phillip."

She felt absurdly grateful when she was with him. He had a way of making her feel he thought of everything. Things she should have thought of. Their safety, for example. And her family's.

"What will you do about my kids?"

"I'll figure it out."

"Can you?"

"I care more about them than Justine does, I can tell you."

Her love was overflowing.

"That makes me so happy."

"Good. Then come here."

"Phillip, I'm not really . . ." she began, but he pulled her to him and reached under her clothes.

He might be too weak to walk, but you wouldn't know it from the strength of his possession. It was always this way now. He awakened feelings in her she thought long dead. She had been too long without a man, and he was as talented sexually as she had fantasized. Insistent and masterful, he swept her into a place where she had no will but his, even now, when she really didn't want to so much. As the days passed he made her do more things, things that once would have shocked her. But she found herself liking them. He talked to her while he was inside her, telling her things, making her respond. It was hypnotic. Her head got fuzzy. The words stoked the fire in her brain. She was addicted. Beyond reason. He knew his power, and he liked it.

Afterwards, lying together, he said, "When this is over we'll be together, Carolyn."

He knew she was at her most vulnerable after she climaxed. Satiated and slow. He used his doctor's ways with her. His man's ways.

"I won't let them hurt you. So we have to make sure they think I'm still sick. Or they might put me on the island with the other men. Then I wouldn't be able to protect you or your kids. You understand that, don't you?"

"Yes, Phillip."

"I'm just not flashy like some others. The time isn't ready yet. We doctors know a thing or two."

She nestled closer. He was what she'd wanted for so long. Her misgivings were gone. She believed in him totally.

"Justine is the enemy. Don't let her fool you again," he instructed.

"If you only knew her . . ."

"I know her type. She'll use us and toss us away. We're expendable. You must see that."

Too many choices. All she wanted was to lie in his arms.

"Just do as I say," he said comfortingly. "And tell me everything she does. That way I can take care of her, too."

"All right, Phillip. I will."

He took her again, to make sure.

The night was calm, the fog swirled overhead. Hiroki was sure he'd find Shuto alone on deck. Shuto was staring out to sea, motionless as a statue, hard as stone.

"There was nothing you could do for Ito," Hiroki said. "It happened too fast. His pain was brief."

"Is that supposed to comfort me?"

Hiroki didn't take offense. "He was a brother to me, too."

Shuto's shoulders slumped. "I know. I'm sorry."

"I want you to reconsider what we're doing. We've already lost Ito. We'll lose Akiro when he finds out. The world will hunt down the rest of us. What do we gain if we lose our whole family?"

"We aren't a family," Shuto said angrily. "How did you feel bring paraded in front of everyone the other day?"

"His motive was good. It saved lives."

"But how did you feel?"

Hiroki hung his head. "Ashamed."

Shuto said triumphantly, "That's all we are to him. Examples. See through his mask, Hiroki."

"I'm a simple person. You and Akiro and the others are the only family I've ever had. I'll never forget how you came and found me and protected me the night the miners wanted to sterilize me."

"You killed three yourself. You were always stronger than you knew."

"But you took ten, my swift brother. You are our power, Shuto. Akiro is our heart. A body must not divide itself."

"Will you follow me or not?"

Hiroki could always read Shuto's energy. It was rising. He wondered if this man who had been a brother to him could kill him. "Ito is gone. The others are unhappy. Let Akiro have his light and be done with it."

Shuto's energy rose again. There was a faint buzz in the air.

"Will you follow me or not?"

Hiroki's big arms were useless here. He could not use them to strangle his own body. He listened to the night sounds.

He bowed. "I will, Shuto-san."

20

Sōfu gan

THE MEN EXTINGUISHED THE FIRE ON THE BEACH. Mac-Kenzie told them what he had learned.

"Shuto's mad," said Rietti flatly. "Bette and Carla must have told your wife what could happen if he ignites the Magnus Field. Devastation."

"That's what he wants," MacKenzie said. "The destructive part of him knows no bounds. I've felt it. If the whole world went up in flames, it wouldn't stop his pain."

"He just might, you know, send it up in flames," Rietti said. "There's no telling what damage would result. Tidal waves could be the least of it."

"Just a minute," Bernhardsen interjected angrily. "Don't fall for this stuff, Mac. Any of you."

"What do you mean?"

Bernhardsen looked at his partner accusingly.

"Tony's a worrier. Ask him if there's ever been an undersea volcano whose heat has even reached the atmosphere, much less caused the kind of destruction he's got you worried about."

"Well, no," said Rietti. "But that doesn't mean—"

"Igniting the Magnus Field is a fairy tale volcanologists use to spice up their courses. Sexy as hell. The world splitting open. But it can't happen."

"If you think a thousand volcanoes erupting at the same time won't affect the surface, Ivor, *you* believe in fairy tales." Rietti turned to the others. "The Field is in an area where the earth's crust is weakest. Like the soft spot in a baby's skull. Ask him how many scientists support the theory."

"About the same number as would have told you the earth was flat back when that was fashionable," said Bernhardsen. "Numbers don't mean anything in science. Truth does."

"So now you're the exclusive agent for truth?"

"We're not going to settle this here, so I want it stopped," MacKenzie cut in. "Our job is to make sure Shuto doesn't get a chance to test the theory. I don't care if you two get along, just cooperate."

Rietti apologized, and Bernhardsen mumbled something about "priorities," but the tension was thicker.

"Nikolai, Commodore, I haven't had a chance to tell you what happened on the other side of the island. You both should probably be sitting down for this."

"You found vodka, Peter?"

"Better. It's hard to believe, but we found the Commodore's old submarine and managed to get her afloat."

"Impossible," said the Commodore. "I saw the *Storm* go down myself."

"The current brought her back up. The hatches were secure and the valves held. There was enough air in her tanks to blow ballast. We winched her to the mining pier. She's waiting there now."

"What shape is she in?" Raskin asked excitedly.

"She's obviously old and rusted. We didn't have time to check her engines, not and get back here for Justine's signal. We'll go back at first light. I need you especially, Nikolai."

"This is great news," said Raskin.

"What do you say to our luck, Commodore?" prompted Rietti. "You're going to be reunited with your sub."

The Commodore's shock was profound. "I don't know what to say. You were actually inside her?"

"Only the control room."

The Commodore seemed to age before their eyes. "I'm sorry, but I cannot countenance this. There were bodies left on board. It's sacrilege to open her. The *Storm*'s a grave ship."

"I understand how you feel," MacKenzie said gently. "You lost brave comrades. But surely they, of all people, would understand."

"I suppose. It seems impossible. When she went down . . . But of course, the fight must continue. She's a warship, after all. I'll help any way I can."

"Thank you, Commodore."

Raskin wanted to cross the island immediately. He was full of energy. The notion of rebuilding the *Storm* seemed to be just the tonic he needed.

"Do you realize there won't be a single plastic piece on her," Raskin said. "No computers, no fiber optics."

"Calm down and get some sleep," MacKenzie advised Raskin. "It's a hike to get there."

"Peter, I'd walk across burning coals to see this ship."

"Remember you said it, pal. Commodore, you and I have first watch."

The squall's passing let the fog back in. Wisps hung over the beach as if the clouds were shedding. Mac and the Commodore sat by the fire. Commodore Rowe stared out to sea, solitary and unreadable.

"Penny for your thoughts, Commodore."

"You'd get a lot for your money, sir. My wife. All that's happened on this trip. Life's ironies."

"You're worried about Lady Emily?"

The Commodore stroked his mustache pensively. "People think she's so strong. It's a facade, you know. She's always been a fragile girl. She leans on me heavily."

"Justine will help her."

"I'm sure that will be a comfort. What is it like being married to one of the strong ones? Different, I imagine."

MacKenzie thrust his cap back. "Not so much. We still have to work at it, like any other couple. The unusual thing for me is how much respect we have for each other. I know she can handle so many things so well, it lets me relax. But she has the same drives and vulnerabilities as any other woman."

And because of that, MacKenzie thought, I know what she must be feeling. The baby was a constant raging undercurrent. Such a small thing compared to the events taking place, yet he could never escape it for long. He was relieved to see her signal. It meant she was still functioning, still clinging to hope. *I prayed for an accident,* she had said. She could have one so easily now. He ached to hold her. Please, he prayed, give it time.

"Still, it's unusual," said the Commodore.

"I love Justine and I admire her skills. I know the price she paid for them. That's probably her greatest liability. She was never sheltered, never protected, and her pain runs deep."

"So you have to be even stronger?"

"Steadier. Her fixed point. It's my responsibility to her."

"You seem able to bear it."

MacKenzie smiled. "Commodore, a day doesn't go by I don't think I'm the lucky one."

"Perhaps if Emily had been strong like that . . ."

MacKenzie heard regret in his voice. "Did something happen?"

"Forgive me. Just the ramblings of an old man. This bloody island does it to me. Brings back too many memories."

"Of that night?"

"Most of all."

"What was it like?" MacKenzie asked. "One submariner to another. I've fought my share of battles."

"I know you have, of course."

The Commodore stared at the dying embers for a while. When he spoke, it seemed to come from a long way away.

"We were on patrol with two T-type subs, *Tarquin* and *Tern*. I was very young to command, only twenty-eight, but this was wartime and we'd lost so many senior captains, I was promoted and given a ship of my own. It was my first cruise as CO. At the time, it wasn't a job with a long life expectancy.

"The *Storm* had a first lieutenant named David Bolliver. Bolliver seemed a good enough man, but I felt he resented me because I was so much younger. It was a different era back then. Age seemed to mean so much. In time I learned my assessment was accurate.

He was a veteran, but he had been passed over for command twice already. This was his last chance to make good. And I was standing in his way.

"It was a difficult period. Everybody desperately hoped the tide of the war was turning, but it was still a guess as to the outcome. Rationing and bombs had sapped the strength of those at home, though certainly not their resolve. There were some developments to take heart over. The 'Black Gap' in the Atlantic where German U-boats had earlier roamed out of reach of our planes was being hit by the long-range Liberator bombers. And we were getting better at training escort groups in sub hunting. In the Pacific, however, the Japanese were still inflicting heavy losses."

The more he spoke, the stronger he became. The man of twenty-eight emerged from the mists of time.

"The *Storm* had some mechanical problems. A week out, we dived on an asdic contact and the planes jammed, causing us to broach. Luckily, the contact was a ghost. Then number two diesel refused to run smoothly. Two weeks into the cruise I thought we had all the bugs out. We had sighted a few ships, but nothing big enough to risk betraying our position. Then we saw smoke on the horizon. We swung the ship around and began tracking. I had a crack navigator named Peterson, and after about an hour, *Storm* was in a favorable position, dead ahead of the enemy. The masts of two ships were just coming over the horizon. We dived and commenced a submerged approach.

"The freighters were making about eight knots on a course which puzzled me because it led to no port. A mile from the lead ship we came up to periscope depth and fired two torpedoes. Twenty seconds later we fired another two at the second freighter. Suddenly I saw a destroyer coming on fast. I had missed him in the setting sun. I submerged to a hundred feet. The destroyer had our range and commenced depth-charging. It was hellish. Just when I thought he was past, he turned towards us again. Our screws were making lots of noise. He obviously had a good contact. I tried a desperate move. I turned towards him. Zero angle on bow. Bolliver thought I was crazy. The weather was rising. It was difficult to see through the periscope. I fired two torpedoes down his throat. A minute later there was an explosion. No good. The torpedoes had detonated prematurely. I commenced evasion tactics, but we were taking a beating. Pipe fittings burst. We were too heavy, and I suspected a leak in the trim tanks. It would have been over for us if not for the *Tarquin*. We heard a great explosion, and the depth charging stopped. When we got our periscope up, the destroyer was burning. *Tarquin* had put two torpedoes amidships. It was too smoky and turbulent to see if we had gotten the freighters. The light was fading fast. With visibility so poor, I surfaced the ship and took Bolliver and a lookout to the bridge."

MacKenzie was fascinated. War from a bygone day. Attacks on the surface, depth charges, all etched in minute detail in the old warrior's memory. He reported it like he was watching it happen.

"What did you find out about their destination?"

"As I said, it surprised me because they weren't heading for any port. Then I saw why. We had fired on a splinter of a much larger convoy heading for a major engagement against our fleet. There were heavy cruisers, battleships, even a carrier. I'd never seen anything like it. All at once we were in the thick of it. Our attack had betrayed our presence and they were coming at us with everything they had. There hadn't been any intelligence on a formation of this type. Wherever they were heading, it was our duty to report it and try to destroy as many ships as possible to weaken the force. We radioed our position and commenced our attack. Given the size of the convoy, I'm sure every man on board *Storm, Tarquin,* and *Tern* knew it was a suicide run. There were just too many.

"We attacked, and attacked, and attacked again. A destroyer sank *Tarquin* making a run on the carrier. *Tern* torpedoed a tanker, but a cruiser rammed her on the surface. The oil fire from the burning ship got her. Smoky red fires lit up the night sky. I dived the ship when the destroyers turned on us, and took evasive action."

The Commodore was sweating even though the air was cool.

"Depth charge triggers made a click that was audible before they exploded. All we could hear were click-bangs for minutes on end. Some screamed from the pressure. Torpedoes broke free and crushed two of the men. We were all knocked about. The explosions pushed the *Storm* sideways and deeper. Our lights went out. Then Bolliver . . ." He stopped abruptly.

"Yes?"

The man who looked back at MacKenzie was old once again.

"Nothing, Admiral. The rest is a matter of fleet record. I was trying to get a better position on a tanker when we were hit in the sail. I managed to bring the *Storm* in here and get off an SOS."

"Remarkable, Commodore. Truly."

"Our action delayed the Japanese. Allied planes were brought to bear. We scored a major victory. I was given credit for five kills. After we were rescued I had to spend some time in the hospital in London, along with others. Our injuries were bad, and they had worsened on the island, you know. Because of them my days of command were over. I was sent on tour to lift the public morale. Soon after, I met Emily and married her."

"What happened to Lieutenant Bolliver?"

"Why do you ask?"

"He's an interesting part of the story."

"I don't know," said the Commodore.

"Did he make it off the island?"

"Yes, but I never saw him again after our return."

MacKenzie thought about a war fifty years ago, so different from his own combat experiences. "I've read a lot of books about your war, Commodore. Thank you for helping me to understand it for the first time."

"Kind of you to say, Admiral."

"Let's get some rest."

"Capital."

They woke the second watch and turned in. MacKenzie lay on the sand, thinking. One chance to go after the *Korlov,* that's what they had. Could they do it?

They could damn well try.

On the other side of the island, the *Storm* waited.

21

NSA Headquarters
Fort Meade, Maryland

MUCH LATER, DEREK BOOKBINDER WAS TO REMARK IT was a cup of coffee and a broken water heater that alerted the National Security Agency and triggered the subsequent events.

Bookbinder was an immaculate man who loved order, logic, and his computers. Computers enabled Bookbinder and the other senior NSA analysts and strategists to collect information on a scale unknown in human history. At the touch of a button Bookbinder could call up just about any database he might need in his constant search for that which military and political leaders required most. Intelligence.

In the vast complex that housed the NSA, the government organization that monitored the world's communications, Bookbinder protected his department's computers with three stringent rules. Keep your machine clean; cover it at night; and never, ever, put your coffee or Coke next to your keyboard. They were simple rules, but over the years he had avoided many of the short circuits and system crashes that had plagued those less punctilious.

Till Friday.

Bookbinder was having a bad morning. He arrived at work with a blinding headache. His allergies began with the blooming of the cherry blossoms everyone else thought so beautiful, but which for Bookbinder signaled a season in purgatory. His nose felt like someone had packed it with a plunger. His sinuses were threatening to explode. He had taken a Comtrex, and when that didn't work, two of his wife, Jane's, Sudafed. He had enough antihistamines in his system to jeopardize a fleet of heavy-equipment operators, but his headache was getting worse. Adding to it, Jane called to tell him their aging hot water heater had defied his latest quick fix with duct tape and was gushing water all over the basement. Bookbinder was a mechanical incompetent. Any attempt to fix things around his house involved duct tape. He was the duct tape world champion. He had been known to try to fix everything from a leaky roof to the family cat with duct tape. The cat hadn't spoken to him since.

"What do I do, Derek?" Jane moaned over the phone. "It's very wet down here."

"Where's the tape?" His head was splitting. He had been at work twenty minutes already and hadn't signed off on the printout from *Korlov*'s satellite relays, or anything else for that matter. He hadn't actually even sat down yet. He was standing in front of his desk juggling coffee and cheese Danish from the truck in the parking lot, along with the printouts he picked up when he came in.

"I already tried," said Jane plaintively. "It won't stick."

"Call Sears. Maybe we're covered."

"What do I tell them?"

"The water heater's broken. Damn it, they know what they are."

"They never do," she said flatly. "They ask what size and what color and what's wrong. How do I know? I won't be questioned by those guys, Derek. They're Gestapo. When did you buy it? From what store? Who was the salesman? I don't need that stress. Dr. Marshall said it wasn't good for me."

Bookbinder knew Dr. Marshall. He got lots of bills from the thrice-divorced ex-pro bowler-turned-therapist who thought everything could be cured by breathing right. And a mean curve.

"It's a white water heater, Jane, you can see that. The installation date is on the little metal plate on the side."

"It's covered with cruddy blue stuff. I can't read it."

Derek's head threatened to burst. "Wait a minute," he said wearily. That's when he made the mistake. He put the coffee and Danish down on his desk and stabbed keys one-handed. The exact installation date of the water heater, along with every other appliance in his house, was neatly filed in the HOME section of his computer. It used about a trillionth of the capacity of the giant mainframe.

"Derek?"

"I've almost got it, Jane." Maybe the air conditioning would dislodge the knife in his forehead.

"By the way, you took my Sudafed? From on the bed stand?"

"Two."

"Actually, you took one. The other was my hormone pill."

As sneezes go, it was a force ten. The phone and the printout went flying and coffee spilled all over his papers and keyboard. The Danish made a nice addition. Bookbinder stared in horror at the mess.

"Don't get hysterical," he cautioned.

"I'm not hysterical," said Jane.

"I meant me. I have to go now, Jane."

"What about the water heater?"

He stifled murderous thoughts. "I'll make the call."

"Have a good day, hon."

"I sure will," said Bookbinder, staring at the sodden mess on his desk.

He got some more antihistamines from the NSA pharmacy downstairs, checked himself in the mirror to make sure his facial hair wasn't falling out, and spoke in a deeper voice than usual all morning. By eleven, he had most of the mess cleaned up. The *Korlov* printout looked fine. The voyage was going as planned. An overflight had tried to make visual contact, but the ship was fogbound. It didn't matter. The hourly codes had been verified by the night watch, the log had been signed. He expected that. Any deviation would have sounded the alarm. Then lots of F-15s would have gone roaring off into the night. Since all was as it should be, he checked NO on the SAT SUR REQ line on the summary sheet, meaning NO SATELLITE SURVEILLANCE REQUIRED, and filed it along with the printout. The papers were a little damp, but they would dry by the time the dispatch boys came. He called his secretary to have them picked up, and was soon engrossed in the rest of his morning's work.

The problem was, Bookbinder hadn't actually checked NO on the SAT SUR REQ line on the damp summary sheet. A side effect of the coffee spill was to make the print on the reverse side of the paper bleed through. The NO Bookbinder had checked in front of SAT SUR REQ was actually the word ON, from a sentence containing the words ON LINE, on back, which disappeared when dry. The spill had also smeared enough ink onto the supervisor's confirmation line for a fair imitation of a hasty initialing. When the report was picked up, the receiving officer saw that the SAT SUR REQ line had been checked by Bookbinder, and countersigned, albeit smudgingly, by his supervisor, so he passed it on to the Reconnaissance Office. There, to accommodate the senior analyst's request, the angle on one of the NSA's Keyhole satellites was ordered changed, and the image series scheduled. It would be ready when Bookbinder came in the next morning, unaware of what he had unwittingly done.

It cost approximately six hundred thousand dollars to change the angle of an orbiting KH-11 satellite. Derek Bookbinder had just spent his salary for the next twelve years on an unauthorized reconfiguration.

The poet Schilling once said that what to us seems merest accident springs from the deepest source of destiny.

Bookbinder had never read Schilling, but very shortly he was going to appreciate the sentiment.

PART THREE

Storm Rising

22

Sōfu gan

THE MEN STARTED ACROSS THE ISLAND AT FIRST LIGHT. The constant rain made everything slippery and dank. Steam wafted off broad green leaves. They used the mining camp's machetes to cut a trail. It was hot, laborious work which took a lot out of them, especially the Commodore, but he was anxious to see the *Storm*, and however many times Mac suggested a rest, he told them to push on.

The rain sizzled on the lava field. The open pit Bernhardsen had almost tumbled into still bubbled with orange magma. They were especially careful during the crossing. Rietti took a cautious lead. MacKenzie and Raskin helped the Commodore. It went without incident, and after the last leg through the rain forest, they reached the mining camp. Raskin was amazed at the bounty. His excitement reached a peak when he saw the array of machines and tools they had to refit the *Storm*. He wanted to spend time cataloging, but everyone was too anxious to get to the pier.

The sight of the *Storm* struck the Commodore forcibly.

"Till this moment, I didn't fully believe it. To see the *Storm* with my own eyes . . ."

His voice trailed off. The water on his cheeks wasn't from the rain. He shook his head as if subconsciously negating all the time and travels between then and now.

"Her valves held. And her hull. We built them strong in those days, Admiral."

"She's testament to that."

"May I have some time in her alone?"

"Of course."

Commodore Rowe's arms and legs were thinner than fifty years ago, his hair whiter, his walk more hesitant, but he seemed to draw strength from the *Storm,* a synergy of two old warriors. He climbed to the bridge and his jaw trembled with emotion till he disappeared down the hatch. Mac could visualize him walking slowly through the corridors. His feet had last been on those decks fifty years before. The men were his long-dead comrades. What would he say to them? What would touch him? And would the *Storm* somehow know her captain had returned after all these years?

Fifteen minutes later he reappeared on the bridge, quiet and somber.

"Permission to come on board, sir."

"Come along, Admiral. Gentlemen. The *Storm* extends her welcome."

"Put on your miner's lights," MacKenzie told the others in the control room. "We'll go forward and work our way back aft. Commodore, you lead."

"Very well."

The hatchways were arched, and every seam was studded with rivets. It was incredibly tight and cramped. Their lights stabbed through the darkness, beams converging when they all looked at the same thing. Dusty human debris was everywhere. Popular novels of the day. Bibles. Backgammon games. Chessmen. Poker dice. Playing cards and cribbage boards. The seamen's mess was a shambles. The mess table was broken. Cups and dishes were strewn about the floor. Torpedoes were stored here, and two had broken free from their moorings. Underneath was the remains of two men. Their skin and clothing were mummified and fused, just like the man in the control room.

"Seamen Blake and Rogers," said the Commodore soberly, spreading a blanket over them. "We stored torpedoes here to save space. The main compressed-air reservoir is below us, with a special tank for firing the torpedoes in the fore ends just ahead, what we call the torpedo room today. An air slug pushed them out the tube. A projecting trigger started the engine."

"Poor fellows didn't have much room in here, did they?" observed Rietti.

"Not until all the torpedoes were fired."

They headed aft through the officers' wardroom, the petty officers' mess, and the engine room artificers' mess. More tables and chairs overturned. Drawers tumbled about. Brass models of ships, wood carvings, even petit point to while away endless hours without television or radio. There were more bodies, too, one an officer's.

"Lieutenant Richards. My engineering officer. A fine man." The Commodore covered the body.

"Any chance we could make the radio work?" Raskin asked as they passed back through the control room to the W/T office.

"It failed after we sent the SOS. It was an old tube set, and we didn't carry many spare parts."

"Too bad," said Rietti. "What's this?"

"My cabin. Please, don't go in."

"Why not?"

"No reason other than I'd like to go through it alone first. My writings would be, I'm sure, quite embarrassing to me now."

"I certainly wouldn't want anyone reading my poetry from those days," chortled Raskin.

"Your prerogative, Commodore," MacKenzie agreed.

The ancient Admiralty-pattern eight-cylinder diesel engines in the engineering space were dusty and silent. They were ponderous machines, all brass and steel, capable of making 950 horsepower at full power. There were bodies alongside.

"Our chief engine room artificer supervised five ERAs, a stoker petty officer, and six leading stokers," Commodore Rowe said. "They were a fine crew. That night they kept the engines running when few could have, blasted about as they were. We were exhausting the batteries regularly."

"I'm confused. Which drove the sub, engines or batteries?" asked Bernhardsen.

"It depended on conditions. The diesel engines and electric motors were both linked to the shaft by clutches. Diesels used up too much air for use underwater. They drove us on the surface, and charged the batteries. Underwater, we used the batteries to power the electric motors. Admiral, I should probably be the one to have a go at the batteries. They're a little tricky."

"Right." MacKenzie gave out assignments and sent them to work.

Hot hours later, MacKenzie and Raskin were near heat stroke, sweating profusely. Even opening the aft hatch didn't provide much relief. They had stripped the twin diesels using the *Storm*'s own tools. Parts lay scattered about the open grid catwalk between them. MacKenzie was struggling with a piston. Raskin opened the lubricating oil tank. The diesel oil on the bottom was a thick, muddy gum.

"I like this work," Raskin said. "My father was a fisherman. I first earned his respect when I wasn't squeamish about baiting hooks. When his old motor was always breaking down, I was the one to fix it. Even on my own boat I wanted to be with the engine room crew seeing to things. I liked to get my hands dirty." He scooped out some brackish muck. "Then I became a captain and had no time for it."

MacKenzie wrenched the piston out. "How do things look?"

"Things are what they are, but I will tell you something, Peter. I am less worried about these engines than about you. You're good at hiding the strain from the others, but not from me."

MacKenzie looked at his wrench as if it would tell him something. It didn't.

"Strain? Nah. Just a pregnant wife and innocent passengers held hostage by terrorists, and eight days left to stop them from killing millions, with a broken-down boat that hasn't seen action in fifty years."

Raskin quickly put a finger to his lips. "Shhh. She'll hear you. Do not anger her."

"Let's talk about something else."

"No. I ask what I want to know."

MacKenzie wiped his hands on a cloth. "I'm worried Justine will abort the baby."

"What chance of that is there here?"

MacKenzie reached into his pocket and showed Raskin the pills Justine had given him.

"RU-486," Raskin read on the smooth coating. "Wait, I know these. They are the French abortion pills. We smuggled them into the Soviet Union for years. But in America . . . Ah, I see. It's a French ship."

"There must be a supply in the infirmary. Justine wanted me to know. I've been worried about her ever since."

"It is dangerous to take them without a proper hospital."

"That's not what's stopping her," MacKenzie said. "She's needed. She can't afford to take herself out of action."

"For the sake of argument, Peter, would it be so wrong? This thing hangs over both your heads. Perhaps it is not the right time. You can have more babies."

"Maybe if I were certain, Nikolai. But we can't be. Not yet. Whatever happened to faith?"

"It's in short supply these days," said Raskin.

"What about you? You're okay?"

Raskin gestured around him. "Better, now that I'm working. Everyone here has a wife. Maybe the *Storm* was waiting all these years to be mine."

It echoed the thought MacKenzie had the first day, in the control room. Was it what the *Storm* had come back for, to give Raskin a purpose and fill the void in his life?

"She certainly needs you."

"I can almost feel that. Is it silly?"

"If anybody can get her in shape, you can."

Raskin closed the tank. "Some more things, I must check, and then we will take stock, yes?"

MacKenzie went back to work. The rings flaked off at his touch. He started working on the next cylinder. Half an hour later Raskin returned, and he could see the Russian was unhappy.

"What's wrong?"

"I will tell you," said Raskin. "First, I do not believe she is capable of diving again. I examined the valves and ballast tanks. That last charge blew too many couplings."

"Not even once?"

"It is too risky," Raskin said firmly.

"So we attack on the surface."

"All right, so far. The steering is workable. The helm will answer."

"What's in the tanks?"

Raskin fingered the muck distastefully. "The fuel is too old to be usable. We'll have to flush it out and use what was left in the mining camp. The Commodore told me the batteries are a waste. There isn't enough lead to make a decent pencil."

"So we can't use the electric motors."

"Another reason to stay on the surface." Raskin patted a diesel. "The engines. Parts are corroded. Gears are frozen. But I've seen many in worse shape, and this is a very simple drive chain. We might scavenge both of them to fix one, make up what we need in the mining camp."

"One engine can drive us."

"That's true enough, but I must add to our troubles. I wish I had better news. Both shafts are bent. Even if we can run an engine, we can't turn the propeller."

"Can't we straighten it?"

"I can't see how. First we'd have to get the propeller off. We don't have diving equipment, or heavy machinery, or a dry dock. Past all that, we'd need an industrial forge to produce enough heat to bend steel. The mine doesn't have one. The nearest is probably in Tokyo."

MacKenzie threw down the cloth. "That's it, then."

Raskin didn't want to disappoint his friend or the *Storm*. "Let me think. I don't want to say that yet."

"Good try, Nikolai, but facts are facts. It was crazy to think we could pull it off. I'm going to call the others. No use in going further."

Rietti, Bernhardsen, and the Commodore were eating lunch on the pier. The rain had stopped, and what passed for sunlight on the island filtered through the mist.

"The forward tank has no leaks," Rietti reported. "We can fill it and the secondary tank from the compressor in the camp. It should be enough to get the torpedoes launched."

"There aren't enough electronics left in the control room, though," said Bernhardsen. "We'll have to jury-rig a circuit."

"You did good work," MacKenzie said, "I'm sorry to tell you we'll have to forget it. There's no way to repair the boat."

MacKenzie saw it on their faces. For a moment it seemed things were turning their way. It was a crushing blow.

"I feel like a fool ever hoping," said Bernhardsen bitterly.

"I'm sorry," said the Commodore. "But after this much time, I didn't hold out much hope. She should never have been violated. Admiral, I'll expect to bury my men now."

"What exactly is the problem?" asked Rietti.

"We can salvage one engine," Raskin said. "But the shaft is too badly bent to turn properly. Probably from the sub resting on the bottom for so long."

"So straighten it."

"Even if we could remove it, a doubtful proposition, we'd need a high-temperature forge. There's nothing in the mining camp like that."

"But we could move her with a straight shaft?" Rietti pressed.

Raskin was irritated. "What's the use of talking about it?"

"Nikolai, don't you see? We have all the heat we need. Look!"

Raskin followed his finger. "My God, Peter . . . ?"

MacKenzie was startled. The volcano!

"Is it feasible, Tony?"

"Why not?"

"No," said the Commodore flatly. "It's enormously precise work. If the shaft's not perfectly straight, the vibrations will tear the hull apart."

"Maybe not for a short distance," Raskin mused, caught up in the idea. "We don't have enough fuel in camp to run even the one diesel for more than a few hours. She might hold for that long. We could rig some protective gear to do the work, and there are metal working tools. I'm willing to try."

"It's a long shot," said MacKenzie.

Rietti was adamant. "We can't let Shuto blow the Magnus Field."

"Is Tony speaking for you, too, Ivor?"

"Why not? You said it yourself, Mac, didn't you? The try's the thing."

"Nikolai?"

"We must try."

"Commodore?"

"I feel it will be fruitless, but yes, all right. I just don't hold out any hope. Sorry, but there it is."

"We'll have to work round the clock. Forget about sleep."

"The computers will help, Mac," said Rietti eagerly.

"Let's get started then," said MacKenzie.

The sun was setting by the time they took a break. He knew only one thing, he had to stop them. He felt for the awl in his pocket. None of them suspected he had it. It pricked his finger. Slippery blood leaked down his hand. Who did he need to kill to stop this madness?

After lunch there had been a lot of technical discussion before they went to bury the Storm's dead. They wrapped the bodies in canvas from the ship's stores. They couldn't bury them at sea, so they carried the corpses up the beach. They were light and crisp, like dried fish. MacKenzie conducted the service. He talked about heroism and sacrifice. He wanted to spit. None of them knew the meaning of the words.

Heroics weren't so brazen. Silence was the greatest sacrifice of all.

Niigata Yakayama towered overhead, blowing smoke and fire, mocking him, mocking him. He felt the needle in his pocket, still oily with his blood. If he couldn't stop them any other way, the time was near he would be using it.

23

Tuscany

KOBIASHI FELT THE STRAIN OF THE VOYAGE DEEPLY.
Every piece of foul weather, every hour of concentration in dense fog, it all wore on him. The crew was
seasick half the time, exhausted the rest. He consoled
himself with the thought that there were just a few
days more till they rendezvoused with the pickup ship
and scuttled the *Tuscany*.

Usually night was his friend, but this night was too
clear. He was worried.

"Any luck?"

"Calm seas, good weather," came his navigator's
response again. "I'm sorry, Captain."

Any second Kobiashi expected to see a jet plane
cross his bow, or a nuclear blast ignite the horizon. He
wondered what was happening on the *Korlov*. He
doubted he would ever see Akiro, Shuto, or any of the
others again. The event was too big. No one would
escape it. They had followed the old man into a
dream, one from which there was no waking.

"Sasaki?"

"My screens are clear, Captain."

"Stay alert."

Hours passed. Kobiashi had stretched his skills to the limit getting them this far, but they were encountering vessels more frequently now as the lanes to Tokyo narrowed. He wondered if they would make it to the rendezvous ship. If they did, he would be free, his debt to Akiro repaid. Then he could begin living his life. All the things he had put aside knowing someday he would have to make this voyage, would be possible. In a few days. If they made it.

"Sasaki?"

"Clear, Captain."

It was getting light, Kobiashi saw.

"Fog ahead," announced Noburu. "A least ten miles thick."

"Lay in a course," ordered Kobiashi, allowing himself the smallest feeling of hope.

24

Sōfu gan

AN OLD STORY ABOUT TESTING OFFICER CANDIDATES FOR creativity has it they were given tools mismatched for the job, like a screwdriver and a sealed bottle, to see if they could adapt to new circumstances. Every part of the operation to restore the *Storm* was like that, MacKenzie decided, rubbing his red-rimmed eyes and regarding the result of their efforts skeptically. Raskin, Rietti, and Bernhardsen were perched on respective ore carts a hundred feet from the end of the pier, all three poised to make a roller-coaster run down the tracks and go flying into the sea just past *Storm*'s bow.

The Commodore was ready to pull the chocks from behind the wheels. "For the record, I can't condone suicide," he said dryly.

"If this works, anything is possible."

"If it doesn't, Peter, you'd better get out of the way fast," warned Raskin.

They'd spent hours moving the mining camp's generator and compressor to the pier, stringing up work lights and the *Storm*'s battle lanterns, and repairing track. MacKenzie and Rietti made the trip back to the other side of the island. Mac apprised Justine of their progress. She in turn told him that the shipment of enriched hydrogen would be arriving the following night, putting Lysenko back on schedule in spite of her sabotage. Eight days left. She would do what she could to delay Lysenko. MacKenzie reluctantly acknowledged that. It meant more danger, more risk to her and the baby. He had to wonder how many times could she do it and not miscarry. Or was that what she hoped for? She signed off: We love you. Plural. She hadn't taken the pills yet.

Frustrated, he fought the impulse to swim to her. At the moment they needed each other most, the link between them was most tenuous. They were a series of flashes in the night, ethereal, noncorporeal. Emotions crossed space bodies could not. Another time of being apart, of their marriage transformed into voices on a phone line, words in a letter, pictures on a desk. Could they stand it again?

We love you. There was still hope.

The *Storm* had to be ready.

He was glad to have company on the trek back across the island. It was frightening at night. Animals screamed across the rain forest. Scamperings in the darkness. In sharp contrast, the lava field sparkled with light. Orange magma glittered through breaks in the rocks, red and yellow gas fires twisted in the air. MacKenzie had never seen anything to compare with it. It looked like hell with Christmas lights.

Back in the forest, MacKenzie could have sworn a

pair of red, beady eyes was tracking them. He saw them at the edge of his vision, but every time he turned to look, they were gone.

"Do you see anything, Tony?"

"Something. Hard to tell, though. Could just be the afterglow."

"Could be." But MacKenzie was relieved to get back to the mining camp. They grabbed an hour's sleep, a quick breakfast, and rejoined the others.

"Promise me I won't drown," said Bernhardsen from the second mining cart.

MacKenzie shook his head. "I'd be lying."

"Just get the hell out of my way before I come in," shouted Rietti in the third and last cart.

Raskin had decreed the number two diesel stood the best chance of being repaired, so it was that shaft and propeller they planned to straighten. In order to remove them, they had to raise the *Storm*'s stern out of the water so the boat wouldn't flood. That was a simple task in dry dock. Here, the submarine's weight made it almost impossible. They used their ingenuity, which was considerable. Bernhardsen replaced the *Storm*'s old ballast pumps with new ones from the mine, and pumped in water to give the bow a pronounced down angle. Shifting trim wasn't enough to bring the stern above water, however, so Raskin had gone into high gear. MacKenzie liked the others seeing his friend's tenacity. Raskin's professed indolence was only a front he'd had to cultivate under his former Soviet masters. First the Russian looped a wire sling under the stern and secured it with a line to the crane. The crane had the height, but not enough power to lift the submarine.

Raskin was sitting on the rest of his idea. The ore

carts were filled with rocks, covered with tarps from the camp. Cable ran from each cart to the capstan on the bow of the *Storm,* and they had removed the heavy brace blocking the end of the tracks. Rietti used much of his computer's remaining battery power to figure the necessary weight. Bernhardsen's had stopped working altogether. The theory was simple. The carts would roll down the tracks, gain sufficient momentum to fly off the end of the pier to the desired spot, and sink to the bottom of the channel, pulling the *Storm*'s bow down with it. Fine. In theory. Except the ore carts needed human hands to steer them. Staring down the tracks that terminated so abruptly above the water, Raskin wasn't sure if he'd invented a brilliant solution to their problem, or the world's most dangerous carnival ride.

"Ready, Commodore," Raskin yelled.

"I'll remember you fondly, Captain."

"Now!"

The Commodore pulled the chocks free. The ore car picked up speed. Its wild bumping almost threw Raskin off. He held on like a bull rider at a rodeo, bucking all the way. He yelled at the top of his lungs as he hit the incline at the end of the tracks and flew out over the water. Outlined against the tree canopy, he and the ore cart separated like the stages of a ballistic missile and hit the water about twenty feet apart. The cart made a thirty-foot-high splash, Raskin's only somewhat smaller. MacKenzie was poised to go in after him, but he needn't have worried. The big Russian burst up through the surface with a huge grin and a raucous yell that would have done a Texan proud.

"I want to do it again!"

MacKenzie smiled wryly. "Obviously a childhood deprived of amusement parks."

Raskin pulled himself onto the pier. "An exhilarating experience. Did it work?"

"See for yourself."

Indeed, the cable was taut and the bow had a steeper angle. The stern was nearer the surface. Rietti's calculations had been right.

Bernhardsen yelled he was ready, and the Commodore yanked out the chocks.

If Raskin was a bull rider, Bernhardsen was a race-car driver. He never even reached for the hand brake to slow the car speeding down the tracks. His eyes were riveted dead ahead. He hit the incline and was launched into the air. His dive was perfectly timed and he sliced the water cleanly. The cart dragged the bow deeper. Bernhardsen swam back to the pier and climbed out as nonchalantly as if he did such gymnastics every day.

"It's depressing how some people can make things look so easy," Raskin confided to MacKenzie.

"You had style."

Rietti made the last run. Whether it was just his usual marked contrast to Bernhardsen or something else, he had trouble from the beginning. His cart swung wildly from side to side and almost tipped over. It hit the incline wrong and the tarp snapped off. Rietti flew out over the water in a shower of rocks, and his cry of pain was clearly audible.

The limp way Rietti fell had MacKenzie diving off the pier even as he disappeared below the surface. Blood leaked from his head like red smoke. Mac followed him down. Rietti was already very deep. The water was clear as glass down to the bottom. Mac could see the three ore carts tethered to the *Storm*. His lungs were beginning to hurt. He managed to get a hand on the back of Rietti's shirt. He was almost out of air. He strained to get back up. The weight on his chest was forcing his mouth open. Suddenly he felt hands lifting, pulling. Raskin and Bernhardsen had found them. Gratefully he let them take over.

Bernhardsen pulled him to the surface. Raskin was already making for the pier with Rietti. Displaying the great strength he preferred to hide, Raskin dragged Rietti onto the pier and started artificial respiration. The Commodore pressed a cloth to Rietti's head to stop the bleeding. Suddenly Rietti coughed and threw up water. His chest heaved and his eyes flickered open. He wiped his face and managed a weak grin.

"I want my money back."

Raskin roared. Bernhardsen muttered something about Italian drivers, but even he seemed relieved.

"Did we make it?" Rietti asked.

No one had actually looked at the *Storm* till that moment. Her tapered stern was high in the air, exposing her twin shafts and propellers underneath the curved propeller guard, and the rudder and hydroplane. The holes and rivets along her deck made her look a creature poised to dive to the bottom.

"Well, I'll be damned," said Raskin proudly. "All we need is some spirits to toast the victory."

The Commodore looked to MacKenzie. "Admiral?"

"Yes, it does seem like a good time."

The Commodore handed Raskin a dusty bottle. "I found the key to the wardroom cabinet this morning.

Compliments of the officers of the *Storm,* aged fifty years."

"Rum!" said Raskin delightedly.

The Commodore poured some for each. "A mug was the highlight of the submariner's day. Up spirits, gentlemen." He gave the traditional toast, "Stand fast the Holy Ghost."

"And the engines," added Raskin, drinking deeply. "The British have a civilized navy, sir."

"The *Storm*'s a sight sitting here with her tail in the air like that," said Rietti.

"Hardly proper," agreed the Commodore.

"She knows it's for love," Raskin assured them.

The rest of the afternoon was spent securing the cables and inspecting the propeller and shaft. They were sweltering. The humidity climbed as the air grew hotter. MacKenzie finally decreed a break.

"Everybody to the bunkhouse for some rest and a meal. We'll go back to work when it cools off. Tony, get a proper bandage on that head wound."

"Right."

They trudged off. MacKenzie looked around for Raskin. He was kneeling by the tracks on the pier.

"Peter, come here, please."

"Problem?"

"I don't know yet."

Raskin handed MacKenzie a metal pin about four inches long.

"I found this between the planks on the pier. It must have caught on the wood. Do you know what it is?"

"A linchpin."

"It's from one of the carts. It holds the wheel on the axle. I wondered why Rietti's cart wobbled so badly, so I took a look at the tracks. I found it on the pier. Just luck. It should have fallen through."

MacKenzie turned the pin over in his hands. "What are you driving at?"

"Peter, see that flange? A pin like this doesn't come loose on its own. It didn't break off, either. It's still in one piece."

"You're saying someone rigged it to come off."

"There is no other explanation."

"Rietti was almost killed, and if the cart had hit the hull and pierced it, we would have lost the *Storm*, too," MacKenzie said grimly.

"I fear we may have a saboteur among us."

"But why would anyone?"

"I don't know. If the pin hadn't caught on the wood, we wouldn't even have suspected."

MacKenzie grew thoughtful. "Any candidates?"

"The list isn't long. Bernhardsen. Rietti, too, covering intention with accident. And the Commodore."

"What link could any of them have to Akiro?"

"I don't know."

"We'll have to be careful," MacKenzie said.

"And watch our backs."

"Make sure you secure the engine room when you're not there, Nikolai."

"I'll stay now. You go back to camp."

MacKenzie put the pin in his pocket. "This is going to make things a lot harder."

"By the way, did you get a look at the propeller?"

MacKenzie nodded. "Frozen solid. Not a chance of getting it off any conventional way I know."

"How are we going to?"

"Maybe you don't want me to tell you. You know how much you hate my plans."

"I am not a young man, Peter. My liver is bad. My hands shake."

"That's a real liability working with explosives, Nikolai. You need to relax."

Raskin turned pale. "I'd prefer to be shot."

MacKenzie clapped him on the back. "Why rush things?"

25

Korlov

FOR A BRIEF TIME THAT EVENING THE FOG LIFTED, DISplaying a sunset that slowly changed the Pacific from blue to red to indigo. It was the third night in a row Akiro had ordered their food brought out to the afterdeck, and a table and chairs set up, so he and Lady Emily could dine together.

"It's good to have someone my own age to talk to. One who remembers the same history."

"Under other circumstances, Mr. Akiro," said Lady Emily, "this would be a lovely evening."

"Permit me." Akiro rearranged the dishes on her tray. He had a way of making even the *Korlov*'s mundane things attractive.

"How do you do that?" she asked.

"Seek function," he explained. "Anything doing what it truly must fulfills its purpose and has beauty."

"You know, I've always thought bridges were like that."

"An excellent example."

Lady Emily poured some tea. "What will happen to us, Mr. Akiro?"

"Shuto will put you all ashore before we leave for the explosion point. I admit to sadness in that. I will be very much alone after you go."

"Why must you be? It's a pity for a man of your intellect."

Akiro remembered his doctors. "I am content."

"You should marry again. I know some very nice women."

Akiro's wizened face creased into an indulgent smile. "I am committed to my task. Shuto's mother understood that"—his face darkened for a moment—"perhaps better than anyone. I have nothing to give anyone else."

"Clearly, not true."

"You flatter me."

"Even less true," said Lady Emily. "You are kind and gentle. And you care very much about others. Isn't that why you're here?"

Akiro watched a cloud drift across the sky. "I am here because of a single event fifty years ago. On that day my destiny was fixed."

"In a way, so was mine," she said.

"How so?"

"I met my husband because of the war. His life was changed by a single day. When we met, his life became mine."

"He was a hero. I was only a victim."

Lady Emily sighed. "It surprises me to find out how often they are the same thing, Mr. Akiro."

"Perspective changes things."

Lady Emily look into his eyes. "That is so often the secret, is it not? Perspective beforehand, and not after. How very much we would do differently."

"A truly Zen thought."

"You're wrong." She touched his thin hand. "It's a very womanly thought."

It was her way to teach him, Akiro thought, usually when he least expected it. At first he was surprised by her wisdom. No longer. He felt great warmth for her, and she knew it. Strange companions to find such solace. The English royal and the Japanese curator. She cared for him, too. How sad to find that here, at the end of his days, having been denied it all his life.

"I'm glad to see you have a good appetite. You usually eat so sparingly," Lady Emily said.

"The air is good for me. The sky is so beautiful at this hour."

"When we can see it."

Akiro laughed. "Saki? I made Shuto bring some."

"Please."

"May I ask you a personal question, Lady Emily?"

"At our age, we have few secrets."

"It is very un-Japanese to be so blunt, but time presses. You spoke of your sadness at the death of your son. Why didn't you have another child?"

"There was difficulty in delivery. The doctors had to operate. I considered myself not so unlucky. After all, I had one."

"You loved him very much."

"He was everything to me." Lady Emily's tears caught the fading sunlight.

"We share that, you know."

"That our children mean so much?"

"No, my dear Lady." Akiro's face looked a thousand years old. "That love is pain. Always and eternal."

Lady Emily cried softly. He made no move to stop her.

After a while Akiro said, "We'll eat out here until the days no longer permit."

Lady Emily dabbed a handkerchief at her eyes. "I'd prefer this to be the last time. I don't care to see the abomination you're building. It makes me think about you differently."

"You should not."

"Nevertheless."

"I thought you of all people would understand."

Lady Emily hated what she had to do next, but Justine had decreed it was necessary. Put aside friendship, the demands of honor, even the shared concerns of old age. Her part of their battle would be fought without violence, but blood would still be spilled.

She said, "I suppose I do understand. Why you work so hard, I mean. Both of us have lost sons."

"What do you mean?"

"I'm sorry. Forget I said it, please."

"You are not usually so cryptic. Has Shuto done something?"

"No."

Akiro studied her. "Like the *katsura* branch, you suggest many things. There is more meaning in your silence than in another's loudest words."

"Don't press me. I have faith in you, Mr. Akiro. When the time comes, you will do the right thing."

Akiro bristled. "If you know something, please tell me. I ask you as a friend."

"I don't wish to hurt you." She averted her eyes. "I have feelings, too."

Akiro drew into himself. His art was the Art of Seeing. What was Lady Emily trying to tell him that would hurt him so much she could not say?

Both of us have lost sons.

Not death. Betrayal.

"I must speak to Shuto," he said.

"If you need me," Lady Emily began.

His frail hand traced the curve of her cheek. Such young eyes. She was indeed the answer to the question the space-that-he-was proposed. Another irony. Life's great insight was often knowing what you were not going to get.

"One of the men will take you to your quarters," he said, and then he was gone.

Lady Emily cried again. Men and their science. Little boys playing at war. A mirthless chuckle of self-derision escaped her lips. This was a woman's art. To set father and son on a collision course, turning them as easily as they might change the direction of a boat. It was a deadly business. She was certain one of them would not survive. She thought about Alex, suffering on the island. What had he felt seeing the *Storm* again after fifty years? In the end she saw that Justine was right. A tranquil relationship with Akiro was an illusion. No one was safe here. Justine was also right in believing their lives were nothing, placed against the number Shuto planned to kill.

Yet, she wondered, would even the beautiful and deadly Justine have asked her to kill Akiro, the second man she had ever loved, if Justine knew, really knew, that Lady Emily had spent a lifetime suffering over killing poor Alex Rowe, her first love?

She sipped her wine to dull the pain. On the horizon the sea engulfed the sun, as life had engulfed her.

Akiro found Shuto in the captain's suite studying oceanic charts with Hiroki.

"I wish to speak to my son."

Hiroki started to go, but Shuto stopped him. "We have no secrets in our family."

"Can that be true, my son? I have just spoken to Dr. Lysenko. He is building two bombs. I want to know why."

Shuto met his gaze. "Enlightenment for the people, Father. I promise you they will have it."

"But that is not all."

"No. That is not all."

"What are you planning?"

"I'm paying back a country, Father. A simple notion, really. My whole life I could never find the ones responsible for what was done to us. To me. Believe me, I tried. But was it the scientists of the day? The politicians? The military men? Then I received enlightenment. I understood. The Americans themselves first advanced the theory of collective guilt at Nuremberg. A nation was responsible for its crimes. Some for planning them, others for executing them, the rest for failing to stop it. I want justice. When a country tries to kill you, you are justified in killing it back."

"Did you plan this from the beginning?"

"At first I thought to go along with you. I understood what you wanted. Then I saw how it could be changed."

"What will happen?"

Shuto told him.

Akiro was horrified. "Those people weren't even alive back then. They aren't responsible."

"The people of Hiroshima and Nagasaki were civilians. They weren't responsible either."

"You can't remember what it was like, Shuto. We were at war."

"Who are you to tell me it's over?"

Akiro had been arguing with his son like a teacher with a stubborn student. His control failed and he slapped Shuto.

"I forbid this!"

Shuto's coldness was a terrible thing. "Go to your cabin, Father."

Akiro was frightened. How could Shuto be capable of this? He thought he knew his son, but he didn't. Does any parent? he wondered.

"How can you kill so many?"

The cry that came from Shuto almost knocked Akiro back. "For my mother!"

"She wouldn't want this."

"You didn't know what she wanted. You didn't love her the way I did. Or the way she loved me. She was the one who held me when I came home from school. She cleaned me and told me I had the right to hate them. You never knew she said that, did you? All your philosophy and understanding. Corridors of Remembrance. Halls of Forgiveness. You never knew how much she hated the Americans for what they had done to us. She never forgave anyone. Never. Not to her dying minute. She told me every night. When I came back from the monastery I promised her I would get revenge. For her. And for Ito and Hiroki and all the others."

"And for yourself."

"For myself, too, damn you. Yes!"

Akiro seemed to fold in on himself as if the air had been sucked out of him.

"Hiroki, you too?"

"Yes, Akiro-san."

"Why didn't you tell me?"

"I have hatred, too, Akiro-san. I want what Shuto wants."

"No, you want *Shuto* to have what he wants. You always have. He was your protector. When the other children ganged up on you, Shuto was your warrior. You have great love for him. But inside you must know this is wrong."

Hiroki said nothing.

"Shuto will betray you as he has me," Akiro warned.

"Hiroki has made up his mind, Father."

"Quiet!" Akiro's voice was like a lash. "I do not know you."

"Yes, you do. I am your son, building my own museum."

"You are a monster. I have no son."

Akiro's words hit Shuto hard. He struck back the only way he could.

"Both of us know how true that is, Father."

Akiro struggled for composure. "I will be in meditation."

Shuto flung a final question at his departing back.

"Tell me who bears the greatest guilt, Father. The monster, or the man who made him?"

Akiro had no answer.

26

Korlov

JUSTINE PUT HER HALTER TOP BACK ON. SHE DIDN'T LIKE the way Keller looked at her during the examination. It wasn't the way a doctor should look. Keller read her test results. "You can't go on stressing your body like this. Sugar's way up. You'll hurt the baby and yourself. I'm going to give you a shot."

"What is it?"

"Light insulin."

Justine winced. "Can you help me with the heat? I can't breathe out there."

"Get more bed rest, and stay inside."

The suggestion, like Keller, was useless. "You know I can't do that."

"You're endangering the child."

She thought about the pills in her cabin. It was dangerous to do it alone. Could she ask Keller to help her?

"I've got to go."

He put a hand on her arm. "I know Carolyn spoke to you. Promise me you won't endanger us."

"Her children could be killed if those bombs go off. Did she tell you that?"

"I'm quite concerned about it."

"I can see how much."

"I'm thinking of everyone, Justine. My advice is—"

Justine shook his hand off. "Stay out of my way, Phillip. For Carolyn's sake and your own. That's my advice."

Justine got the daily ration of salt pills and headed for the construction tent on the main deck. It was near a hundred degrees, and raining. It rained so often, no one bothered to avoid it anymore. Clothing was always damp anyway. The dead calm made it worse. Not even the slightest breeze for relief. Lysenko's team baked as they worked, even with the tent sides raised. Their only relief was to swim several times a day.

The bombs were guarded day and night. Justine and the other women weren't allowed any closer than the lifeboats. The "trigger" bomb was housed in a stainless steel receptacle awaiting the plutonium. The fusion bomb was larger, composed of several prefabricated units and computers. The mounting platform was designed to float in high seas. Track from the damaged crane had been rerouted by Shuto's men to launch it from the side of the ship.

"You don't look well, my dear."

Lady Emily was their royal water lady, complete with bucket and dipper. The back of her neck was covered by a white cloth pinned to her hat, like a Foreign Legion cap.

Justine accepted a drink gratefully. "I know this heat gets to everybody, but I just feel miserable."

"It's your condition. Try and stay in the shade as much as possible."

Justine knew it wasn't only her physical strength that was fading. She was sinking emotionally, too. She wanted to take the abortion pills. Mac's faith stopped her, and the memory of those few moments underwater when she felt a connection to the baby. But those things were less and less easy to draw upon. Her own faith was gone.

Shuto was on her mind, too. She felt if only she could reach him, she might be able to dissuade him. But ever since his brief display of emotion for her, he'd been closed. Passing him was like being close to a furnace. She felt his rage. When Ivan, one of Lysenko's men, grabbed Carla Bernhardsen, Shuto almost broke his arm. The Russians were frightened of Shuto, but it didn't change them. Ill will came off Lysenko in waves, and he pawed Bette when she served lunch.

Emotions on the boat were boiling. Hot tempers on a sizzling ship. Word of the blowup between Akiro and Shuto spread quickly. Lady Em had aged perceptibly since turning father and son against each other. She cared very much for the old man. Akiro would not speak to Shuto, and had refused all meals since. He spent his time meditating in the bow, growing weaker by the hour. Akiro was held in high respect by the Japanese, especially Hiroki. Grumbling had already made Shuto discipline two of his men. Discontent was a potent weapon.

The Russians and Japanese weren't the only ones giving off bad feelings, Justine thought. Carolyn had once been her ally, but she was her enemy now.

Phillip's work, no doubt. Justine couldn't escape the feeling that for all his weakness and self-pampering, Keller was a dangerous man.

Less than a week remained. Mac needed time to fix the *Storm*. She had to slow Lysenko down without arousing Shuto's suspicions.

She got permission from the guard to go to the tent. Lysenko and his people wore sweat-stained white lab coats over half-naked bodies. None of the men wore shirts anymore, just cloths wrapped around their waists, sarong style. She had gotten rid of her uniform and wore shorts and a halter top like the other women.

Lysenko stopped working at a console and ogled her openly. He tapped the woman assisting him.

"The nurse who ministers to us is back."

"Krasiva," Kiri observed with a leer. "Pretty."

"Perhaps she'll join us tonight?" Ivan wondered aloud.

Kiri was a long-boned blonde with a wide mouth and green eyes. "I can ask her."

"She'd be the life of the party," said Ivan with a leer that belied his sweet face and small hands.

Justine knew what they were talking about. The whole ship heard the sounds coming out of Lysenko's cabin.

"The question is, would *she* like it?" Lysenko said.

Justine handed Kiri a salt pill. "Things must be pretty bad at home for you to join this outfit."

"Kiss these," said Kiri nastily, lifting her shirt.

Justine had hoped to see vulnerability, or that Lysenko had coerced them. Then she would have thought twice about what she was going to do. But Kiri and the others were willing partners in his corporation of destruction.

"The bitch should be taught a lesson," said Vera. "Like this."

"Ow!"

Justine hated she couldn't react fast enough to stop Vera from poking the soldering iron into her arm. Ivan held her hands. She was too weak to do much about it, and couldn't break cover even if she weren't.

"Uncreative, but direct, Vera," Ivan said, enjoying it.

"Predators and prey, Justine," said Lysenko. "Always the same. We will all retire in a few years, quite rich. What will you have for your years of serving fat, rich passengers who rightly regard you as their social inferior?"

"I wasn't sure till now," Justine admitted.

"And now?" Kiri asked triumphantly.

"Now I'll know I actually did meet the biggest assholes in the world."

Lysenko reddened and slapped her.

"Make a spot for her on the platform. Let her be on it when the bombs explode, Viktor," suggested Vyachslav.

"Or just let me have her," said Vera, running her hands over Justine's breasts.

"Get away from me."

"Don't you like Vera?"

"Honey, I'll be laughing about this long after you're gone."

Lysenko's eyes narrowed. "Why do you say that?"

Justine laughed. "You think Shuto is going to let you go?"

Lysenko studied her closely. "You know something. Tell me."

"Let me go."

Lysenko motioned Ivan to release her. "You strike

me as smarter than most of your kind. Help us and you'll profit."

"How much?"

"A quarter of a million dollars when we're off this ship."

"I could never make that much money in my whole life. Can I trust you?"

"I care only for my survival, and that of my friends, and to go on selling my skills. Help me and I'll give you the money."

Nice speech, Justine thought, you lying pig.

"Shuto has help you don't know about. It's where he's going after he explodes the bombs. Iran, that's where. I heard him talking. They're behind all this. You're dead meat as soon as your work is finished."

"What about you and the others?"

"Shuto says he'll leave us on the island with the men. But I don't trust him. That's the other thing I want. To go with you."

"You're assuming I have another way off this ship."

Justine arched her eyes in a way she hoped was sexy. It had been a long time. "You're a genius, right?"

"Of course."

"I figure a genius would have been figuring how to get another ship the minute Shuto blew up the *Odessa*. And maybe even how to pay him back for it, hmm?"

Lysenko seemed pleased. "You surprise me. That's rare these days. Brains, beauty. What else?"

"Temper," Justine said, hitting Vera hard enough to roll the dark-haired woman's eyes up in her head and drop her to the deck. It wasn't karate, nothing fancy, and it took all the strength she had. She figured it was in character for the smart operator she was portraying herself to be. Even if it wasn't, some things you had to allow yourself.

"I'll see what else I can find out," she said.

She left him and the others openmouthed, and went to the kitchen. Carla and Bette were sweating over steaming racks of dishes.

"Before that creep grabbed me, I heard them talking about the Magnus Field at lunch," Carla said. "They're really going to blow it."

Carla's and Bette's fears about the volcanic region, the pressures of spying, and the physically depleting kitchen work were wearing both women out.

"I need more of that stuff we're putting in the food," Bette said.

"Skip a day," Justine advised her. "I don't want them getting suspicious. Five Japanese came to the infirmary today with stomach problems."

"I'd make it ground glass instead of laxative," Carla said viciously. She pushed limp strands of hair off her sweaty face. "Look at me. I can't stand much more of this."

"Maybe we could take a swim?" suggested Bette.

"I don't think you want to," Justine said.

"Is it tonight?" asked Bette.

"If you're ready."

"Couldn't happen to a nicer bunch," said Carla. "I can still feel their filthy hands on me."

"I ran into them, too." Justine showed them the burn. "It makes it easier."

"You're shaking. Have you eaten?"

"Later."

"We're depending on you," Bette said, concerned. "You have to take care of yourself."

"I'm trying, but I feel awful. I spent half the

morning throwing up. I hate this." Justine had tears in her eyes.

Bette put her arms around her. "Morning sickness goes away, I promise. Carla and I were pregnant with our second kids almost at the same time. We sat around and complained for a year. No one should have to do what you're doing carrying a child."

Justine sniffled. "Thanks."

Carla handed her three sealed plastic bags. "We did our best. Had to defrost a damn lot of beef to get it."

"Serve hamburgers tonight." Justine covered the bags with a towel. "Be waiting for me?"

"We won't let you down."

"That's it, everybody," said Lysenko. "We'll begin loading the plutonium day after tomorrow. Ivan, how do the readings on the explosives look?"

"Symmetrical, Viktor. Everything is in order."

"Kiri?"

"I want to recalibrate the temperature sensor."

"Do it tomorrow. Vera?"

"Sectors one through eight are clear." She rubbed her jaw. "Viktor, I want that bitch."

"You'll have her," he promised. An angry Vera was capable of exquisite torment. "But come now. It's too hot to stay here another minute."

Lysenko led them down to the diving platform alongside the ship. It was dusk and the sea was still. The sunset was filtered by fog. Dying violet light colored the water.

"First one in," he directed. He liked to be the last so he could watch the others take off their clothes. They all swam naked. His orders. A swim, dinner, and then a night in his cabin, the best he could do on this horrid freighter. The nurse had guessed right. He intended to preserve his life. His delivery network was sending two ships. One carried the enriched hydrogen, the other would take them off the *Korlov* as soon as the work was finished. A simple transmitter would summon it.

Kiri had her clothes off first, as always. He liked those long legs wrapped around his head. She was a master at taking two men at a time. Ivan and Vyachslav were naked, too, embracing. Vera paused to stroke both before she dove in. They were all bisexual. Lysenko still hadn't exhausted the sexual permutations. Finding them had been simple. He'd requested the KGB files of men and women who had the scientific talent he needed for the Institute, and instead of rejecting the deviants, he hired them.

The water was warm, but it washed away the sweat and it was still cooler than the damn air.

"Come, Viktor. Swim!"

They were about a hundred feet from the ship, bobbing inside life preservers. They'd roped themselves together, which gave him some interesting ideas. He pulled one of the white circles off the float and paddled towards them.

Justine sidestroked quietly alongside the ship. The bags Carla had given her were tied to a string around her waist.

She reached the stern and swam past the propellers, under the curved afterdeck. The fog was too thick to see the top railing. She could hear them now, cavorting in the water. They were playing some kind of game, spinning Kiri in her life preserver. Wherever she stopped . . .

Justine struck out from the ship. How far could she go and still make it back? She took the first bag off the string and broke it open. The blood from the beef Bette and Carla had defrosted spread quickly in the water.

She changed location and broke the second bag. The Russians were still playing. This time Ivan was in the middle. Lysenko was telling them what to do. Always the director. If she'd primed him right, he wouldn't wait for the explosion to get off the *Korlov*, he'd call his ship. If she could get anywhere near it, she'd make short work of him, and use the radio to call help. It was only a possibility, but you never knew what was going to work.

She broke the last bag. More blood spilled. Four or five pints in all. She swam back to the stern and waited. There. Ripples in the water. Things moving. She shuddered. Her fear was real. A line hit the water, startling her. Bette and Carla hadn't forgotten. She grabbed it and they pulled her up to the deck.

Lysenko felt the cares of the day fading. He bobbed contentedly in the life preserver, feeling a lovely sexual glow. Time for dinner. Playing with Kiri and Vyachslav had worked up an appetite. Kiri was floating, head back, arms hanging limply in the water. Vera was trying to coax some life out of Ivan.

"Come on," she said petulantly. "Mama wants some more . . ."

The expression on her face changed suddenly. Her eyes glazed. She jerked sideways. Her mouth moved, but no sound came out.

Lysenko was confused. "What's wrong? Ivan, what are you doing?"

Then they saw the red stain bubbling up under Vera, and Kiri started screaming.

"Oh, my God. Sharks! Get back to the ship!"

Something brushed Lysenko's legs. They were dangling like bait. Kiri and Vyachslav were already swimming hard. Vyachslav suddenly stopped with a horrid gurgle and was sucked underwater as if giant hands had pulled him. Fear erupted inside Lysenko. He threw his arms around himself in panic. It saved his life. He slid through the life preserver just as a shark took a chunk out of it. The last things he saw before going under were those huge jaws and jagged teeth.

It was a madhouse below. The sharks were in a feeding frenzy. The water was streaked with blood. Vyachslav wasn't dead. He was struggling for the surface. One of his legs was nearly severed. Blood poured out of the stump. He grabbed Lysenko to stay afloat, his face mad with fear. Lysenko saw a shark coming and thrust his assistant in front of him like a shield. The shark tore Vyachslav's arm off. The light in his eyes dulled and went out. Lysenko pushed him away and swam for the ship with all his might.

Kiri and Ivan were ahead of him. Kiri was still screaming. The guards must have heard her because they were shooting from the ship. A shark went belly up. Others tore it to shreds. Lysenko was only twenty feet from the ship. Shuto was on the platform firing. Lysenko felt a shark's sandpaper skin graze him. Pain exploded across his back. Hiroki pulled Kiri and Ivan onto the platform. The fog echoed with screams and gunshots. Lysenko was propelled by terror. Vyachslav passed him, and some part of Lysenko wondered how it was possible, till he saw it was only a head on a severed torso dragged by a feeding shark.

The sharks were right behind him homing on his dangling genitals, wanting to bite them off. He kicked harder than ever. The Japanese yanked him on board sobbing. Kiri was catatonic. Ivan was locked into an embryo position, rocking. Lysenko threw up.

Shuto continued to shoot sharks even after the Russians were out of the water. His anger was so great, he knew he wasn't ready to go among people. The slightest provocation and he'd hurt someone. It soothed him to kill.

First Ito, then his father, now this. More delays he couldn't afford. At any moment their ruse with the *Tuscany* might be discovered. The *Korlov* herself was due in Tokyo in five days. The Americans would begin a global search when she didn't arrive. He had to get back on schedule. His father was getting to him. The old man knew him too well. Hiroki had been right. Shuto wasn't immune to feelings. Suffering this way, dying by degrees, Akiro put it all on Shuto's shoulders. The men didn't like it. It created friction. He had hoped to fool his father till it was over. Then it wouldn't have mattered.

We are such fools, Shuto thought. I'm about to destroy so many, and the death of one man bothers me.

"Excuse me, Mr. Shuto?"

It was Dr. Keller, with his medical bag.

"You've recovered. That's good."

"I'm still fighting an infection, but my nurse couldn't handle the injuries alone."

"How are the Russians?"

"Two dead," said Keller. "Dr. Lysenko was bitten, but I closed the wounds. Kiri is in shock. We gave her sedatives. It could take her days to come out of it. Ivan lost a hand."

Shuto shot another shark. It lay on the surface jerking from side to side as other sharks ripped chunks from it.

"They're lucky to be alive," Shuto said.

Keller said idly, "Luck seems a big part of things these days."

"What do you mean?"

"Nothing."

Shuto jabbed a finger into the nerve bundle in Keller's shoulder. Agony coursed along his side.

"Ow! Why did you do that?" he cried.

"Never fence with me. What did you mean?"

"Ow. Nothing! I heard about Ito. Now this. You've had a string of bad luck. That's all."

Shuto surveyed him closely. A weak man. Pampered. Selfish. With a cruel streak. A doctor for the power and status it gave him. He saw he had frightened him. It was the wrong way to play a man like this. Fear would drive him into a shell. Flattery and reward, those were his keys.

"Tell me about yourself," Shuto said, and shot another shark.

Justine watched them from on deck. She'd come out to tell Shuto about the Russians, but Keller had gotten to him first. She'd been grateful for Keller's help. The wounds were more than she and Carolyn could handle. Now she was worried. He'd turned Carolyn against her. Was he trying to do the same with Shuto?

The sharks were still swimming around the ship, demons she had summoned to kill the killers. She leaned heavily against the railing. Something was wrong. She felt strangely light-headed. She came to a decision about Keller. Her promise to Carolyn that she wouldn't hurt him was a promise she couldn't keep.

She was thinking about that when she heard someone yelling to Shuto that she had fallen. She hadn't felt it. Footsteps reached her. Concerned voices, one of them Shuto's. Phillip Keller's face swam into her darkening vision. He was kneeling over her.

"I'll help you."

She saw it in his eyes. The shot he gave her in the infirmary. She tried to yell not to let him touch her.

"Take her inside," Keller said.

She felt Shuto pick her up, then the prick of a needle. Her last conscious thought was that she had badly misjudged Dr. Phillip Keller.

27

NSA Headquarters

BOOKBINDER HAD SPENT MOST OF THE NIGHT WITH HIS face under a towel, breathing steam from a teapot of herbal brew made by one of his wife's friends from group therapy. At first he approached the home remedy with a scientist's skepticism and refused to take it. Around three in the morning he relented because his sinuses were threatening to blow the top of his head off, and Jane said she was leaving for her mother's because she couldn't get any sleep.

An hour later he could feel the logjam in his head breaking up. By five, he could see straight. By seven he took the first breath through his nose in days.

"It's a miracle." Maybe the ex-pro bowler knew something after all.

"Call Sears," Jane said. "The tape just blew off the water heater."

Bookbinder took a shower and headed for work. Even the water heater didn't bother him. He could *breathe*. That is, until he reached his desk. The packet of satellite photos was labeled CLASSIFIED. Bookbinder's first thought was that they had been routed incorrectly to his desk. Then he saw his name on the tag and on the request sheet. Backtracking the paperwork, he soon had the authorization in his hands and saw what had happened. That's when he couldn't breathe.

Bookbinder knew what it cost to reposition a KH-11. Like every other service in the government, the NSA was having to make do with less and less money. Heads had rolled over screwups far less costly. He checked the night report. The *Korlov*'s transmissions had come in right on the hour. There wasn't a reason in hell to order these shots.

He spilled the photos out on his desk. Nice clear eight-by-tens, computer-enhanced, the works. He couldn't look at them. He shoved them back into the folder. He was glad he hadn't called Sears. Let the next owners of his house fix the damn water heater. He punched up RESUME on his computer, to update it.

The phone rang. He regarded it like it was a snake poised to bite.

"Bookbinder here."

"Derek, David Farley. Can you come to my office?"

It would have been bad enough if it were his supervisor. This was the head of the entire division. Ask not for whom the bell tolls . . .

"Sir?"

"Right away, Derek."

"Yes, sir. On my way."

Farley had a big corner suite. Bookbinder was directed into the conference room. One entire wall was a map of the world. Bookbinder swallowed hard. Farley's secretary was serving coffee to the men and women seated at the long table. The Director of the

NSA, his chief assistant, and the head of the recon office all had copies of the satellite photos in front of them. So did a navy Admiral he didn't recognize. Farley introduced him.

"Have a seat, Derek. This is Admiral Ben Garver, Chief of Naval Operations. One of the men who planned the *Korlov*'s route. The others, you know. Well?"

Bookbinder wanted to be a man about it. "Sir, I can only say that I acted on my own, without anyone's permission. I'm ready to—"

Farley nodded. "And don't think that initiative won't be rewarded. How did you know, Derek?"

"I beg your pardon?"

"The photos. I got my copies as usual and saw it right away. The French just forwarded the passenger list. When were you going to tell us? Is there more?"

Bookbinder picked up the photos. What was going on? No one seemed mad at him. He stalled.

"May I, sir?"

"Of course."

Bookbinder put them under the magnifier trying to figure out what the hell was happening. There was the *Korlov* steaming along happily. Wait a minute. He turned up the power. The OBO freighter was at least a hundred feet longer than this ship. The hull shape was wrong, too. That wasn't the *Korlov!* He could just make out the name in the computer enhancement. *Tuscany.* He scanned the data Farley had handed him. The French ship's course track had brought it close to the *Korlov*'s route. Perfect for a hijacking.

Bookbinder wasn't a religious man, but at that moment he began to believe in a God who loved and protected poor fools like him. He was also smart enough to see that the biggest mistake of his career might just have turned into his greatest success. He grabbed at it with both hands, and lied like a champion.

"It was perfect, sir."

"Excuse me?" said the head of the NSA.

"No mistakes in the code. When we set this project up, we figured we'd have at least one mistake in sending. There haven't been any. I wanted to check."

As a lie, it was a beaut. Careers had been made on less.

"Remarkable," said the head of the NSA.

"The intuition of our people is one of our biggest assets," agreed Farley proudly.

Bookbinder smiled modestly.

"I don't want to break up this mutual admiration society," said the Admiral darkly. "But where the hell is the *Korlov?*"

"Derek?" asked Farley.

"Yes, Derek," said the Director. "How are you going about it?"

Bookbinder was thinking faster than he ever had in his life. Despite the pressure, he was surprisingly clearheaded and relaxed. Maybe it was the tea. He spoke extemporaneously, working it out as he went.

"Our last confirmed visual fix for *Korlov* was off Nauru. So the relay had to be put on the *Tuscany* after that. Probably a terrorist attack, well-planned, executed fast. They sailed the *Korlov* away, and we continued to track the *Tuscany,* never knowing about the switch. It stands to reason there are still terrorists on *Tuscany.* I think we very much want to talk to them. This isn't my area, Admiral, but I've heard your SEALs are pretty good at that sort of thing."

Garver said, "We have a team on the *Kennedy.* They'll be in the air within the hour. One thing I'll add. Admiral MacKenzie is like a son to me. His wife, Justine, is like a daughter." He punctuated his words with a big unlit cigar. "Don't hold a single resource back."

"Of course," said the NSA Director.

"What else, Derek?" asked Farley.

"I'd like to use the new heat trackers. Those satellites can get a big scan of ocean, see if we can pick her up. There aren't that many places to hide a hundred-thousand-ton ship."

"Fine," pronounced the NSA head. "I know you won't let us down. Ben, we'll patch you into your carrier. Start the ball rolling. Gentlemen, we'll meet as soon as we have something from the *Tuscany*."

"You're cleared for whatever you need, Derek," said Farley. "Go to it."

Bookbinder nodded gamely.

28

Sōfu gan

BADLY SUNBURNT AND ACHING ALL OVER, MACKENZIE wiped the sweat off his body and took a long drink. It was a never-ending cycle; drink it in, sweat it out. The heat and humidity were unwelcome partners in everything they did. Grime embedded itself in their pores, no matter how many times they swam. Their shorts were ripped and oil-stained. Days without shaving had given everyone a thick beard.

"I heard the crew of the *Threadfin* tried this once, back in the late fifties," he said. "They were hit by a Greek freighter in the Suez Canal. Bent their shaft."

"Did it work?" Bernhardsen's fair complexion was a hardship in this climate. His skin was cracked and blistered.

The Commodore waggled a finger at him. "Doesn't matter. If we damage the propeller, we're finished." There was no shade on the pier. Sweat dripped off him.

MacKenzie looked at their expectant faces. "Everybody knows their job. Okay, let's do it like we rehearsed."

The *Storm* sat bow down in the water, her stern in the air. It had taken almost two days to remove the conical "dunce cap" on the end of the shaft, and the propeller nut, and clear the shaft for removal. The next step was blowing off the propeller. It took six hours to prepare the shape charge and rig a harness to catch the propeller. They used a wire sling attached to the crane arm, similar to the one the stern was resting on. The propeller would fall into it once it came free.

If they didn't blow it to bits.

They were using a small detonator charge from one of the *Storm*'s Mark VIII torpedoes. The Mark VIII weighed over a ton and a half, so they stripped it right in the fore ends. Exposed, one fifth of its length was explosive. The rest was air tank, engine, and a gyroscope–pendulum–depth pressure valve arrangement that kept the torpedo running straight and at the correct depth.

Rietti brought up the detonator. MacKenzie watched for signs of panic, but his hands were steady as he passed it to Raskin.

"It's ready," Rietti said. "Leads shorted."

"Nikolai, place the detonator," MacKenzie ordered.

Raskin walked the device gingerly to the stern. The charge was big enough to blow his hands off. Rietti had shorted the leads together to prevent accidental detonation, but the explosive itself was unstable. Raskin placed the detonator against the blade of the propeller six inches from the hub.

"Tape it."

Bernhardsen leaned past Raskin and fixed the detonator to the shaft with electrical tape. His hands were just as steady as his partner's. MacKenzie was reminded they routinely braved volcanoes. At least one of them would again.

"Get back. I'm going to wire it. Nikolai?"

Raskin knew what he wanted. With someone responsible for one act of sabotage, MacKenzie wasn't going to complete the wiring with anyone but Raskin near the detonator. Rietti passed him the two-wire conductor, telephone wire taken from the mining camp. MacKenzie connected the detonator leads. It was very quiet on the pier. The air was still and heavy.

"Signal the Commodore to start the generator," MacKenzie ordered, trailing the wire back. "Everybody take cover. Make the connection, Nikolai."

Raskin connected the wires to the generator and the firing switch.

"Set, Peter."

"Arm it," said MacKenzie.

"Armed," responded Raskin, connecting the final leads. He looked up expectantly.

"Fire," MacKenzie ordered, and Raskin closed the switch.

There was a loud crack, and a plume of black smoke rose from the *Storm*. They ran down the pier. The propeller had been blown clean off the shaft and sat snugly in the sling. They hooted and clapped each other on the back, and even the normally taciturn Bernhardsen grinned.

"Admiral, I'm amazed at your utility," said the Commodore. "An inspired piece of work."

They boarded the *Storm*. With the propellor off, they could begin removing the shaft. The Commodore directed the operation with confidence. Fifty years hadn't dimmed his knowledge of his boat.

"Begin with that connecting link. You'll have to remove the pin, and that saddle has to be cut."

MacKenzie sparked an acetylene torch into life. The white glare flickered on the old engines and thick bulkheads. Sparks showered to the deck.

"You're through." Bernhardsen shoved a brace under the remaining section of shaft to support it.

"Tell Nikolai we're ready, Commodore."

Bernhardsen helped him work the shaft loose. MacKenzie couldn't help but wonder if he had sabotaged the ore cart. Long partnerships, like long marriages, had their own stresses and strains. Maybe he didn't want a weak partner weighing him down anymore. Or had Rietti himself done it? Was he so afraid of going into a volcano again that he'd try and keep them here to end their final expedition? And what about the Commodore? His reaction to finding the *Storm* had been surprise bordering on shock. Did it indicate something deeper?

"It's free," said Bernhardsen with relief.

"Nikolai's got the winch on it," MacKenzie said. "Guide it out."

The shaft slid through the hull.

Bernhardsen said with feeling, "Now the real fun begins."

The tracks had ended only a hundred yards back, but it had already taken them more time to carry the shaft a few hundred yards into the rain forest than it had to get the shaft to the end of the tracks from the pier. The eight-foot piece of steel weighed over three hundred pounds. All things being equal, that meant they each had to support sixty pounds. The tools each man had to carry added at least another twenty, and with the Commodore unable to manage a full load, the total weight was probably close to ninety pounds. In this heat, on this terrain, it was a killer.

"Stay in step," MacKenzie cautioned. "Slow and steady."

There were only five days left. He wanted Raskin working on the engines, but he needed every man here. They walked single file, holding the shaft on their right shoulders. MacKenzie, Rietti, the Commodore, Bernhardsen, and then Raskin. It was treacherous. Vines clutched at their feet. The terrain was uneven, shifting the weight burden constantly. MacKenzie's shoulder felt like it was breaking. The steel was slick with sweat.

It was like riding a bicycle built for five through a jungle. Broad leaves smacked them in the face because they were unable to free their hands. Insects bit them unmercifully. The path rose steeply on one side, and dropped about ten feet on the other to a stream below. Rietti stumbled and almost knocked them over.

"Watch it," said Bernhardsen angrily.

"Easy now," said Raskin. "Stay in line."

The few rays of sunlight piercing the tree canopy illuminated clouds of insects. Twice they had to stop for snakes, waiting with the metal shaft on their shoulders in that hot, steamy, and utterly joyless place.

MacKenzie found himself lulled into a weary rhythm. One step at a time. One step. One more. The pain in his knees was growing steadily. He was about to order a rest break when he heard a cry of pain and Rietti slammed into him from behind. The weight of the shaft greatly increased. MacKenzie stumbled. If he fell with it on him, he would be crushed.

"Push!" yelled Raskin from behind. MacKenzie shoved it with all his might. The shaft crashed to the ground and rolled down to the stream, flattening brush.

"What the hell happened . . . ?" MacKenzie started to yell, but a flicker of red eyes in the dark bushes sounded an alarm and he barely managed to shout, "Into the trees!" before a wild boar sprang from the bush. It blocked the trail, snorting fiercely. The Commodore was in its path. It looked ready to charge. Bernhardsen and Rietti threw tools. A hammer connected and the animal squealed in pain. MacKenzie shoved the Commodore unceremoniously up into a tree.

"Mac, behind you!" yelled Bernhardsen.

MacKenzie turned. The boar's red eyes were fixed on him. Spittle dripped from its bristly snout. It was poised to attack. He had no chance against a wild boar and he knew it. Its tusks would rip him apart. MacKenzie's back was to the stream. He stood totally still, trying not to panic, desperate not to let himself be spooked by his fear. The boar hesitated. Prey was supposed to run. It snarled, uncertain.

MacKenzie heard Raskin whisper behind him, "Back and to the right, Peter."

The wild boar lowered its snout and growled from deep in its throat.

"Mine or yours?" MacKenzie whispered.

"For the love of . . . Yours. Now!"

The boar charged and MacKenzie threw himself back. He had a brief glimpse of Raskin wielding a steel pry bar like a lance as he tumbled downhill into the water. There was a horrible squealing above him. Screams filled the jungle. He swiped at his eyes to clear them, and when he did, he would remember what he saw for the rest of his life. Raskin's face was contorted by the strain of holding the squealing boar on the ground, impaled on the end of the pry bar like it was an hors d'oeuvre on a toothpick. The pull on his muscles must have been incredible. He had caught the animal in midair as it leaped for MacKenzie. The boar's own weight drove the bar in.

"Mac, catch!"

Bernhardsen threw him the other pry bar. Mac drove the point into the boar and it screamed with rage. Blood spattered on his arms and legs as it writhed. He went to strike again.

Raskin said, "Wait." He was breathing deeply, his voice barely audible.

MacKenzie had ample evidence of Raskin's enormous strength over the years, but he had never seen anything like this. The boar struggled to free itself. The angle of the bar never changed. The boar went mad. With a final huge effort Raskin drove the bar all the way through the boar into the ground. Spittle flew, but it couldn't dislodge the bar. Its eyes faded. It gave a final quiver, and died.

Raskin dropped to the ground, exhausted. He didn't have strength left to lift his head.

"Nikolai, you saved my life."

"Did you . . . ?" Raskin gasped.

"Did I what? Please, Nikolai, anything."

"Did you . . . bring the rum?"

"A *case* when we get home. No, a barrel!"

"Stop fawning over me. You were of some small help. Where are the others?"

"Right here," said Bernhardsen. "Nikolai, I never saw anyone so big move so fast."

"I'm giving up all forms of exercise," said Rietti.

"Captain," said the Commodore. "I lost a man to

those boars during my last stay. I wish you'd been here."

"Accolades gratefully accepted," said Raskin.

The shaft lay in the stream. They were going to lose more time getting it back up here. And they couldn't work in the lava field after dark. It meant waiting till dawn tomorrow to begin. Almost a full day lost. They'd be down to four. Could they do it?

"We're fairly close to the lava field, aren't we?" Raskin asked.

MacKenzie figured Raskin was thinking along the same lines. He was wrong.

Raskin was eyeing the pig.

"Comrades, after all the canned goods, I have an excellent idea for dinner."

29

Sōfu gan

THEY GOT THE SHAFT TO THE LAVA FIELD JUST BEFORE nightfall. The boar made a fine meal roasted over a magma pit. After eating, the men slept soundly. MacKenzie needed sleep, too. Desperately. There had been too many days without it. But he'd have to wait.

He didn't relish traveling at night, not after the attack of the wild boar, but he had a lot of distance to cover and he had to be back before morning. He crossed the lava field and struck down the path to the other side of the island. He cinched his belt tighter because his shorts were sliding around. No trick to losing weight in this climate. They were all looking skeletal with their hollow, bearded cheeks, sunken eyes, and ribs showing. Even Nikolai had lost his share of pounds.

"A shadow of my former self," he had proclaimed miserably, tearing into the roast pig with a hunter's savage joy. MacKenzie could still smell the meat roasting. Few meals had ever tasted better. He felt a deep sense of gratitude towards Raskin. It was the second time the Russian had saved his life. The first was on the *Kentucky* when a KGB agent had tried to kill him. Raskin watched over him like an older brother, sure that he was going to get into some trouble or other and need saving. From the looks of things, he wasn't so wrong. Mac hoped the *Storm* would keep his friend's private grief assuaged.

MacKenzie got to the beach, lit a fire, and retrieved his flashlight from the Hotel. How was Justine? Had she taken the pills? They both wanted what every parent wanted, a normal, healthy child. Was he wrong to tell her not to abort it? Did mothers know things fathers didn't? Endless questions. All the world's problems in miniature.

He waited long past the time for her signal. The ship remained dark. He grew worried. He might make it to the ship if he swam, but there was the riptide to contend with, and an unplanned visit could easily endanger everyone. His job was to stay here and raise the *Storm*. There were only four days left. He signaled, hoping she might be able to receive even if she couldn't send. There was no acknowledgment. God, what he wouldn't give for a radio to call for help. Radio . . . Suddenly something that had been subconsciously nagging at his mind broke through. The British called the radio the wireless telegraph, or W/T. Radio for help. The realization hit him hard. So simple. Why hadn't he seen it sooner?

He wanted to stay, but his night was far from over. He had to check his hunch.

"Be safe," he whispered.

He extinguished the fire and plunged back into the rain forest, heading for the *Storm*.

Korlov

Shuto saw MacKenzie's signal from shore. Ito would have been able to read the Morse code, he was sure. He couldn't, but it didn't matter. He already knew what it said.

"This time *you* underestimated *me*, Admiral," he said to no one in particular.

He had been sure someone of MacKenzie's resources wouldn't accept imprisonment on the island without trying to stop him. According to the reports, he was working very hard on the old submarine, but it didn't pose a real threat. Shuto admired his spirit. Under other circumstances they might have been friends. Same with the nurse. Their ties had been forged on a level even he didn't fully understand.

He glanced over to the tent to make sure guards were posted. Cabinets and consoles and boxes of death. The shark attack had slowed things down, cost him precious time. Lysenko and his team had worked on the bombs only sporadically yesterday and today. Even so, it would be over soon. He felt very much alone. His grief over Ito's death was limitless. He had lost his father. He even felt Hiroki slipping away. Shuto began to understand about revenge. It was never a small thing. It was a raging mindless beast. Unleashed, it devours everyone, including those who invoke it. *Especially* those who invoke it.

"My path leads to self-destruction, Father. You were right about that," he said aloud. He wondered why it wasn't a disturbing notion, why it felt so fitting. He, Akiro, Lysenko, the Americans, even the *Korlov* herself, could be engulfed by one supreme act of destruction if he wished. Like Hiroshima. It was the perfect balance. Zero sum. Truly Zen. He should have seen from the beginning there could be no survivors.

The fire on the beach went out.

"Good night, Admiral. I don't know if I can keep my promise to you."

"Who are you talking to?" asked Hiroki, behind him.

Shuto had felt him. "A friend."

"There's no one here."

Shuto shrugged. "Depends on how you look at it."

Hiroki couldn't follow that kind of logic. "I've been thinking."

"Oh?"

"I don't think you're after revenge, or justice. You're trying to destroy yourself."

Shuto laughed. "All this, just for that?"

"Be clever with someone else, Shuto. I'm not smart enough."

"You're smarter than you think, Hiroki." Shuto looked at him kindly. "Hiroki, you remember how you accepted all those beatings from the people Akiro found you with?"

"I don't like to think about it."

"You were bigger than most of them. Stronger. How come you never fought back?"

"They told me I was supposed to work, so I worked."

"Hauling coal fourteen hours a day without shoes in winter? Gruel for meals. Beaten if you fell. Didn't you think something was wrong?"

Hiroki looked away. "Sort of, I guess."

Shuto put a hand on his shoulder. "I can always tell when you're lying. You're lying now. You didn't fight back because you thought you deserved it. It was your punishment for being different. Right?"

Hiroki's big shoulders slumped. "Yes."

"Even after Akiro took you in, did it ever stop hurting?"

"No."

"For me either, Hiroki. It hurts the same even now. Am I mad? I don't know. Does it even matter? Maybe pain makes you clearheaded. Did you know for a long time I thought about killing myself?"

"Really? You?"

"In the monastery. I didn't because the priests showed me it would have been the cruel ones' victory. They showed me how clever the cruel ones had been. They broke my body and stole my spirit until life hurt so much, I was ready to cooperate with them by destroying myself. Do you see the irony?"

"What happened?"

"The priests taught me that a man has a flame inside. It can grow large or small. It can burn brightly, or low. It can be fed, or it can be extinguished. My flame was almost gone. Many hours I stared at the candles in the temple. My flame was no bigger than theirs. Then I learned how to make it grow. You know I can't have a wife or children. I am no scholar like Akiro. What was left? I found the more I hated, the larger I was. Hatred has fed me all my life. I punished the ones who beat me, and the ones who tormented you and Ito. I saved the others when Akiro found them, and each time I made the bad ones pay. When I became large enough, I chose this course. It is the culmination of my life. But there is a price. I see that now. If the inner flame grows too large, it consumes you. That is what you sense. But there is no turning back."

"I love you, Shuto. Let it go."

"I can't."

Hiroki balled his big fists. "Sometimes I could just take you and beat the sense into you."

Shuto's energy crackled. Hiroki put his hands down.

"I'll let you go if you want," Shuto said softly. "Take a boat."

"I'll stay with you."

"I hope you survive it, Hiroki-my-brother."

Hiroki bowed deeply. What would be, would be.

30

Sōfu gan

MACKENZIE PASSED THE LAVA FIELD WITHOUT WAKING the men. After all the physical exertion, it would have taken a fire siren to rouse them. His legs felt like lead. All he wanted was to lay his head down and sleep, but he had more miles to go. He sipped water and ate some food, moving as fast as he could.

So simple, MacKenzie thought. We were struck in the sail, the Commodore had said, so I took the *Storm* here and sent an SOS to base. But the shell had destroyed the W/T mast. He had seen it. It would have been impossible to send an SOS after such a hit. The damage had to have happened *after* he radioed his SOS. Captain Rowe had taken his warship out of action before it was hit. I must be even tireder than I thought for it to take so long to come to me, Mac thought. If one of Alex Rowe's lies had come to the surface with the *Storm*, were there others? Had the Commodore tried to sabotage the *Storm* to hide them?

He made the mining camp and walked down to the ocean. The sea beckoned to him as it always had. It was where he felt most alive. The *Storm* floated beside the pier, the final repository of their hopes and dreams. He patted her dark hull.

"Will you share your secrets with me, old girl? It's just us now."

He wasted no more time on conjecture. He turned on the generator to power the lights inside *Storm,* and searched every compartment. He didn't like having to do it. It was rifling a grave. Personal articles. Half-finished needlepoint. A faded newsletter the captain had typed himself. Letters stiff with age crumbled at his touch. He found secret fears revealed in a journal hidden under a mattress. There was a stash of rum in the seamen's mess. It was a record of human frailties and brave endeavor. Testimony to men under pressure, fighting to survive. There was ample evidence of courage. *We'll fight till this war is over,* one boy wrote to his mother. *Never fear,* he told her.

In the control room his inch-by-inch inspection revealed dried blood on the lower conning tower hatch. Another of *Storm*'s secrets. What did it mean?

The captain's cabin was the only place the Commodore had asked them not to enter. Mac checked the entire cabin but didn't find anything. Then he realized he should have found the *Storm*'s log. It was missing. The Commodore had been alone for fifteen minutes the first day. He could have taken it. Mac-Kenzie went forward. What could the *Storm* tell him that Commodore Rowe would sink her to hide it? He checked the compressed-air reservoir and the ballast tanks. He found what he was looking for under the number one battery plate.

The skeleton still wore the reefer jacket and insignia

of a lieutenant in the British submarine service. Asymmetrical shrinkage of the skull had fixed his officer's cap at a rakish angle. It was insolent in death. The desiccated corpse weighed hardly anything, which had enabled the Commodore to carry it here. The *Storm*'s log was there, too. It had fallen into the battery acid, lost forever.

MacKenzie saw why the Commodore had hidden the corpse, as soon as he pulled it free. The officer's sweater was fused to his body; there was no way to remove it. The others would have seen the bullet hole at once. MacKenzie removed the ID tags and regarded them soberly because they exposed another lie. Lieutenant David Bolliver had never left the ship, never made it to the island, or gone back to London. But no depth charge or destroyer shell had killed him. The hole in the breast of his sweater was surrounded by the same brown stain that was on the hatch, blood, oxidized dry as dust after all these years, which had welled up behind the path of the bullet.

There was a metal rod in the engine room. MacKenzie inserted it into the hole and probed. The bullet tore through the papier-mâché skin and clothing and fell to the deck. A .38-caliber. He put it in his pocket.

"What can you tell me, Lieutenant?" MacKenzie asked softly. "From the looks of things, the Commodore took his ship out of action, sailed it here, and scuttled her. I don't know why he shot you, but you managed to secure the hatches before she went under. That's where the blood on them came from. You saved her, Lieutenant. You died before you could blow enough ballast to get her back up.

"Were you rightly shot for some action against the

Storm? Did you lose your nerve and try and scuttle her yourself and just botch the job?"

MacKenzie could keep asking, but he'd get no answers. He returned the body to its hiding place and secured the plate.

Captain Alex Rowe and First Lieutenant David Bolliver. Which was the hero, which the coward? He had four days left to find out.

PART FOUR

The Storm's Secret

31

U.S.S. Kennedy

FORTY-FIVE MINUTES BEFORE SUNRISE, THE HELO PILOT got the high sign from the flight boss.

"There's the go, sir."

"Take her up," said the SEAL leader, Commander Lee Jackson. "Signal Bravo to follow."

Two specially equipped RH-53D Sea Stallion helicopters leaped off the carrier's deck and flew out to sea. It had been a hasty summons, Jackson thought. From the CNO, Admiral Ben Garver, no less. One minute they were playing poker, the next they were grabbing their weapons and ammunition from special storage. Jackson finished checking his combat gear and tucked his longish hair under his collar. It was no affectation. It hid the mottled skin around his neck and ears which looked badly burned. It was actually frostbite from a mission on the polar ice cap. Only the knowledge of a Russian ice specialist trained by Inuit Eskimos, and the combat skills of Justine MacKenzie, had saved his life.

"Everybody set, Pepper?"

Lt. Juan Peppito Torres, Jackson's number two, was a strapping man with dark wavy hair and an engaging smile. Pepper looked back to the rest of the team. He sensed their confidence.

"All set, sir."

Jackson leaned close, for his ears alone. "One more thing. I got the word right before we left. Justine MacKenzie was on the ship when it was taken. She might still be. Thought you'd like to know."

Pepper remembered the beautiful, deadly CIA operative well. She'd led their mission to rescue the family of a legendary Russian submarine commander who had been taken hostage to force him to deliver his submarine to terrorists. Pepper would never forget the *Northern Star*'s violent end, or the sacrifices that enabled them to survive. He owed her too.

The pilot looked at the radar screen. "Bravo's in position. ETA five minutes."

"Pepper, pass the word. Final check."

Each SEAL had a custom Beretta semiautomatic pistol in his holster, with extra clips of ammo in a special mag holder. Their special combat vests or their fatigues held flash grenades and thundersticks for disorienting Tangos, and six hundred rounds of jacketed hollow-point ammunition in thirty-round magazines for the MP5 machine guns which hung on straps around their necks. They wore night-vision goggles. Miniaturized communications gear was strapped to each man's waist: Motorola walkie-talkies with lip mikes and earpiece.

Jackson spoke into his lip mike. "How's it look, Pony?"

"Got 'em in our sights, Skipper," came the voice through his earpiece.

"Pony" Mareska was Bravo team's leader. His Sea Stallion was approaching the *Tuscany* from the opposite direction.

"One mile," said the pilot. The sun was just creeping over the horizon.

"Good hunting, Bravo," said Jackson, taking his place by the exit hatch. "Execute now."

Bravo team's Sea Stallion dove on the *Tuscany* from the stern, raking it with machine-gun fire. Hovering twenty feet above the water, SEAL sharpshooters picked off targets. Tangos dove for cover. The withering fire held them down. Exactly ten seconds into Bravo's assault, with all eyes aft, Jackson's Sea Stallion swooped down from the opposite direction, almost invisible with the sun behind them, and landed on *Tuscany*'s bow. Alpha team poured out.

"Everybody go!"

SEALs learn to fire on the run, or coming into a room, or out of the sea, or leaping from a helicopter. A terrorist came down the stairway, firing. Jackson shot him. The heavy load spun the man around and drove him to the deck. They worked quickly and efficiently, the best shots in the world. The opposition was brave enough, but their skills were weak. Jackson realized they didn't have their first team manning the *Tuscany*. They would be on the *Korlov*.

"Passenger deck secure, Skipper. Two Tangos down," Jackson heard in his earpiece.

"Engine room secure, Skipper. Hostages clear. No Ts."

"Keep some alive, damn it," Jackson said sharply.

"Bridge secure, Skipper. One tried to get off a radio message to his buddies. He didn't."

That was important. The terrorists on the *Korlov* mustn't know the *Tuscany* had been taken.

"Got the captain. He's wounded, Skipper."

"Fix him up. I want to talk to him. Pepper, any word on our friend?"

"I wish," Pepper said in his ear. "Nada."

"Keep at it."

One by one his men reported in as the ship was secured. Four more terrorists dead, seven in all. Three wounded. Two captured.

"Ship's ours, Pony," radioed Jackson to Bravo copter. "Nice work."

"We aim to please."

"You're outta here."

"Roger."

The Sea Stallion veered away. Jackson sat in a deck chair and lit a cigar. Pepper and two of his men brought the wounded captain to him on a stretcher. Blood was seeping through the bandage on his chest.

"Skipper, the *Tuscany*'s chief engineer says the captain and his officers were executed. The passengers were transferred to the *Korlov*, including our friend."

"Sorry to hear it." Jackson kneeled beside the wounded captain. "I'm Commander Jackson, U.S. Navy. What's your name?"

"Captain Kobiashi." He coughed up foamy red spittle. "Your men are trained very well, Commander."

"You're part of the group that boarded the *Korlov*?"

Kobiashi nodded weakly. "How are my crew?"

Jackson thought about the *Tuscany*'s officers. It affected his sympathy.

"Seven dead. Five wounded."

"A sad day. One more question, please?"

Jackson knew what it was. He caught Pepper's eye and read the answer.

So did Kobiashi. "Thank you for your honesty," he said.

"Where is the *Korlov*?" Torres demanded.

Kobiashi felt his secret hope leave him. "I was so close to the end."

"What's he talking about, Skipper?"

"He's wandering."

"Where is the *Korlov*?" Torres asked again.

"Forget it, Pepper. Let him be."

Home was so far away. Noburu gone. Sasaki. He raised his hand. Sunlight backlit the veins in what was left of his webs. No music for this child.

Jackson saw the deformity.

"The others have things, too," said Torres. "Weird, huh?"

"Who are you all?" Jackson asked.

"Part of Akiro's dream." A darkness deeper than the factory basement's was falling. Kobiashi's eyes closed.

Pepper felt for a pulse.

"He's gone, Lee."

Jackson took the SATCOM transmitter from his vest pocket and called the carrier. They wanted the remaining terrorists brought back double quick for debriefing. Jackson signed off and spoke into his lip mike, heading for the Sea Stallion. His men had the Japanese prisoners and the chief engineer and two of his crew secured. Jackson left Torres to sail the *Tuscany* back to port, along with two other SEALs and the rest of the engine room crew. Three days of sailing in the South Pacific. Tough life.

The helicopter rose off the deck. It had been good work, perfectly executed, but not finding Justine MacKenzie left it unfinished.

The *Tuscany* dwindled in the distance. The rest was up to others.

32

Korlov

JUSTINE KEPT COMING IN AND OUT OF A FOG. EVERYTHING was hazy. Voices were a long way off. There was something she had to do, but she couldn't remember what it was.

"You can't keep her under like this," someone was saying. Carolyn, she thought. "It will hurt the baby."

"I'm the doctor. Be quiet."

"What did you tell Shuto?" Carolyn demanded.

"I realized I better not tell him anything, not after what Justine did." Keller massaged the spots Shuto had poked. They still throbbed. "He'd kill us for not telling him about her sooner. That's why I decided to stop her myself."

Carolyn was crying. How sad a strong woman like her could be reduced to tears by this bully.

"What about all those people? How can Justine stop him laid up like this?"

"She can't, and neither can we. She would have

gotten us killed. We're a doctor and a nurse. We're not equipped for this. We have to save ourselves."

"But what about my kids?"

"Shuto promised to let me make a radio call to the States to tell them to move."

"Why would he do that?" Carolyn asked suspiciously.

"I promised to be their doctor. Clever, no? With Justine sick, he needs me. I guess you could call that killing two birds with one stone."

Across the room, Justine stirred. If she could just concentrate . . .

Keller noticed it. "Time for another shot. That blue bottle, please."

"She could go into shock."

"Whose side are you on?"

"Yours. I've chosen. You know it. None of the women will even speak to me anymore. But it's not wrong to ask you to remember Justine's condition, is it? You're clever enough to hold her without hurting her."

Justine felt a pinch in her arm. She tried to remember how many pinches there had been. Five? No, six. Two full days had gone by.

"Carolyn, I told you I'd take care of everything. Come inside."

Justine wondered if Keller's drugs would do the difficult part for her. It didn't seem to matter anymore. Nothing did. The fog was closing in again. She was angry at herself. She'd been so intent on Shuto and Lysenko, she hadn't watched Keller closely enough. Two whole days gone. Three days left. Just three days before the bombs were completed and the *Korlov* sailed. For a moment her mind cleared. She tried to roll off the bunk, fight back somehow. Then the drug took effect and she felt herself slipping. Tears leaked from her eyes for herself, for the child, for Mac, for all the people Shuto was going to kill.

The door to Phillip and Carolyn's quarters closed, cutting off the sound of their lovemaking, a now familiar cadence of slaps and moans. She couldn't hold her thoughts together anymore.

She slept.

Bette, Carla, and Lady Em gathered around the wooden chopping block in the steamy galley and held a council of war.

"Admiral MacKenzie signaled again from the beach last night," Bette said, slicing onions. "There was nothing I could do. He must be terribly worried."

Lady Em sighed. "I wish I could remember my Morse code, dears. It was just too long ago."

"Two days Keller's had Justine under sedation." Carla fumed. "Lysenko's finishing the bombs. Shuto's almost ready to sail. The men are nowhere to be seen. And we stand here boiling rice and cutting vegetables."

Lady Em was troubled. "What would you have us do?"

"What Justine would," Carla said firmly.

"She'd slit his throat." Bette brought her knife down hard against the wood. "I don't know if I'm ready for that."

"None of us are," admitted Carla. She dropped the vegetables into a pot of boiling water.

"Dr. Keller's been very smart cozying up to Shuto. Shuto trusts him, I think." Lady Em shook her head sadly. "I thought better of him. Carolyn, too."

"He's just using her," Bette said. "I don't know why she can't see it."

"I tried to tell her," said Lady Em. "She called me old and dried up."

"Don't mind her," Carla said. "She won't be the first woman to love a creep. He's slick, I'll give him that."

"Do we know what he's giving Justine?" Lady Em asked.

Bette said, "No. Why?"

"If we did, why couldn't we substitute something for it? Get Justine up and around. She'll know what to do."

"It's a good thought," said Bette, brightening. "Do let's try."

Carla checked her watch. "Carolyn will be handing out the salt pills in a few minutes. Keller will be alone. It's as good a time as any."

"How do we distract him?" asked Lady Em.

Carla pushed back her stringy hair and cocked a hip. "From what I've seen of Dr. Keller, that won't be a problem. Anybody got a comb?"

Lysenko refused to swim anymore. No matter how hot it got in the tent, he wouldn't go near the water. He doubted he would ever swim in anything but a pool again. He walked with a makeshift cane, hunched over, a result of the shark bites. In her free time Kiri walked around dropping food over the side. When the sharks came she scolded them about having killed her friends. Ivan's shakes were worse.

"Kiri, pay attention," he admonished. No one else could wire this section, but she kept drifting. "You want to blow us up?"

"Sorry, Viktor. It's this heat. I can't concentrate. Ask Vera."

"Vera's dead," he snapped.

"Oh, yes. I forgot."

"Ivan, watch her, damn it."

"Sure, Viktor."

Kiri hadn't been the same since the shark attack. No more fun. Nightmares had her shaking and coming to him for comfort. Who the hell did she think he was, her father? He'd replace her as soon as they got off this damn ship. And he had to get away soon. Shuto was as ruthless as he was mad. After the shipment of enriched hydrogen Lysenko ordered had arrived and been off-loaded, Shuto and his men had blown up the ship. How could you deal with a person like that?

He was working faster than he should have to make up for the loss of Vera and Vyachslav. Problems kept cropping up. Without the delays, he would have been finished ahead of schedule. Now it was all he could do to finish on time. At least he had the transmitter. It had come with the shipment. The new yacht was waiting over the horizon. His rage at Shuto threatened to consume him at times. It had made him especially nasty to Kiri. He would have sabotaged the bombs if he thought he could get away with it, but the idea of Shuto coming after him was terrifying. He wondered where the nurse was. He hadn't seen her in days. He had rewired the bombs to require a second trigger, to protect himself after her warning. Maybe he would take her with him after all. He was tired of sleeping with Ivan.

Shuto came into the tent looking strained. Akiro was dying of hunger to protest what Shuto was doing. Tempers were flaring. If this kept up, they wouldn't need a bomb to blow up the *Korlov*. She'd self-destruct.

"How soon will you be done?" Shuto asked, barely civil.

"We'll be done with the wiring in two days. One more for testing. Then it's ready," said Lysenko.

"What about the plutonium?"

"We can bring it up now. I'll need Mori and Hiroki."

Shuto pointed to Kiri. "Is there a reason for that?"

Lysenko looked. Kiri was idly raising and lowering her shirt, seemingly unaware she was exposing her breasts.

"Snap out of it, woman," he said irritably. "Ivan, don't let her touch anything till I get back."

Out on deck Lysenko took a moment to look back at his work. The bombs were a variation on a basic design he had invented years before, smaller than the WW II relics that had made Akiro's men what they were, but immensely more powerful. Lysenko hated art and found music immensely boring, but his bombs, even on the deck of a rattrap freighter in the middle of fogbound nowhere, were things of beauty to him. The technical architecture was striking. The physics of the universe in three-foot cubes. His ability to re-create the power of the sun. Glorious.

Hiroki and Mori were waiting nervously in the containment area.

"Put on radiation suits," Lysenko directed.

They struggled into the ungainly protection. It was difficult for Lysenko to straighten up in the suit with his back hurting as much as it did. The Geiger counter showed only normal background radiation. He cycled the airlock open.

"Breathe normally and follow me. This isn't dangerous if you're careful."

Lysenko made sure their suits were properly sealed

before entering the inner chamber. He found beauty here, too. The stainless steel cylinders and rainbow-colored coils of wire seemed cheerful. He unlocked the computer controls and engaged the heavy motor. The storage rack turned slowly, extending a canister. A pneumatic arm placed it onto a platform. Lysenko unclasped the turnbuckle around the middle of the cylinder to reveal a seam.

"Turn the top half slowly. They're threaded together."

Hiroki put his arms around the container. There was a sudden pop and he leaped back. The container rocked precariously.

"Steady it," Lysenko commanded sharply.

Hiroki grabbed it and froze.

"I should have warned you," said Lysenko. "Negative air pressure to prevent leakage after an accidental rupture. Go on."

Hiroki hugged the container again and did a kind of step-around. It slowly separated.

"Put the top down."

Inside, a small, ovoid cylinder was suspended in the center of a webbed harness to prevent shocks. Black and yellow radiation decals glared warnings.

"That's the core," said Lysenko. "Forty pounds of plutonium. In all, two tons of it here. Ito, get the tongs."

Lysenko wheeled over a transfer cart that moved smoothly on heavy rubber rollers. There were ovoid depressions on its polished steel surface for the cores, like an egg crate.

"One of you on each side," Lysenko ordered. "The tongs fit into those holes in the core. Use them to lift the core out. Put it in the first receptacle."

Hiroki and Mori were sweating visibly behind their

face shields. Besides the hard work, there was a psychological component to their reaction. The radioactive material was the poison of their lives. It didn't help to have Shuto staring at them, either.

"Careful," Lysenko warned.

Hiroki muttered something in Japanese that required no translation.

The core fit snugly into the first depression. Each had a cover that rotated over it, like a serving dish. Lysenko slid it shut.

"One down."

In the corridor by the infirmary, Bette took the napkin off the tray of food she was holding.

"I'm ready."

"Me, too." Carla smoothed down her skirt and loosened her halter.

Bette knocked. "Dr. Keller?"

Keller opened the door. "Yes?"

Bette smiled brightly. "We came to see Justine. We made something for her. She's still not feeling well, is she?"

"No. What is it?"

"Bread pudding. We found a mix in the galley."

"It's not possible for her to—"

"There's enough for two," Carla purred. "She could eat hers later."

"I'm sorry. She's sleeping."

"But Bette and I made it special. And I need some medical advice." Carla folded her arms. Her breasts swelled enticingly.

"All that work shouldn't go to waste. Come in."

Justine was asleep in one of the beds, sweat-drenched and pale.

"She looks terrible," Bette said.

Keller's face held nothing but professional concern.

"I'm doing my best. The diabetes is complicated by her pregnancy."

And you, you bastard, thought Carla viciously. "Doctor, could I see you privately for a moment?"

"Of course."

"I'll stay with her," volunteered Bette.

Carla and Keller went inside. Bette put the tray down and listened at the door.

"It's my chest, I think," Carla was saying. Bette heard Keller tell her to undress. Carla was tough. Bette had to make her friend's sacrifice worth something. She went over to Justine. She was breathing shallowly. Her skin was slack and gray. Bette shook her.

"Justine, wake up."

"Hmmm."

"Come on. Wake up." Bette had never hit another person in her life. She slapped Justine tentatively, then harder. Justine's eyelids fluttered open.

"Wha . . . ?"

"It's me. Bette. What is Keller giving you to keep you like this?"

"Drug . . ." she managed weakly. "Can't wake up . . ."

"Which one?"

Justine's eyes closed.

Bette slapped her. "Wake up. Carla's in there with him. You've got to tell me what he's giving you."

Bette wasn't sure Justine heard her, then, "Bottle . . ."

The medical supply cabinet was filled with them.

"Which?" She shook Justine hard. "Which bottle?"

"Blue . . ."

There was a blue bottle in the cabinet, on a tray

with syringes. She emptied it out and refilled it with water from the tap.

"Listen to me, Justine. I put water in. You'll be up and around in a while. We'll be waiting for you. We don't know what to do without you. Please be okay."

She hoped Justine heard her. She had to get Carla out of there. She knocked hard on the connecting door.

"Carla? We have to go. Carla?"

She kept banging till the door opened. Carla tugged at her clothing, moving quickly, as if there was something behind her. There was.

"Take those pills," Keller was saying. His face was flushed. "They should help."

"Thank you, Phillip. Enjoy the pudding."

He stuck a finger in the dish and licked it. "Delicious. Come back if you need me. Any time."

Carla closed the door behind them.

"I hope the filthy bastard chokes on it," she said bitterly when they were alone in the corridor.

"Are you all right?"

Carla turned away. "Sure, why not?"

"You're crying."

"I've been pawed before. At least this was for a good cause."

"Brave girl." Bette used her apron to dab at Carla's eyes. "Let's get back."

"At least I found out what Carolyn sees in him," Carla said as they walked. "He's got an animal kind of sexiness. He wants to devour you. Control everything. Make you beg. It isn't love and affection. It isn't *friendship.*"

"How can she like that?"

"Some women do. I think she's one of the ones who'll do anything for love. Did you get it?"

"I can't be sure. Justine is out of it. I hope so."

Carla said with real feeling, "If this doesn't work, I vote for cutting his throat."

Bette was saved a reply. Lady Em came rushing up to them, terribly upset.

"Please, I don't know what to do. You have to come up on deck."

"What's wrong?"

Lady Em's hands fluttered in front of her like frightened birds. "It's Akiro. He's going to kill himself."

It was very hot. The fog drifted overhead. The ocean was very still.

The scene on deck was a collision of worlds. The ancient conflicted with the modern. Akiro was dressed in a traditional *gi,* a white cloth filled with Japanese characters tied around his forehead, sitting cross-legged on the tracks leading from the hold to the bombs, blocking Lysenko's way. Lysenko was hunched over, wearing a containment suit, a high-tech warrior ready to push the plutonium cart through him. Ancient and modern collided in other ways. The most destructive weapon science ever built sat twenty feet behind Akiro, but everyone was focused on the long knife in his lap. Both his hands were wrapped around the handle. The point touched his belly. His eyes were closed in meditation.

Lady Em made to run for Akiro, but Mori stopped her.

"Akiro!" she shouted. His face was impassive and resigned. He made no acknowledgment he even heard her.

"You must not interfere," Mori said. "It is tradition."

"Blast tradition," said Lady Em. "We can't let him die."

"We can't take his dignity either," Mori said. "You have spent much time together. Can you not understand why he is doing this?"

"Let me talk to him," she pleaded.

"If he chooses. He knows you are here."

Across the deck, Lysenko ripped off his suit helmet. "I'm dying in here," he shouted angrily. "I'll run this cart right over him if he doesn't move." But he wasn't talking to Akiro. Hiroki had extended the tableau further by thrusting himself between the two.

"This is radioactive plutonium," Lysenko said furiously. "Do you want to die? Get out of my way."

"Let him pass, Hiroki-san." It was Shuto.

"I cannot let your father be hurt."

"My father made his choice. You must, too. Stand aside."

"I cannot."

Mori and the other Japanese watched silently. Akiro was their father, Shuto their elder brother. Akiro had found all of them over the years, in clinics and hospitals, in sweatshops and factories, usually abandoned, often abused, and hid them in his museum. Shuto had protected them. The conflict between the two was tearing them apart.

"Shuto, this is the result when the body turns against itself. You ask me to choose between my heart and my strength. If I tear out my heart, I have no strength. And what good is strength without heart? Don't you see? Either way, we'll die."

"I beg you. Don't let it come to that."

"Shuto, my brother, you can change it. Heal the body. Forget revenge. Give Akiro his Light, and let us go home."

Shuto's only response was to slide to the deck cross-legged without ever moving his feet, duplicating Akiro's meditative posture. His hands rested on his knees, palms up. His eyes closed. He breathed in through his nose, out through his mouth. A moment later, Hiroki did the same. All three looked asleep. Lysenko took it as an opportunity to push the cart forward. The sound of the guards cocking their automatic weapons stopped him. Mori motioned him back.

Lysenko shook his head. "You're all crazy. I swear it."

"What are they doing?" Carla asked Mori.

"Meditating, to find answers," he said.

"How long will it take?" asked Carolyn.

Mori shrugged.

"Lady Em, why not go inside and wait," Bette advised. "It's so hot out here."

"I won't leave him."

Mori sent a man for a chair.

The tableau continued, the fog drifting overhead, the ocean very still.

33

ADMIRAL GARVER SENT BOOKBINDER THE RAW PRODUCT from the *Tuscany* debriefings. Bookbinder pored over it, hoping for a lead. The terrorists were Japanese, well trained and financed, heavily armed. Not members of any known group. Independents, all with some kind of genetic mutation caused by radiation, motive for them to stop the plutonium shipments by panicking the country with a nuclear blast. Unfortunately for Bookbinder, knowing when and why they took the *Korlov* didn't tell him where it was. He drew a circle on his map with a radius of how far the *Korlov* could sail since the switch had been made. It was still a vast area. He kept trying not to think about the odds of finding anything at all if the terrorists had airlifted the plutonium to a land base and scuttled the ship.

Satellite photos were spread out all over his desk. Word spread quickly, and several colleagues offered their help. He took it gladly. They brainstormed for hours, reworked satellite tracks, logged currents and tidal drifts, listed islands, the works. But two days after he had been summoned to Farley's office, Bookbinder didn't have anything to show for his work except a lot of pictures of empty ocean.

"It isn't anywhere," Bookbinder said, frustrated, to no one, because everyone else had gone home.

He rubbed his sleepy eyes. Getting a good night's sleep would have been good for him, but with his allergies, he was afraid to leave the ultra-air-conditioned NSA building. Try thinking with his sinuses packed to the brim. He'd stuck the satellite pictures on the wall to form a map of the sailing area, the South Pacific in miniature. It covered half the length of the room. He looked at it as he wandered around the office drinking coffee and eating his fourth sweet little cake from the lunchroom. His stomach felt like a vat of acid.

"Please tell me where the hell you are."

Maybe some kind of fortuitous accident would occur, like the cup of coffee that had started all this. Something mystical like throwing a dart and having it hit the exact right spot. He tried it with a sharp pencil, eyes closed. He broke a bud vase on one of the other analysts' desks. He tried it again, facing forward, eyes still closed, praying. Nothing but a lousy volcanic island. Well, they'd photographed the hell out of *every* island, on every wavelength in the spectrum. No *Korlov*.

The freighter was due in Japan in three days. The terrorists could logically expect a search to begin at that time. Bookbinder had to assume they were planning to set off their bomb before then.

Three days.

The acid feeling was spreading.

34

Sōfu gan

MACKENZIE COULD FEEL THE SCORCHING HEAT OF THE lava field fifty feet away. He was listless and mentally slow. It had been too long without sleep, and the ever-present heat and humidity were catching up with him. Like the others, he had sores on his arms that wouldn't heal in the damp air. They were all exhausted. The Commodore's lush silver hair was a dull gray tangle and he was stick-thin. Bernhardsen looked like a burn patient, with red blistery patches all over his skin.

"Can you make it?" MacKenzie asked the Commodore.

"Go on, Admiral. Let me fetch the water and be what help I can."

MacKenzie didn't know if Lord Rowe was going to make it off Sōfu gan a second time. He was beginning to wonder if any of them would. Heating the shaft in the lava field was working slowly. They'd cut down trees for a track to roll the shaft across the magma pit.

The wood burned away, leaving the shaft in place. When the steel glowed white-hot, they began to hammer it straight. It was brutal work. The air itself blistered their lungs. They had to change position frequently in a kind of hip-hop dance to keep their shoes from burning, despite using asbestos from the mining camp to pad their soles. It was impossible to work over the pit for long.

"My turn to hit," said Bernhardsen.

"You wash, I'll dry," murmured MacKenzie. His eyes were on fire. His skin was hot to the touch, feverish.

MacKenzie had three sets of the *Storm*'s oven mits on his hands, and an asbestos pad between the pry bar and his shoulder. The heat burned all the hairs off their arms, legs, and torsos. Their muscles were clearly defined on lean, toughened frames. He got his weight under the bar and shoved as hard as he could.

"Hold it," said Bernhardsen. He worked the shaft with the sledge. The metal rang in the boiling air. They had been at it for almost forty hours and they were groggy and short-tempered. Raskin and Rietti were repairing the diesels, waiting for them to finish the shaft. There were only two days left till the *Korlov* sailed for the explosion point, and they all knew it.

Mac hadn't gotten any response from the *Korlov* again last night. He tortured himself worrying. And with Justine missing, he couldn't count on any more delays.

"We're close, Mac." Sweat dripped off Bernhardsen's body and hissed into steam when it hit the rocks.

"I'm reaching my limit, Ivor."

"I can't take much more of this either."

Daylight was going fast. The rain forest shimmered

in the heat. They couldn't work in the dark. And they couldn't wait till morning.

"Let's get it this time," MacKenzie said.

He swung the heavy sledge. It didn't have to be pretty. It just had to be straight enough not to tear the hull apart.

"Paul Bunyan." MacKenzie felt the shock in his burning feet.

"Who?"

"American folklore . . . big guy. Cut down a lot of trees."

"Typical American," said Bernhardsen, changing position.

"Make it John Henry, then."

"Who's that?"

"Steel-drivin' man."

"Oh."

Bernhardsen took the sledge. More hammerblows rang out. The heat rose off the black rocks in waves.

"Ever hear of Thor? He'd make your Paul Bunyan and John Henry look sick." He hit the shaft over and over till it was almost a steady note.

"Honor's at stake." MacKenzie took the sledge and spit into his hands.

"Why did you do that?"

"I haven't the slightest idea. I saw it on television."

"Oh."

MacKenzie swung the sledge. There was a rhythm to it. A shock and a bounce as the sledge came off the steel. He felt loose and powerful.

"More," Bernhardsen said.

They might have been building a railroad across the country, two men poised on either side of the track, driving spikes. They pushed each other. Bernhardsen pounded the shaft till he had no more strength, then passed the sledge to Mac. When it seemed MacKenzie couldn't pick up the hammer one more time, Bernhardsen took it back. It ceased being a contest. They had one purpose, one goal.

The heat was a living thing to be taunted and fought off. For longer than they thought possible, they pounded the steel into submission. When at last exhaustion set in, and neither could do any more, MacKenzie measured it.

"That's it," he pronounced.

"I won't argue."

"Let's roll it off."

Moving three hundred pounds of white-hot steel almost broke them. Sparks flew.

"What's the difference between magma and lava?" MacKenzie asked.

"Push!"

"I am pushing. This takes my mind off how much I hurt."

"Magma's below the surface," Bernhardsen grunted. "As soon as it's aboveground, it's lava."

"I never knew that," MacKenzie admitted.

"I'll die satisfied."

They got the shaft over the jagged rocks. The Commodore was standing by with water from the nearby stream to cool it.

"Last one," said MacKenzie. "Together, now!"

The shaft rolled off the lava field. What followed was totally unexpected. The foliage burst into flames.

"More water!" MacKenzie was furious at himself. He should have realized the steel was hot enough to ignite anything it touched. He helped the Commodore and Bernhardsen throw water on the fire. It didn't help. It began to spread.

"We need a fire break," Bernhardsen yelled. "Start in the middle and work outward."

Rain forest trees are tall and thin. They felled enough to create a break. But MacKenzie didn't see the fire cross overhead by way of the vines till a blast of heat scorched him from behind. He was surrounded by flames. Exhausted, he wasn't thinking properly. His carelessness had created a murderous situation.

"Mac!"

Bernhardsen was up in a tree beyond the fire ring. He threw a tool with a line attached, and it wrapped around a branch over MacKenzie's head. The fire lapped at it. MacKenzie piled dead branches on the ground to make a mound.

"Set?" Bernhardsen yelled.

"Go!"

MacKenzie had been firing torpedoes for years. He knew how to lead a target. He got a running start from ten feet back and charged the mound as Bernhardsen swung the line down. MacKenzie leaped for it and momentum carried him up and over the wall of flames. He felt his legs sizzle, and then he was in clear air. The foliage was thick and forgiving. He came down in a tangle of brush and vines soft enough to prevent broken bones.

Behind him the jungle was still burning, but contained between the break and the lava field, it began to burn itself out.

"That's another one for the books, Ivor," MacKenzie said gratefully.

The Commodore rushed water to them. MacKenzie drank some and poured the rest over his head.

Bernhardsen drenched himself and sprawled on the ground.

"Just get me a three-inch-thick steak with onions and two gallons of champagne. Call room service."

"I'd settle for a decent bed," said the Commodore. "For my aching back."

"First, I'd . . . Hey, what are you doing?"

MacKenzie had Bernhardsen's computer across his lap. "I want to recheck the torpedo figures."

"Mine isn't working, remember?"

"Sorry, right. Did Tony take his?"

"I think so."

"Forget it, then. It's not important." MacKenzie lay down, too. "Wake me when Nikolai and Tony get here."

Raskin and Rietti arrived two hours later with the rain and good news. The evening meal was spiced up with some whiskey from the wardroom closet.

"We got the engine together," Raskin told them. "I think it will run, but to be honest, I would measure its life in hours. Ten, if we're lucky. Not more than that."

"Top speed?"

"Three knots. Maybe four."

MacKenzie grew thoughtful. "It'll have to be a daylight attack. Come around and get as close as we can, shoot. What about the torpedoes?"

"Of the *Storm*'s original sixteen," Rietti said, "four were left. We stripped one to blow the propeller. I checked the remaining three as best I could, replaced the oil, and charged the compressed-air tanks."

"Shouldn't we test one?" Bernhardsen asked. "If I remember right, there were a lot of duds in those days."

"Not as many as the Germans had," responded the

Commodore. "But admittedly, more than we would have liked."

"There's no way to test one unless we fire it," Rietti argued. "We have too few for that."

"We'll rig all three to fire in a salvo," MacKenzie said. "They'll either work or they won't. The only test the *Storm*'s going to get is in actual combat."

"I just want to remind you all that we have to get our wives off the ship first," said Bernhardsen. "Or am I the only one worrying about that?"

"Justine is ready to get them off," said MacKenzie. "She's waiting for our signal."

"Capital," said the Commodore.

"That's good enough for me," agreed Rietti.

MacKenzie hated to lie to them, but he couldn't tell them the truth, that concern for the women's safety had plagued him ever since he had lost contact with his wife. It wasn't the first time in his marriage he and Justine had been caught in a balancing act. He was a naval officer on a mission. He had to weigh his pregnant wife's life, and the lives of the other women, against the millions who might perish if Shuto were to succeed. He knew his duty and responsibility. He also knew his heart. Did any person, any number of people, matter more than Justine? He didn't want to answer that, didn't think he could.

"Time to go," he said.

They marched the shaft back and loaded it into the ore cart. It was raining. They crowded alongside. MacKenzie released the hand brake and they rolled down the tracks.

"Breeze feels good," said the Commodore.

"Simple pleasures." Rietti turned his face in to

the wind. "It seems like a long time since we had them."

"I just want to see Carla again."

"And Lady Emily."

It was a collective hurt. The loneliness of separation, the worry about their wives' safety. MacKenzie tried not to think of the sacrifice they might have to make.

Raskin sang a sad verse, in deep, guttural Russian. It seemed to blend with the clack-clack of the cart on the tracks, and the hot air suddenly turned cool. No one knew what the words meant, but MacKenzie heard his friend's grief for his lost wife, and felt his own longings. The Commodore looked haunted. Rietti's eyes brimmed. Even Bernhardsen grew quiet.

"Tell us what it means, Nikolai," said Rietti. "Can you?"

Raskin nodded. He spoke softly, just over the wind:

"I will never love you more than in the
early morning darkness, or be as lost
in the deep anguish, or treasure more the
simple faith that pulls me back from the cliff
and heals my empty, foolish, suffering wounds.

I will never love you more than in the
space before dawn. I cannot see your face.
Forced to stare, we expose what we believe.
What works when sense fails? Can we trust?
Can we trust?

I will never love you more than in the
tiny, worldless chamber of shadows.
Crumpled sheets deny nothing.

I remember. I remember. Creeping bodiless inside you, and feeling you return from the mist.

I will never love you more than by that ocean, in a place where there was no time."

No one spoke as they rolled down to the sea. The *Storm* was waiting.

35

Korlov

KELLER TOOK JUSTINE'S PULSE. SHE WAS QUITE PALE, TOO weak to awaken from her restive sleep. The drug would kill her soon. Too bad to waste such a beautiful woman, far better than Carolyn. But Justine didn't have the same tastes. He wondered why some women responded so well to obedience. Françoise, his nurse in Paris, and later his fiancée, was a prime example. She liked to be forced. Then she was like a cat in bed, supple and agile, fierce in her pleasures. Unfortunately, like the proverbial cat, curiosity had killer her, too.

Keller tightened the restraints. Justine's vulnerability sent a tingle across his scrotum. He let his soft hands roam her body. She was strong, almost masculine in the way she took control. He'd seen the way Carolyn looked up to Justine. It troubled him Carolyn was still fighting for this woman and her unborn child. His control wouldn't be complete till he had destroyed Justine.

He crooned to her in German, his first language. "Such a pretty tongue, eh, *liebchen?* We spoke it at home. I used to take Françoise to my mother's house in Paris. That's where she heard it. It made her curious. She had lost her father in the war. One day she searched the house and found my father's old SS papers. That was very bad of her, don't you think?"

Keller traced her lips. They were dry, but provocative. He wondered if he had the time to take her like this, bound and semiconscious.

"I'm telling you all this, *liebchen,* because in spite of being a remarkable woman, you won't last much longer. You'd sacrifice us all to stop Shuto. I won't let you sacrifice me. I let you think I was weak so you'd underestimate me. I am not weak. My father was a German SS colonel. My mother was an exemplar of the Hitler Youth. They met at a concentration camp. You're surprised? Why? People must meet somewhere. Mother was sent from Berlin to teach the Jewish prisoners to sew German flags. She was a sensitive girl. She made lovely little kerchiefs to welcome the people coming off the railroad cars so they wouldn't be alarmed by the armed men and guard dogs.

"My father was one of those who saw the end coming. He created a new identity for them as rich French Jews with money taken from the prisoners. The past was simply a family secret. Françoise was shocked. She wanted to expose us. But she was pregnant. And Father had died years before. What would be gained by ruining her child's family? She relented, but we could see she was hesitant. Mother told me what had to be done. At first I didn't want to. I loved Françoise."

Women were like boxes. You closed one, opened another, forgot about the first. "I put a drug in her wine that aborted the fetus. She bled to death on the living room floor while Mother and I were in the upstairs parlor. There was talk about the accident. After all, I was a doctor. We managed to cover it up, but it was prudent for me to leave the country for a while. Do you think I'd have been on the *Tuscany* if I didn't have to?"

Justine roused somewhat. "Phillip . . . ?"

"Thank you for reminding me, *liebchen.* Time for another shot. One more, later, then the long sleep."

Shuto had to believe she died from a complication of her pregnancy. She was close. Depleted, weakened, diabetic. It was truly ironic. Shuto protected Justine, unaware she was responsible for every death and delay he had suffered. Even a mutant's love was blind.

Justine moaned more throatily. "Phillip . . . itch . . . bad."

"Tell me where."

"Between . . ."

"Here?" No response, but she was squirming so nicely. "Maybe you should scratch it yourself, *liebchen.*"

He untied one wrist. Her muscle control returned slowly. She had been restrained for almost three days. Her hand moved to her hair.

"Liebchen, scratch *all* the places—"

Justine struck with all her strength, hitting the nerve bundle behind the jaw with the *pesas.* Keller's eyes went blank and he crashed to the floor.

"Scratch *that, liebchen,"* she said savagely.

She undid the restraints and got herself up. Thank God for Carla and Bette. She was shaky, but she had to find out what was happening. Mac would be beside himself after three days of not hearing from her. She tied Keller's wrists and ankles. He was a real bastard, all right. He'd pay for what he'd done, too. She'd see to it. Psychopaths were always so clever. That poor girl. She felt for her own baby. Had it been hurt? She slammed the *pesas* into Keller's knee. Even though he was unconscious, it tore an agonized moan from his lips. She breathed a little easier. It wasn't good procedure to lose control like this.

"Sue me for excessive force," she said, and went to find the others.

Shuto rose from the lotus position. Almost four hours had passed. It was dusk. The red color again suffused the fog. There was no breeze. The entire ship's company was on deck, waiting, a ship of ghosts hoping to be set free. Kiri walked around dropping food over the side and conducting increasingly shrill shark scoldings. Ivan refused to leave the tent, and Carolyn had to monitor the frequent sedatives he needed. Lysenko was working on the last settings alone, crumpling calculations and throwing them away like a frustrated child. Carla and Bette stood beside Lady Em, separated from Akiro by Mori and the rest of the Japanese.

Hiroki's eyes fluttered open, somehow in tune with Shuto. A silent understanding seemed to settle over both, terrible and sad. Hiroki bowed, and moved into fighting position.

"Hear this first, Hiroki. Akiro-san!" Shuto called.

Akiro's face was bloodless, his breathing shallow. He was somewhere between life and death, not belonging to either.

"What is it, Shuto?"

"I want you to tell them the truth."

Akiro said softly, "I'm an old man. Who knows the truth anymore? What I wanted, even that seems vanity now."

"All dreams are vain, Father. Tell them about me. It may save Hiroki's life."

"I don't know what you mean."

"Yes, you do, Akiro-san. Tell them you aren't my father."

"It's not true!"

"Don't dishonor yourself further by continuing the lie. I always knew. My mother told me, though you swore her not to."

Akiro seemed to shrink inside himself.

"But we grew up together," Hiroki said, confused.

"It was before you came," said Shuto. "Tell him, Akiro-san!"

The knife quivered in Akiro's hands. The point never moved from his belly. For a moment it appeared he might use it.

"It was so long ago. What can any of you know about it? My fiancée died that day in Hiroshima. The light that took her eyes, took her life. I wandered in the city, lost. We tended to the dead and dying and created the Museum for the reasons you know. But Shuto is telling the truth. He is not my son. I found him later, in a hospital where the first mutated babies were born, and adopted him."

"Tell him what I could have been, *Father.*" The word was venomous on his lips. "Tell him!"

Akiro bowed his head. "You all know how he suffered. He did not have to. The doctors wanted to try plastic surgery. I refused to let them. I told myself it was a very new art. It often made conditions worse. Instead, I took him and his mother into my home, married her, and raised him as my son."

Shuto's resentment boiled over. "He *used* me, Hiroki. He didn't hide me, or protect me, or even cure me. He thrust me out to be hurt and abused so he could sell my pain as his own. I was living proof of the need for the Museum. I was an example for the cause. And if I was maimed and crippled in the process, it only made the great Akiro more noble. I didn't matter. He sacrificed me willingly. He had his truth. He had his dream. I was never his son. I was his *advertisement.*"

"What about Ito and me? And the rest?"

"He did the same to you, just without the lie."

Hiroki's face was grave. "Akiro?"

"Hiroki, I was young. I thought our goals were worth the sacrifice. When you're young, you do. Would you have preferred the mine? Or Ito, the factory? Or any of you where I found you? I gave you something to believe in. Something to fight for. As *I* fought!" His voice was stronger. *"You* are the Museum. They will remember you for generations to come."

Hiroki bowed his head. "I don't know what to say."

"Shuto, I take your hatred to the grave. Accept that as my punishment. Don't make the world pay for what I did."

Shuto might have been listening to the wind for all it moved him. His face was like stone.

Justine heard it all. Her seeds of destruction had borne fruit. She forced herself to stay to see the ending. Her joints were stiff and sore. Her sweat didn't evaporate in the still, humid air.

Lady Em was crying. Carla put an arm around her frail shoulders for comfort. Justine came up behind them.

Bette exclaimed, "You're all right."

"You and Carla saved my life."

"I was so worried."

"Where's Phillip?" asked Lady Em.

"Tied up in the infirmary. How long has this been going on?"

Bette told her about the past three days.

"What do we do now?" asked Carla.

"Wait and see. Lady Em, are you okay?"

"We did this," she said bitterly. "I take no pleasure in it."

"We didn't do it for pleasure. We did it to stop them. Our husbands are still on the island. And those bombs are capable of killing millions. No one's safe yet."

The elderly woman drew herself straighter. "You're right, of course."

Justine said in a kinder voice, "For what it's worth, I'm sorry."

"Thank you for that, my dear."

"They're starting again," said Bette.

Across the deck, Shuto said, "Hiroki, stand aside."

The bomb tent and bridge bounded their arena. Alongside the *Korlov,* the sea was steel gray.

"I've followed you all my life, Shuto. But Akiro is right. It must end here." He bowed and dropped into cat stance, his weight on his back leg, his front foot ready to strike. His expression was unreadable.

Shuto flowed forward. There was an exchange of blows almost too quick to follow. Justine was glad she was there to witness it. She had never seen anyone so fast. Hiroki threw a front kick to Shuto's midsection, and at the last minute changed its direction into a roundhouse kick to his head. It would have brought down most men, but Shuto blocked it and hit Hiroki in the stomach. Hiroki was tough. He took it with a deep grunt and grabbed Shuto's wrist and twisted. Shuto broke his grip and launched a back-fist to Hiroki's head. Hiroki blocked it and drove his knee towards Shuto's groin. Shuto blocked it and flowed away.

They circled warily, hesitant. These were brothers, fighting each other for the first time in their lives. They both knew it was to the death. Reconciliation wasn't possible. Hiroki had to kill Shuto to save Akiro. Shuto had to kill Hiroki to have his revenge. Hiroki attacked when Shuto came into range of his powerful arms. Shuto reacted too quickly and spun inside Hiroki's grip, driving an elbow into Hiroki's ribs. Hiroki winced in pain, but managed to catch Shuto with a knife-hand to Shuto's neck before he was out of range. The force was incredible, but Shuto slid away. He threw a punch at Hiroki's head. Hiroki fell for the feint and brought his hands up. It enabled Shuto to drive a side-kick into Hiroki's already damaged ribs, emptying Hiroki's breath out of him like a burst paper bag. A broken rib might have punctured his lung. He staggered back. Shuto drove in hard with combination kicks to his head and face. Blood spurted from Hiroki's nose. He tried to block the onslaught. Shuto pursued him.

Hiroki was like a wounded bear, huge and ferocious, snarling with rage, but Shuto had been faster and stronger all his life. Hiroki held off Shuto's steady advance as best he could, blocking and moving, trying not to take the full force of the blows. Shuto was a perfect fighter, no excess energy, not a wasted motion. Justine watched enviously a level of skill she would never have. But Hiroki was smarter than she gave him credit for. All the while he was taking Shuto's punishment, he had a plan of his own. He couldn't outfight Shuto, so he did the one thing Shuto never expected of him. Hiroki tried to outthink him.

Hiroki let his arms drop, exposing his neck. It looked perfectly natural after all the punishment. His face was bleeding heavily. The pain from his ribs must have been excruciating. Shuto dove in with a chop. That's when Hiroki made his play. He caught Shuto's descending arm, locked on to his wrist, and pulled it down sharply. Shuto was caught off guard. Momentum carried him forward, off balance. Hiroki executed a hip throw and Shuto hit the deck hard, stunned. Hiroki hit him squarely below the abdomen, seemingly knowing just where he was aiming. Shuto writhed in pain. Justine caught her breath. It was suddenly possible for Hiroki to finish Shuto, something she wouldn't have thought possible when they started. Do it! she wanted to scream. End it here and now! Shuto was exposed for a killing blow. But as Hiroki raised his hand to deliver it, their eyes met, and Shuto said something. Hiroki hesitated.

The edge of Shuto's hand sliced across Hiroki's throat, crushing his windpipe. Hiroki reared up, unable to breathe, clutching at his neck. He clawed the air wildly. A high, hoarse wheeze came from his torn throat. He was dying even as he staggered across the deck. He hit the gunwale and tumbled over the side. A cry of pain and betrayal followed him. There was a wet, roiling, thrashing sound. Justine didn't need to look over the side to know the sharks still swam here.

Shuto turned to Akiro, grief-stricken, hoping for

solace, but the old man had cheated him of that, too. Akiro's *gi* was blood-soaked from the ceremonial cut across his stomach. His head lolled against his chest. He had departed from Shuto the same way he had raised him, leaving him to fend for himself.

Justine was torn. It would have been over if Hiroki had won, but she felt oddly relieved. It bothered her. How could she still have feelings for Shuto? Maybe after the likes of Keller, she could pity the man. In his own way, he was as much a victim as anyone. Mori let her go to him.

"Are you hurt?" she asked.

"I will heal."

"Death follows you, Shuto. Stop it now," she said.

It began to rain. Lady Em was helping Mori settle Akiro to the deck and cover him. She was crying. Carolyn was nowhere to be seen.

"I have lost a father and two brothers," Shuto said, watching them bear his father away. "Who will cry for me, I wonder?"

"I will," Justine said. "But I'll hate you, too. For not stopping it."

"I'll settle for that."

He turned to go. She grabbed his arm.

"What did you say to Hiroki? Why did he hesitate?"

"I said, please. He had never heard me say it before."

Justine shook her head. "You don't believe that stopped him, do you? He *let* you kill him."

Shuto shrugged. "Our ends will be the same. The family Akiro created, its purpose. Look what we have become. He who wins is the last to die."

Lysenko came up and stuck his face in Shuto's.

"If this tiring display of familial affection is over,

I'd like to get back to work. We can be done by tomorrow if there aren't any more interruptions."

Shuto took Lysenko's shirt in his hand and yanked him close. For a second, Justine thought he was going to kill the Russian. Instead, he lifted him effortlessly and held him over the side. Sharks thrashed in the water below.

"For God's sake, Shuto! Stop!" Lysenko cried.

"Finish it," Shuto said bleakly, and thrust the man away so hard, he did a stumbling run back to the tent.

Justine felt so faint, she would have slid to the deck, but Shuto lifted her and carried her to a chair. The women came over, concerned, but he waved them back.

"Are you all right?" he asked.

"No."

"What is it?"

"It's the baby . . . you . . . this ship . . . I can't *fight* anymore."

Rain coursed down her face and blended with her tears. She was furious with herself for her weakness, crying to the man she had secretly fought since he took over the ship. She had betrayed him just like everyone else had, even killed his family. Now she was asking him for comfort. She couldn't remember what was right and wrong anymore, what her commitments were. The baby. Loyalty to Mac. Stopping Shuto. Sick and depleted, she had nothing left to fight with. It was suddenly all too much and she burst into tears, crying with deep, wracking sobs.

He held her till it subsided. Awkwardly at first, then with compassion. Finally she broke away.

"I can't stand myself!"

He said nothing.

She sniffled. "I'm sorry."

"Don't be."

She saw something change in his eyes. She wiped her nose and looked at him curiously. "What is it?"

He held out his wet hands. "Your tears. Holding you when you cried. No one ever . . . ever asked that of me before. On the day I had to kill my brother, it means more to me than you can imagine."

"It can't," she said miserably.

"It does."

"You don't know anything about me."

He touched her belly. She froze, but he was the gentle Shuto again. He placed both hands on her, palms down, and felt for the life inside her. He searched as the Old Ones had shown him. There. A pulse beat. Tentative. Growing. Alive, but . . . He had no gift to repay this woman for letting him feel what it was like to be a normal man, even for so short a time, so he gave what he could to her child.

"What do you feel?" she asked.

A miracle, he wanted to say. Something forever denied him. He broke the contact before the child could feel his bitterness. It was no way to start life. He of all people knew.

"What did you do?" she asked.

He lifted her. "Nothing you didn't deserve. I have learned much from you, Justine."

"I am not your friend, Shuto." It was as close as she could come to the truth.

"You have no idea what you are to me," he said simply.

Her confusion was paralyzing her. He was her enemy, she had to remember that. Yet her compassion for him was real.

"Shuto, I'll die if I don't get off this ship," she begged him unashamedly. "The baby, too. Let me

288

take the others and go." She leaned against him to stand. Her vision was dark at the edges.

He motioned Carla and Bette to help her. Justine watched him go. The women helped her on the slippery deck.

"Get me to the infirmary," Justine told them.

"Hang on, honey," Carla urged.

They made it before Carolyn did, but not by a big enough margin. Keller was lying on the floor, bound and gagged, making angry noises when the door flew open and Carolyn rushed in. She shielded him protectively.

"I saw you on deck. What did you do to him?"

"He's still alive," Justine said coldly. "You know what he planned for me."

"He kept you from hurting us."

"Wake up, Carolyn. Look at yourself. He's using you."

Carolyn pulled off Keller's gag.

"Carolyn, thank God. These horrible women trapped me. My leg's broken!"

Carolyn pointed an accusing finger at Justine. "You always had it in for us. You're jealous. Let us go or I'll tell Shuto all about your little games."

Bette blocked the infirmary door. "We won't let you."

Carla said, "Ask your lover how he examined me. I still have his paw prints on me."

"She's lying," Keller swore.

"You threw yourself at him," Carolyn said defensively. "That sexy body. Always strutting around. I saw you on the *Tuscany.*"

"I never—"

"Stop it, Carla," said Justine. "It's nonsense."

"Consider this, my dear," Lady Em implored Carolyn. "You knew what he was doing to Justine. You didn't even try to stop him. That's what he's done to you."

"I don't care. Leave me alone. I can't think anymore."

Justine had no strength to argue. Carolyn had chosen. The *pesas* flashed out and Carolyn fell on top of Keller. He started to yell. Justine shoved the gag back in his mouth.

"Tie and gag her too," she ordered.

"Neat trick, that," said Carla appreciatively.

"Where do we put them?" Bette asked.

"There's a storage room down the corridor. Can you manage it yourselves?" She felt the dizziness again.

"Sure. Then you've got to eat something," Bette insisted.

Justine lay down. Lady Em mopped her forehead.

One day left.

PART FIVE

Storm Ahead

36

Sōfu gan

It took till nighttime for MacKenzie and Rietti to finish wiring a circuit to fire the torpedoes from the *Storm*'s bridge. The fog was patchy. Moonlight made shadows move along the hull. Mac couldn't help thinking that if all went well, it was their last night on Sōfu gan. None too soon. They were at the limit of their endurance, tense and shaky. Even Niigata Yakeyama was rumbling uneasily.

"The circuit looks good, Tony."

"It should work. But how do you aim this thing?"

"The angle on the bow matches the angle in the tubes. The torpedoes go the way the sub is pointed."

"Sounds primitive."

"'Elegantly simple' might be a better description. Any change with you and Ivor?"

Rietti shook his head. "He told me he still expects me to go on the expedition, assuming we get out of here. I told him I still wouldn't, and that was it again."

"It means a lot to him."

"It doesn't mean as much to me," Rietti said. "Look, I'm done with the wiring. The red button arms the circuit. The green one fires the torpedoes."

"Thanks. Go down and help the Commodore. And, Tony?"

"Yes?"

"Every man has to know his limits."

"Sure, Mac. Thanks."

MacKenzie blew into the voice tube. "Nikolai, stand by to answer bells on main engine."

A cloud spurted back out the tube. "First I've got to get the dust out of my eyes."

"Sorry."

The shaft was back in place and the propeller and dunce cap secured. It seemed a good fit, but there was only one way to know. One by one they cut the cables tethering the bow to the ore carts and returned the *Storm* to trim. Bernhardsen and Rietti completed work on the steering. Raskin and the Commodore were ready to try the engine on his command.

The lights strung over the pier showed *Storm*'s rough, pitted hull. Phosphorescent water lapped at her saddle tanks. Tendrils of fog wafted by. It was a fine night for a ghost ship.

"Once more, old girl," MacKenzie whispered, looking down her gray length. "You can do it."

"Ready for testing," came Raskin's voice through the tube. He sounded like an old gramophone record.

"Start number two engine," MacKenzie ordered. "Nice and easy, Nikolai."

The engine started roughly, and stalled. Nikolai would be pumping more oil. MacKenzie crossed his fingers. After a moment, another few turns. And another stall.

"Come on, Nikolai . . ."

Suddenly the big diesel kicked into life, caught, held, and kept running. The hull began to shake, and acrid exhaust poured out of the aft escape tube. A strong wind blew into the ship through the conning tower hatches as the powerful diesel sucked air in to feed on. The *Storm* vibrated with power, alive again. Mac pounded the railing with joy. The others were cheering. It was the lift they needed.

"Peter, it's working!" came Raskin's beaming voice. "Should we test the shaft?"

"Better know now. Make minimum turns."

He heard the change in pitch as soon as Raskin engaged the clutch. The shaft was turning unevenly. The deck underfoot began to vibrate like a buzzsaw. When the propeller bit into the water, the entire boat shuddered. At first MacKenzie thought the boat couldn't stand the stress, but it steadied down. The *Storm* strained forward under its own power for the first time in fifty years.

Raskin's teeth sounded like they were chattering. "I don't know how long she can take this vibration. Or I can. But we're making turns as ordered, Captain."

"Secure the engine, Nikolai. My compliments."

MacKenzie looked at himself. The captain of a fifty-year-old sub, and his uniform was a torn T-shirt and filthy shorts. He'd lost enough weight to be able to count his ribs. His face had a thick growth of beard and his hair was wildly unkempt.

Bernhardsen called up. "Mac, we've got the torpedoes loaded. The Commodore wants you to check the settings."

"I'm coming," he said, and went below.

* * *

An hour later, MacKenzie drew Raskin aside in engineering.

"I'm going across the island with Tony. Take Ivor and the Commodore back to the camp and don't let them near the boat. Especially the Commodore."

"Why?"

MacKenzie told him about the W/T, and finding Lieutenant Bolliver's body.

"I can't believe it," Raskin said, the implications setting in. "It changes everything."

"If he's going to make another try at sabotage, it'll have to be tonight."

"I understand, Peter. I'll watch him."

MacKenzie put a hand on his friend's shoulder. "The *Storm* owes you a lot, Nikolai."

"Is it perverse to say I'm almost sorry we're finished?"

"No. You feel alone again."

"And worried. Will she work, or have I failed her like I did Irina?"

"She'll work. She has to," Mac declared.

"I will try to believe."

"Good. I'll be back in a couple of hours."

MacKenzie and Rietti headed across the island. The elation that energized them was soon replaced by crushing fatigue.

"Does the lava field seemed hotter?" he asked Rietti.

"It's possible. There's been a lot of rumbling these past two days. With volcanoes, you never know."

"Do you miss your work?" MacKenzie asked.

"More than anything except Bette. But like you say. A man has his limits."

"That's not what I said."

"Excuse me?"

"I said a man has to *know* his limits."

"What's the difference?"

"We'll talk about it later." MacKenzie heard the surf ahead. He got the flashlight and went to the beach. They built the fire. He said his nightly prayer and waited.

"Look," Rietti pointed. "There."

Sure enough, a light flashed from the *Korlov*.

I'm okay.

MacKenzie's heart soared.

She was hurting, he could see that even before she told him. Her hand was unsteady, she made mistakes. She reported her physical and emotional condition as a fact, something he had to know to plan effectively. That didn't make it any easier on his feelings. He understood the significance of Akiro's death and the loss of Hiroki. Shuto was unopposed. The bombs were almost ready. There was nothing more she could do to delay Lysenko except a suicide play. Shuto was sailing tomorrow. Would Mac be able to attack?

He told her the *Storm* was ready. He would wait till she got the women off the ship, but he couldn't wait longer than two hours before darkness. He had no radar or sonar. He had to have light. If she and the other women weren't off the ship by then, he had no choice but to attack. He didn't want to ask if she had taken the pills, if that was why she'd been gone for three days.

We love you, she sent, and signed off.

We.

MacKenzie doused the fire and headed back across the island for what he hoped was the final time.

37

Sōfu gan

MacKenzie knew something was wrong as soon as they reached the mining camp. The bunkhouse was dark and seemingly deserted.

"Could they be at the *Storm*?" Rietti wondered.

"No, I told—"

"Mac, over there! Nikolai's hurt."

Raskin was sprawled on a bunk. There was a wicked gash on his head. MacKenzie covered him. Rietti lit a lantern and checked his vital signs.

"He's lost some blood, but his pulse is strong. He'll make it," he said, dressing the wound.

MacKenzie was angry at himself. "I shouldn't have left him."

"But Ivor and the Commodore were here."

"Exactly."

"I don't understand, Mac. Where are they?"

"I think I know. Stay with Nikolai."

"No, I'm coming with you."

MacKenzie was filled with foreboding as they raced

down to the *Storm*. Ivor Bernhardsen was lying unconscious on the pier.

Rietti seemed frozen. "Is he?"

MacKenzie turned him over. "He's breathing."

Bernhardsen was still alive, but his shirt was soaked with blood seeping from a hole in his chest. Red froth bubbled from his lips.

"Mac," he gasped.

"Easy now. Don't talk."

Rietti tore open Bernhardsen's shirt. "We have to stop the bleeding. Hang on, Ivor."

Mac was wadding the torn shirt over the bullet hole when a sudden sharp voice commanded his attention.

"Get away from him, Admiral. You, too, Dr. Rietti."

Commodore Rowe was pointing an old English Webley .38-caliber pistol from the *Storm*'s armory at them. His face was hard, and there was a determination in him that MacKenzie hadn't seen before.

"Get away from him," the Commodore repeated.

"He'll die if we don't help him."

The Commodore's voice was cold. "He deserves to die. He tried to sink the *Storm*. I got my gun from my cabin when he went into the boathouse. I didn't want to shoot him, but he gave me no choice."

"Sink the *Storm*?" Rietti exclaimed. "Why would Ivor do such a thing?"

"I don't know. But take a look."

MacKenzie realized sickly there were several blocks of CVX explosive from the mine taped to the hull. Wires led from the generator in the boathouse to a firing switch on the pier. It would have blown her wide open.

"I caught him," said the Commodore. "He damaged the engine, too."

"Wasn't . . . me," Bernhardsen gasped. "Him . . ."

"Absurd on the face of it," said the Commodore. "Why would I want to sink my own ship?"

MacKenzie knew why, but he wasn't going to say it. He had to get the pistol away from the Commodore.

"Tell me what happened," he said.

"Ivor found a bottle of the *Storm*'s whiskey. He and Captain Raskin drank heavily. I turned in, but after the day's events, I couldn't sleep. For a while I watched Dr. Bernhardsen fixing his computer. Then I heard a noise and saw him leave. An hour later he still wasn't back. I went to rouse Captain Raskin. That's when I saw his head wound. I went out looking for Ivor and found him here, sabotaging the *Storm*."

"He's lying." Bernhardsen managed to prop himself up to a sitting position. "He did it all. He shot me when I tried to stop him."

"Give me the gun, Commodore," MacKenzie said.

The Commodore shook his head. "This is war, Admiral."

"What are you going to do?"

"He's a dangerous man. I plan to execute him."

MacKenzie held out his hand. "That's my decision. Give me the gun."

"The *Storm* is still my command."

"And he wouldn't be the first man to die on her to cover up your mistakes, would he?" MacKenzie wanted to shake him. "That was Lieutenant Bolliver."

The Commodore's eyes grew wide.

"What are you talking about?" demanded Rietti.

"Tell him, Commodore."

The Commodore's voice wavered. "It has nothing to do with this."

"You've lied to us all along. You've lied for over fifty years." MacKenzie stepped in front of him, shielding Bernhardsen. "Give me the gun."

The Commodore looked shocked. "You believe him?"

"Once more I'm going to ask you—" MacKenzie began.

"Mac!" yelled Rietti.

MacKenzie was hit hard from behind and he went sprawling into the Commodore, knocking the gun from his hand even as it went off with a crackling blast. Mac managed to get the gun and point it at the Commodore, sure he had the right of it.

"You don't understand!" protested the Commodore. "Help Tony!"

Rietti cried out. Confused, MacKenzie spun around to see Rietti on his knees bleeding profusely, his face contorted with pain. Bernhardsen was standing over him, pulling a long needle out of Rietti's arm. He raised it to drive it in again. Understanding hit MacKenzie. Rietti hadn't been warning him about the Commodore at all, he'd been warning him about Bernhardsen!

MacKenzie fired. Bernhardsen sagged and fell to the planks. He thought the Norwegian was finished. He should have remembered Bernhardsen's tenacity. In a last effort, Bernhardsen grabbed the firing switch and pressed it before Rietti could knock it out of his hands.

MacKenzie leaped across the water to the *Storm.* He wasn't about to lose her now. The detonators had to be set for specific times or number of turns. He was betting Bernhardsen hadn't known how to short out that circuit as MacKenzie had done to blow the prop.

He had maybe twenty seconds. He counted them in his head as he clambered past the sail and almost fell, but he grabbed the holes on top of the saddle tanks to stop his slide. He tore the CVX charges away and threw them as far as he could. They exploded in the sea not fifty feet from them, sending a geyser of water over the sub.

"Quickly, man," called the Commodore. "Tony needs help."

MacKenzie felt like the world was spinning around him. How could it have been Bernhardsen?

"Commodore, I don't understand. I thought—"

"We'll discuss that later. You know how to apply a tourniquet?"

"Yes."

"Do it. Tony saved your life. Hurry. He's going into shock. I'll be back."

MacKenzie worked on Rietti's arm. The Commodore came back with a cup of *Storm*'s rum and held it to Rietti's lips. Rietti coughed and spluttered, but it brought his color back.

"Take it easy. You're going to be okay," MacKenzie said.

"My arm hurts."

The Commodore showed him the needle. "It should."

"I thought Ivor couldn't even walk," Rietti said. "Then he had that thing in his hand and he was going for your back. I got between you and he stabbed me."

MacKenzie picked up the awl. "One of the *Korlov*'s tools. It was supposed to be in the buoy."

Bernhardsen's strained voice behind them said, "I took it to stop you."

"Help me over to him, please," Rietti asked.

Bernhardsen lay in a pool of blood. He was dying.

Rietti knelt by him. "Why, Ivor? What's going on?"

"Tony . . . I needed money . . . for the expedition. No one else would . . . but Shuto."

"Shuto!?"

"I went everywhere for money after Peru. Shuto heard. He came . . . asked about the Magnus Field. I figured out what he wanted. I knew it wouldn't work. I told him it would . . . even agreed to help . . . to get the money."

"Why did you take us on board the *Tuscany*?"

"Shuto wanted us close till it was over . . . then we were free."

MacKenzie appreciated Akiro and Shuto's planning again. Knowing you were going to put the hostages on the island, what better move than to have Bernhardsen for a spy among them?

"Did you report to him about us?" MacKenzie demanded.

"Had to . . . He threatened the women."

"How?"

Bernhardsen's face was ashen white. "Computer battery compartment . . ."

MacKenzie opened it. No wonder it hadn't worked. There was a ship-to-shore transmitter where the battery should have been. The sight of it hit MacKenzie hard.

"Then Shuto knows about the *Storm*."

Bernhardsen nodded. "Shuto told me I had to be ready to kill you if you became a threat. So I took the awl . . . Then we found the *Storm*. He told me to sink it instead. Tried the other day."

"Did you tell him what Justine and the women were doing?"

Bernhardsen rallied, pained. "Never. I swear . . . Said we signaled just to . . . to let wives know we were all right . . . Would never hurt Carla . . . She doesn't know."

There were tears in Rietti's eyes. "You could have come to me."

Bernhardsen shook his head. "Lost you, Tony . . . New expedition would have made it right . . . If it matters, I didn't want to hurt you. You either, Mac."

Bernhardsen was fading fast.

"Listen to me, Ivor. You've got one chance to make up for this." MacKenzie handed him the transmitter. "Tell Shuto you sank the *Storm*. Tell him!"

For a moment he thought the Norwegian was gone. Then Bernhardsen stirred and he took the transmitter. His hand shook as he punched in a number and hit SEND.

"Yes?"

MacKenzie recognized Shuto's voice.

"The sub's gone." By a supreme effort of control, Bernhardsen's voice was steady.

"I will release the women. Good-bye, Dr. Bernhardsen. Good luck on your expedition."

The connection broke with a hiss of static. MacKenzie replaced the transmitter.

When he looked back, Bernhardsen's eyes were dull and lifeless. He was dead.

They cut wood for a funeral pyre and brought Bernhardsen to the lava field. It was time and energy they could scarcely afford, but Rietti insisted.

Raskin was pale and subdued.

"I'm responsible for this," he said to MacKenzie as they worked.

"He fooled all of us, Nikolai."

"Still, if I hadn't drank so much."

"Bernhardsen was smart. He would have found some way to get to the *Storm.*" Raskin started to protest, but MacKenzie cut it off. "Don't start the I'm-not-the-man-I-was speech. None of us are. I need you, Nikolai. I can't do this without you. And I have to. You understand?"

"I'll just fail you like I failed Irina."

"You didn't fail Irina. Cancer killed her."

"It doesn't feel like that."

"To hell with what you feel," MacKenzie said furiously. There comes a time feelings don't matter a damn. My problems, your problems. We have to put a hold on them, don't you see? Too much depends on it."

"Admiral?"

"Yes, Tony?"

"We're ready."

"Coming." MacKenzie turned to Raskin. "You're getting another chance, Nikolai. Take it. Give me the *Storm* and one good engine for ten hours. I know that boat. She wants to do it. She wants *you* to do it. Don't give up now."

"I'll try. Ten hours. For that much I will try."

They put branches across the magma pit and lay Bernhardsen's body on top. Rietti spoke quietly.

"I don't know why Ivor did what he did. Only that he always thought he knew what was right. Maybe that blinded him. Or maybe those people dying hurt him more than I knew and he had to make up for it somehow. Anyway, I was his friend, so I ask You to forgive him. I hope he made up for things by doing right in the end."

The wood began to burn and flames engulfed the

body. Within minutes it tumbled into the pit. There was a final burst of flame.

Niigata Yakeyama rumbled fiercely. It had lost one of its own.

It was dawn when they got back to the *Storm*. The fog was changing color again with the rising sun. MacKenzie felt a mounting sense of fear and loss. Bernhardsen had done considerable damage. He'd stripped one of their three torpedoes to make his]bomb, and he hedged his bet by damaging the diesel. Raskin didn't know if he could get the *Storm* back in working order before the *Korlov* sailed.

The Commodore found him on the pier.

"May I speak to you, Admiral?"

"Of course, Commodore."

"How is the work going?"

"Slowly. Bernhardsen was thorough."

There was silence between them for a while, but each knew what the other was thinking.

"When did you find out about me?" the Commodore asked.

"I realized the sail damage and the SOS were out of order. Later, I searched the *Storm* and found Bolliver's body. That's why I didn't believe you about Bernhardsen. I figured you were the one with reason to sink her."

"I thought about it," admitted the Commodore. "But I couldn't let my personal problems jeopardize our mission."

"I should have known that. I'm sorry."

"Dash it all, man, what else could you have thought?"

MacKenzie remembered Bernhardsen saving his life at the lava field, only to be desperate enough to try to take it hours later. Who knew what motivated anyone? Their reflections shimmered in the water, dissolving and re-forming like the mists of time.

"Do you want to know what happened that night fifty years ago?" asked the Commodore.

"Yes, I do."

"I froze." It was a terrible admission. The Commodore twisted his hands together savagely. "I believe to this day I would have been able to command if I'd just had time, but I'll never know. With all those ships approaching, and the odds against us, it was just too much." His voice was filled with self-contempt. "I ran to my cabin to collect myself. Bolliver followed me. I ordered him back to his station and told him to dive out of harm's way. I thought in a few minutes I'd be back in control. He refused. He called me a coward. God knows, I was frightened enough. Again I ordered him to dive. He still refused. It was mutiny, during wartime. I would have been within my rights to shoot him. But the destroyer was bearing down on us and we had to do something. There were forty-eight men's lives to be thought of."

"What happened?"

"Instead of diving, Bolliver assumed command, and I let him. Sadly, happily—I don't really know which after all these years—he was brilliant. He took risks no prudent commander would ever countenance, but Providence was on his side that night. He made a down-the-throat shot against the destroyer bearing down on us and caught it napping. Blew it to pieces. He came around under her smoke and put a salvo of torpedoes into the battleship and dove right under the burning hull. The explosion almost shook us apart, but when we surfaced amidst all that smoke and fire, we had a perfect shot at a tanker. He fired and sank her. The Oerlikon gun accounted for another kill. Of course, we were taking terrific punishment. You saw with your own eyes what the depth charges did. I don't know what kept our engines running. No one had ever put on a fight like this. It was mad, almost insane, but Bolliver pulled it off."

Ten feet away, the *Storm* bore silent witness. The Commodore was almost talking to himself, pleading a case to his conscience. MacKenzie suspected he had done so countless times over the years.

"There comes a time when it is militarily unwise to continue the fight, and we had reached it. A commanding officer is required not to throw men's lives away needlessly. *Tarquin* and *Tern* were already down. Our batteries were depleted, the diesels were shot. There were three destroyers on us, all depth-charging. Two of my men drowned when pipes burst, then two more. Bolliver was mad. We were finished, but he kept issuing orders, kept maneuvering to attack. My head had cleared by then. I knew I had no choice. We were doomed with Bolliver in command. I had to save my boat and my crew. I ordered Bolliver to stand down. He refused. I got my revolver from the armory and forced him into the W/T room. He refused again and ordered me aside. I had no choice but to shoot him. I left him there and went to take evasive action. I sent an SOS over the W/T. There was so much noise in the area, we were able to dive and sneak away. I suppose you saw the damage to the sail. We were caught by one of the destroyer screws as we dove. The W/T operator was killed. It almost finished us. I had to take her back up to the surface."

"What happened to Bolliver?"

"I put him in my cabin and gave him the best medical attention I could under the circumstances, but he was dying. I was tormented. A squall had moved in. I couldn't risk diving with all that damage; we might not be able to surface again. We were in danger of capsizing. I managed to bring us here and got the crew out. I couldn't leave the boat on the surface for enemy planes to spot. I had to scuttle her."

"Along with Bolliver," said MacKenzie softly.

"Don't you think I knew that? I was burying the evidence of my weakness. My inability to command. The terrible embarrassment of it all. My second officer had been killed, as well as the W/T operator who had seen the gun. The only other men on the bridge during the engagement had serious wounds and probably wouldn't make it. Bolliver and I had been alone in my cabin when he removed me from command, and he would be entombed with my boat. Who was to say what had happened during those desperate hours? I looked within myself to see if I was sinking the *Storm* for those reasons. Maybe I wasn't thinking clearly. At twenty-eight, who can say he truly understands himself? I was sick and tired, in terrible pain. My shoulder had been broken during the depth charging. I had to take morphine to be able to function at all. Was I a good commander, or a murderer? To this day I don't know. Bolliver fought the greatest engagement I have ever seen on the high seas. I couldn't escape the conviction that I had shot a hero, and now I was burying him. I've lived with that uncertainty ever since."

MacKenzie said, "You flooded the ballast tanks and left the conning tower hatches open. The *Storm* went down, but Bolliver managed to get up and secure the hatches before dying. I found his blood there. It left her intact for fifty years. What about the five enemy ships?"

"Four were Bolliver's. The first freighter that started it all was the only one which was truly mine. I never wanted credit for his kills. It was just the time, you must see that. The country needed heroes. People were dying in the streets. I was lauded for the victories before I really knew what was happening. They made me go out on tour. I hated the terrible fraud. Once it got started, though, I suppose I just let it happen."

"Did Lady Em know?"

"Yes." He sat a bit straighter. "It was a matter of self-respect. I told Emily before we were married. I couldn't let her think I was something I wasn't. I had that much pride. I said if she would stand by me, I'd make a clean breast of it. She begged me not to, said I mustn't, that it had all happened under impossible circumstances. Our engagement had already been announced. She couldn't bear anyone to know the truth. It would embarrass her father and her family. If I truly loved her, I would go on keeping it secret."

What's it like being married to one of the strong ones? the Commodore had once asked him. Now MacKenzie knew why.

"So you did as she asked."

"Public humiliation would have destroyed her. I lived the lie. I know what you're wondering. Was it for her sake or for mine? It's another question I never stopped asking. Over the years there were many times I thought of telling the truth, but something always seemed to come up. One of Emily's illnesses, the death of our son. There was always a reason not to hurt her, not to tell."

"Then the past took over and put it all out of reach. Till now," said MacKenzie. "I'm sorry, Commodore."

"Do you judge me harshly, Admiral MacKenzie?"

"I can't judge you at all, sir. The events and circumstances are beyond my knowing. If Bolliver was a mutineer, you could have shot him with impunity, but he was a hero, saving a boat whose captain had lost the capacity to command. Yet, knowing you as I do, perhaps if Bolliver had tried to help you, given you some of his courage, you would have recovered. And consider this. In a few hours the *Storm* will be able to sail into battle for larger stakes than anyone could have imagined in those years because, in the end, you saved it that night. I wish I could give you absolution, but I can't."

"I understand, Admiral." The truth set free was a burden he could no longer carry. "Thank you for listening."

MacKenzie stroked his beard. The Commodore walked away, head bowed. Ironically, living a lie had probably hurt him more than anyone. MacKenzie marveled at the pools and eddies Fate created. The final sum of the cowardice and heroism on board the *Storm* still remained to be tallied. A sudden vibration in the hull cut MacKenzie's reverie short. Raskin had the diesel running.

"How does it look, Nikolai?" he called down.

"Your ten hours starts now," Raskin's voice was hopeful.

"Good work. Stand ready. Commodore Rowe!" Mac called to his departing back.

"Yes?"

"Get on board, Commodore. Today the *Storm* needs every hero she can get."

The Commodore straightened and looked at him gratefully. "Thank you, Admiral."

"Cast off those lines. Make ready to sail." MacKenzie blew into the tube. "Nikolai, prepare to answer all bells."

"Aye, Captain."

The Commodore climbed into the bridge. "The *Storm* is under your command, Admiral MacKenzie. I'd like to be your number one."

"Proud to have you, Commodore. Nikolai, all ahead slow. Keep her running no matter what."

"If I have to turn the shaft myself."

"Steady as she goes," MacKenzie ordered.

They inched away from the dock. The last voyage of the *Storm* was under way.

PART SIX

Voyage of the Storm

38

Korlov

SHUTO LOOKED OVER THE WATER TO SŌFU GAN. FOG hung over the sea and embraced the ship as if urging it not to go. The volcano blew angry white smoke. The air was thick and hot. He was glad to be leaving.

Bernhardsen had done his job. He might go on his expedition yet. Killing the men was Shuto's preferable solution, but this worked out just as well and allowed him to let the Admiral live. The submarine had occupied MacKenzie. Besides the nurse, he was the only one he didn't want to kill, and he would have had to if he'd made an attempt at him. But there was nothing the Admiral could do to stop him now. The *Korlov* would be ready to sail within the hour.

He respected the Admiral's leadership. Bernhardsen respected it, too. Shuto had heard it in his voice. Imagine using the volcano to straighten the sub's shaft. It must have been a grand venture raising the sub. He wished he could have been with them. But he wasn't entitled to that kind of camaraderie. He had come to this place for vengeance, it was near, and he was ready to die.

Two more matters needed to be disposed of first. The first was heading for him now like a cloud of insects.

"We're ready," said Lysenko. "I'll show you how to detonate the bombs."

"Proceed."

"They were originally designed for battlefield conditions, so they can be programmed simply." Lysenko showed him the digital timer. "You can set it for a minimum of ten minutes, up to a maximum of eight hours."

Lysenko was feebler, the limp more pronounced. Since the attack, it was almost as if his corruption could no longer be contained and was rotting him from the inside.

"How do I know it will work?"

"I guarantee it."

"That's not good enough. I want you with me till after the explosion."

Lysenko mustered his courage. "I have another ship. I've called it."

"I can just as easily send it away."

"But you won't. The bombs need a second trigger. I'll only give it to you after I'm on board. With my money."

"You're threatening me?"

"The *Korlov* is a death ship. I'll die if I stay here. Or go mad like Kiri and Ivan. I have nothing to lose."

It was the first honest thing Shuto had heard the Russian say.

"If the device doesn't work, Dr. Lysenko, there is nowhere on earth you can hide from me."

"You are a rare motivator," Lysenko said dryly. "I'm a logical man. Fulfilling my contract was the fastest way off this ship and away from you. It guarantees my life. Believe me, the bombs will work."

Shuto studied him. "All right. You may go."

"And my money?"

"When I have the trigger."

Lysenko picked up his attaché case. "Fair enough. I'll need some men to help with Kiri. Unless you want her."

"You are vile."

Lysenko shrugged. "Insert the trigger here to activate the system. I won't offer to shake your hand, Shuto. Our contract is satisfied."

"Good-bye, Doctor."

A yacht similar to the *Odessa* was steaming towards them. Shuto wished he hadn't used up the last of the missiles, but it couldn't be helped.

"Mori, bring the yacht alongside and transfer the money. Wait for the trigger."

Shuto felt the *Korlov*'s engines. His men were preparing to sail. They were fewer now. Akiro, Ito, Hiroki, all gone. Lysenko was right. It was a death ship.

Mori's men had to carry Kiri, screaming. The money case needed three men to bring it over. Lysenko opened it curiously and his expression changed to delight. Akiro's gold had finally found its way into Russian hands. Lysenko handed Mori the trigger and gave the order to sail in the same breath. There was nothing more to be done. The yacht churned a wide wake behind it, anxious to be gone.

"I am glad to be rid of them, Mori," Shuto said. "Tell the women to get ready."

* * *

Lysenko sipped a glass of ice-cold vodka in the yacht's air-conditioned bridge and watched the *Korlov* dwindle. It wasn't until it disappeared totally that he felt safe.

"There is fresh clothing in your suite, Dr. Lysenko," said the captain. "And correspondence from your office."

"Have the men bring the gold there." Lysenko compared his own sweaty face and filthy clothing to the captain in his crisp white uniform. "Christ, it wasn't until now I see how horrible this whole thing has been."

"We're glad to have you back, sir."

The suite was perfect. Silk hangings, caviar, and a magnum of Tattingers in a bucket of ice. The chest of gold sat in the middle of the living room, almost three hundred pounds. He deserved every penny of it after what that maniac had put him through. Lysenko had to admit there was something exciting about the shiny stuff. Kingdoms had fallen over it. Certainly it was a lot sexier than negotiable bonds. He took a bar out. It had a cold, oily feel. He put a few on the table. One on the desk. Used another as a doorstop. He made a big pile. He liked the look of it.

He reached for another bar and frowned. What was this? Next to the last layer was a dull gray brick that certainly wasn't gold. Had Shuto stiffed him? Lysenko examined it more closely. Then he saw. The bar dropped from his hand and he ran into the shower to scrub himself madly where he had touched it, even knowing it was too late. He never stopped scrubbing.

Hours later the captain and his men found Lysenko in the living room sprawled over his pile of gold. He and the gold were covered with blood from his having opened his wrists with the razor the yacht broker had conveniently provided. Shuto had been subtle. A speck of plutonium could cause cancer. A bar of plutonium like the one Shuto had placed in the gold, and Lysenko had inadvertently handled, exposed him to enough radiation to kill dozens. There was no escape, no cure. Lysenko had seen too many agonized victims of radiation poisoning to be able to face it himself. He took the easy way out.

The captain called Ivan. He saw the bar and had enough presence of mind left to warn the others. They sealed the suite, leaving Lysenko lying on top of his gold in a last embrace.

39

Korlov

THE WOMEN WERE WAITING WITH THEIR FEW POSSESSIONS
when Mori came to tell them the boat was ready to
take them to the island. He bowed to Justine.

"Thank you for treating our wounds."

"You're welcome," she said, thinking: I inflicted
most of them.

"That's it then," said Lady Em. "Can you make it,
my dear?"

"I'll use the wheelchair."

Carla covered her lap with a blanket. They looked
like prisoners of war. But the end to their imprisonment was near.

Justine said, "Fell it? The engines are running."

Carla pushed her. "We did everything we could."

Smoke poured from the *Korlov's* stacks. The ship
was alive and ready. Shuto was on deck. He motioned
Carla and Bette to help Lady Em down to the lifeboat
and get in themselves. The motor was already running. Carla took up the tiller. They sat bobbing on the

water. Justine remained on deck in the chair. She understood. Shuto wanted to be the one to grant her freedom. He bowed formally.

"Good-bye, Nurse."

"Please change your mind."

"Thank you for what you gave me. It was more than most."

She looked down the steps. "I can't make it on my own."

"I'll help you."

"Stop. Don't let her go!"

Five minutes later and she would have been in the boat, she told herself, but Carolyn and Keller ran on deck, Keller limping badly. Twine still hung from their wrists and ankles. Shuto looked at them in surprise.

"She's the one responsible for what happened," Keller yelled. "The fire in the crane, the sharks. And you're letting her go. Ask her!"

Shuto turned to her. "Is this . . . ?"

The gun Justine had taken from the terrorist that first night and had hidden under the blanket was aimed straight at him. His eyes blazed as the truth sank in. Her betrayal was an all-consuming fire.

"Let the women go," she said.

It was like facing an exploding star. She'd never confronted anger like this. The veins on his neck pulsed. His terrible energies engulfed her in a silent onslaught of his will against hers. She trembled, almost dropping the gun.

"Let them go," she said. "You're fast, but nobody beats a bullet at this range. And I'm very good."

"Better than I could have imagined to have betrayed me so thoroughly." Shuto made the motion. Mori released the line.

"Justine," Bette called urgently. "Come on!"

"Go. I can't make it."

"Not without you!"

"You *must* come, my dear," yelled Lady Em.

"Go, damn it!"

Carla hit the throttle and the boat buzzed off into the rain. Justine waited till they were out of firing range. They would be safe on the island. Shuto couldn't take the time to hunt for them.

Shuto turned away from her, and Justine knew she should have shot him, but she couldn't. It was one betrayal too many. Her hesitation cost her dearly. Shuto was already moving, but even he was too late. The weakness that came over her had a finality about it this time. The gun fell from her nerveless fingers. Darkness came fast, like a sack yanked over her head.

On the last day, she had run out of time.

40

H.M.S. Storm

SLOWLY, PAINFULLY, THE *STORM* GATHERED SPEED. Heavy waves slammed into the bridge one after the other. The rain squall beat at her mercilessly, making her pay for every yard of ocean she sailed.

The wind and rain made being on the bridge miserable for MacKenzie and the Commodore. The turbulence grew stronger as the waves picked up, blasting white water along the bulging curve of her saddle tanks. The *Storm* struggled mightily, making almost four knots, even better than Raskin had estimated. But they were rolling badly and the hull vibration had increased along with the shaft's revolutions. MacKenzie heard Raskin retching violently below, not even long submarine service a protection against the malady. He pitied his friend for what he was going through in the hot, cramped space.

MacKenzie peered into the rain, searching ahead for the *Korlov* as they came around the island. He was also continuously monitoring the tiny signal light

Rietti had rigged. He had sent the wounded Rietti to the beach, waiting to see if Justine and the women got off the ship. If they did, he would signal the *Storm* using the transmitter Bernhardsen had hidden in his computer, switched to a different frequency to avoid Shuto's detecting it.

MacKenzie pressed the test switch on the signal light. It glowed briefly.

"Clever fellow, our Tony," the Commodore said, piloting from the auxiliary steering unit.

"I'll be relieved when we get his signal."

"She'll get them off, that wife of yours. Then it'll be up to us."

It had been fifty years since the Commodore had been at the helm, but he handled the *Storm* as if they were both just out of Cammell Laird's, brand spanking new and ready for battle.

"I see you haven't lost your touch. Steer port ten."

"Thank you, Admiral. Port ten, aye."

MacKenzie would have liked to dive to avoid the rain squall, which was making them wallow badly on the surface, but it was an option closed to him. He bit his lip anxiously. It would be several miles yet before they would know if the *Korlov* was still anchored beyond the breakers. If the women were off the ship, he could safely attack. But what if they weren't? Could he do his job if it demanded such a heavy price? He cupped his hands over the light to keep it dry.

"Starboard ten, Commodore."

"Starboard ten, aye . . . Admiral, look!"

A lightning fork speared down the sky, and for a minute MacKenzie couldn't be sure he was seeing the signal light, or an afterimage. But there it was, holding steady. Rietti's signal. The women were off the ship.

"Bless Mrs. MacKenzie," said the Commodore fervently.

"And just in time. Look!"

The *Korlov* lay ahead, a dim shape, hazy through the sheets of rain, but still at anchor. The sight lifted MacKenzie's heart and made him feel like he could carry the *Storm* himself.

Steer port fifteen," he ordered, calling down, "Nikolai, this is it. We're going in."

"Aye, Peter," came Raskin's voice over the tube.

"Starboard ten, Commodore. Hug the island as long as possible."

"Watch the breakers. They can tear our guts out," warned the Commodore.

"I can barely see. You're directed to steer clear of any obstacles on your own."

"Aye."

For the first time the squall was on their side. The *Storm* blended in with the gray sea. The black-painted sections of her hull broke up her silhouette. In the rain they were almost impossible to spot. The *Korlov* grew closer, still anchored where they left her more than ten days ago. MacKenzie's anxieties were high. His hand hovered over the torpedo release button. Normal attack distance was a mile. He wanted to be well under that with an aging ship and untested weapons. He was going to make a straight shot on the surface at the stationary target as soon as he was in range. Nothing fancy. No tricks. The bow angle was the only thing that mattered. Get close, aim, launch.

The *Storm*'s bow wave crested out and flowed over the deck up to her sail. The sound of her passage was like the crashing of a great waterfall. MacKenzie felt an almost religious sensation riding the *Storm*. He had a feeling the boat was glad he was here; that she was telling him she'd break her back to see him through. He wondered if it was why she had come back, to give him this mission. Had she always known he was coming to raise her, waiting under the waves since before he was born so he could captain a submarine in the service of his country one last time? He wasn't alone. The *Storm* had given each of them something important. For Raskin, a reason to go on. For Bernhardsen, a chance at redemption. Tony Rietti had found a way to face his fears. And the Commodore had finally been unburdened of the lie that had weighed so heavily on him for fifty years.

MacKenzie stepped onto the raised platform alongside the periscope standards and took a dead reckoning on the freighter. The wind swept by. The rain tasted sweet. He slicked back his wet hair and raised his face to it, letting it wash him, feeling clean for the first time in weeks. His beard was a tangle of soggy ringlets. The rain mingled with the salt spray. It wasn't until this moment, here at sea, that he fully appreciated the enormity of what they had accomplished. Despite all that had happened on the island, death and dark secrets, separations and betrayals, he felt breathless and alive.

"I'd almost forgotten what it felt like," said the Commodore reverently.

MacKenzie thought of his own days on the bridge, of battles fought and won, of enemies defeated.

"I never forgot," he said softly.

The beat of the engine blended with his own racing pulse as the *Storm's* great bulk shouldered aside the sea to make her final run. The fore planes were folded back. Her long white wake astern fountained out like freshly fallen snow. The island slipped away, leaving palm trees, beaches, sweltering heat, and the body of

Ivor Bernhardsen. Over the all, Niigata Yakeyama blew smoke and fire.

MacKenzie corrected their course, always aware of the tenuous throb of the *Storm*'s engine.

"The *Storm* came here in a squall fifty years ago, and now she's leaving in one."

"Two miles," said the Commodore.

"Starboard ten."

"Starboard ten, aye."

The *Storm* plunged on. MacKenzie could see men in the *Korlov*'s bridge. Others were moving about on deck. They still hadn't seen the *Storm*. The rain streamed down the Commodore's haggard face. His words were mostly lost in the wind, but MacKenzie thought he was praying.

"Steady as she goes." MacKenzie's eyes never left the *Korlov*. A mile and a half and closing. The squall whipped the sea into whitecaps.

"Admiral, we're too late!" The Commodore pointed wildly. "They're sailing."

MacKenzie wiped his eyes. The freighter was making smoke. He yelled to Raskin to coax more speed out of the diesel. Desperate, he watched the *Korlov* inscribe a slow arc along the breakers, heading for open sea.

"She's slow," MacKenzie fumed. "We'll catch her."

"Not at this speed," the Commodore said miserably. "They've got us by at least four knots."

In truth, the *Korlov* was opening the distance. Her ponderous stern rolled in the squall.

"Can you give me any more speed, Nikolai?"

"Peter, she's overheating as it is."

"We can't shoot from this distance," the Commodore reminded him bleakly.

"We'll give chase as long as we can."

Rain slashed across the bow. Walls of water crashed into the bridge, soaking them. Lighting flashed overhead.

"We'll capsize if you take her into open sea in this weather and the engines give out," the Commodore warned.

MacKenzie stared straight ahead. He had a warship and a target.

"Till then, we follow. Steady as she goes."

41

Sōfu gan

RIETTI HAD PRESSED THE TRANSMIT BUTTON WHEN HE SAW
the women's lifeboat coming. His joy at their return
was mixed with concern. He couldn't wait to see
Bette, but how was he going to tell Carla that Ivor had
betrayed them by being part of Shuto's scheme from
the beginning, and that if Shuto succeeded in blowing
the Magnus Field, her husband was to blame? After so
many years, it was a shame Ivor had gone so wrong.
As much as he didn't want to tell Carla what he had
done, he owed her the truth. Peru had damaged Ivor
more than anyone. She had a right to know.

By the time the lifeboat breached the breakers and
buzzed into the bay, the *Korlov* was ready to sail.
Rietti worried the *Storm* wasn't coming until he saw it
come surging around the island. It was a beautiful
sight, but as he watched, the *Korlov* began to pull
away. The *Storm* struggled to keep up, but she was
losing the race. All their work for nothing, he thought
bitterly.

The wound in his shoulder throbbed painfully, but their failure hurt far worse. The Magnus Field would be a global catastrophe. He paced anxiously. Behind him, Niigata Yakeyama roared in evil delight. He had been around volcanoes all his professional life. This one gave all the signs it was going to erupt. Too bad Ivor wasn't here to see it. He would have been on the rim taking measurements to support their theory, waiting for the other volcanologists to arrive. *A volcanic eruption shows up on every seismograph in the world,* Rietti remembered saying. *Everyone comes flocking to see it within hours.* The irony was that Ivor would have been first, the authority. Niigata Yakeyama would have restarted his career.

Carla grounded the boat and the women waded ashore. Bette ran up the beach and into his arms.

"Tony!"

He hugged her fiercely. "Bette, you're all right. Carla, too. And Lady Emily."

They all hugged and cried with relief.

"Where is the Commodore, please?" asked Lady Em.

"With the Admiral and Captain Raskin on board the *Storm*. Look, there."

Lady Em turned towards the sea and saw the ancient sub. Memories echoed from long ago. The *Storm* was fading, out beyond the mist. It might well have been fifty years before on the English coast when she watched the submarines sailing out to do battle.

"Good luck this time, my darling," she said softly.

"Wait, Justine isn't with you," Rietti suddenly realized.

"She's still on the *Korlov*," Bette said. "She held off Shuto so we could escape."

"But I signaled Admiral MacKenzie she was safe. If he attacks . . ." The enormity of it hit him hard.

"Tony, where's Ivor?" Carla asked.

"Yes, Tony," said Bette. "Where?"

Rietti knew he had to tell her, but he couldn't. Although he felt she deserved the truth, the weary, bedraggled woman who had been his friend for over fifteen years deserved compassion more. Suddenly he realized what he had to do, for Justine as well as Carla, what he should have been doing all along.

Everyone comes flocking to see it. Within hours.

"Tony, where's Ivor?" Carla asked again.

"Up there." Rietti pointed to the volcano. "Waiting for me."

Korlov

Carolyn and Keller were pressed together like spoons, on the bed in the captain's stateroom. These were grand quarters compared to their former compartment. Shuto had even given them extra food and bottles of wine.

"We're safe now," Keller said. "You did well with those knots. Did it hurt much?"

"It doesn't matter. It was for you, Phillip."

"Now, if Shuto would just let me at that horrible woman. Look at my knee!" It was all swollen and bruised.

"Did you see how angry he was? It looked like he wanted to kill her. She was lucky she passed out," Carolyn said.

"I wouldn't want to be in her shoes," Keller agreed.

Carolyn walked over to the table and refilled their glasses.

"It's like a honeymoon," she said happily. "You made the call to the States, right?"

"What call?"

Carolyn stopped in mid pour. "What do you mean, what call?"

"Oh, *that*. Yes, of course. I promised, didn't I?"

"To what number?" Carolyn asked suspiciously.

"I don't like to be questioned, Carolyn."

"To what number!"

"Yours. I had it in my records."

"Your records were in the *Tuscany*. My kids are at my mother's. You're lying!"

He was off the bed in one stride and grabbed her wrists so tightly they hurt.

"What's wrong with you? The bomb probably won't even work. We'll be in Japan while the others rot on that island. You think Shuto will send anyone to rescue them? We're safe. Enjoy it."

Carolyn was in a state of shock. "It isn't possible."

"What isn't?"

"Justine and the others. They were right about you."

He shrugged. "I'm simply logical. And you're no different. You didn't care who died, as long as you got what you wanted. Me."

"I didn't know those people. I thought it wouldn't matter. But those are my kids!"

"I hate children. We're better off without them."

Carolyn's laugh was bitter. "I defended you. What could I have been thinking? I never should have listened. No, don't touch me like that. I'm going to Shuto."

"No, you're not." He slapped her viciously.

"Phillip, don't!"

He picked up a belt and used it to emphasize every word.

"Don't . . . ever . . . threaten . . . me . . . again!"

"No more, Phillip. Please! Oh, God, don't hit me again."

He drove her across the room till she cringed in the corner. When he was done with the belt, he punched and kicked her. She was bruised and hurt in a dozen places. Her face was a bloody mess.

She was crying. "No more, Phillip . . ."

"You see what you made me do?" he shouted.

She hid her face from him, fearing more punishment.

His voice softened. "Come to bed. I'll fix it."

She whimpered softly. "Okay, Phillip. Whatever you say. Just don't hit me anymore."

He led her across the room. "That's a good girl."

Carolyn grabbed the bottle of wine off the table as she passed and swung it against his head as hard as she could. The bottle was heavy, almost full. It burst and sprayed wine over the walls. Keller's eyes went blank and he crumpled to the deck. Blood from his crushed skull mingled with the wine. Carolyn knew she had killed him the way he fell, so completely limp, as if all the messages from his brain had been canceled at once. She checked for a pulse and couldn't find any. She felt dazed. He'd hurt her terribly, but beyond the physical pain, her shame was overpowering. Her stupidity. Lady Em had been right. Look what she had become.

Her face in the mirror was a horror show. She cleaned herself as best she could, but she would never be the same. His destruction of her was complete, physically and spiritually. There was only one consolation, one thing left to hold on to. She knew she was capable of depraved acts, things she once wouldn't have dreamed of doing, but letting her kids die without trying to save them wasn't one of them.

"So long, Phillip. The honeymoon's over."

She took his keys. The Japanese were too busy sailing the ship to bother with her. She stole a pistol from the unguarded weapons room, then went to the infirmary and unlocked it. Carolyn had witnessed Justine's collapse. Without insulin, the diabetes had progressed to its coma state. Justine was ketotic and in shock, close to complete kidney failure as the chemical poisons in her blood built up too fast to be cleaned out. She needed a hospital. Her only chance for survival was to get off the ship.

Carolyn started an IV to bring up Justine's fluid level, and prepared two syringes. The first contained insulin to restore her blood chem. The second was a powerful stimulant. It would either get her up on her feet, or kill her. It was a gamble, but there was no time for anything else. She made the injections, waited, changed the drip and began another. She put a little sugar on Justine's tongue. Twenty minutes went by. She was worried the Japanese would find Keller. After half an hour she saw the first signs that Justine was starting to recover.

"Come on, honey. You're tough. Wake up now."

"Mmmm?"

"It's Carolyn. I'm so sorry. You've got to get up. You can still make the island."

Justine's eyes fluttered open. "Carolyn . . . ?"

"Thank God. Listen, I've been wrong about everything."

"Where's Phillip?"

"He's dead."

"Carolyn, your face . . . !?"

She turned away so Justine couldn't see how bad it was.

"Forget me. Can you get up?"

"I think so."

Carolyn put Justine's arm over her shoulder. As they walked, she told her about Keller.

"Can you ever forgive me?"

Justine managed a weak smile. "Look what a mess *I* made of things. I keep ending up here."

"If not for Phillip and me, you would have gotten away."

"Doesn't matter now. Mac's coming. We have to go."

On deck the squall was hitting the ship hard. The rain was cold and clean on Justine's face. Her mind was beginning to clear and she felt stronger. But with clarity came a sudden awareness.

"We're under full steam!"

Sheets of rain billowed across the sea. Once the women were off, the *Storm* should have attacked. Shuto must have sailed before Mac could strike. Unknowingly, it had saved her life. But where was Mac?

"Can you see another ship anywhere?"

Carolyn squinted. "Wait a minute . . . Justine, what the hell is that, a submarine?"

Justine's heart beat stronger.

"It's Mac on the *Storm.*" But she could see the *Korlov* was drawing away. "Carolyn, remember how the Commodore said his sub sank near the island?"

"Yes."

"The men raised it. I couldn't tell you when you were with Phillip. Mac is in command and he's coming to sink this ship. But the *Storm* must not have the speed to close on us. We've got to slow the *Korlov* down."

"How?"

"You know those bottles of alcohol in the infirmary?"

"For sterilizing. Sure."

Justine explained how to build a firebomb. "Do it and bring them to me."

Carolyn looked skeptical. "What are you going to do with them? You can barely walk."

The wind whipped Justine's long hair around her face.

"Just make those bombs and meet me in the engine room. Mac's depending on me."

The rain hid Carolyn's tears. The way Justine said it, like if Mac had needed her to walk on water, she damn well would have, was everything Carolyn wanted in life and would never have. Keller had seen to that.

"I can make them, honey. But that's not the way we'll do it. I know the engine room better than you do. I delivered their salt pills every day." She handed Justine the pistol. "Get in a lifeboat. If I'm not back in twenty minutes, take it and go."

"I won't."

Carolyn took her arm. Justine was too weak to fight. Lightning flashed the world white.

"This is my job," Justine insisted furiously.

"Look at me," Carolyn said bitterly. The wind blew her wet hair away, and Justine winced to see her face. "I'll never be pretty again. Phillip's last gift. If I don't get back, leave without me. Save your baby. My babies, too. Promise me."

"I promise."

Carolyn put her in the boat. "One more thing. Your

blood chem's shot. You need a hospital. In a few hours the stimulant I gave you is going to fade and you'll go down for the count. You have to get medical help before that. Don't wait too long. You could pass out any minute. Tell my kids . . . you know."

The rain swirled around them.

"I'll tell them."

The two women embraced, and then Carolyn was gone.

42

Sōfu gan

RIETTI MANAGED TO CARRY NINETY POUNDS OF CVX explosive from the mining camp in his knapsack. After the first few hundred feet up the volcano, he found himself crying. It wasn't only the straps cutting so badly into the wound Ivor had inflicted, he was so frightened he was sobbing almost continuously as he climbed. He never wanted anything in his life as much as he wanted to go back down the volcano. His hands were shaking. His bladder and bowels had already given way. He knew he was very near hysteria. He clamped down hard with the last of his self-control to avoid it.

Niigata Yakeyama had thrown up a column of fire and smoke. Lava flowed down ancient channels. If not for the rain, the CVX on his back might easily have ignited. He felt like he was back in Peru, revisiting his nightmare. The volcano was going to erupt soon. He felt it the same way he had felt it then. He kept seeing bodies falling into the magma. One of them was always his own. He climbed because he believed the *Storm* wasn't going to make it and he couldn't permit Shuto to explode the Magnus Field. Ivor was wrong. It would be a cataclysm. Rietti knew if he could coax the volcano into erupting, the first scientific teams would be here within hours, with radios.

The rock face was hot enough to burn the skin on his hands. He used asbestos pads to climb with, but they slipped, and he had already fallen once. Lava coursed down a dozen channels. A pipe blew out near him and he had to scramble out of the way of molten rock that flowed past not ten feet away. He wrapped his body with strips of asbestos from the camp and kept wetting them. The rain helped there too. Even so, his outer clothes kept smoldering. He climbed away from the lava. The rim was in sight.

Rietti was betting the crust covering the main magma core inside the volcano was close to cracking. He was going to speed it up with the CVX. He knew this volcano. It was ready to blow. His conviction was formed by years of experience. Then the world would hear it. He thought about what MacKenzie had said as he climbed. The Admiral was quite a man. He'd gotten them through everything, even raising the *Storm*. It wasn't his fault Ivor had cost him those last precious hours. MacKenzie had told him the truth, it had just taken him time to see it. Knowing your limits didn't mean you had to accept them. Rietti had accepted his fear far too easily.

The island was a long way below. The rain forest canopy spread out as far as he could see. The rumblings were stronger, coming quicker, as if birth were imminent. A pipe blew above him. He was in immediate danger. An overhang jutted out about fifteen feet away. He scampered across the hot stone face and ducked under it just as the lava hit. It shot into space like a waterfall. A lavafall, more accurately. He was *under* a lava flow! It was a sight no volcanologist had ever seen before. He waited till the pipe exhausted itself, and started climbing again.

Niigata Yakeyama tried to throw him from its face three more times, but each time he held on. The summit was less than a hundred feet overhead, then fifty, and then he was standing on the rim looking down into a cauldron of fire hell would envy.

Nothing in nature can match an erupting volcano's fury. A hundred A-bomb blasts are dwarfed by a single explosion, which can vaporize ten square miles of rock. It was different up here, he had once said to MacKenzie. You had to see it with your own eyes, feel the raw power with your own senses, to know it. White-orange magma geysers shot hundreds of feet up from the crown, which glowed orange along its fault lines. Earth flowed like water. This was how the world was born. Flame erupted in the air as gases ignited, twisting together in glowing ribbons. It was Fire's mating ritual. Devils romped behind pillars of molten rock, red and orange in the shadows. The wind created by the heat roared up at him, sweeping his hair back, singeing his face and lungs.

The volcano roared and he roared back at it. It couldn't frighten him anymore. It had done its best to dislodge him, but it had failed. He had sworn he would never come back here, but he had come nonetheless. The volcano could be beaten if he had the will. He shucked off the knapsack. The CVX needed only to be dropped in. Raindrops hit all around him, turning to steam with a staccato hiss. It could rain forever and not extinguish one bit of the volcano's fury. Rietti faced the cauldron of fire and wind defiantly. His fear burned away. His mind was a pure white light. He felt Ivor's presence close by. His last thoughts were of Bette as he pushed the knapsack into the fire and began his descent in almost the same motion.

The first explosions reached him before he was halfway down, and he felt his spirit burning along with his flesh.

43

BOOKBINDER FELT LIKE HIS EYES WERE FALLING OUT OF [
head. He readjusted the lamp to get more light on
image he was viewing. It was still too dark. Had t[
switched to smaller bulbs around here? There wer[
lot of economy moves he could tolerate, but t[
wasn't one of them. It should have been a hi[
intensity bulb. He turned the fixture up to see. [
couldn't make out the numbers in the glare, and the
afterimage left black spots on his vision. Great, another set of photos to go through and he was blind.

Rachel Kronitz, one of his colleagues, was striding
purposefully towards him. She was the woman whose
vase he broke when he threw the pencil at the map.

"Rachel," he said hastily. "It was late and I was
stupid. I meant to tell you . . ."

"If this isn't a declaration of undying love," said
the pretty analyst, "I don't know what the hell you're
talking about."

"Your vase the other day."

Her blue eyes got mean. "So it was *you*. Put ten bucks on my desk by morning. But that isn't why I came in."

"I should keep my mouth shut," he said, thinking it was probably the best advice he never took. He'd already had three calls from Farley this morning. The NSA chief was glaring at him instead of smiling. And Admiral Garver was blowing steam like an angry whale. Bookbinder had put his RÉSUMÉ file back on active.

"We just got this," Rachel said. "I don't know if it means anything, but you said you wanted everything that came in about the area. And you underlined *everything*. Well, here."

He scanned the transmission. "A volcano erupting? Good God, Rachel, so what?"

"Look where."

"Southern Japan?"

She showed him on the map. "One of the islands in the extreme southern chain. It's within the *Korlov*'s sailing radius."

"They wouldn't have stayed so close," he said. "Would they?"

"Somebody very clever might."

Bookbinder sat back in his chair. "Got a printout?"

"Right here."

He got out the corresponding satellite pictures of the area and put them in the viewer.

"What's that, fog?" Bookbinder asked.

"Yeah. Pretty thick, too."

"Hard to get anything clear with such a big temperature inversion, you know?" He was getting interested.

"The other feature is the volcano. It overshadows the area," Rachel observed. "Maybe the heat seekers didn't track so well with all that temperature bleeding all over the place. I never thought of it."

Bookbinder blinked rapidly. He was excited.

"The fog knocks out the visuals, and the volcano hides the heat. Even a big ship's heat. Kind of like not being able to see the writing on the bulb because of the glare."

"Do you think . . . ?"

Bookbinder picked up the phone and called Farley.

"Sir, I think we've got a possible."

He listened, then covered the phone and said to Rachel, "He wants to know if it's worth a satellite look-see."

Rachel shrugged. "Your call, Kimosabe."

Bookbinder took a deep breath. His sinuses were clear. His instincts were screaming.

"Better still, sir. Is that SEAL team still in the area?"

44

H.M.S. Storm

FOAMING WAVES SHATTERED AGAINST THE BRIDGE. THE
wind whipped at them. MacKenzie was worried
about Raskin. It was hell below. The diesel had been
running for hours and the vibration was a torment.

"Nikolai, are you okay?" he called down.

"I'm managing. There is nothing left in my stomach
to lose."

The waves continued to flood the bridge. Water
dripped down their bodies, pooled in their shoes. The
cutting wind gave them a bad chill. The Commodore
shivered, near his limit.

"I thought I'd welcome this. Instead I feel so brittle,
my teeth are chattering."

"Want to go below?"

"On the surface, in this sea?" The Commodore
looked horrified.

A sudden bass rumbling filled the air, deeper than
the thunder or even *Storm*'s vibration. A loud crack

was followed by a blast of flame and smoke. Behind them, a roiling dust cloud grew in the sky.

"It's the volcano!" MacKenzie had to shout over the noise of the eruption.

"Tony was right," said the Commodore. "It was ready."

MacKenzie was awed. For a few moments the eruption dwarfed even the squall. A huge fireball engulfed the summit. Smoke poured into the air. He remembered the thick ash in the mining camp, and the heat of the lava field. He could only hope Rietti and the women would be all right on the beach.

He turned back. They were a gray submarine on a gray sea under a gray sky. A wave hit them, slamming the conning tower hatch shut. Mac heard Raskin's painful yell over the tube. The Commodore realized what was happening and quickly threw the hatch back open.

"The diesel sucked the air out of the boat, making a partial vacuum," he explained. "Hell on the ears."

The *Korlov* slowed a bit in the high seas, but it wasn't enough to let the *Storm* close the gap. They plunged on like a faithful hound. MacKenzie checked his watch. They were almost out of daylight.

"We'll lose the *Korlov* if it gets dark."

"We might lose her before that," the Commodore said. "Listen."

The *Storm*'s engine pitch stuttered, fell, then rose to a piercing whine.

"Nikolai, what's wrong?"

Raskin sounded worried. "She's breaking down, Peter."

"You've got to hold her together."

"How much longer?"

"I wish I knew."

MacKenzie ducked another wall of water. The *Korlov* was still well out of range. A floating bomb. His responsibility. How many would die if they couldn't catch it? Had they come this far only to fail? He remembered the first time he'd seen the *Storm*. In her last battle she'd proved herself a great warship. But the end of her story had yet to be written. She'd been taken out of action before she was ready. She wanted one more battle. Every time he came on board, he felt it. Once more against the enemy to fulfill her destiny.

He wiped the water off his face. The *Storm*'s white wake spread out like wings. The throb of her engine was strained. She was running her heart out.

"Give her the chance," he prayed softly.

Korlov

Carolyn made the bombs easily enough, and she knew her way to the engine room. It was incredibly loud. The big shafts pounded mightily. She stepped onto one of the overhead catwalks. Steam hissed like nasty whispers. Below her the men watched the gauges carefully, opening and closing valves. Oil drums were stacked against a bulkhead. She had three bottle bombs. Gauze drooped out of the neck of each. She lit the first one.

"Hey! What are you doing?"

She recognized Mori. He was lifting his gun. Almost without thinking, she threw the bomb at him. It hit as he fired, exploding on the catwalk, covering him with burning alcohol. His arms jerked wildly, engulfed in flames, and he fell over the catwalk. Men looked to see where he had come from and spotted her. An alarm rang out. Men were shouting, coming for her, shooting.

She lit the second bomb and dropped it. Fire dripped through the grating, starting smaller fires. She watched it all as if it were happening to somebody else. Only recently an arsonist, she was a better nurse. Her blood spurting in pulses from her thigh told her that Mori had hit the big femoral artery. Life was rushing out of her body. She lit the third bomb and heaved it away. It burst over the engine. She felt the heat come up and reach for her. There was a sudden jolt and men started yelling as the oil drums began to burn.

Carolyn lay down and thought about her kids. Her face no longer hurt. It was getting quieter. Much quieter.

She felt very much at peace when the end came.

In the bridge, Shuto felt the change in speed even before he heard the alarms. The *Korlov* lurched violently and began to slow. Then the panicked voice of the engine room chief spilled out of the speaker, reporting what had happened. Fires were raging. He needed more men to control them.

"It was Dr. Keller's wife. She had firebombs. Mori's dead."

Shuto heard men screaming in the background. He felt cold. Mori was the last. The coldness gave way to anger. How was this possible? The woman was Keller's, certainly not one to go against him. And Justine was comatose in the infirmary.

"Maintain course and speed," he ordered.

"I can't. We're losing rpm's. It will be hard even to hold her steady in this sea."

"Put everyone on the fire."

"The fires are out of control. One of the main engines just shut down."

"Fix it!"

Shuto tore open the door to the captain's suite. Keller lay facedown in a pool of blood and wine, dead. A bloodied belt was still wrapped around his hand. There was blood on the bathroom towels and in the sink. Carolyn would want to look at herself if she'd been beaten. Shuto ran to the infirmary. Justine was gone. The IV bottles and syringes told the story. Keller's wife was a nurse, too. She'd managed to bring Justine back, then freed her. But it was out on deck that he got his greatest shock. Closing fast was the ancient submarine Bernhardsen had reported destroyed. He grabbed his binoculars. MacKenzie and that doddering old Commodore stood in the bridge. He thought he'd beaten the Admiral, but MacKenzie had outmaneuvered him. He must have found out about Bernhardsen and turned him. The *Storm* had been following them ever since they left the island. The *Korlov* had probably escaped a torpedo by minutes.

His Chief Engineer ran up to him, sooty and glazed with sweat. "Shuto, we can't control the fire. All the electrical systems are down. If the fuel tanks blow . . ."

"How much time?"

"Fifteen minutes. Maybe twenty."

Shuto had hated people all his life, but it reached a peak here. Revenge, once so large, became a narrow, concentrated thing, like a laser beam.

"Take the men to the lifeboats."

"What about you?"

"Tell them I wish them well."

The remaining crew needed little urging. They

lowered the lifeboats and streamed away from the freighter like a line of water bugs. Shuto knew he had only given them the illusion of safety. No lifeboat could get far enough away from what was going to happen in ten minutes. The world would still take notice. The island, the ship, very likely the entire region, would be consumed. This was ground zero. This was Hiroshima.

The fire was spreading rapidly inside the ship without men to fight it. Like the bombs on the main deck, Shuto was rapidly approaching critical mass, ready to explode. The Admiral's submarine was closing. He wished he had a missile left to greet it. Instead he sent his undying rage along the connection to the Admiral, and to Justine, wherever she was. Especially to Justine. He had let her look into his heart. Shown her kindness. Her betrayal was greatest.

The rain squall tore at him. He raised his arms and let it. He deserved the lashing. A feral moan escaped his lips. He heard the rage in it. In a flash of understanding he saw how his hatred had been his weakness. It kept him from people all his life so he never learned to understand them. The Admiral and the nurse had used that to trick him. A bitter laugh escaped him. He had studied the martial arts till he was the supreme fighter, yet he'd been beaten without a single punch or kick. He had been bested by emotions, the most basic ones of all. Trust. Kindness. Even love.

He was surprised to see the Chief Engineer returning, even more surprised by the semiconscious figure he slung to the deck.

"We found the nurse in the lifeboat. She is very weak. Do we take her?"

Justine's voice was barely a whisper. "Let me go."

Shuto almost laughed. The final irony. Justine had been too weak to complete her escape. Her eyes were pleading. She could not even struggle.

"Leave her," he said.

"Come, too. The ship is dying."

"Then go before it takes you with it."

The Chief Engineer bowed, then fled.

Shuto knelt beside Justine. Her life flame was barely a flicker.

"So you could not leave me?"

The ghost of a smile crossed her face. "Believe me, I tried."

"We are bound together, you and I. And the Admiral. He's coming, you know."

"I know. He's my husband."

"What?"

"My name is Justine MacKenzie."

It took a moment for it to sink in. After the initial shock, Shuto managed a rueful grin.

"Yet another level to the game. From the beginning, the two of you against me?"

"Yes."

"Even apart, you knew?"

"We are bound, too, Shuto. It's what you couldn't see."

Again he saw how hatred had been his weakness. Such bonds till now were beyond him. He tried to hate this woman who had betrayed him. He picked her up and strode across the wet deck through the blinding rain to the tent.

"What are you doing?"

"Finishing it," he said.

"The *Storm* is coming. It's too late."

"You're carrying his child in your belly. I don't believe he will shoot with you on board."

"He will, Shuto," she said sadly. "He has to."

"Then the responsibility will be his."

He slid the trigger in the way Lysenko had showed him and set the timer to its minimum. Ten minutes. He felt the spirits of the dead all around him. His father. Ito. Hiroki. Mori. The rest who had died to bring him to this spot. He pushed the detonator button and the timer began its steady progression:

9:59 . . . 9:58 . . . 9:57 . . .

Akiro would soon have his Light.

45

H.M.S. Storm

"She's slowing!" MacKenzie strained to see through the rain. "There's smoke coming from her."

"It looks like she's on fire," said the Commodore. "But blast it all, Admiral. We've got problems, too."

There was a heavy smell of burning oil, and the color of their exhaust had changed. The diesel was giving out.

"What's our range?"

"One mile and closing."

MacKenzie called to the engine room. "Nikolai, the *Korlov*'s almost dead in the water. We're closing."

"Thank God. The engine is tearing itself to pieces."

"I need ten more minutes."

"If I have to row us," Raskin said fervently.

MacKenzie was focused, deliberate. He didn't attack in anger. It was a cold and terrible thing. The panorama before him became vividly alive. The *Korlov* dead ahead. The *Storm* crashing through the sea. Wind and rain engulfed them both. Lightning turned the sky white.

"We'll fire at a thousand yards, Commodore."

"That's very close."

"We can't afford to miss. Starboard thirty. Swing us around. I want the *Storm*'s tubes aimed at their broadside."

"Coming around. Range fifteen hundred yards and closing."

"Port ten."

"Port ten, aye."

"Prepare to fire," MacKenzie said.

The Commodore scanned the ship through binoculars. "Twelve hundred yards."

"Hold her steady."

"Eleven hundred yards."

"Maintain angle on the bow," MacKenzie ordered. The *Korlov* was dead ahead.

"One thousand yards."

The steel hull loomed before him. MacKenzie put his hand on the firing switch.

"Admiral, wait! Look astern. Shuto has your wife up there with him!"

MacKenzie raised his glasses and felt an icy hand seize his chest. He had assumed Justine had gotten away with the women, yet there she was. Lifeboats were leaving the burning ship. Only Shuto and Justine were left. He must have learned somehow she was his wife and was using her as a shield to stop him. The fire was out of control. The freighter was doomed. But Shuto's hatred was so great, MacKenzie was sure he would set the bombs to detonate before the *Korlov* sank. The devastation would be immeasurable if the tons of plutonium on board were spread by a nuclear blast. He had to shoot to stop it, to send the ship to the bottom, where it posed no threat. He had to.

"Nine hundred yards."

"I can't hold her much longer, Peter."

Every fear Mac had conjured since the mission began came back to haunt him. If he fired, he would be killing his wife and child. But countless lives hung in the balance. He was sworn to protect those lives, to put personal concerns aside. It was the code he had lived by all his professional life. But here, now, what did any of it mean?

"Eight hundred yards," said the Commodore.

Shuto was supporting Justine. MacKenzie could feel his wife's weakness.

"What are your orders, Admiral? I say, Admiral?"

"I told you he wouldn't fire," Shuto said triumphantly.

"He will."

The rain coursed down Justine's cheeks along with her tears. "He'll fire because he's the most principled man I've ever known. And after it's all over, even if he lives, he'll be dead along with the rest of us, one more casualty of your need for revenge."

"He won't," Shuto said firmly.

"Shuto, look at him on that boat. Think of what he's done to get here. Do you think a man like that can be blackmailed? Do you think the bravery you've felt in him, the essential goodness, can be bought even at the cost of himself? It can't. If you were more of a man, you'd know it."

The words stung Shuto. Despite his hatred, he felt a oneness with his enemy. He could be in the conn of the submarine himself, coming for this woman, hating him for everything he had caused.

"He's sending his fear," he lied.

"He's sending his good-bye," Justine said softly. "In the end, Shuto, all you'll destroy is a man that would have fought those terrible boys for you. You feel that in him, I know it. It's why he can't stop." She looked at her husband standing in the bridge. "It's why I love him."

Shuto tried to break the connection, but it was too strong. He felt what Justine's presence on the ship was costing the Admiral, felt his conflict. MacKenzie would indeed die if he had to kill her. What was it like to love someone that much? Yet MacKenzie didn't turn the *Storm*. Did honor and responsibility mean that much to him? The joining went deeper. For one terrible moment he saw himself as MacKenzie did. One of those awful boys who hurt others, who killed and tormented. The vision almost sent him screaming.

The timer glowed in the tent:

6:59 . . . 6:58 . . . 6:57 . . .

The fire reached the bridge.

A terrible quiet surrounded MacKenzie. The noise of the squall, the *Storm*'s straining engines, even the Commodore calling out the distance to him, were all diminished. Again he was one with Shuto. Their rage and fear combined in silent struggle. The link grew deeper. They were fighting on a higher plane, a struggle without arms, beyond the conflict of their ships. Countless lives hung on the outcome. MacKenzie offered the code he had lived by his whole life. Honor. Sacrifice. Courage. Shuto had lived in torment his whole life. He sent his pain.

MacKenzie urged peace. Shuto refused it. There

could be none without revenge. MacKenzie deflected the thought as if it were a blow.

All the while, the flames backlit Shuto as if he were standing in hell.

Shuto felt the fire approaching. Not even the rain could put it out. He could no longer separate Justine, the Admiral, and himself. He felt the irrevocable change Justine had made in him. The words were ripped from his heart.

"I love you," Shuto said for the first time in his life.

He put Justine in a lifeboat and lowered it to the sea. He felt the depth of the Admiral's gratitude, but the conflict wasn't over. Like his crew, Justine couldn't make it to safety before the bombs exploded. His gift meant nothing. Shuto felt the Admiral's honor, his willingness to sacrifice. Shuto wondered if he had ever truly understood either. The *Storm* was still coming. MacKenzie made no attempt to veer away. He couldn't.

1:00 . . . :58 . . . :57 . . .

The link grew deeper. Shuto demanded revenge, MacKenzie countered with responsibility. It made Shuto wonder what his life would have been like if he hadn't tried to extract payment from the world for his injuries. He had gained nothing for it. Seen through MacKenzie's eyes, he was still striking out like an angry child, even now with his plans in ruins, selfish, without virtue. Akiro had seen that, and rather than be a part of it, had chosen death. His father's contempt added to the Admiral's. They shamed him.

:15 . . . :14 . . . :13 . . .

Peace. Honor. He had one last chance to find both. His gift could not be meaningful unless he sacrificed.

He understood that at last, and with that understanding he knew he had lost the struggle. The Admiral had won without a single blow. Shuto bowed his head in defeat.

The tent was burning. The canvas was curled and blackened. The flames reached for him as he walked inside.

MacKenzie felt the connection break. The outer world rushed in. Sound, fury.

"Admiral?" The Commodore shook him. "Admiral, what are your orders?"

"Fire."

The Commodore hit the switch. For a moment nothing happened, then the high-pitched shriek of misfiring engines reached them.

"Nikolai!" MacKenzie called down. "Check the tubes."

Raskin's frightened voice came back almost at once. "The torpedoes are running hot in the tubes with the outer doors open. They don't have enough power to break free."

The torpedoes were stuck half out of the tubes, burning up their engines. The *Storm* was still running fast at the *Korlov*, but they couldn't shoot. MacKenzie had to make a decision. He turned to the Commodore—only to be facing the octagonal barrel of his Webley .38 a second time.

"What are you doing, Commodore?"

"There's only one way to do this now and we both know it, Admiral. This happened frequently in the old days. After fifty years, it was a good bet it might happen again. I'm taking back my ship."

"I forbid it."

The Commodore's face was peaceful. He might have been a man of twenty again.

"I've suffered a lifetime because of that night. You and the *Storm* have given me the chance to make up for it. Let me do this, my friend. Take Captain Raskin in the small boat. Your wife needs you. Go quickly. Only eight hundred yards left."

MacKenzie saw his determination. It couldn't be shaken.

"Nikolai, lock up the engine and get up here on the double. Launch the small boat. Move!"

"What will you tell everyone, Admiral?"

"Only what happened here today. The *Storm* kept your secret for fifty years. So will I."

"You're a kind man."

MacKenzie saluted. "It's been an honor serving with you, Captain Rowe."

The old man's eyes were shining. "Good-bye, Admiral."

Raskin launched the boat. MacKenzie climbed down from the bridge and they rowed hard for Justine. The length of the *Storm* shot past, heading towards its final fate.

Justine managed to lift herself in the lifeboat. The *Storm* rushed dead on at the *Korlov*. She feared Mac was making a suicide run until she saw the small boat launched. He was coming for her. The Commodore was alone in the bridge, tall and proud. But would his sacrifice be in time? How many minutes had passed since Shuto set the timer? Flames crackled over the *Korlov*. Justine looked for Shuto. He was standing in the stern, alone. He never took his eyes off the *Storm*. Then she saw what was in his hand. That's when she knew. There would be time. Shuto had come to his truth at last, in the final moments of his life. The battle was over. An ending with honor.

Shuto was holding the trigger for the bombs. On his face was the first look of peace she had ever seen there.

In the small boat, MacKenzie watched Alex Rowe steer the *Storm* straight at the *Korlov.*

"Give 'em hell, Commodore," Mac said softly.

The Commodore never wavered or looked back. In those last moments MacKenzie finally knew why the *Storm* had waited all these years. She'd waited for Alex Rowe. What she'd given the rest of them was only to enable them to reach this moment, to give her frightened captain the chance to be the hero he should have been, the hero she had always wanted him to be. She'd waited to right the wrongs committed in the heat of battle, and to restore the infinitely fine cosmic balance that Lt. David Bolliver had upset. Perhaps somewhere the able first lieutenant had found his own boat and his own battles to win, free of conflict. This last victory was Captain Alex Rowe's alone.

The *Storm* rammed the *Korlov,* setting off the torpedoes in her bow. The charges in the fore end went up along with them. Captain Rowe picked his spot perfectly. There was a secondary explosion as the *Korlov*'s fuel tanks went up with enough force to lift the ship out of the water and break the keel in two. As if in sympathy, Niigata Yakeyama erupted again. A new column of fire and smoke shot a thousand feet into the air and spread out in a gray wave. A great wind blew over the ocean.

Locked together, both ships were dying. The sea

rushed into open compartments greedily. The *Korlov* sank slowly aft, then dived vertically stern first, taking the *Storm* with her. Echoes from the final explosions rolled over the sea. Moments later there was no trace of either ship.

The last voyage of the *Storm* had ended.

EPILOGUE

Bethesda Naval Hospital

IT WAS KIND OF AN UNOFFICIAL GATHERING. THIS MANY people weren't supposed to be waiting in the Delivery Lounge, but since doctors in the Public Health Service were commissioned officers, when the Chief of Naval Operations said to cordon off the area, they hopped to it.

"How long does it take?" Raskin asked Lady Emily.

"Relax, Captain. You can't rush some things."

"My first labor was eighteen hours," volunteered Carla Bernhardsen.

"And you survived?" Raskin was shocked.

"We're tougher than men think," Bette said.

"This is *hell*," said Ben Garver, pacing like a nervous cat. "Why can't somebody *do* something?"

He stormed over to Dr. Teitel, the head of the hospital, to make his objections known.

"But, Ben," they heard the doctor saying. "Babies don't *take* orders."

Raskin went over to play with the kids. He and

363

Lady Emily had been adopted as official grandparents. There were six altogether. Bette and Carla's four, and Carolyn Carter's two. One was playing a computer game with Derek Bookbinder by the bottles of champagne arrayed on the table under bunches of pink and blue balloons. The rest were playing tag-and-kill with the SEAL, Lee Jackson. A nurse looked disapprovingly at the noise; Raskin gave the tag players a stern look and they quieted down. Even Jackson. Raskin decided he was getting good at this.

How different everybody looked from that last day on the island, he thought. Bette and Carla wore tailored wool suits. Lady Emily was casually elegant in slacks and a silk shirt with a gold brooch. They showed few signs of the ordeal seven months before that had cost two of them their husbands. He thought about that last day. They had gotten to Justine after the *Storm* sank the *Korlov*. She was in bad shape. He and MacKenzie had taken turns rowing, neither talking, listening to her labored breathing, and praying. Raskin heard the helicopter first.

"Peter?"

MacKenzie shielded his eyes against the sun. "Maybe."

Moments later a big Sea Stallion swooped down. SEALs dropped into the sea with harnesses and they were winched up to the helo. They were taken right to the carrier. A second helo went to the island, where the volcano was increasingly active. Rietti's setting it off was the reason Bookbinder and the NSA had found them, of course, and they had picked him up, badly burned, but alive. After seeing the crater from the air, Raskin could only shudder at what he must have gone through.

Ivor Bernhardsen's secret, and the Commodore's,

were buried, and Rietti's courage was praised. All three had been given heroes' honors by their respective governments. MacKenzie had spoken quietly to Lady Emily on the plane back. It seemed to give her a great sense of peace. Raskin himself was dickering with Garver about a job in Washington.

Justine's obstetrician, Dr. Fox, strode past. The tall, handsome redhead exuded a sense of calm Raskin didn't feel.

"Any news?" he asked.

"Soon," was all Fox would say, passing through the doors to the delivery unit.

Inside, MacKenzie held Justine's hand as Dr. Glicke wheeled her from the labor to the delivery room. He and the doctors and nurses were fully gowned. It was happening quickly now.

"Just a little more," urged Fox. "Push."

Justine moaned and bore down. Mac hadn't let go of her hand for the last hour. She was weak and pale.

"Mac?!"

"I'm here, honey. Just a little more."

"Push."

She panted with the exertion, bathed in sweat. "I can't."

"I've got the head," Fox announced, concentrating. "Once more."

Justine pushed. MacKenzie never let her go. It was messy and noisy and chaotic, everything the human family is.

"And the shoulders . . . Got her!"

The baby was covered in blood and vernix, slightly blue, crying loudly, with the face of a rhesus monkey. She was the most beautiful thing MacKenzie had ever seen.

"Honey, look," he whispered.

"Oh, Mac, she's perfect.".

Somewhere in her tired brain she remembered the way Shuto had touched her that day. *Thank you . . .*

Tears flowed freely down MacKenzie's face. In those first few seconds his brain took a flash picture he would never forget. One magical stop-motion instant counting fingers and toes and eyes and ears to know that his daughter was healthy. Nothing had ever seemed as important.

The nurse put a funny little monk's cap on the baby and laid her on Justine's chest.

"Hello, Alexandra," she crooned. "Hello, my sweet."

"As beautiful as her mother," Fox said happily. "We'll take her in a few minutes and clean her up. You guys rest now. Get to know each other. Those folks outside warned me if I didn't tell them when the baby came, they'd attack the unit. Especially the SEALs."

Mac and Justine held the tiny miracle, all sticky and warm and quiet now.

Outside, they could hear the party starting.

"A CRAM COURSE IN THE ART OF KILLING. THE BEST AGAINST THE BEST IN A COMPELLING YET THOUGHTFUL THRILLER THAT DRAWS YOU THROUGH A LABYRINTH OF DECEPTIONS UNTIL THE EXPLOSIVE CLIMAX."

— CLIVE CUSSLER

WHITE STAR

A Novel

JAMES THAYER

Now available from Pocket Books

POCKET
BOOKS

1161